THE AGE OF INNOCENCE

Edith Wharton (1862-1937) was born into a distinguished New York family and was privately educated in America and abroad. In 1905 she published *The House of Mirth* and two years later moved to France. The author of *Ethan Frome* (1911), *The Reef* (1912), and *The Custom of the Country* (1913), she won the Pulitzer Prize in 1920 for *The Age of Innocence*. In addition to many novels, she wrote short stories—which in brief used her major themes of nineteenth-century New York, the standards of high society, and the supernatural—and poetry, travel books, and an autobiography.

Cynthia Griffin Wolff received her undergraduate and graduate degrees from Harvard University. She has taught at Boston University, Queens College, Manhattanville College, and The University of Massachusetts at Amherst; currently, she holds the Class of 1922 Chair of Humanities at MIT. She has written three books: *Samuel Richardson and the Eighteenth Century Puritan Character*, *A Feast of Words: The Triumph of Edith Wharton* (the second edition of which was published in 1995 by Addison-Wesley), and *Emily Dickinson*. She has edited more than a dozen books and has authored monographs and several dozen essays—most recently examinations of mid-nineteenth-century slave and abolitionist narratives.

Currently, she is engaged in the research for a literary biography of Willa Cather.

PENGUIN BOOKS
Published by the Penguin Group
Penguin Books USA Inc., 375 Hudson Street,
New York, New York 10014, U.S.A.
Penguin Books Ltd, 27 Wrights Lane, London W8 5TZ, England
Penguin Books Australia Ltd, Ringwood, Victoria, Australia
Penguin Books Canada Ltd, 10 Alcorn Avenue,
Toronto, Ontario, Canada M4V 3B2
Penguin Books (N.Z.) Ltd, 182–190 Wairau Road, Auckland 10, New Zealand

Penguin Books Ltd, Registered Offices: Harmondsworth, Middlesex, England

First published in the United States of America by
D. Appleton and Company 1920
This edition with an introduction by Cynthia Griffin Wolff
published in Penguin Books 1996

15 17 19 20 18 16 14

Introduction copyright © Cynthia Griffin Wolff, 1996
All rights reserved

LIBRARY OF CONGRESS CATALOGING-IN-PUBLICATION DATA
Wharton, Edith, 1862–1937.
The age of innocence/Edith Wharton; edited with an introduction
by Cynthia Griffin Wolff and notes by Laura Dluzynski Quinn.
p. cm.—(Penguin twentieth-century classics)
Includes bibliographical references (p.).
ISBN 0 14 01.8970 X
1. New York (N.Y.)—Social life and customs—Fiction.
2. Man-woman relationships—New York (N.Y.)—Fiction.
3. Married people—New York (N.Y.)—Fiction. 4. Upper class—New York
(N.Y.)—Fiction. I. Wolff, Cynthia Griffin. II. Title. III. Series.
PS3545.H16A7 1996
813'.52—dc20   95-30951

Printed in the United States of America
Set in Adobe Stempel Garamond

THE AGE OF INNOCENCE

EDITH WHARTON

EDITED WITH AN INTRODUCTION BY
CYNTHIA GRIFFIN WOLFF
AND NOTES BY
LAURA DLUZYNSKI QUINN

PENGUIN BOOKS

CONTENTS

INTRODUCTION

On the eleventh hour of the eleventh day of the eleventh month of 1918, the guns fell silent. World War I came to an end, and the preparations for peace began. Yet despite the Allied nations' sense of relief and gratitude, even happiness had its melancholy aspect. Old orders had fallen in this *first* "world" war: dreams had been demolished; the world had been irrevocably changed; and no artist understood the contradictions and complexities of the war and its "tragic victory" more keenly or comprehensively than the great American novelist, Edith Wharton. She recorded her vivid reaction in *Fighting France* (1915): "It is one of the most detestable things about war," she wrote, "that everything connected with it, except the death and ruin that result, is such a heightening of life, so visually stimulating and absorbing. 'It was gay and terrible,' is the phrase forever recurring in [Tolstoy's novel] 'War and Peace.' "

Edith Wharton began drafting *The Age of Innocence* almost as soon as the gunfire had finished, and the narrative assumed its final form only fourteen months later. In many ways, this was Wharton's "war novel": it was a salute to the new age and a memorial to the age departed; but most of all, it was a study of the complex, intimate connections between social cohesion and individual growth, and its insights were saddened, deepened, and enriched by Edith Wharton's own recent acquaintance with conflict and devastation.

Never tainted by sentiment, most of Wharton's narratives explore the uncertain terrain between two opposite dangers. At one extreme there is anarchy, the eradication of all systems of order. Wharton's first novel, *The Valley of Decision*, a saga of Napoleonic uprisings in Italy, had depicted the chaotic results: "Man was free at last—freer than his would-be liberators had ever dreamed of making him—and he used his freedom like a beast!" At the other extreme there is stifling, suffocating repression; well-known masterpieces like *The House of Mirth* and *Ethan*

Frome depict the potentially fatal consequences. Yet if both of these extremes are lethal, the territory between them is filled with uncertainty, and it can never offer more than partial answers to our human problems and mortal woes. Edith Wharton consistently held that the notion of "perfect" happiness—like that of "perfect" freedom—is nothing but an alluring phantom that leads us to inevitable destruction; and virtually all of her prewar fictions center upon the individual dilemma of discovering and accepting some form of partial (and necessarily *imperfect*) happiness.

The new dimension introduced by the First World War was a concern for the survival not merely of individual men and women, but of a culture—an entire society. Just before the war began—and throughout its duration—Wharton educated herself in the fields of archaeology and anthropology. She learned about ancient and primitive cultures; but perhaps most important, she also realized with new clarity that cultures can die, become "extinct," like species who have failed the test of evolution. Unlike any other experience in her life, the war demonstrated what happens when an entire society and its traditions are subjected to unrelenting assault. The war's conclusion had revealed France's heroic ability to withstand this assault—to endure and even to grow stronger. Yet it had disclosed very little about the fortitude of Edith Wharton's native land, the United States, which had refused to enter the war until shortly before its conclusion. What might be America's sources of strength? What elements of American culture could provide not merely real happiness for individuals, but enduring strength for this still-unproven nation?

Wharton's experiences during the war changed her forever; and it is no accident that *The Age of Innocence* is a post–*Civil War* novel, set in the 1870s, but designed to discover those cultural strengths that might enable America to survive the postwar years of the 1920s.

Wharton, who resided in Europe permanently after her divorce in 1913, had taken up residence in Paris; for the already renowned author, these war years were not a time of artistic creativity. Instead, she turned her energies to working for the Allied cause, and in this, as in so many things, she was prodigiously energetic and exceptionally successful. Indeed, her achievements were so remarkable that in 1916 she was made a chevalier of the French Legion of Honor, probably the most notable award for her work, but only one of many. Throughout the conflict, Edith Wharton played an extraordinary role in providing help and support for civilians and soldiers alike.

Shortly after war broke out, Wharton became head of the American Hostels for Refugees. Always astute in her own professional matters, but without any prior experience in the general world of business, she was now the chief executive officer of a large international organization. The hostels ministered to the many thousands of displaced persons who poured into Paris weekly—providing them with housing, food, medical care, jobs (or, when necessary, job training), child care, eventually even a hospital specifically for tubercular patients. As the director of this organization for four years, Wharton worked to exhaustion, often imperiling her own health. During this time she put her novel-writing career almost entirely aside, publishing only one full-length work, *Summer* (1917). However, she did not stop writing altogether, for in addition to administering this immense network of patriotic charities and raising the money to support them, she became an excellent war correspondent.

In *Fighting France*, the descriptions of Paris—a city that was sometimes giddy with the unique urgency of men preparing for the front, but often engulfed in leaden melancholy—enable us to understand the passionate sensitivity that had propelled Wharton into such remarkable activity:

Wherever one goes, in every quarter and at every hour, among the busy confident strongly-stepping Parisians one sees these other people, dazed and slowly moving—men and women with sordid bundles on their backs, shuffling along hesitatingly in their tattered shoes, children dragging at their hands and tired-out babies pressed against their shoulders: the great army of the Refugees. Their faces are unmistakable and unforgettable. No one who has ever caught that stare of dumb bewilderment—or that other look of concentrated horror, full of the reflection of flames and ruins—can shake off the obsession of the Refugees.

Many things were exceptional about Wharton's exertions during the war, but one thread runs throughout. She was in no sense of the word a society "do-gooder": for Edith Wharton, these Allied soldiers and refugees were complex people whose joys and horrors she felt as keenly as her own. In *No Gifts from Chance* (Scribner's, 1994), one of Wharton's biographers, Shari Benstock, has recorded an unforgettable tale.

> A woman, "Mme Marguerite M.," had spent fourteen months in a straw kennel in a German prison with some five thousand civilian prisoners. During that time, she received the news that her husband, a soldier, had died in a military prison camp. She watched her seven-year-old daughter die before her eyes. She heard the screams of her sister, lodged in an adjoining kennel, as she was raped by German officers in front of her two children. The sister died; her children were taken away and never seen again. "Mme Marguerite M." fell ill with grief and, thinking her insane, the guards released her. Discovered in a Paris railway station by a policeman, she was sent to one of the hostels' rest homes. "She had been there for several weeks when I first saw her," Edith wrote, "but even then I could not wonder that her gaolers thought her mad. Today, she is quiet and has recovered her self-control; but she remains an irreparable wreck, a wasted life. . . . I could tell of many others like her.

Few learned more immediately and circumstantially than Edith Wharton that the battle lines of war do not begin and end somewhere "out there," somewhere "far away," in some archetypal field where heroic young men vie with each other for "honor." War is "gay"; but it is also "terrible": it disrupts our fundamental harmonies; and if war can produce exhilaration, energy, and a sense of purpose, it can also threaten all of us with despair and madness.

Having seen the "reflection of flames and ruins" in the faces of her refugees, Wharton determined to witness combat firsthand. During 1915, she made several trips to the front, walked the lines, spoke with the soldiers, and meditated upon the fragility of that always uncertain balance between coherence and chaos. Often, she had a specific mission to fulfill, such as delivering supplies to hospitals and inspecting the conditions in them. Sometimes, the plight of orphaned children commanded her attention, as another of her biographers, R. W. B. Lewis, attests:

> Like the older refugees, they arrived sick with privation and filth, and stupid with terror: one child had been rescued from a farm where she had been left alone without food for five days; two other girls were lifted from the arms of their dead father. They were bathed, clothed and fed, and turned out into the garden to play. The [hastily assembled accommodations were] so successful that the Belgian government asked if Mme. Wharton could take in another six hundred. [Soon] the Children of Flanders Rescue Committee . . . was running an organization almost as large as that of the American Hostels.

Eventually, the plight of individual refugees became an almost familiar horror.

What these sojourns along the front revealed in addition was a larger horror—wholesale, systematic destruction: villages leveled as part of a scorched-earth policy; the helpless—women, the elderly, children—brutalized "for fun." These were calculated steps in the campaign to annihilate a nation's civilization, and thereby to destroy its will to resist.

As Wharton repeatedly asserted throughout *Fighting France*, the enemy's ultimate intent was to eradicate the Allies' sense of community. In village after village,

> one had . . . most hauntingly, the vision of all the separate terrors, anguishes, uprootings and rendings apart involved in the destruction of the obscurest of human communities. The photographs on the walls, the twigs of withered box above the crucifixes, the old wedding-dresses in brass-clamped trunks, the bundles of letters laboriously written and as painfully deciphered, all the thousand and one bits of the past that give meaning and continuity to the present.

Thus it is perhaps not surprising that she also remarked upon a "domestic" impulse among the soldiers at the front. Men who lived with uncertainty, men who had marched and fought across the scarred countryside, men who risked mutilation and death —these were also men who repeatedly put together makeshift homes and villages.

> The houses are partly underground, connected by deep winding "bowels" over which light rustic bridges have been thrown, and so profoundly roofed with sod that as much of them as shows above ground is shell-proof. Yet they are real houses, with real doors and windows. . . . In other cheery catacombs we found neat rows of bunks, mess-tables, sizzling sauce-pans over kitchen-fires. Everywhere were endless ingenuities.

It seemed to Wharton that the impulse to establish community had become an indispensable component of sanity at the front. Thus as quickly as the enemy destroyed those trivial mementos which, when taken together, had created a "past," new connections and new mementos were assembled to take their place. What she observed and reported, then, was the soldiers' resolute determination to establish a network of relationships and home-like spaces—society's most primitive response to the threat of extermination.

Edith Wharton was fifty-three when she witnessed the pan-orama of violence and brutality that had given rise to this do-mesticity in the trenches. The bold concern that had led her to the front lines and the vigorous ingenuity with which she had taken charge of Allied charities would have been unusual for anyone; for a woman—and especially for a woman of Wharton's age and circumstances—they were extraordinary. Not only had her background failed to prepare her for it; everything in the world of her childhood had explicitly forbidden any such bold and resourceful behavior.

Wharton was born Edith Newbold Jones on January 24, 1862. Her parents were distinguished members of an exclusive coterie with inherited money and social privilege, a compact realm called "Old New York."

If any Americans can be said to have aristocratic origins, Edith Wharton would have a plausible claim to such lineage: her great-grandfather, Ebenezer Stevens, had participated in the Boston Tea Party. Later, as an officer in the Revolutionary War, he took part in the victories of Saratoga and Yorktown, and his ingenious maneuvers were said to have been responsible for foiling the British blockade at Annapolis. Although he settled in New York and pursued a very profitable career as an East Indies merchant after the war, he continued to act upon his sense of civic duty. Thus even while in business, he also distinguished himself in numerous areas of public service: he went on confidential missions for both the French and American governments and served on innumerable committees for the city of New York. Edith Wharton admired General Stevens for his cunning, his success, and his high sense of honor. She commemorated him by naming her home in Lenox "The Mount"—the same name that Great-Grandfather Stevens had given to his own country home; and in her autobiography, *A Backward Glance*, she described her illustrious ancestor at great length, explaining:

> If I have dwelt too long on the career of this model citizen it is because of a secret partiality for him. . . . I like above all the abounding energy, the swift adaptability and the *joie de vivre* which hurried him from one adventure to another, with war, commerce and domesticity (he had two wives and fourteen children). . . . But perhaps I feel nearest to him when I look at my eagle andirons, and think of the exquisite polychrome mantels that he found the time to bring all the way from Italy, to keep company with the orange-trees on his terrace.

Wharton took deep pleasure in her distant kinsman's aesthetic sensibility; she respected his ability to combine militant energy and business acumen with familial devotion and peacetime public service; indeed, to some extent her emulation of him, even her identification with him in her own active adult life, seems to have gone well beyond merely the naming of her home after his.

Yet if General Ebenezer Stevens provided inspiration for his great-granddaughter (and perhaps especially so during and after the tumultuous years of World War I), he was a distant and indistinct role model. The more immediate influences in Wharton's life had been her parents and their friends; and the Old New York of Edith Jones Wharton's youth was a society that had generally fallen away from its era of bold vigor and active virtue. True, a few of its members still attempted to live as vitally as Ebenezer Stevens had lived, and contributed in large and small ways to the honor and betterment of their community. In Wharton's estimation, Theodore Roosevelt, a deeply respected personal friend, exemplified the best of such citizens. Yet far too many in this privileged class had become enervated and complacent—narrow and rigid and sometimes pointlessly punitive. By the time Edith Jones was born, the once-vibrant little world of Old New York provided a generally stifling environment, even for men; and for women, its mores had become suffocating.

The author's father, George Frederic Jones, received an abundant allowance until his father died; then he inherited a substantial fortune. By all accounts he was a kind and generous man; his talented daughter was devoted to him. Yet his life betrayed no force or direction. He never worked for a living, and he occupied his time with the leisurely hobbies of his set—"sea-fishing, boat-racing and wild-fowl shooting." Insofar as he had faults, they were sins of omission: indifference and the propensity to be dominated by the strong will of his wife.

Although the author's mother, Lucretia Rhinelander Jones, could boast a distinguished heritage, she had been reared in comparatively straitened circumstances: her father had died at the age of thirty, leaving his young widow and their four children dependent upon the generosity of the family. Lucretia was a great beauty in her youth, and when she married George Jones, she could finally afford to indulge that beauty. The couple took an extended European vacation for their honeymoon, and Edith Wharton later recorded the tales she had been told of their early married life and especially of their initial trip to Paris:

[Mother's] sloping shoulders and slim waist were becomingly set off by the wonderful gowns brought home from that first visit to the capital of fashion. All this happened years before I was born; but the tradition of elegance was never abandoned, and . . . [eventually] I shared the excitement caused by the annual arrival of the "trunk from Paris," and the enchantment of seeing one resplendent dress after another shaken out of its tissue-paper. Once, when I was a small child, my mother's younger sister, my beautiful and serious-minded Aunt Mary Newbold, asked me, with edifying interest: "What would you like to be when you grow up?" and on my replying in all good faith, and with a dutiful air: "The best-dressed woman in New York," she uttered the horrified cry: "Oh, don't say that, darling!" to which I could only rejoin in wonder: "But, Auntie, you know Mamma *is*."

Lucretia and George Jones were gregarious; they very much enjoyed entertaining; and it is rumored that the expression "Keeping up with the Joneses" was coined to describe the splendid social enthusiasm of Edith Jones Wharton's parents!

The home of such parents would *seem* to offer a daughter at least the promise of lighthearted, social-butterfly fun. Yet the reality was far from fun for the daughter of the Jones household. Lucretia's two older children, both boys, had been born thirteen and fifteen years earlier than their sister, and Edith appears to have been an unplanned and largely unwelcome addition to the family. Mother made no secret of the fact that she preferred her sons.

Toward her daughter, Lucretia was disapproving and distant; she was inclined to ridicule everything from the child's red hair and supposedly "big feet" to her serious nature. When the little girl's literary talents emerged (as they did at a very young age), Lucretia's reaction was one of fascinated horror. And when her daughter actually began to write tentative fiction, Lucretia's response was to stifle the impulse as sternly as possible:

It was not thought necessary to feed my literary ambitions with foolscap, and for lack of paper I was driven to begging for the wrappings of the parcels delivered at the house. After a while these were regarded as belonging to me, and I always kept a stack in my room. It never occurred to me to fold and cut the big brown sheets, and I used to spread them on the floor and travel over them on my hands and knees.

Thus while Edith Wharton ultimately voiced admiration for her mother's beauty and sense of taste and for her fastidious attention to the elegance of precise language, she had few other positive recollections of "Mamma"; indeed, the adult author consistently described Mamma's manner with images of icy coldness, as indifferent at best and at worst contemptuous. A mother with Lucretia's hostile habits would have been difficult under any circumstances; in the atmosphere of Old New York, her attitude reinforced the effect of an environment already infected with pernicious elements.

All of Wharton's childhood memories, then, acknowledge a peculiar mixture of strengths and deficiencies in the society into which she had been born.

On the one hand, many of the ancient values remained: the honor, loyalty, and devotion to family that had characterized Ebenezer Stevens's life could still be discerned in the lives of his descendants. Old New York's merits, Wharton would assert,

lay in upholding two standards of importance in any community, that of education and good manners, and of scrupulous probity in business and private affairs. New York has always been a commercial community, and in my infancy the merits and defects of its citizens were those of a mercantile middle class. The first duty of such a class was to maintain a strict standard of uprightness in affairs; and the gentlemen of my father's day did maintain it, whether in the law, in banking, shipping, or wholesale commercial enterprises. . . . I should say that the qualities justifying the existence of our old society were social amenity and financial incorruptibility.

On the other hand, however, Old New York had become unimaginative and lethargic and potentially rigid in the exercise of these virtues.

A little world so well-ordered and well-to-do does not often produce either eagles or fanatics, and both seem to have been conspicuously absent from the circle in which my forebears moved.
. . . Conformity is the bane of middle-class communities. . . .
Looking back at that little world, and remembering the "hoard
of petty maxims" with which its elders preached down every sort
of initiative, I have often wondered at such lassitude in the descendants of the men who first cleared a place for themselves in
a new world. What had become of the spirit of the . . . revolu-
tionaries?

It was, perhaps, precisely this conformity that the potential author Edith Jones found most personally oppressive.

Her parents and their friends were not interested in music or
the visual arts; they regarded authors as potentially dangerous,
"bohemian" individuals—people to be excluded from polite circles. Paradoxically, Old New Yorkers had a deep reverence for
beauty; however, they fixed their veneration almost entirely
upon the appearance of their children—and especially, of course,
upon their daughters.

In that simple society there was an almost pagan worship of physical beauty, and the first question asked about any youthful new-
comer on the social scene was invariably: "Is she pretty?" or: "Is
he handsome?"—for good looks were as much prized in young
men as in maidens. . . . Most vivid is my memory of the picturesque archery club meetings. . . . And a pretty sight the meeting
was, with parents and elders seated in a semicircle on the turf
behind the lovely archeresses in floating silks or muslins, with
their wide leghorn hats, and heavy veils flung back only at the
moment of aiming. These veils are associated with all the summer
festivities of my childhood. . . . No grace was rated as high as "a
complexion." . . . Beauty was unthinkable without "a complexion," and to defend that treasure against sun and wind and the
arch-enemy sea air, veils as thick as curtains . . . were habitually
worn.

Other than its respect for youthful grace, this society's capacity
to appreciate beauty had become almost comically circumscribed.

Young couples often acquired elaborately framed oil copies of the "old masters" while on their European honeymoon; young matrons sometimes collected china or old lace; and when newlyweds settled down, they generally lived in houses whose interiors were so uncomfortable and formal that the very rooms themselves seemed to have been upholstered. Such were their notions of culture and taste.

In this environment, young women had a specific and ruthlessly prescribed relationship to beauty: they were meant to become, themselves, supremely beautiful objects. Thus the veiling that protected young archeresses can be taken to represent a more general practice of confinement and prohibition. Young women were intended to *be* beautiful. *Creating* beauty—becoming an *artist—writing novels!* (For money!) These would have been unsavory pursuits even in a man; in a woman, they were utterly unthinkable!

Thus in the world of Edith Jones Wharton's girlhood—that is, the world in which she set her great novel *The Age of Innocence*—the acceptable course for a young woman's life was as rigid as her corsets (which could stand by themselves); the expectations and prospects in life of a proper young man were almost equally limited; and the result was mutilating—potentially lethal—to the spirit of *both* men and women.

In Edith Wharton's own life, gaining freedom from the constrictions of this world and overcoming the particular patterns of meanness that had dominated her mother's house were feats of heroic strength. The account of her personal struggle is, itself, an engrossing narrative that can offer insight and inspiration to all of us, even today.

Perhaps it is not surprising that at the beginning of her writing career, it was the deficiencies of Old New York—and particularly the scarcity of options for talented and vigorous *women* in these circumstances—that dominated Edith Wharton's imagination. As I have elsewhere written: "The little girl had spent years watching in rapt wonder as Mother's annual box of dresses from Paris was opened. She had a hunger for beauty in all its forms and must have been unnaturally susceptible to an image of the woman as a beautiful work of art." Little by little, however, Wharton became "confident that 'doing' was a source of strength, while 'being' merely diminished individual resources. Yes, there were objective problems that confronted the woman who chose to create beauty; but on balance, writing offered no intrinsic obstacle to emotional intimacy . . . , and it offered strengths that could be found nowhere else."

Early short stories like "The Muse's Tragedy" and "The Valley of Childish Things and Other Emblems" explore the tragic consequences of the injunction to "*be*" rather than the encouragement to "*do*"; in this early fiction, Wharton often paid particular attention to the relationship between women and beauty or art, even as she was becoming more and more determined to realize her own full potential as an active and successful artist. The most magnificent and complex exploration of this tragic "feminine" heritage is Wharton's first New York novel (and one of her finest pieces of fiction), *The House of Mirth* (1905); its heroine, Lily Bart, suffers the ruinous consequences of a tradition that has allowed its females only one responsibility, that of becoming the embodiment of beauty and artistic perfection, and only one "career," that of marrying well.

Yet this account of Wharton's indictment of the world from which she had come is in some ways misleading. She always had an abhorrence of glib "solutions" to difficult problems; thus her condemnation of Old New York's narrowness was consistently balanced by her appreciation of the difficulties encountered in any attempt to discover practical alternatives. She had little interest in flamboyant acts of individual daring: she never admired defiance for its own sake, nor did she believe that any person could find "fulfillment" entirely free from the burden of social constraints.

In Wharton's judgment, the relationship between self and society was *intrinsic* and *inescapable;* to become a mature "self"— a fulfilled and happy adult—everyone (both male and female) must have rewarding and viable social roles to play. Moreover, she believed that an individual's failure to find some genuinely meaningful place in a vital and admirable community would ultimately have fatal consequences: exclusion from the society of significant others was tantamount to some form of death. Thus the seductive desires for "absolute personal fulfillment" or "utter freedom" could never be more than alluring, lethal phantoms; and anyone who pursued such illusions would find only catastrophe.

Insofar as Wharton's novels have "happy endings," the happiness is circumscribed because (as she often observed) in real life, joy always *is* limited. The *real* challenge that confronts each man and woman, then, can never be that of finding perfect happiness; rather, it must be that of creating some form of *possible* happiness—achieving self-respect and the partial realization of one's hopes and aspirations. In this life, no one can expect more.

Wharton's understanding of the human condition, always balanced and sober, was deeply affected by her experiences during World War I. The American novelists whom we usually associate with the mood of disillusionment following the war were younger than Wharton because it was generally only the young, like Fitzgerald and Hemingway, who had witnessed its carnage firsthand. Edith Wharton was unique: she could remember the "old ways" of the post–Civil War world that had comprised her childhood in New York; yet she could understand the "new ways" too. She could share the "lost generation"'s disenchantment and even understand their sense of betrayal during the 1920's; yet perhaps as a consequence of her maturity, this confrontation with the melancholy realities of destruction led not to despair, but rather to a more complex understanding of the human condition and a more fully developed sense of compassion.

While Edith Wharton watched the French continue to fight despite the privation and devastation they had suffered, she marveled at their resilience and strength as a nation. "In great trials a race is tested by its values," she wrote, "and the war has shown the world what are the real values of France." She wondered how had it been possible for the people of this embattled country to survive, to be strong, to endure; and she concluded that it was because they had preserved their sense of "larger meanings": "They have understood life to be made up of many things past and to come, of renunciation as well as satisfaction, of traditions as well as experiments, of dying as much as of living."

France had triumphed over war because of its honesty, its realistic sense of values, and its devotion to a coherent set of traditions. "The whole civilian part of the nation seems merged in one symbolic figure," Wharton observed in *Fighting France*, "carrying help and hope to the fighters or passionately bent above the wounded. The devotion, the self-denial seem instinctive; but they are really based on a reasoned knowledge of the situation and on an unflinching estimate of values. All France knows today that *real 'life'* consists in the things that make it worth living."

In the end, Wharton's experiences during World War I affirmed a powerful but paradoxical truth. There must always be a balance between "renunciation" and "satisfaction": personal happiness depends upon the survival of the community; yet the survival of the community depends upon the willingness of each individual to surrender some portion of his or her own personal gratification to the general good. Without this balance, *both* individual rights and civilized communal existence will be lost.

Thus while the young American novelists of the postwar generation danced into the hectic frenzy of the jazz age, with its "free" love and its endless, giddy quest for pleasure, Edith Wharton embraced maturity. In a short, postwar book entitled *French Ways and Their Meaning* (1919), she recollected a conversation with William Dean Howells that had occurred in 1906:

We had been talking of that strange exigency of the American public which compels the dramatist (if he wishes to be played) to wind up his play, whatever its point of departure, with the "happy-ever-after" of the fairy-tales. . . .

"Yes," said Mr. Howells; "what the American public wants is *a tragedy with a happy ending*. . . ."

"A tragedy with a happy ending" is exactly what the child wants before he goes to sleep . . . , but as long as he needs it he remains a child, and the world he lives in is a nursery-world. Things are not always and everywhere well with the world, and each man has to find it out as he grows up. It is the finding out that makes him grow, and until he has faced the fact and digested the lesson he is not grown up. . . .

The same thing is true of countries and peoples. The "sheltered life," whether of the individual or of the nation, must either have a violent and tragic awakening—or never wake up at all.

After the war had ended, Wharton hoped that America too would embrace maturity—that as a country it would begin to seek a balance between "tradition" and "experiment," between "renunciation" and "satisfaction"—and would ultimately achieve the judicious wisdom that had fortified France in her mortal peril.

In the early postwar years, she was optimistic about America's future. "We are growing up at last; and it is only in maturity that a man glances back along the past, and sees the use of the constraints that irritated his impatient youth. So with races and nations; and America has reached the very moment in her development when she may best understand what has kept older races and riper civilizations sound." Thus Edith Wharton's best and most subtle "war novel" was neither a brutal battlefield tragedy nor an apocalyptic jazz-age satire. It was a glance "back along the past" to examine the "constraints" that had bedeviled her own "impatient youth." By now, Wharton had the advantage of age and perspective; and her "war novel" was as singular as her own active, middle-aged American presence in Paris throughout the conflict. Perhaps her most personal novel, perhaps her most American novel, perhaps even her greatest novel: *The Age of Innocence* is Edith Wharton's unique postwar narrative.

Critics who have seen *The Age of Innocence* as a sentimental return to her youth miss this point. One might do well, for example, to note every time the words *real* and *realistic* are used, especially toward the novel's conclusion; for if it is nothing else, this piece of fiction is an urgent, encouraging appeal for its readers to abandon unrealizable fantasies for the actual, deep pleasures that "real life" can afford. *Newland* Archer is Wharton's quintessentially American hero, recalling, perhaps, Christopher *Newman* in Henry James's novel *The American*. Like many of James's heroes, Newland Archer can learn about himself and his native land only after an encounter with the perversions of ancient European civilizations—an encounter that is provided in *The Age of Innocence* not by a journey abroad, but by a series of negotiations with a foreign visitor, Ellen, wife of the depraved Count Olenska.

If Edith Wharton had the example of her dear friend Henry James in mind when she wrote this novel, she was also mindful of other novelists, particularly Tolstoy. The phrase "it was gay and terrible" from *War and Peace* had echoed in her mind throughout the years of combat; now, in these postwar years, the echoes of another of Tolstoy's masterpieces captured her imagination: *Anna Karenina*. The latter novel explores the very tensions about which Wharton herself wrote so often—the conflict between the claims of tradition and those of individual freedom. At this point in her career, she was so intent upon capturing the tension between these antitheses in a precise and powerful way that she experimented with several different narrative possibilities before she settled upon the final version of *The Age of Innocence*.

In the Edith Wharton archives of the Beinecke Library at Yale University, there are two fully developed alternative plot plans for the novel. In the first, Archer is engaged when he meets Mme. Olenska and falls in love with her; he marries his fiancée, settles down in New York, and finds that his passion remains unabated. He runs away for a passionate tryst in Florida with Mme. Olenska and intends to break with everything else. Yet gradually he realizes that he is profoundly *uncomfortable* trying to live outside of the society he has always known. On her part, Mme. Olenska quickly becomes bored with Archer. Eventually, both realize that *in reality,* they have nothing in common. They return to New York without anyone's knowing of their romantic adventure, and shortly thereafter, Mme. Olenska returns forever to Europe.

In the second version, May releases Newland from his engagement; she marries another man, and he marries Mme. Olenska. Newland and Ellen have a rapturous honeymoon, but when they return to New York, the radical differences in their personalities and interests become apparent. Archer is happy only in the world that has shaped him; Ellen is miserably bored out-side of the sophisticated, cultured world of Europe. The couple agrees upon a formal separation: Ellen takes up permanent res-idency abroad, and Newland returns home to live the rest of his life with his mother and sister.

Of course, what both of these alternate plots sketch is the inevitable failure of the purely romantic vision, a story very much along the lines of *Anna Karenina* (but perhaps even more dreary because it lacks the crisp conclusion of a suicide). The first of the two is deeply poignant; the second might have been profoundly, dismally tragic.

What Wharton could see, with charity and utter clarity, is that Newland and Ellen *both* perceive the other primarily in terms of some romanticized personal need. Thus, although Ellen Olen-ska may indeed seem the fulfillment of Newland Archer's *dreams*—representing "freedom," mystery, and the unknown world of art and intellect—she is an actual woman with whom he has little or nothing in common. Similarly, although Ellen, in her vulnerable and weakened situation, is drawn to Newland—who represents safety, order, and protection—it is the security and honor he seems to embody that she "loves," and not the particularities of his personality. (Actually, Ellen consistently finds Beaufort's sophisticated companionship more engaging than Newland Archer's.)

The core of the novel is Newland's quest for real happiness, a quest that coincides with the pursuit of maturity. One uncom-promising fact constrains this quest: the deepest and most in-delible components of Newland Archer's nature have been formed and nourished within the narrow confinements of the very world against whose strictures he frets. He may be capable of improvement, of growth—even of achieving wisdom and con-tentment. However, he will never be capable of some funda-mental transformation. Insofar as he can find happiness, the nature of his satisfactions will always, necessarily, be limited by the kind of person he is.

Because of Newland's shortcomings, it is important to realize how much of the story is told from his point of view. It is even more important to recognize how often his judgment is seriously mistaken, especially throughout the opening portions of the novel. When we first encounter him, Newland is decent and honorable enough—so long as these virtues require very little beyond good manners. The most appalling possibility presented by the novel is that Newland might never grow beyond this smug, limited understanding of his duties in the world and his relationships within it, that he might become a kind of carbon copy of Larry Lefferts and his friends. The opening chapter hints clearly at such a possibility. Wharton's rendering of the young man's inventorial appreciation of his young fiancée and his plans for her future—"He meant her (thanks to his enlightening companionship) to develop a social tact and readiness of wit enabling her to hold her own with the most popular married women of the 'younger set' "—captures nothing so forcefully as the potential fatuousness of the young man's personality. Such opinions are anything but an informed or reliable index to the moral and emotional possibilities of actual situations; a wary reader must be mindful of the severe limitations of the romantic, self-serving, visionary tendencies that becloud Newland's perceptions of his world.

By contrast, May and Ellen are both uncompromising realists; ironically, at every point in the novel, they may both know more than Newland does about what is "actually" happening. Wharton's study of *The Golden Bough* just before she wrote *The Age of Innocence* had taught her about the ruthless power of the Cult of Diana—a force used to protect mothers and children—and May, who becomes an "Archer" when she marries, embodies the single-minded vigor that is represented by this protector of the domestic realm. In order to call her readers' attention to this suggestion, Wharton fills her narrative both with allusions to ancient cultures and classical mythology, and with references to the various forms of combat that might be associated with this militant goddess and her Olympian peers. May is far from ignorant, a fact that she attempts to disclose to Newland without success. (Indeed, it is an interesting exercise to peruse the novel and take note, at each crucial moment, of what May probably *knows*—despite Newland's consistent belief in her ignorance and "innocence.") Moreover, she can be capable of great generosity;

even after the engagement, she knows that Newland has become emotionally involved with some other woman, and she offers him his freedom when he appears to want it. Yet once she and Newland have entered into a binding commitment, she becomes as fierce in her protection of home and hearth as the goddess Diana herself. May has no knowledge of the dark, depraved world in which Ellen has suffered and from which she has recently escaped; yet she does understand many of Newland Archer's limitations, and she agrees with Ellen about life's necessities—particularly those pertaining to loyalty and honor.

Paradoxically, then, May and Ellen often voice similar sentiments. When Newland rashly proposes an elopement, May sensibly punctures his romantic scheme: "We can't behave like people in novels." Much later in the novel, when Newland proposes to Ellen that they escape to a place where they can be perfectly free, she dismisses his scheme with weary skepticism: "Where is that country?"

Moreover, Ellen is, in her own way, surely as "innocent" as May; throughout much of her visit to America, Ellen allows herself to suppose that in New York she can find a world where people are uncomplicated and, in some simple way, merely "kind" and "generous." Despite the dark initiation of her marriage, she has evidently failed to acknowledge two intractable facts; that dangerous, primitive passions are everywhere because they lurk at the core of humanity itself, and that it is principally the rituals that have been designed to control and contain the violent expression of these feelings which vary from culture to culture. What Ellen does appreciate, even to the center of her being, is that everyone—everywhere—needs the security that only a structured society can offer. In the end, part of May's generosity (and a signal indication of Old New York's "kindness") is the family's willingness to offer Ellen precisely the "tribal" protection and support that she will require if she is to have a contented and relatively free existence once she returns to Europe.

Wharton was far from blind to the limitations of the world she had depicted in this novel: she understood that its brutality was merely discreetly clothed in the genteel customs of cordiality. On the other hand, she also recognized not only that this world had its positive components, but also that it was caught in a process of inevitable change. New families were invading the realm of Old New York; stale customs and restrictions were gradually yielding to innovations and improvements. Change was slow, painfully slow. Nonetheless, there was a distinct possibility that this steady process of evolution would ultimately produce a new kind of society, one that retained the admirable qualities of Old New York and combined them with more enlightened practices. Most important, there was hope that this commingling of moral rectitude with more generous freedoms would create a stronger community and a culture whose values could endure.

The Age of Innocence, then, is a patient, compassionate novel. It never argues that Old New York was an idyll to which hectic modern society should return (instead, it lays bare the flaws of Old New York with ruthless precision). However, neither does the novel suggest that the world of the inheritors is ideal. Instead it offers growth and balance and tolerance. And in the case of Newland Archer, it presents the unforeseeable, incomparable gift of middle-aged self-respect: "There was good in the old ways. . . . There was good in the new order too."

Finally, as much of the novel is designed to suggest, few people—even "way back then"—were as "innocent" as we moderns may ingenuously suppose. Edith Wharton has wrapped her novel in a gentle joke to make this point. *The Age of Innocence* is the title of a well-known painting by Sir Joshua Reynolds. It depicts a little girl, perhaps four or five years old. This is the only *real* "age of innocence," Wharton slyly suggests. Beware of supposing an intricate social system to be innocent; if you do, you will almost certainly be ensnared by its subtle complexities.

SUGGESTIONS FOR
FURTHER READING

I. WORKS BY WHARTON THAT ARE RELEVANT TO
THE AGE OF INNOCENCE

The House of Mirth (1905)
The Reef (1911)
The Custom of the Country (1913)
Fighting France (1915)
Summer (1917)
The Marne (1918)
French Ways and Their Meaning (1919)
A Son at the Front (1920)
Old New York (4 vols, 1924): *False Dawn* (*The Forties*); *The Old Maid* (*The Fifties*); *The Spark* (*The Sixties*); *New Year's Day* (*The Seventies*)
A Backward Glance (1934)

II. SECONDARY WORK RELATED TO WHARTON AND TO
THE AGE OF INNOCENCE

Ammons, Elizabeth. *Conflicting Stories: American Women Writers at the Turn into the Twentieth Century.* New York: Oxford University Press, 1991.

———. *Edith Wharton's Argument with America.* Athens: University of Georgia Press, 1980.

Bell, Millicent. "Edith Wharton in France," in *Wretched Exotic,* ed. Katherine Joslyn and Alan Price. New York: Peter Lang, 1993.

Benstock, Shari. *No Gifts from Chance: A Biography of Edith Wharton.* New York: Charles Scribner's Sons, 1994.

Dwight, Eleanor. *Edith Wharton: An Extraordinary Life.* New York: Harry N. Abrams, 1994.

Fracasso, Evelyn E. "The Transparent Eyes of May Welland in Wharton's *The Age of Innocence,*" *Modern Language Studies,* 21:4 (Fall, 1991).

Gargano, James W. "Tableaux of Renunciation: Wharton's Use of The Shaughran in *The Age of Innocence,*" in *Studies in American Fiction* 15:1 (Spring, 1987).

Goodman, Susan. *Edith Wharton's Women: Friends and Rivals*. Hanover and London: University Press of New England, 1990.

Heller, Adele, and Lois Rudnick, eds. *1915: The Cultural Moment*, New Brunswick, NJ: Rutgers University Press, 1991.

Lewis, R. W. B. *Edith Wharton: A Biography*. New York: Harper and Row, 1975.

Lewis, R. W. B., and Nancy Lewis, eds. *The Letters of Edith Wharton*. New York: Charles Scribner's Sons, 1988.

Martin, Robert A. and Linda Wagner-Martin. "The Salons of Wharton's Fiction: Wharton and Fitzgerald, Hemingway, Faulkner, and Stein," in *Wretched Exotic*, ed. Katherine Joslyn and Alan Price. New York: Peter Lang, 1993.

Pizer, Donald. "American Naturalism in Its 'Perfected' State: *The Age of Innocence* and *An American Tragedy*, in *Edith Wharton: New Critical Essays*, ed. Alfred Bendixen and Annette Zilversmit. New York & London: Garland Publishing, Inc., 1992.

Price, Alan. "Wharton Mobilizes Artists to Aid the War Homeless," in *Wretched Exotic*, ed. Katherine Joslyn and Alan Price. New York: Peter Lang, 1993.

———. "Edith Wharton at War with the American Red Cross: The End of *Noblesse Oblige*," in *Women's Studies*, Special Issue: Reading the Letters of Edith Wharton, Guest Ed. Annette Zilversmit, 20:1 (1991).

Sensibar, Judith. " 'Behind the Lines' in Edith Wharton's *A Son at the Front: Re-writing a Masculinist Tradition*, in *Wretched Exotic*, ed. Katherine Joslyn and Alan Price. New York: Peter Lang, 1993.

Wolff, Cynthia Griffin. *A Feast of Words: The Triumph of Edith Wharton*, 2nd ed. Reading, MA: Addison Wesley Publishing Co., 1994.

A NOTE ON THE TEXT

The text of this edition of *The Age of Innocence* follows the text of the Scribner's edition (1993), based in turn on the authoritative Library of America edition (1985) of the novel.

THE AGE OF INNOCENCE

BOOK ONE

1

On a January evening of the early seventies, Christine Nilsson was singing in Faust at the Academy of Music in New York.

Though there was already talk of the erection, in remote metropolitan distances "above the Forties," of a new Opera House which should compete in costliness and splendour with those of the great European capitals, the world of fashion was still content to reassemble every winter in the shabby red and gold boxes of the sociable old Academy. Conservatives cherished it for being small and inconvenient, and thus keeping out the "new people" whom New York was beginning to dread and yet be drawn to; and the sentimental clung to it for its historic associations, and the musical for its excellent acoustics, always so problematic a quality in halls built for the hearing of music.

It was Madame Nilsson's first appearance that winter, and what the daily press had already learned to describe as "an exceptionally brilliant audience" had gathered to hear her, transported through the slippery, snowy streets in private broughams, in the spacious family landau, or in the humbler but more convenient "Brown *coupé*." To come to the Opera in a Brown *coupé* was almost as honourable a way of arriving as in one's own carriage; and departure by the same means had the immense advantage of enabling one (with a playful allusion to democratic principles) to scramble into the first Brown conveyance in the line, instead of waiting till the cold-and-gin congested nose of one's own coachman gleamed under the portico of the Academy. It was one of the great livery-stableman's most masterly intuitions to have discovered that Americans want to get away from amusement even more quickly than they want to get to it.

When Newland Archer opened the door at the back of the club box the curtain had just gone up on the garden scene. There was no reason why the young man should not have come earlier, for he had dined at seven, alone with his mother and sister, and had lingered afterward over a cigar in the Gothic library with

glazed black-walnut bookcases and finial-topped chairs which
was the only room in the house where Mrs. Archer allowed
smoking. But, in the first place, New York was a metropolis,
and perfectly aware that in metropolises it was "not the thing"
to arrive early at the opera; and what was or was not "the thing"
played a part as important in Newland Archer's New York as
the inscrutable totem terrors that had ruled the destinies of his
forefathers thousands of years ago.

The second reason for his delay was a personal one. He had
dawdled over his cigar because he was at heart a dilettante, and
thinking over a pleasure to come often gave him a subtler satisfaction than its realisation. This was especially the case when
the pleasure was a delicate one, as his pleasures mostly were; and
on this occasion the moment he looked forward to was so rare
and exquisite in quality that—well, if he had timed his arrival in
accord with the prima donna's stage-manager he could not have
entered the Academy at a more significant moment than just as
she was singing: "He loves me—he loves me not—*he loves
me!*—" and sprinkling the falling daisy petals with notes as clear
as dew.

She sang, of course, *"M'ama!"* and not "he loves me," since
an unalterable and unquestioned law of the musical world required that the German text of French operas sung by Swedish
artists should be translated into Italian for the clearer understanding of English-speaking audiences. This seemed as natural
to Newland Archer as all the other conventions on which his
life was moulded: such as the duty of using two silver-backed
brushes with his monogram in blue enamel to part his hair, and
of never appearing in society without a flower (preferably a gardenia) in his buttonhole.

"M'ama . . . non m'ama . . ." the prima donna sang, and
"M'ama!", with a final burst of love triumphant, as she pressed
the dishevelled daisy to her lips and lifted her large eyes to the
sophisticated countenance of the little brown Faust-Capoul, who
was vainly trying, in a tight purple velvet doublet and plumed
cap, to look as pure and true as his artless victim.

Newland Archer, leaning against the wall at the back of the

club box, turned his eyes from the stage and scanned the opposite side of the house. Directly facing him was the box of old Mrs. Manson Mingott, whose monstrous obesity had long since made it impossible for her to attend the Opera, but who was always represented on fashionable nights by some of the younger members of the family. On this occasion, the front of the box was filled by her daughter-in-law, Mrs. Lovell Mingott, and her daughter, Mrs. Welland; and slightly withdrawn behind these brocaded matrons sat a young girl in white with eyes ecstatically fixed on the stagelovers. As Madame Nilsson's "M'ama!" thrilled out above the silent house (the boxes always stopped talking during the Daisy Song) a warm pink mounted to the girl's cheek, mantled her brow to the roots of her fair braids, and suffused the young slope of her breast to the line where it met a modest tulle tucker fastened with a single gardenia. She dropped her eyes to the immense bouquet of lilies-of-the-valley on her knee, and Newland Archer saw her white-gloved finger-tips touch the flowers softly. He drew a breath of satisfied vanity and his eyes returned to the stage.

No expense had been spared on the setting, which was acknowledged to be very beautiful even by people who shared his acquaintance with the Opera houses of Paris and Vienna. The foreground, to the footlights, was covered with emerald green cloth. In the middle distance symmetrical mounds of woolly green moss bounded by croquet hoops formed the base of shrubs shaped like orange-trees but studded with large pink and red roses. Gigantic pansies, considerably larger than the roses, and closely resembling the floral pen-wipers made by female parishioners for fashionable clergymen, sprang from the moss beneath the rose-trees; and here and there a daisy grafted on a rose-branch flowered with a luxuriance prophetic of Mr. Luther Burbank's far-off prodigies.

In the centre of this enchanted garden Madame Nilsson, in white cashmere slashed with pale blue satin, a reticule dangling from a blue girdle, and large yellow braids carefully disposed on each side of her muslin chemisette, listened with downcast eyes to M. Capoul's impassioned wooing, and affected a guileless incomprehension of his designs whenever, by word or glance, he persuasively indicated the ground floor window of the neat brick villa projecting obliquely from the right wing.

"The darling!" thought Newland Archer, his glance flitting back to the young girl with the lilies-of-the-valley. "She doesn't even guess what it's all about." And he contemplated her absorbed young face with a thrill of possessorship in which pride in his own masculine initiation was mingled with a tender reverence for her abysmal purity. "We'll read Faust together . . . by the Italian lakes . . ." he thought, somewhat hazily confusing the scene of his projected honey-moon with the masterpieces of literature which it would be his manly privilege to reveal to his bride. It was only that afternoon that May Welland had let him guess that she "cared" (New York's consecrated phrase of maiden avowal), and already his imagination, leaping ahead of the engagement ring, the betrothal kiss and the march from Lohengrin, pictured her at his side in some scene of old European witchery.

He did not in the least wish the future Mrs. Newland Archer to be a simpleton. He meant her (thanks to his enlightening companionship) to develop a social tact and readiness of wit enabling her to hold her own with the most popular married women of the "younger set," in which it was the recognised custom to attract masculine homage while playfully discouraging it. If he had probed to the bottom of his vanity (as he sometimes nearly did) he would have found there the wish that his wife should be as worldly-wise and as eager to please as the married lady whose charms had held his fancy through two mildly agitated years; without, of course, any hint of the frailty which had so nearly marred that unhappy being's life, and had disarranged his own plans for a whole winter.

How this miracle of fire and ice was to be created, and to sustain itself in a harsh world, he had never taken the time to think out; but he was content to hold his view without analysing it, since he knew it was that of all the carefully-brushed, white-waistcoated, buttonhole-flowered gentlemen who succeeded each other in the club box, exchanged friendly greetings with him, and turned their opera-glasses critically on the circle of ladies who were the product of the system. In matters intellectual and artistic Newland Archer felt himself distinctly the superior of these chosen specimens of old New York gentility; he had probably read more, thought more, and even seen a good deal more of the world, than any other man of the number. Singly they betrayed their inferiority; but grouped together they represented "New York," and the habit of masculine solidarity made him accept their doctrine on all the issues called moral. He instinctively felt that in this respect it would be troublesome— and also rather bad form—to strike out for himself.

"Well—upon my soul!" exclaimed Lawrence Lefferts, turning his opera-glass abruptly away from the stage. Lawrence Lefferts was, on the whole, the foremost authority on "form" in New York. He had probably devoted more time than any one else to the study of this intricate and fascinating question; but study alone could not account for his complete and easy competence. One had only to look at him, from the slant of his bald forehead and the curve of his beautiful fair moustache to the long patent-leather feet at the other end of his lean and elegant person, to feel that the knowledge of "form" must be congenital in any one who knew how to wear such good clothes so carelessly and carry such height with so much lounging grace. As a young admirer had once said of him: "If anybody can tell a fellow just when to wear a black tie with evening clothes and when not to, it's Larry Lefferts." And on the question of pumps versus patent-leather "Oxfords" his authority had never been disputed.

"My God!" he said; and silently handed his glass to old Sillerton Jackson.

Newland Archer, following Lefferts's glance, saw with surprise that his exclamation had been occasioned by the entry of a new figure into old Mrs. Mingott's box. It was that of a slim young woman, a little less tall than May Welland, with brown hair growing in close curls about her temples and held in place by a narrow band of diamonds. The suggestion of this headdress, which gave her what was then called a "Josephine look," was carried out in the cut of the dark blue velvet gown rather theatrically caught up under her bosom by a girdle with a large old-fashioned clasp. The wearer of this unusual dress, who seemed quite unconscious of the attention it was attracting, stood a moment in the centre of the box, discussing with Mrs. Welland the propriety of taking the latter's place in the front right-hand corner; then she yielded with a slight smile, and seated herself in line with Mrs. Welland's sister-in-law, Mrs. Lovell Mingott, who was installed in the opposite corner.

Mr. Sillerton Jackson had returned the opera-glass to Lawrence Lefferts. The whole of the club turned instinctively, waiting to hear what the old man had to say; for old Mr. Jackson was as great an authority on "family" as Lawrence Lefferts was on "form." He knew all the ramifications of New York's cousinships; and could not only elucidate such complicated questions as that of the connection between the Mingotts (through the Thorleys) with the Dallases of South Carolina, and that of the relationship of the elder branch of Philadelphia Thorleys to the Albany Chiverses (on no account to be confused with the Manson Chiverses of University Place), but could also enumerate the leading characteristics of each family: as, for instance, the fabulous stinginess of the younger lines of Leffertses (the Long Island ones); or the fatal tendency of the Rushworths to make foolish matches; or the insanity recurring in every second generation of the Albany Chiverses, with whom their New York cousins had always refused to intermarry—with the disastrous exception of poor Medora Manson, who, as everybody knew . . . but then her mother was a Rushworth.

In addition to this forest of family trees, Mr. Sillerton Jackson carried between his narrow hollow temples, and under his soft thatch of silver hair, a register of most of the scandals and mysteries that had smouldered under the unruffled surface of New York society within the last fifty years. So far indeed did his information extend, and so acutely retentive was his memory, that he was supposed to be the only man who could have told you who Julius Beaufort, the banker, really was, and what had become of handsome Bob Spicer, old Mrs. Manson Mingott's father, who had disappeared so mysteriously (with a large sum of trust money) less than a year after his marriage, on the very day that a beautiful Spanish dancer who had been delighting thronged audiences in the old Opera-house on the Battery had taken ship for Cuba. But these mysteries, and many others, were closely locked in Mr. Jackson's breast; for not only did his keen sense of honour forbid his repeating anything privately imparted, but he was fully aware that his reputation for discretion increased his opportunities of finding out what he wanted to know.

The club box, therefore, waited in visible suspense while Mr. Sillerton Jackson handed back Lawrence Lefferts's opera-glass. For a moment he silently scrutinised the attentive group out of his filmy blue eyes overhung by old veined lids; then he gave his moustache a thoughtful twist, and said simply: "I didn't think the Mingotts would have tried it on."

2

Newland Archer, during this brief episode, had been thrown into a strange state of embarrassment.

It was annoying that the box which was thus attracting the undivided attention of masculine New York should be that in which his betrothed was seated between her mother and aunt; and for a moment he could not identify the lady in the Empire dress, nor imagine why her presence created such excitement among the initiated. Then light dawned on him, and with it came a momentary rush of indignation. No, indeed; no one would have thought the Mingotts would have tried it on!

But they had; they undoubtedly had; for the low-toned comments behind him left no doubt in Archer's mind that the young woman was May Welland's cousin, the cousin always referred to in the family as "poor Ellen Olenska." Archer knew that she had suddenly arrived from Europe a day or two previously; he had even heard from Miss Welland (not disapprovingly) that she had been to see poor Ellen, who was staying with old Mrs. Mingott. Archer entirely approved of family solidarity, and one of the qualities he most admired in the Mingotts was their resolute championship of the few black sheep that their blameless stock had produced. There was nothing mean or ungenerous in the young man's heart, and he was glad that his future wife should not be restrained by false prudery from being kind (in private) to her unhappy cousin; but to receive Countess Olenska in the family circle was a different thing from producing her in public, at the Opera of all places, and in the very box with the young girl whose engagement to him, Newland Archer, was to be announced within a few weeks. No, he felt as old Sillerton Jackson felt; he did not think the Mingotts would have tried it on!

He knew, of course, that whatever man dared (within Fifth Avenue's limits) that old Mrs. Manson Mingott, the Matriarch of the line, would dare. He had always admired the high and mighty old lady, who, in spite of having been only Catherine Spicer of Staten Island, with a father mysteriously discredited, and neither money nor position enough to make people forget it, had allied herself with the head of the wealthy Mingott line, married two of her daughters to "foreigners" (an Italian marquis and an English banker), and put the crowning touch to her audacities by building a large house of pale cream-coloured stone (when brown sandstone seemed as much the only wear as a frock-coat in the afternoon) in an inaccessible wilderness near the Central Park.

Old Mrs. Mingott's foreign daughters had become a legend. They never came back to see their mother, and the latter being, like many persons of active mind and dominating will, sedentary and corpulent in her habit, had philosophically remained at home. But the cream-coloured house (supposed to be modelled on the private hotels of the Parisian aristocracy) was there as a visible proof of her moral courage; and she throned in it, among pre-Revolutionary furniture and souvenirs of the Tuileries of Louis Napoleon (where she had shone in her middle age), as placidly as if there were nothing peculiar in living above Thirty-fourth Street, or in having French windows that opened like doors instead of sashes that pushed up.

Every one (including Mr. Sillerton Jackson) was agreed that old Catherine had never had beauty—a gift which, in the eyes of New York, justified every success, and excused a certain number of failings. Unkind people said that, like her Imperial namesake, she had won her way to success by strength of will and hardness of heart, and a kind of haughty effrontery that was somehow justified by the extreme decency and dignity of her private life. Mr. Manson Mingott had died when she was only twenty-eight, and had "tied up" the money with an additional caution born of the general distrust of the Spicers; but his bold young widow went her way fearlessly, mingled freely in foreign society, married her daughters in heaven knew what corrupt and fashionable circles, hobnobbed with Dukes and Ambassadors, associated familiarly with Papists, entertained Opera singers, and was the intimate friend of Mme. Taglioni; and all the while (as Sillerton Jackson was the first to proclaim) there had never been a breath on her reputation; the only respect, he always added, in which she differed from the earlier Catherine.

Mrs. Manson Mingott had long since succeeded in untying her husband's fortune, and had lived in affluence for half a century; but memories of her early straits had made her excessively thrifty, and though, when she bought a dress or a piece of furniture, she took care that it should be of the best, she could not bring herself to spend much on the transient pleasures of the table. Therefore, for totally different reasons, her food was as poor as Mrs. Archer's, and her wines did nothing to redeem it. Her relatives considered that the penury of her table discredited the Mingott name, which had always been associated with good living; but people continued to come to her in spite of the "made dishes" and flat champagne, and in reply to the remonstrances of her son Lovell (who tried to retrieve the family credit by having the best *chef* in New York) she used to say laughingly: "What's the use of two good cooks in one family, now that I've married the girls and can't eat sauces?"

Newland Archer, as he mused on these things, had once more turned his eyes toward the Mingott box. He saw that Mrs. Welland and her sister-in-law were facing their semicircle of critics with the Mingottian *aplomb* which old Catherine had inculcated in all her tribe, and that only May Welland betrayed, by a heightened colour (perhaps due to the knowledge that he was watching her) a sense of the gravity of the situation. As for the cause of the commotion, she sat gracefully in her corner of the box, her eyes fixed on the stage, and revealing, as she leaned forward, a little more shoulder and bosom than New York was accustomed to seeing, at least in ladies who had reasons for wishing to pass unnoticed.

Few things seemed to Newland Archer more awful than an offence against "Taste," that far-off divinity of whom "Form" was the mere visible representative and vicegerent. Madame Olenska's pale and serious face appealed to his fancy as suited to the occasion and to her unhappy situation; but the way her dress (which had no tucker) sloped away from her thin shoulders shocked and troubled him. He hated to think of May Welland's being exposed to the influence of a young woman so careless of the dictates of Taste.

"After all," he heard one of the younger men begin behind him (everybody talked through the Mephistopheles-and-Martha scenes), "after all, just *what* happened?"

"Well—she left him; nobody attempts to deny that."

"He's an awful brute, isn't he?" continued the young enquirer, a candid Thorley, who was evidently preparing to enter the lists as the lady's champion.

"The very worst; I knew him at Nice," said Lawrence Lefferts with authority. "A half-paralysed white sneering fellow—rather handsome head, but eyes with a lot of lashes. Well, I'll tell you the sort: when he wasn't with women he was collecting china. Paying any price for both, I understand."

There was a general laugh, and the young champion said: "Well, then——?"

"Well, then; she bolted with his secretary."

"Oh, I see." The champion's face fell.

"It didn't last long, though: I heard of her a few months later living alone in Venice. I believe Lovell Mingott went out to get her. He said she was desperately unhappy. That's all right—but this parading her at the Opera's another thing."

"Perhaps," young Thorley hazarded, "she's too unhappy to be left at home."

This was greeted with an irreverent laugh, and the youth blushed deeply, and tried to look as if he had meant to insinuate what knowing people called a *"double entendre."*

"Well—it's queer to have brought Miss Welland, anyhow," some one said in a low tone, with a side-glance at Archer.

"Oh, that's part of the campaign: Granny's orders, no doubt," Lefferts laughed. "When the old lady does a thing she does it thoroughly."

The act was ending, and there was a general stir in the box. Suddenly Newland Archer felt himself impelled to decisive action. The desire to be the first man to enter Mrs. Mingott's box, to proclaim to the waiting world his engagement to May Welland, and to see her through whatever difficulties her cousin's

anomalous situation might involve her in; this impulse had
abruptly overruled all scruples and hesitations, and sent him hurrying through the red corridors to the farther side of the house.

As he entered the box his eyes met Miss Welland's, and he
saw that she had instantly understood his motive, though the
family dignity which both considered so high a virtue would not
permit her to tell him so. The persons of their world lived in an
atmosphere of faint implications and pale delicacies, and the fact
that he and she understood each other without a word seemed
to the young man to bring them nearer than any explanation
would have done. Her eyes said: "You see why Mamma brought
me," and his answered: "I would not for the world have had
you stay away."

"You know my niece Countess Olenska?" Mrs. Welland enquired as she shook hands with her future son-in-law. Archer
bowed without extending his hand, as was the custom on being
introduced to a lady; and Ellen Olenska bent her head slightly,
keeping her own pale-gloved hands clasped on her huge fan of
eagle feathers. Having greeted Mrs. Lovell Mingott, a large
blonde lady in creaking satin, he sat down beside his betrothed,
and said in a low tone: "I hope you've told Madame Olenska
that we're engaged? I want everybody to know—I want you to
let me announce it this evening at the ball."

Miss Welland's face grew rosy as the dawn, and she looked
at him with radiant eyes. "If you can persuade Mamma," she
said; "but why should we change what is already settled?" He
made no answer but that which his eyes returned, and she added,
still more confidently smiling: "Tell my cousin yourself: I give
you leave. She says she used to play with you when you were
children."

She made way for him by pushing back her chair, and
promptly, and a little ostentatiously, with the desire that the
whole house should see what he was doing, Archer seated himself at the Countess Olenska's side.

"We *did* use to play together, didn't we?" she asked, turning
her grave eyes to his. "You were a horrid boy, and kissed me
once behind a door; but it was your cousin Vandie Newland,
who never looked at me, that I was in love with." Her glance

swept the horse-shoe curve of boxes. "Ah, how this brings it all back to me—I see everybody here in knickerbockers and pantalettes," she said, with her trailing slightly foreign accent, her eyes returning to his face.

Agreeable as their expression was, the young man was shocked that they should reflect so unseemly a picture of the august tribunal before which, at that very moment, her case was being tried. Nothing could be in worse taste than misplaced flippancy; and he answered somewhat stiffly: "Yes, you have been away a very long time."

"Oh, centuries and centuries; so long," she said, "that I'm sure I'm dead and buried, and this dear old place is heaven;" which, for reasons he could not define, struck Newland Archer as an even more disrespectful way of describing New York society.

It invariably happened in the same way.

Mrs. Julius Beaufort, on the night of her annual ball, never failed to appear at the Opera; indeed, she always gave her ball on an Opera night in order to emphasise her complete superiority to household cares, and her possession of a staff of servants competent to organise every detail of the entertainment in her absence.

The Beauforts' house was one of the few in New York that possessed a ball-room (it antedated even Mrs. Manson Mingott's and the Headly Chiverses'); and at a time when it was beginning to be thought "provincial" to put a "crash" over the drawing-room floor and move the furniture upstairs, the possession of a ball-room that was used for no other purpose, and left for three-hundred-and-sixty-four days of the year to shuttered darkness, with its gilt chairs stacked in a corner and its chandelier in a bag; this undoubted superiority was felt to compensate for whatever was regrettable in the Beaufort past.

Mrs. Archer, who was fond of coining her social philosophy into axioms, had once said: "We all have our pet common people—" and though the phrase was a daring one, its truth was secretly admitted in many an exclusive bosom. But the Beauforts were not exactly common; some people said they were even worse. Mrs. Beaufort belonged indeed to one of America's most honoured families; she had been the lovely Regina Dallas (of the South Carolina branch), a penniless beauty introduced to New York society by her cousin, the imprudent Medora Manson, who was always doing the wrong thing from the right motive. When one was related to the Mansons and the Rushworths one had a *"droit de cité"* (as Mr. Sillerton Jackson, who had frequented the Tuileries, called it) in New York society; but did one not forfeit it in marrying Julius Beaufort?

The question was: who *was* Beaufort? He passed for an Englishman, was agreeable, handsome, ill-tempered, hospitable and witty. He had come to America with letters of recommendation from old Mrs. Manson Mingott's English son-in-law, the banker, and had speedily made himself an important position in the world of affairs; but his habits were dissipated, his tongue was bitter, his antecedents were mysterious; and when Medora Manson announced her cousin's engagement to him it was felt to be one more act of folly in poor Medora's long record of imprudences.

But folly is as often justified of her children as wisdom, and two years after young Mrs. Beaufort's marriage it was admitted that she had the most distinguished house in New York. No one knew exactly how the miracle was accomplished. She was indolent, passive, the caustic even called her dull; but dressed like an idol, hung with pearls, growing younger and blonder and more beautiful each year, she throned in Mr. Beaufort's heavy brown-stone palace, and drew all the world there without lifting her jewelled little finger. The knowing people said it was Beaufort himself who trained the servants, taught the *chef* new dishes, told the gardeners what hot-house flowers to grow for the dinner-table and the drawing-rooms, selected the guests, brewed the after-dinner punch and dictated the little notes his wife wrote to her friends. If he did, these domestic activities were privately performed, and he presented to the world the appearance of a careless and hospitable millionaire strolling into his own drawing-room with the detachment of an invited guest, and saying: "My wife's gloxinias are a marvel, aren't they? I believe she gets them out from Kew."

Mr. Beaufort's secret, people were agreed, was the way he carried things off. It was all very well to whisper that he had been "helped" to leave England by the international banking-house in which he had been employed; he carried off that rumour as easily as the rest—though New York's business conscience was no less sensitive than its moral standard—he carried everything before him, and all New York into his drawing-rooms, and for over twenty years now people had said they were "going to the Beauforts'" with the same tone of security as if they had said they were going to Mrs. Manson Mingott's, and with the added satisfaction of knowing they would get hot canvas-back ducks and vintage wines, instead of tepid Veuve Clicquot without a year and warmed-up croquettes from Philadelphia.

Mrs. Beaufort, then, had as usual appeared in her box just before the Jewel Song; and when, again as usual, she rose at the end of the third act, drew her opera cloak about her lovely shoulders, and disappeared, New York knew that meant that half an hour later the ball would begin.

The Beaufort house was one that New Yorkers were proud to show to foreigners, especially on the night of the annual ball. The Beauforts had been among the first people in New York to own their own red velvet carpet and have it rolled down the steps by their own footmen, under their own awning, instead of hiring it with the supper and the ball-room chairs. They had also inaugurated the custom of letting the ladies take their cloaks off in the hall, instead of shuffling up to the hostess's bedroom and recurling their hair with the aid of the gas-burner; Beaufort was understood to have said that he supposed all his wife's friends had maids who saw to it that they were properly *coiffées* when they left home.

Then the house had been boldly planned with a ball-room, so that, instead of squeezing through a narrow passage to get to it (as at the Chiverses') one marched solemnly down a vista of enfiladed drawing-rooms (the sea-green, the crimson and the *bouton d'or*), seeing from afar the many-candled lustres reflected in the polished parquetry, and beyond that the depths of a conservatory where camellias and tree-ferns arched their costly foliage over seats of black and gold bamboo.

Newland Archer, as became a young man of his position, strolled in somewhat late. He had left his overcoat with the silk-stockinged footmen (the stockings were one of Beaufort's few fatuities), had dawdled a while in the library hung with Spanish leather and furnished with Buhl and malachite, where a few men were chatting and putting on their dancing-gloves, and had finally joined the line of guests whom Mrs. Beaufort was receiving on the threshold of the crimson drawing-room.

Archer was distinctly nervous. He had not gone back to his club after the Opera (as the young bloods usually did), but, the night being fine, had walked for some distance up Fifth Avenue before turning back in the direction of the Beauforts' house. He was definitely afraid that the Mingotts might be going too far; that, in fact, they might have Granny Mingott's orders to bring the Countess Olenska to the ball.

From the tone of the club box he had perceived how grave a mistake that would be; and, though he was more than ever determined to "see the thing through," he felt less chivalrously eager to champion his betrothed's cousin than before their brief talk at the Opera.

Wandering on to the *bouton d'or* drawing-room (where Beaufort had had the audacity to hang "Love Victorious," the much-discussed nude of Bouguereau) Archer found Mrs. Welland and her daughter standing near the ball-room door. Couples were already gliding over the floor beyond: the light of the wax candles fell on revolving tulle skirts, on girlish heads wreathed with modest blossoms, on the dashing aigrettes and ornaments of the young married women's *coiffures,* and on the glitter of highly glazed shirt-fronts and fresh glacé gloves.

Miss Welland, evidently about to join the dancers, hung on the threshold, her lilies-of-the-valley in her hand (she carried no other bouquet), her face a little pale, her eyes burning with a candid excitement. A group of young men and girls were gathered about her, and there was much hand-clasping, laughing and pleasantry on which Mrs. Welland, standing slightly apart, shed the beam of a qualified approval. It was evident that Miss Welland was in the act of announcing her engagement, while her mother affected the air of parental reluctance considered suitable to the occasion.

Archer paused a moment. It was at his express wish that the announcement had been made, and yet it was not thus that he would have wished to have his happiness known. To proclaim it in the heat and noise of a crowded ball-room was to rob it of the fine bloom of privacy which should belong to things nearest the heart. His joy was so deep that this blurring of the surface left its essence untouched; but he would have liked to keep the surface pure too. It was something of a satisfaction to find that May Welland shared this feeling. Her eyes fled to his beseechingly, and their look said: "Remember, we're doing this because it's right."

No appeal could have found a more immediate response in Archer's breast; but he wished that the necessity of their action had been represented by some ideal reason, and not simply by poor Ellen Olenska. The group about Miss Welland made way for him with significant smiles, and after taking his share of the felicitations he drew his betrothed into the middle of the ball-room floor and put his arm about her waist.

"Now we shan't have to talk," he said, smiling into her candid eyes, as they floated away on the soft waves of the Blue Danube.

She made no answer. Her lips trembled into a smile, but the eyes remained distant and serious, as if bent on some ineffable vision. "Dear," Archer whispered, pressing her to him: it was borne in on him that the first hours of being engaged, even if spent in a ball-room, had in them something grave and sacramental. What a new life it was going to be, with this whiteness, radiance, goodness at one's side!

The dance over, the two, as became an affianced couple, wandered into the conservatory; and sitting behind a tall screen of tree-ferns and camellias Newland pressed her gloved hand to his lips.

"You see I did as you asked me to," she said.

"Yes: I couldn't wait," he answered smiling. After a moment he added: "Only I wish it hadn't had to be at a ball."

"Yes, I know." She met his glance comprehendingly. "But after all—even here we're alone together, aren't we?"

"Oh, dearest—always!" Archer cried.

Evidently she was always going to understand; she was always going to say the right thing. The discovery made the cup of his bliss overflow, and he went on gaily: "The worst of it is that I want to kiss you and I can't." As he spoke he took a swift glance about the conservatory, assured himself of their momentary privacy, and catching her to him laid a fugitive pressure on her lips. To counteract the audacity of this proceeding he led her to a bamboo sofa in a less secluded part of the conservatory, and sitting down beside her broke a lily-of-the-valley from her bouquet. She sat silent, and the world lay like a sunlit valley at their feet.

"Did you tell my cousin Ellen?" she asked presently, as if she spoke through a dream.

He roused himself, and remembered that he had not done so. Some invincible repugnance to speak of such things to the strange foreign woman had checked the words on his lips.

"No—I hadn't the chance after all," he said, fibbing hastily.

"Ah." She looked disappointed, but gently resolved on gaining her point. "You must, then, for I didn't either; and I shouldn't like her to think—"

"Of course not. But aren't you, after all, the person to do it?"

She pondered on this. "If I'd done it at the right time, yes: but now that there's been a delay I think you must explain that I'd asked you to tell her at the Opera, before our speaking about it to everybody here. Otherwise she might think I had forgotten her. You see, she's one of the family, and she's been away so long that she's rather—sensitive."

Archer looked at her glowingly. "Dear and great angel! Of course I'll tell her." He glanced a trifle apprehensively toward the crowded ball-room. "But I haven't seen her yet. Has she come?"

"No; at the last minute she decided not to."

"At the last minute?" he echoed, betraying his surprise that she should ever have considered the alternative possible.

"Yes. She's awfully fond of dancing," the young girl answered simply. "But suddenly she made up her mind that her dress wasn't smart enough for a ball, though we thought it so lovely; and so my aunt had to take her home."

"Oh, well—" said Archer with happy indifference. Nothing about his betrothed pleased him more than her resolute determination to carry to its utmost limit that ritual of ignoring the "unpleasant" in which they had both been brought up.

"She knows as well as I do," he reflected, "the real reason of her cousin's staying away; but I shall never let her see by the least sign that I am conscious of there being a shadow of a shade on poor Ellen Olenska's reputation."

In the course of the next day the first of the usual betrothal visits were exchanged. The New York ritual was precise and inflexible in such matters; and in conformity with it Newland Archer first went with his mother and sister to call on Mrs. Welland, after which he and Mrs. Welland and May drove out to old Mrs. Manson Mingott's to receive that venerable ancestress's blessing.

A visit to Mrs. Manson Mingott was always an amusing episode to the young man. The house in itself was already an historic document, though not, of course, as venerable as certain other old family houses in University Place and lower Fifth Avenue. Those were of the purest 1830, with a grim harmony of cabbage-rose-garlanded carpets, rosewood consoles, round-arched fire-places with black marble mantels, and immense glazed book-cases of mahogany; whereas old Mrs. Mingott, who had built her house later, had bodily cast out the massive furniture of her prime, and mingled with the Mingott heirlooms the frivolous upholstery of the Second Empire. It was her habit to sit in a window of her sitting-room on the ground floor, as if watching calmly for life and fashion to flow northward to her solitary doors. She seemed in no hurry to have them come, for her patience was equalled by her confidence. She was sure that presently the hoardings, the quarries, the one-story saloons, the wooden green-houses in ragged gardens, and the rocks from which goats surveyed the scene, would vanish before the advance of residences as stately as her own—perhaps (for she was an impartial woman) even statelier; and that the cobblestones over which the old clattering omnibuses bumped would be replaced by smooth asphalt, such as people reported having seen in Paris. Meanwhile, as every one she cared to see came to *her* (and she could fill her rooms as easily as the Beauforts, and without adding a single item to the *menu* of her suppers), she did not suffer from her geographic isolation.

The immense accretion of flesh which had descended on her

in middle life like a flood of lava on a doomed city had changed her from a plump active little woman with a neatly-turned foot and ankle into something as vast and august as a natural phenomenon. She had accepted this submergence as philosophically as all her other trials, and now, in extreme old age, was rewarded by presenting to her mirror an almost unwrinkled expanse of firm pink and white flesh, in the centre of which the traces of a small face survived as if awaiting excavation. A flight of smooth double chins led down to the dizzy depths of a still-snowy bosom veiled in snowy muslins that were held in place by a miniature portrait of the late Mr. Mingott; and around and below, wave after wave of black silk surged away over the edges of a capacious armchair, with two tiny white hands poised like gulls on the surface of the billows.

The burden of Mrs. Manson Mingott's flesh had long since made it impossible for her to go up and down stairs, and with characteristic independence she had made her reception rooms upstairs and established herself (in flagrant violation of all the New York proprieties) on the ground floor of her house; so that, as you sat in her sitting-room window with her, you caught (through a door that was always open, and a looped-back yellow damask portière) the unexpected vista of a bedroom with a huge low bed upholstered like a sofa, and a toilet-table with frivolous lace flounces and a gilt-framed mirror.

Her visitors were startled and fascinated by the foreignness of this arrangement, which recalled scenes in French fiction, and architectural incentives to immorality such as the simple American had never dreamed of. That was how women with lovers lived in the wicked old societies, in apartments with all the rooms on one floor, and all the indecent propinquities that their novels described. It amused Newland Archer (who had secretly situated the love-scenes of "Monsieur de Camors" in Mrs. Mingott's bedroom) to picture her blameless life led in the stage-setting of adultery; but he said to himself, with considerable admiration, that if a lover had been what she wanted, the intrepid woman would have had him too.

To the general relief the Countess Olenska was not present in her grandmother's drawing-room during the visit of the betrothed couple. Mrs. Mingott said she had gone out; which, on a day of such glaring sunlight, and at the "shopping hour," seemed in itself an indelicate thing for a compromised woman to do. But at any rate it spared them the embarrassment of her presence, and the faint shadow that her unhappy past might seem to shed on their radiant future. The visit went off successfully, as was to have been expected. Old Mrs. Mingott was delighted with the engagement, which, being long foreseen by watchful relatives, had been carefully passed upon in family council; and the engagement ring, a large thick sapphire set in invisible claws, met with her unqualified admiration.

"It's the new setting: of course it shows the stone beautifully, but it looks a little bare to old-fashioned eyes," Mrs. Welland had explained, with a conciliatory side-glance at her future son-in-law.

"Old-fashioned eyes? I hope you don't mean mine, my dear? I like all the novelties," said the ancestress, lifting the stone to her small bright orbs, which no glasses had ever disfigured. "Very handsome," she added, returning the jewel; "very liberal. In my time a cameo set in pearls was thought sufficient. But it's the hand that sets off the ring, isn't it, my dear Mr. Archer?" and she waved one of her tiny hands, with small pointed nails and rolls of aged fat encircling the wrist like ivory bracelets. "Mine was modelled in Rome by the great Ferrigiani. You should have May's done: no doubt he'll have it done, my child. Her hand is large—it's these modern sports that spread the joints—but the skin is white.—And when's the wedding to be?" she broke off, fixing her eyes on Archer's face.

"Oh—" Mrs. Welland murmured, while the young man, smiling at his betrothed, replied: "As soon as ever it can, if only you'll back me up, Mrs. Mingott."

"We must give them time to get to know each other a little better, mamma," Mrs. Welland interposed, with the proper affectation of reluctance; to which the ancestress rejoined: "Know each other? Fiddlesticks! Everybody in New York has always known everybody. Let the young man have his way, my dear; don't wait till the bubble's off the wine. Marry them before Lent;

I may catch pneumonia any winter now, and I want to give the wedding-breakfast."

These successive statements were received with the proper expressions of amusement, incredulity and gratitude; and the visit was breaking up in a vein of mild pleasantry when the door opened to admit the Countess Olenska, who entered in bonnet and mantle followed by the unexpected figure of Julius Beaufort.

There was a cousinly murmur of pleasure between the ladies, and Mrs. Mingott held out Ferrigiani's model to the banker. "Ha! Beaufort, this is a rare favour!" (She had an odd foreign way of addressing men by their surnames.)

"Thanks. I wish it might happen oftener," said the visitor in his easy arrogant way. "I'm generally so tied down; but I met the Countess Ellen in Madison Square, and she was good enough to let me walk home with her."

"Ah—I hope the house will be gayer, now that Ellen's here!" cried Mrs. Mingott with a glorious effrontery. "Sit down—sit down, Beaufort: push up the yellow armchair; now I've got you I want a good gossip. I hear your ball was magnificent; and I understand you invited Mrs. Lemuel Struthers? Well—I've a curiosity to see the woman myself."

She had forgotten her relatives, who were drifting out into the hall under Ellen Olenska's guidance. Old Mrs. Mingott had always professed a great admiration for Julius Beaufort, and there was a kind of kinship in their cool domineering way and their short-cuts through the conventions. Now she was eagerly curious to know what had decided the Beauforts to invite (for the first time) Mrs. Lemuel Struthers, the widow of Struthers's Shoe-polish, who had returned the previous year from a long initiatory sojourn in Europe to lay siege to the tight little citadel of New York. "Of course if you and Regina invite her the thing is settled. Well, we need new blood and new money—and I hear she's still very good-looking," the carnivorous old lady declared.

In the hall, while Mrs. Welland and May drew on their furs, Archer saw that the Countess Olenska was looking at him with a faintly questioning smile.

"Of course you know already—about May and me," he said,

answering her look with a shy laugh. "She scolded me for not giving you the news last night at the Opera: I had her orders to tell you that we were engaged—but I couldn't, in that crowd."

The smile passed from Countess Olenska's eyes to her lips: she looked younger, more like the bold brown Ellen Mingott of his boyhood. "Of course I know; yes. And I'm so glad. But one doesn't tell such things first in a crowd." The ladies were on the threshold and she held out her hand.

"Good-bye; come and see me some day," she said, still looking at Archer.

In the carriage, on the way down Fifth Avenue, they talked pointedly of Mrs. Mingott, of her age, her spirit, and all her wonderful attributes. No one alluded to Ellen Olenska; but Archer knew that Mrs. Welland was thinking: "It's a mistake for Ellen to be seen, the very day after her arrival, parading up Fifth Avenue at the crowded hour with Julius Beaufort—" and the young man himself mentally added: "And she ought to know that a man who's just engaged doesn't spend his time calling on married women. But I daresay in the set she's lived in they do —they never do anything else." And, in spite of the cosmopolitan views on which he prided himself, he thanked heaven that he was a New Yorker, and about to ally himself with one of his own kind.

The next evening old Mr. Sillerton Jackson came to dine with the Archers.

Mrs. Archer was a shy woman and shrank from society; but she liked to be well-informed as to its doings. Her old friend Mr. Sillerton Jackson applied to the investigation of his friends' affairs the patience of a collector and the science of a naturalist; and his sister, Miss Sophy Jackson, who lived with him, and was entertained by all the people who could not secure her much-sought-after brother, brought home bits of minor gossip that filled out usefully the gaps in his picture.

Therefore, whenever anything happened that Mrs. Archer wanted to know about, she asked Mr. Jackson to dine; and as she honoured few people with her invitations, and as she and her daughter Janey were an excellent audience, Mr. Jackson usually came himself instead of sending his sister. If he could have dictated all the conditions, he would have chosen the evenings when Newland was out; not because the young man was un-congenial to him (the two got on capitally at their club) but because the old anecdotist sometimes felt, on Newland's part, a tendency to weigh his evidence that the ladies of the family never showed.

Mr. Jackson, if perfection had been attainable on earth, would also have asked that Mrs. Archer's food should be a little better. But then New York, as far back as the mind of man could travel, had been divided into the two great fundamental groups of the Mingotts and Mansons and all their clan, who cared about eating and clothes and money, and the Archer-Newland-van-der-Luyden tribe, who were devoted to travel, horticulture and the best fiction, and looked down on the grosser forms of pleasure.

You couldn't have everything, after all. If you dined with the Lovell Mingotts you got canvas-back and terrapin and vintage wines; at Adeline Archer's you could talk about Alpine scenery and "The Marble Faun"; and luckily the Archer Madeira had

gone round the Cape. Therefore when a friendly summons came
from Mrs. Archer, Mr. Jackson, who was a true eclectic, would
usually say to his sister: "I've been a little gouty since my last
dinner at the Lovell Mingotts'—it will do me good to diet at
Adeline's."

Mrs. Archer, who had long been a widow, lived with her son
and daughter in West Twenty-eighth Street. An upper floor was
dedicated to Newland, and the two women squeezed themselves
into narrower quarters below. In an unclouded harmony of
tastes and interests they cultivated ferns in Wardian cases, made
macramé lace and wool embroidery on linen, collected American
revolutionary glazed ware, subscribed to "Good Words," and
read Ouida's novels for the sake of the Italian atmosphere. (They
preferred those about peasant life, because of the descriptions of
scenery and the pleasanter sentiments, though in general they
liked novels about people in society, whose motives and habits
were more comprehensible, spoke severely of Dickens, who
"had never drawn a gentleman," and considered Thackeray less
at home in the great world than Bulwer—who, however, was
beginning to be thought old-fashioned.)

Mrs. and Miss Archer were both great lovers of scenery. It
was what they principally sought and admired on their occasional travels abroad; considering architecture and painting as
subjects for men, and chiefly for learned persons who read Ruskin. Mrs. Archer had been born a Newland, and mother and
daughter, who were as like as sisters, were both, as people said,
"true Newlands"; tall, pale, and slightly round-shouldered, with
long noses, sweet smiles and a kind of drooping distinction like
that in certain faded Reynolds portraits. Their physical resemblance would have been complete if an elderly *embonpoint* had
not stretched Mrs. Archer's black brocade, while Miss Archer's
brown and purple poplins hung, as the years went on, more and
more slackly on her virgin frame.

Mentally, the likeness between them, as Newland was aware,
was less complete than their identical mannerisms often made it
appear. The long habit of living together in mutually dependent
intimacy had given them the same vocabulary, and the same
habit of beginning their phrases "Mother thinks" or "Janey

thinks," according as one or the other wished to advance an opinion of her own; but in reality, while Mrs. Archer's serene unimaginativeness rested easily in the accepted and familiar, Janey was subject to starts and aberrations of fancy welling up from springs of suppressed romance.

Mother and daughter adored each other and revered their son and brother; and Archer loved them with a tenderness made compunctious and uncritical by the sense of their exaggerated admiration, a id by his secret satisfaction in it. After all, he thought it a good thing for a man to have his authority respected in his own house, even if his sense of humour sometimes made him question the force of his mandate.

On this occasion the young man was very sure that Mr. Jackson would rather have had him dine out; but he had his own reasons for not doing so.

Of course old Jackson wanted to talk about Ellen Olenska, and of course Mrs. Archer and Janey wanted to hear what he had to tell. All three would be slightly embarrassed by Newland's presence, now that his prospective relation to the Mingott clan had been made known; and the young man waited with an amused curiosity to see how they would turn the difficulty.

They began, obliquely, by talking about Mrs. Lemuel Struthers.

"It's a pity the Beauforts asked her," Mrs. Archer said gently. "But then Regina always does what he tells her; and Beaufort—"

"Certain *nuances* escape Beaufort," said Mr. Jackson, cautiously inspecting the broiled shad, and wondering for the thousandth time why Mrs. Archer's cook always burnt the roe to a cinder. (Newland, who had long shared his wonder, could always detect it in the older man's expression of melancholy disapproval.)

"Oh, necessarily; Beaufort is a vulgar man," said Mrs. Archer. "My grandfather Newland always used to say to my mother: 'Whatever you do, don't let that fellow Beaufort be introduced to the girls.' But at least he's had the advantage of associating with gentlemen; in England too, they say. It's all very mysterious—" She glanced at Janey and paused. She and Janey knew every fold of the Beaufort mystery, but in public Mrs. Archer continued to assume that the subject was not one for the unmarried.

"But this Mrs. Struthers," Mrs. Archer continued; "what did you say *she* was, Sillerton?"

"Out of a mine: or rather out of the saloon at the head of the pit. Then with Living Wax-Works, touring New England. After the police broke *that* up, they say she lived—" Mr. Jackson in his turn glanced at Janey, whose eyes began to bulge from under her prominent lids. There were still hiatuses for her in Mrs. Struthers's past.

"Then," Mr. Jackson continued (and Archer saw he was wondering why no one had told the butler never to slice cucumbers with a steel knife), "then Lemuel Struthers came along. They say his advertiser used the girl's head for the shoe-polish posters; her hair's intensely black, you know—the Egyptian style. Anyhow, he—eventually—married her." There were volumes of innuendo in the way the "eventually" was spaced, and each syllable given its due stress.

"Oh, well—at the pass we've come to nowadays, it doesn't matter," said Mrs. Archer indifferently. The ladies were not really interested in Mrs. Struthers just then; the subject of Ellen Olenska was too fresh and too absorbing to them. Indeed, Mrs. Struthers's name had been introduced by Mrs. Archer only that she might presently be able to say: "And Newland's new cousin—Countess Olenska? Was *she* at the ball too?"

There was a faint touch of sarcasm in the reference to her son, and Archer knew it and had expected it. Even Mrs. Archer, who was seldom unduly pleased with human events, had been altogether glad of her son's engagement. ("Especially after that silly business with Mrs. Rushworth," as she had remarked to Janey, alluding to what had once seemed to Newland a tragedy of which his soul would always bear the scar.) There was no better match in New York than May Welland, look at the question from whatever point you chose. Of course such a marriage was only what Newland was entitled to; but young men are so foolish and incalculable—and some women so ensnaring and unscrupulous—that it was nothing short of a miracle to see one's only son safe past the Siren Isle and in the haven of a blameless domesticity.

All this Mrs. Archer felt, and her son knew she felt; but he knew also that she had been perturbed by the premature announcement of his engagement, or rather by its cause; and it was for that reason—because on the whole he was a tender and indulgent master—that he had stayed at home that evening. "It's not that I don't approve of the Mingotts' *esprit de corps;* but why Newland's engagement should be mixed up with that Olenska woman's comings and goings I don't see," Mrs. Archer grumbled to Janey, the only witness of her slight lapses from perfect sweetness.

She had behaved beautifully—and in beautiful behaviour she was unsurpassed—during the call on Mrs. Welland; but Newland knew (and his betrothed doubtless guessed) that all through the visit she and Janey were nervously on the watch for Madame Olenska's possible intrusion; and when they left the house together she had permitted herself to say to her son: "I'm thankful that Augusta Welland received us alone."

These indications of inward disturbance moved Archer the more that he too felt that the Mingotts had gone a little too far. But, as it was against all the rules of their code that the mother and son should ever allude to what was uppermost in their thoughts, he simply replied: "Oh, well, there's always a phase of family parties to be gone through when one gets engaged, and the sooner it's over the better." At which his mother merely pursed her lips under the lace veil that hung down from her grey velvet bonnet trimmed with frosted grapes.

Her revenge, he felt—her lawful revenge—would be to "draw" Mr. Jackson that evening on the Countess Olenska; and, having publicly done his duty as a future member of the Mingott clan, the young man had no objection to hearing the lady discussed in private—except that the subject was already beginning to bore him.

Mr. Jackson had helped himself to a slice of the tepid *filet* which the mournful butler had handed him with a look as sceptical as his own, and had rejected the mushroom sauce after a scarcely perceptible sniff. He looked baffled and hungry, and

Archer reflected that he would probably finish his meal on Ellen Olenska.

Mr. Jackson leaned back in his chair, and glanced up at the candlelit Archers, Newlands and van der Luydens hanging in dark frames on the dark walls.

"Ah, how your grandfather Archer loved a good dinner, my dear Newland!" he said, his eyes on the portrait of a plump full-chested young man in a stock and a blue coat, with a view of a white-columned country-house behind him. "Well—well—well . . . I wonder what he would have said to all these foreign marriages!"

Mrs. Archer ignored the allusion to the ancestral *cuisine* and Mr. Jackson continued with deliberation: "No, she was *not* at the ball."

"Ah—" Mrs. Archer murmured, in a tone that implied: "She had that decency."

"Perhaps the Beauforts don't know her," Janey suggested, with her artless malice.

Mr. Jackson gave a faint sip, as if he had been tasting invisible Madeira. "Mrs. Beaufort may not—but Beaufort certainly does, for she was seen walking up Fifth Avenue this afternoon with him by the whole of New York."

"Mercy—" moaned Mrs. Archer, evidently perceiving the uselessness of trying to ascribe the actions of foreigners to a sense of delicacy.

"I wonder if she wears a round hat or a bonnet in the afternoon," Janey speculated. "At the Opera I know she had on dark blue velvet, perfectly plain and flat—like a night-gown."

"Janey!" said her mother; and Miss Archer blushed and tried to look audacious.

"It was, at any rate, in better taste not to go to the ball," Mrs. Archer continued.

A spirit of perversity moved her son to rejoin: "I don't think it was a question of taste with her. May said she meant to go, and then decided that the dress in question wasn't smart enough."

Mrs. Archer smiled at this confirmation of her inference. "Poor Ellen," she simply remarked; adding compassionately:

"We must always bear in mind what an eccentric bringing-up Medora Manson gave her. What can you expect of a girl who was allowed to wear black satin at her coming-out ball?"

"Ah—don't I remember her in it!" said Mr. Jackson; adding: "Poor girl!" in the tone of one who, while enjoying the memory, had fully understood at the time what the sight portended.

"It's odd," Janey remarked, "that she should have kept such an ugly name as Ellen. I should have changed it to Elaine." She glanced about the table to see the effect of this.

Her brother laughed. "Why Elaine?"

"I don't know; it sounds more—more Polish," said Janey, blushing.

"It sounds more conspicuous; and that can hardly be what she wishes," said Mrs. Archer distantly.

"Why not?" broke in her son, growing suddenly argumentative. "Why shouldn't she be conspicuous if she chooses? Why should she slink about as if it were she who had disgraced herself? She's 'poor Ellen' certainly, because she had the bad luck to make a wretched marriage; but I don't see that that's a reason for hiding her head as if she were the culprit."

"That, I suppose," said Mr. Jackson, speculatively, "is the line the Mingotts mean to take."

The young man reddened. "I didn't have to wait for their cue, if that's what you mean, sir. Madame Olenska has had an unhappy life: that doesn't make her an outcast."

"There are rumours," began Mr. Jackson, glancing at Janey.

"Oh, I know: the secretary," the young man took him up. "Nonsense, mother; Janey's grown-up. They say, don't they," he went on, "that the secretary helped her to get away from her brute of a husband, who kept her practically a prisoner? Well, what if he did? I hope there isn't a man among us who wouldn't have done the same in such a case."

Mr. Jackson glanced over his shoulder to say to the sad butler: "Perhaps . . . that sauce . . . just a little, after all—"; then, having helped himself, he remarked: "I'm told she's looking for a house. She means to live here."

"I hear she means to get a divorce," said Janey boldly.

"I hope she will!" Archer exclaimed.

The word had fallen like a bombshell in the pure and tranquil atmosphere of the Archer dining-room. Mrs. Archer raised her delicate eye-brows in the particular curve that signified: "The butler—" and the young man, himself mindful of the bad taste of discussing such intimate matters in public, hastily branched off into an account of his visit to old Mrs. Mingott.

After dinner, according to immemorial custom, Mrs. Archer and Janey trailed their long silk draperies up to the drawing-room, where, while the gentlemen smoked below stairs, they sat beside a Carcel lamp with an engraved globe, facing each other across a rosewood work-table with a green silk bag under it, and stitched at the two ends of a tapestry band of field-flowers destined to adorn an "occasional" chair in the drawing-room of young Mrs. Newland Archer.

While this rite was in progress in the drawing-room, Archer settled Mr. Jackson in an armchair near the fire in the Gothic library and handed him a cigar. Mr. Jackson sank into the armchair with satisfaction, lit his cigar with perfect confidence (it was Newland who bought them), and stretching his thin old ankles to the coals, said: "You say the secretary merely helped her to get away, my dear fellow? Well, he was still helping her a year later, then; for somebody met 'em living at Lausanne together."

Newland reddened. "Living together? Well, why not? Who had the right to make her life over if she hadn't? I'm sick of the hypocrisy that would bury alive a woman of her age if her husband prefers to live with harlots."

He stopped and turned away angrily to light his cigar. "Women ought to be free—as free as we are," he declared, making a discovery of which he was too irritated to measure the terrific consequences.

Mr. Sillerton Jackson stretched his ankles nearer the coals and emitted a sardonic whistle.

"Well," he said after a pause, "apparently Count Olenski takes your view; for I never heard of his having lifted a finger to get his wife back."

6

That evening, after Mr. Jackson had taken himself away, and the ladies had retired to their chintz-curtained bedroom, Newland Archer mounted thoughtfully to his own study. A vigilant hand had, as usual, kept the fire alive and the lamp trimmed; and the room, with its rows and rows of books, its bronze and steel statuettes of "The Fencers" on the mantelpiece and its many photographs of famous pictures, looked singularly home-like and welcoming.

As he dropped into his armchair near the fire his eyes rested on a large photograph of May Welland, which the young girl had given him in the first days of their romance, and which had now displaced all the other portraits on the table. With a new sense of awe he looked at the frank forehead, serious eyes and gay innocent mouth of the young creature whose soul's custodian he was to be. That terrifying product of the social system he belonged to and believed in, the young girl who knew nothing and expected everything, looked back at him like a stranger through May Welland's familiar features; and once more it was borne in on him that marriage was not the safe anchorage he had been taught to think, but a voyage on uncharted seas.

The case of the Countess Olenska had stirred up old settled convictions and set them drifting dangerously through his mind. His own exclamation: "Women should be free—as free as we are," struck to the root of a problem that it was agreed in his world to regard as non-existent. "Nice" women, however wronged, would never claim the kind of freedom he meant, and generous-minded men like himself were therefore—in the heat of argument—the more chivalrously ready to concede it to them. Such verbal generosities were in fact only a humbugging disguise of the inexorable conventions that tied things together and bound people down to the old pattern. But here he was pledged to defend, on the part of his betrothed's cousin, conduct that, on his own wife's part, would justify him in calling down on her all the thunders of Church and State. Of course the dilemma was purely hypothetical; since he wasn't a blackguard Polish nobleman, it was absurd to speculate what his wife's rights would be if he *were*. But Newland Archer was too imaginative not to feel that, in his case and May's, the tie might gall for reasons far less gross and palpable. What could he and she really know of each other, since it was his duty, as a "decent" fellow, to conceal his past from her, and hers, as a marriageable girl, to have no past to conceal? What if, for some one of the subtler reasons that would tell with both of them, they should tire of each other, misunderstand or irritate each other? He reviewed his friends' marriages—the supposedly happy ones—and saw none that answered, even remotely, to the passionate and tender comradeship which he pictured as his permanent relation with May Welland. He perceived that such a picture presupposed, on her part, the experience, the versatility, the freedom of judgment, which she had been carefully trained not to possess; and with a shiver of foreboding he saw his marriage becoming what most of the other marriages about him were: a dull association of material and social interests held together by ignorance on the one side and hypocrisy on the other. Lawrence Lefferts occurred to him as the husband who had most completely realised this enviable ideal. As became the high-priest of form, he had formed a wife so completely to his own convenience that, in the most conspicuous moments of his frequent love-affairs with other men's wives, she went about in smiling unconsciousness, saying that "Lawrence was so frightfully strict"; and had been known to blush indignantly, and avert her gaze, when some one alluded in her presence to the fact that Julius Beaufort (as became a "foreigner" of doubtful origin) had what was known in New York as "another establishment."

Archer tried to console himself with the thought that he was not quite such an ass as Larry Lefferts, nor May such a simpleton as poor Gertrude; but the difference was after all one of intelligence and not of standards. In reality they all lived in a kind of hieroglyphic world, where the real thing was never said or done or even thought, but only represented by a set of arbitrary signs; as when Mrs. Welland, who knew exactly why Archer had pressed her to announce her daughter's engagement at the Beaufort ball (and had indeed expected him to do no less), yet felt obliged to simulate reluctance, and the air of having had her hand forced, quite as, in the books on Primitive Man that people of advanced culture were beginning to read, the savage bride is dragged with shrieks from her parents' tent.

The result, of course, was that the young girl who was the centre of this elaborate system of mystification remained the more inscrutable for her very frankness and assurance. She was frank, poor darling, because she had nothing to conceal, assured because she knew of nothing to be on her guard against; and with no better preparation than this, she was to be plunged overnight into what people evasively called "the facts of life."

The young man was sincerely but placidly in love. He delighted in the radiant good looks of his betrothed, in her health, her horsemanship, her grace and quickness at games, and the shy interest in books and ideas that she was beginning to develop under his guidance. (She had advanced far enough to join him in ridiculing the Idyls of the King, but not to feel the beauty of Ulysses and the Lotus Eaters.) She was straightforward, loyal and brave; she had a sense of humour (chiefly proved by her laughing at *his* jokes); and he suspected, in the depths of her innocently-gazing soul, a glow of feeling that it would be a joy to waken. But when he had gone the brief round of her he returned discouraged by the thought that all this frankness and innocence were only an artificial product. Untrained human nature was not frank and innocent; it was full of the twists and defences of an instinctive guile. And he felt himself oppressed by this creation of factitious purity, so cunningly manufactured by a conspiracy of mothers and aunts and grandmothers and long-dead ancestresses, because it was supposed to be what he wanted, what he had a right to, in order that he might exercise his lordly pleasure in smashing it like an image made of snow.

There was a certain triteness in these reflections: they were those habitual to young men on the approach of their wedding day. But they were generally accompanied by a sense of compunction and self-abasement of which Newland Archer felt no trace. He could not deplore (as Thackeray's heroes so often ex-

asperated him by doing) that he had not a blank page to offer
his bride in exchange for the unblemished one she was to give
to him. He could not get away from the fact that if he had been
brought up as she had they would have been no more fit to find
their way about than the Babes in the Wood; nor could he, for
all his anxious cogitations, see any honest reason (any, that is,
unconnected with his own momentary pleasure, and the passion
of masculine vanity) why his bride should not have been allowed
the same freedom of experience as himself.

Such questions, at such an hour, were bound to drift through
his mind; but he was conscious that their uncomfortable per-
sistence and precision were due to the inopportune arrival of the
Countess Olenska. Here he was, at the very moment of his
betrothal—a moment for pure thoughts and cloudless hopes—
pitchforked into a coil of scandal which raised all the special
problems he would have preferred to let lie. "Hang Ellen Olenska!" he grumbled, as he covered his fire and began to undress.
He could not really see why her fate should have the least bearing on his; yet he dimly felt that he had only just begun to
measure the risks of the championship which his engagement
had forced upon him.

A few days later the bolt fell.

The Lovell Mingotts had sent out cards for what was known
as "a formal dinner" (that is, three extra footmen, two dishes for
each course, and a Roman punch in the middle), and had headed
their invitations with the words "To meet the Countess Olenska," in accordance with the hospitable American fashion, which
treats strangers as if they were royalties, or at least as their
ambassadors.

The guests had been selected with a boldness and discrimi-
nation in which the initiated recognised the firm hand of Catherine the Great. Associated with such immemorial standbys as
the Selfridge Merrys, who were asked everywhere because they
always had been, the Beauforts, on whom there was a claim of
relationship, and Mr. Sillerton Jackson and his sister Sophy (who
went wherever her brother told her to), were some of the most
fashionable and yet most irreproachable of the dominant "young

married" set; the Lawrence Leffertses, Mrs. Lefferts Rushworth (the lovely widow), the Harry Thorleys, the Reggie Chiverses and young Morris Dagonet and his wife (who was a van der Luyden). The company indeed was perfectly assorted, since all the members belonged to the little inner group of people who, during the long New York season, disported themselves together daily and nightly with apparently undiminished zest.

Forty-eight hours later the unbelievable had happened; every one had refused the Mingotts' invitation except the Beauforts and old Mr. Jackson and his sister. The intended slight was emphasised by the fact that even the Reggie Chiverses, who were of the Mingott clan, were among those inflicting it; and by the uniform wording of the notes, in all of which the writers "regretted that they were unable to accept," without the mitigating plea of a "previous engagement" that ordinary courtesy prescribed.

New York society was, in those days, far too small, and too scant in its resources, for every one in it (including livery-stable-keepers, butlers and cooks) not to know exactly on which evenings people were free; and it was thus possible for the recipients of Mrs. Lovell Mingott's invitations to make cruelly clear their determination not to meet the Countess Olenska.

The blow was unexpected; but the Mingotts, as their way was, met it gallantly. Mrs. Lovell Mingott confided the case to Mrs. Welland, who confided it to Newland Archer; who, aflame at the outrage, appealed passionately and authoritatively to his mother; who, after a painful period of inward resistance and outward temporising, succumbed to his instances (as she always did), and immediately embracing his cause with an energy redoubled by her previous hesitations, put on her grey velvet bonnet and said: "I'll go and see Louisa van der Luyden."

The New York of Newland Archer's day was a small and slippery pyramid, in which, as yet, hardly a fissure had been made or a foothold gained. At its base was a firm foundation of what Mrs. Archer called "plain people"; an honourable but obscure majority of respectable families who (as in the case of the Spicers or the Leffertses or the Jacksons) had been raised above their level by marriage with one of the ruling clans. People, Mrs.

Archer always said, were not as particular as they used to be; and with old Catherine Spicer ruling one end of Fifth Avenue, and Julius Beaufort the other, you couldn't expect the old traditions to last much longer.

Firmly narrowing upward from this wealthy but inconspicuous substratum was the compact and dominant group which the Mingotts, Newlands, Chiverses and Mansons so actively represented. Most people imagined them to be the very apex of the pyramid; but they themselves (at least those of Mrs. Archer's generation) were aware that, in the eyes of the professional genealogist, only a still smaller number of families could lay claim to that eminence.

"Don't tell me," Mrs. Archer would say to her children, "all this modern newspaper rubbish about a New York aristocracy. If there is one, neither the Mingotts nor the Mansons belong to it; no, nor the Newlands or the Chiverses either. Our grandfathers and great-grandfathers were just respectable English or Dutch merchants, who came to the colonies to make their fortune, and stayed here because they did so well. One of your great-grandfathers signed the Declaration, and another was a general on Washington's staff, and received General Burgoyne's sword after the battle of Saratoga. These are things to be proud of, but they have nothing to do with rank or class. New York has always been a commercial community, and there are not more than three families in it who can claim an aristocratic origin in the real sense of the word."

Mrs. Archer and her son and daughter, like every one else in New York, knew who these privileged beings were: the Dagonets of Washington Square, who came of an old English county family allied with the Pitts and Foxes; the Lannings, who had intermarried with the descendants of Count de Grasse, and the van der Luydens, direct descendants of the first Dutch governor of Manhattan, and related by pre-revolutionary marriages to several members of the French and British aristocracy.

The Lannings survived only in the person of two very old but lively Miss Lannings, who lived cheerfully and reminiscently among family portraits and Chippendale; the Dagonets were a considerable clan, allied to the best names in Baltimore and Philadelphia; but the van der Luydens, who stood above all of them, had faded into a kind of super-terrestrial twilight, from which only two figures impressively emerged; those of Mr. and Mrs. Henry van der Luyden.

Mrs. Henry van der Luyden had been Louisa Dagonet, and her mother had been the granddaughter of Colonel du Lac, of an old Channel Island family, who had fought under Cornwallis and had settled in Maryland, after the war, with his bride, Lady Angelica Trevenna, fifth daughter of the Earl of St. Austrey. The tie between the Dagonets, the du Lacs of Maryland, and their aristocratic Cornish kinsfolk, the Trevennas, had always remained close and cordial. Mr. and Mrs. van der Luyden had more than once paid long visits to the present head of the house of Trevenna, the Duke of St. Austrey, at his country-seat in Cornwall and at St. Austrey in Gloucestershire; and his Grace had frequently announced his intention of some day returning their visit (without the Duchess, who feared the Atlantic).

Mr. and Mrs. van der Luyden divided their time between Trevenna, their place in Maryland, and Skuytercliff, the great estate on the Hudson which had been one of the colonial grants of the Dutch government to the famous first Governor, and of which Mr. van der Luyden was still "Patroon." Their large solemn house in Madison Avenue was seldom opened, and when they came to town they received in it only their most intimate friends.

"I wish you would go with me, Newland," his mother said, suddenly pausing at the door of the Brown *coupé*. "Louisa is fond of you; and of course it's on account of dear May that I'm taking this step—and also because, if we don't all stand together, there'll be no such thing as Society left."

Mrs. Henry van der Luyden listened in silence to her cousin Mrs. Archer's narrative.

It was all very well to tell yourself in advance that Mrs. van der Luyden was always silent, and that, though non-committal by nature and training, she was very kind to the people she really liked. Even personal experience of these facts was not always a protection from the chill that descended on one in the high-ceilinged white-walled Madison Avenue drawing-room, with the pale brocaded armchairs so obviously uncovered for the occasion, and the gauze still veiling the ormolu mantel ornaments and the beautiful old carved frame of Gainsborough's "Lady Angelica du Lac."

Mrs. van der Luyden's portrait by Huntington (in black velvet and Venetian point) faced that of her lovely ancestress. It was generally considered "as fine as a Cabanel," and, though twenty years had elapsed since its execution, was still "a perfect likeness." Indeed the Mrs. van der Luyden who sat beneath it listening to Mrs. Archer might have been the twin-sister of the fair and still youngish woman drooping against a gilt armchair before a green rep curtain. Mrs. van der Luyden still wore black velvet and Venetian point when she went into society—or rather (since she never dined out) when she threw open her own doors to receive it. Her fair hair, which had faded without turning grey, was still parted in flat overlapping points on her forehead, and the straight nose that divided her pale blue eyes was only a little more pinched about the nostrils than when the portrait had been painted. She always, indeed, struck Newland Archer as having been rather gruesomely preserved in the airless atmosphere of a perfectly irreproachable existence, as bodies caught in glaciers keep for years a rosy life-in-death.

Like all his family, he esteemed and admired Mrs. van der Luyden; but he found her gentle bending sweetness less approachable than the grimness of some of his mother's old aunts, fierce spinsters who said "No" on principle before they knew what they were going to be asked.

Mrs. van der Luyden's attitude said neither yes nor no, but always appeared to incline to clemency till her thin lips, wavering into the shadow of a smile, made the almost invariable reply: "I shall first have to talk this over with my husband."

She and Mr. van der Luyden were so exactly alike that Archer often wondered how, after forty years of the closest conjugality, two such merged identities ever separated themselves enough for anything as controversial as a talking-over. But as neither had ever reached a decision without prefacing it by this mysterious conclave, Mrs. Archer and her son, having set forth their case, waited resignedly for the familiar phrase.

Mrs. van der Luyden, however, who had seldom surprised any one, now surprised them by reaching her long hand toward the bell-rope.

"I think," she said, "I should like Henry to hear what you have told me."

A footman appeared, to whom she gravely added: "If Mr. van der Luyden has finished reading the newspaper, please ask him to be kind enough to come."

She said "reading the newspaper" in the tone in which a Minister's wife might have said: "Presiding at a Cabinet meeting"— not from any arrogance of mind, but because the habit of a life-time, and the attitude of her friends and relations, had led her to consider Mr. van der Luyden's least gesture as having an almost sacerdotal importance.

Her promptness of action showed that she considered the case as pressing as Mrs. Archer; but, lest she should be thought to have committed herself in advance, she added, with the sweetest look: "Henry always enjoys seeing you, dear Adeline; and he will wish to congratulate Newland."

The double doors had solemnly reopened and between them appeared Mr. Henry van der Luyden, tall, spare and frock-coated, with faded fair hair, a straight nose like his wife's and the same look of frozen gentleness in eyes that were merely pale grey instead of pale blue.

Mr. van der Luyden greeted Mrs. Archer with cousinly affability, proffered to Newland low-voiced congratulations couched in the same language as his wife's, and seated himself in one of the brocade armchairs with the simplicity of a reigning sovereign.

"I had just finished reading the Times," he said, laying his long finger-tips together. "In town my mornings are so much occupied that I find it more convenient to read the newspapers after luncheon."

"Ah, there's a great deal to be said for that plan—indeed I think my uncle Egmont used to say he found it less agitating not to read the morning papers till after dinner," said Mrs. Archer responsively.

"Yes: my good father abhorred hurry. But now we live in a constant rush," said Mr. van der Luyden in measured tones, looking with pleasant deliberation about the large shrouded room which to Archer was so complete an image of its owners.

"But I hope you *had* finished your reading, Henry?" his wife interposed.

"Quite—quite," he reassured her.

"Then I should like Adeline to tell you—"

"Oh, it's really Newland's story," said his mother smiling; and proceeded to rehearse once more the monstrous tale of the affront inflicted on Mrs. Lovell Mingott.

"Of course," she ended, "Augusta Welland and Mary Mingott both felt that, especially in view of Newland's engagement, you and Henry *ought to know*."

"Ah—" said Mr. van der Luyden, drawing a deep breath.

There was a silence during which the tick of the monumental ormolu clock on the white marble mantelpiece grew as loud as the boom of a minute-gun. Archer contemplated with awe the two slender faded figures, seated side by side in a kind of vice-regal rigidity, mouthpieces of some remote ancestral authority which fate compelled them to wield, when they would so much rather have lived in simplicity and seclusion, digging invisible weeds out of the perfect lawns of Skuytercliff, and playing Patience together in the evenings.

Mr. van der Luyden was the first to speak.

"You really think this is due to some—some intentional interference of Lawrence Lefferts's?" he enquired, turning to Archer.

"I'm certain of it, sir. Larry has been going it rather harder than usual lately—if cousin Louisa won't mind my mentioning it—having rather a stiff affair with the postmaster's wife in their village, or some one of that sort; and whenever poor Gertrude Lefferts begins to suspect anything, and he's afraid of trouble, he gets up a fuss of this kind, to show how awfully moral he is, and talks at the top of his voice about the impertinence of inviting his wife to meet people he doesn't wish her to know. He's simply using Madame Olenska as a lightning-rod; I've seen him try the same thing often before."

"The *Leffertses!*—" said Mrs. van der Luyden.

"The *Leffertses!*—" echoed Mrs. Archer. "What would uncle Egmont have said of Lawrence Lefferts's pronouncing on anybody's social position? It shows what Society has come to."

"We'll hope it has not quite come to that," said Mr. van der Luyden firmly.

"Ah, if only you and Louisa went out more!" sighed Mrs. Archer.

But instantly she became aware of her mistake. The van der Luydens were morbidly sensitive to any criticism of their secluded existence. They were the arbiters of fashion, the Court of last Appeal, and they knew it, and bowed to their fate. But being shy and retiring persons, with no natural inclination for their part, they lived as much as possible in the sylvan solitude of Skuytercliff, and when they came to town, declined all invitations on the plea of Mrs. van der Luyden's health.

Newland Archer came to his mother's rescue. "Everybody in New York knows what you and cousin Louisa represent. That's why Mrs. Mingott felt she ought not to allow this slight on Countess Olenska to pass without consulting you."

Mrs. van der Luyden glanced at her husband, who glanced back at her.

"It is the principle that I dislike," said Mr. van der Luyden. "As long as a member of a well-known family is backed up by that family it should be considered—final."

"It seems so to me," said his wife, as if she were producing a new thought.

"I had no idea," Mr. van der Luyden continued, "that things had come to such a pass." He paused, and looked at his wife again. "It occurs to me, my dear, that the Countess Olenska is already a sort of relation—through Medora Manson's first husband. At any rate, she will be when Newland marries." He turned toward the young man. "Have you read this morning's Times, Newland?"

"Why, yes, sir," said Archer, who usually tossed off half a dozen papers with his morning coffee.

Husband and wife looked at each other again. Their pale eyes clung together in prolonged and serious consultation; then a faint smile fluttered over Mrs. van der Luyden's face. She had evidently guessed and approved.

Mr. van der Luyden turned to Mrs. Archer. "If Louisa's health allowed her to dine out—I wish you would say to Mrs. Lovell Mingott—she and I would have been happy to—er—fill the places of the Lawrence Leffertses at her dinner." He paused to let the irony of this sink in. "As you know, this is impossible." Mrs. Archer sounded a sympathetic assent. "But Newland tells me he has read this morning's Times; therefore he has probably seen that Louisa's relative, the Duke of St. Austrey, arrives next week on the Russia. He is coming to enter his new sloop, the Guinevere, in next summer's International Cup Race; and also to have a little canvasback shooting at Trevenna." Mr. van der Luyden paused again, and continued with increasing benevolence: "Before taking him down to Maryland we are inviting a few friends to meet him here—only a little dinner—with a reception afterward. I am sure Louisa will be as glad as I am if Countess Olenska will let us include her among our guests." He got up, bent his long body with a stiff friendliness toward his cousin, and added: "I think I have Louisa's authority for saying that she will herself leave the invitation to dine when she drives out presently: with our cards—of course with our cards."

Mrs. Archer, who knew this to be a hint that the seventeen-hand chestnuts which were never kept waiting were at the door, rose with a hurried murmur of thanks. Mrs. van der Luyden beamed on her with the smile of Esther interceding with Ahasuerus; but her husband raised a protesting hand.

"There is nothing to thank me for, dear Adeline; nothing whatever. This kind of thing must not happen in New York; it shall not, as long as I can help it," he pronounced with sovereign gentleness as he steered his cousins to the door.

Two hours later, every one knew that the great C-spring barouche in which Mrs. van der Luyden took the air at all seasons had been seen at old Mrs. Mingott's door, where a large square envelope was handed in; and that evening at the Opera Mr. Sillerton Jackson was able to state that the envelope contained a card inviting the Countess Olenska to the dinner which the van der Luydens were giving the following week for their cousin, the Duke of St. Austrey.

Some of the younger men in the club box exchanged a smile at this announcement, and glanced sideways at Lawrence Lefferts, who sat carelessly in the front of the box, pulling his long fair moustache, and who remarked with authority, as the soprano paused: "No one but Patti ought to attempt the Sonnambula."

It was generally agreed in New York that the Countess Olenska had "lost her looks."

She had appeared there first, in Newland Archer's boyhood, as a brilliantly pretty little girl of nine or ten, of whom people said that she "ought to be painted." Her parents had been continental wanderers, and after a roaming babyhood she had lost them both, and been taken in charge by her aunt, Medora Manson, also a wanderer, who was herself returning to New York to "settle down."

Poor Medora, repeatedly widowed, was always coming home to settle down (each time in a less expensive house), and bringing with her a new husband or an adopted child; but after a few months she invariably parted from her husband or quarrelled with her ward, and, having got rid of her house at a loss, set out again on her wanderings. As her mother had been a Rushworth, and her last unhappy marriage had linked her to one of the crazy Chiverses, New York looked indulgently on her eccentricities; but when she returned with her little orphaned niece, whose parents had been popular in spite of their regrettable taste for travel, people thought it a pity that the pretty child should be in such hands.

Every one was disposed to be kind to little Ellen Mingott, though her dusky red cheeks and tight curls gave her an air of gaiety that seemed unsuitable in a child who should still have been in black for her parents. It was one of the misguided Medora's many peculiarities to flout the unalterable rules that regulated American mourning, and when she stepped from the steamer her family were scandalised to see that the crape veil she wore for her own brother was seven inches shorter than those of her sisters-in-law, while little Ellen was in crimson merino and amber beads, like a gipsy foundling.

But New York had so long resigned itself to Medora that only a few old ladies shook their heads over Ellen's gaudy clothes, while her other relations fell under the charm of her high colour and high spirits. She was a fearless and familiar little thing, who asked disconcerting questions, made precocious comments, and possessed outlandish arts, such as dancing a Spanish shawl dance and singing Neapolitan love-songs to a guitar. Under the direction of her aunt (whose real name was Mrs. Thorley Chivers, but who, having received a Papal title, had resumed her first husband's patronymic, and called herself the Marchioness Manson, because in Italy she could turn it into Manzoni) the little girl received an expensive but incoherent education, which included "drawing from the model," a thing never dreamed of before, and playing the piano in quintets with professional musicians.

Of course no good could come of this; and when, a few years later, poor Chivers finally died in a madhouse, his widow (draped in strange weeds) again pulled up stakes and departed with Ellen, who had grown into a tall bony girl with conspicuous eyes. For some time no more was heard of them; then news came of Ellen's marriage to an immensely rich Polish nobleman of legendary fame, whom she had met at a ball at the Tuileries, and who was said to have princely establishments in Paris, Nice and Florence, a yacht at Cowes, and many square miles of shooting in Transylvania. She disappeared in a kind of sulphurous apotheosis, and when a few years later Medora again came back to New York, subdued, impoverished, mourning a third husband, and in quest of a still smaller house, people wondered that her rich niece had not been able to do something for her. Then came the news that Ellen's own marriage had ended in disaster, and that she was herself returning home to seek rest and oblivion among her kinsfolk.

These things passed through Newland Archer's mind a week later as he watched the Countess Olenska enter the van der Luyden drawing-room on the evening of the momentous dinner. The occasion was a solemn one, and he wondered a little nervously how she would carry it off. She came rather late, one hand still ungloved, and fastening a bracelet about her wrist; yet she entered without any appearance of haste or embarrassment the drawing-room in which New York's most chosen company was somewhat awfully assembled.

In the middle of the room she paused, looking about her with a grave mouth and smiling eyes; and in that instant Newland Archer rejected the general verdict on her looks. It was true that her early radiance was gone. The red cheeks had paled; she was thin, worn, a little older-looking than her age, which must have been nearly thirty. But there was about her the mysterious authority of beauty, a sureness in the carriage of the head, the movement of the eyes, which, without being in the least theatrical, struck his as highly trained and full of a conscious power. At the same time she was simpler in manner than most of the ladies present, and many people (as he heard afterward from Janey) were disappointed that her appearance was not more "stylish"—for stylishness was what New York most valued. It was, perhaps, Archer reflected, because her early vivacity had disappeared; because she was so quiet—quiet in her movements, her voice, and the tones of her low-pitched voice. New York had expected something a good deal more resonant in a young woman with such a history.

The dinner was a somewhat formidable business. Dining with the van der Luydens was at best no light matter, and dining there with a Duke who was their cousin was almost a religious solemnity. It pleased Archer to think that only an old New Yorker could perceive the shade of difference (to New York) between being merely a Duke and being the van der Luydens' Duke. New York took stray noblemen calmly, and even (except in the Struthers set) with a certain distrustful *hauteur;* but when they presented such credentials as these they were received with an old-fashioned cordiality that they would have been greatly mistaken in ascribing solely to their standing in Debrett. It was for just such distinctions that the young man cherished his old New York even while he smiled at it.

The van der Luydens had done their best to emphasise the importance of the occasion. The du Lac Sèvres and the Trevenna George II plate were out; so was the van der Luyden "Lowestoft" (East India Company) and the Dagonet Crown Derby.

Mrs. van der Luyden looked more than ever like a Cabanel, and Mrs. Archer, in her grandmother's seed-pearls and emeralds, reminded her son of an Isabey miniature. All the ladies had on their handsomest jewels, but it was characteristic of the house and the occasion that these were mostly in rather heavy old-fashioned settings; and old Miss Lanning, who had been persuaded to come, actually wore her mother's cameos and a Spanish blonde shawl.

The Countess Olenska was the only young woman at the dinner; yet, as Archer scanned the smooth plump elderly faces between their diamond necklaces and towering ostrich feathers, they struck him as curiously immature compared with hers. It frightened him to think what must have gone to the making of her eyes.

The Duke of St. Austrey, who sat at his hostess's right, was naturally the chief figure of the evening. But if the Countess Olenska was less conspicuous than had been hoped, the Duke was almost invisible. Being a well-bred man he had not (like another recent ducal visitor) come to the dinner in a shooting-jacket; but his evening clothes were so shabby and baggy, and he wore them with such an air of their being homespun, that (with his stooping way of sitting, and the vast beard spreading over his shirt-front) he hardly gave the appearance of being in dinner attire. He was short, round-shouldered, sunburnt, with a thick nose, small eyes and a sociable smile; but he seldom spoke, and when he did it was in such low tones that, despite the frequent silences of expectation about the table, his remarks were lost to all but his neighbours.

When the men joined the ladies after dinner the Duke went straight up to the Countess Olenska, and they sat down in a corner and plunged into animated talk. Neither seemed aware that the Duke should first have paid his respects to Mrs. Lovell Mingott and Mrs. Headly Chivers, and the Countess have conversed with that amiable hypochondriac, Mr. Urban Dagonet of Washington Square, who, in order to have the pleasure of meeting her, had broken through his fixed rule of not dining out between January and April. The two chatted together for nearly twenty minutes; then the Countess rose and, walking alone across the wide drawing-room, sat down at Newland Archer's side.

It was not the custom in New York drawing-rooms for a lady to get up and walk away from one gentleman in order to seek the company of another. Etiquette required that she should wait, immovable as an idol, while the men who wished to converse with her succeeded each other at her side. But the Countess was apparently unaware of having broken any rule; she sat at perfect ease in a corner of the sofa beside Archer, and looked at him with the kindest eyes.

"I want you to talk to me about May," she said.

Instead of answering her he asked: "You knew the Duke before?"

"Oh, yes—we used to see him every winter at Nice. He's very fond of gambling—he used to come to the house a great deal." She said it in the simplest manner, as if she had said: "He's fond of wild-flowers"; and after a moment she added candidly: "I think he's the dullest man I ever met."

This pleased her companion so much that he forgot the slight shock her previous remark had caused him. It was undeniably exciting to meet a lady who found the van der Luydens' Duke dull, and dared to utter the opinion. He longed to question her, to hear more about the life of which her careless words had given him so illuminating a glimpse; but he feared to touch on distressing memories, and before he could think of anything to say she had strayed back to her original subject.

"May is a darling; I've seen no young girl in New York so handsome and so intelligent. Are you very much in love with her?"

Newland Archer reddened and laughed. "As much as a man can be."

She continued to consider him thoughtfully, as if not to miss any shade of meaning in what he said, "Do you think, then, there is a limit?"

"To being in love? If there is, I haven't found it!"

She glowed with sympathy. "Ah—it's really and truly a romance?"

"The most romantic of romances!"

"How delightful! And you found it all out for yourselves—it was not in the least arranged for you?"

Archer looked at her incredulously. "Have you forgotten," he asked with a smile, "that in our country we don't allow our marriages to be arranged for us?"

A dusky blush rose to her cheek, and he instantly regretted his words.

"Yes," she answered, "I'd forgotten. You must forgive me if I sometimes make these mistakes. I don't always remember that everything here is good that was—that was bad where I've come from." She looked down at her Viennese fan of eagle feathers, and he saw that her lips trembled.

"I'm so sorry," he said impulsively; "but you *are* among friends here, you know."

"Yes—I know. Wherever I go I have that feeling. That's why I came home. I want to forget everything else, to become a complete American again, like the Mingotts and Wellands, and you and your delightful mother, and all the other good people here tonight. Ah, here's May arriving, and you will want to hurry away to her," she added, but without moving; and her eyes turned back from the door to rest on the young man's face.

The drawing-rooms were beginning to fill up with after-dinner guests, and following Madame Olenska's glance Archer saw May Welland entering with her mother. In her dress of white and silver, with a wreath of silver blossoms in her hair, the tall girl looked like a Diana just alight from the chase.

"Oh," said Archer, "I have so many rivals; you see she's already surrounded. There's the Duke being introduced."

"Then stay with me a little longer," Madame Olenska said in a low tone, just touching his knee with her plumed fan. It was the lightest touch, but it thrilled him like a caress.

"Yes, let me stay," he answered in the same tone, hardly knowing what he said; but just then Mr. van der Luyden came up, followed by old Mr. Urban Dagonet. The Countess greeted them with her grave smile, and Archer, feeling his host's admonitory glance on him, rose and surrendered his seat.

Madame Olenska held out her hand as if to bid him goodbye.

"Tomorrow, then, after five—I shall expect you," she said; and then turned back to make room for Mr. Dagonet.

"Tomorrow—" Archer heard himself repeating, though there had been no engagement, and during their talk she had given him no hint that she wished to see him again.

As he moved away he saw Lawrence Lefferts, tall and resplendent, leading his wife up to be introduced; and heard Gertrude Lefferts say, as she beamed on the Countess with her large unperceiving smile: "But I think we used to go to dancing-school together when we were children—." Behind her, waiting their turn to name themselves to the Countess, Archer noticed a number of the recalcitrant couples who had declined to meet her at Mrs. Lovell Mingott's. As Mrs. Archer remarked: when the van der Luydens chose, they knew how to give a lesson. The wonder was that they chose so seldom.

The young man felt a touch on his arm and saw Mrs. van der Luyden looking down on him from the pure eminence of black velvet and the family diamonds. "It was good of you, dear Newland, to devote yourself so unselfishly to Madame Olenska. I told your cousin Henry he must really come to the rescue."

He was aware of smiling at her vaguely, and she added, as if condescending to his natural shyness: "I've never seen May looking lovelier. The Duke thinks her the handsomest girl in the room."

The Countess Olenska had said "after five"; and at half after the hour Newland Archer rang the bell of the peeling stucco house with a giant wisteria throttling its feeble cast-iron balcony, which she had hired, far down West Twenty-third Street, from the vagabond Medora.

It was certainly a strange quarter to have settled in. Small dress-makers, bird-stuffers and "people who wrote" were her nearest neighbours; and further down the dishevelled street Archer recognised a delapidated wooden house, at the end of a paved path, in which a writer and journalist called Winsett, whom he used to come across now and then, had mentioned that he lived. Winsett did not invite people to his house; but he had once pointed it out to Archer in the course of a nocturnal stroll, and the latter had asked himself, with a little shiver, if the humanities were so meanly housed in other capitals.

Madame Olenska's own dwelling was redeemed from the same appearance only by a little more paint about the window-frames; and as Archer mustered its modest front he said to himself that the Polish Count must have robbed her of her fortune as well as of her illusions.

The young man had spent an unsatisfactory day. He had lunched with the Wellands, hoping afterward to carry off May for a walk in the Park. He wanted to have her to himself, to tell her how enchanting she had looked the night before, and how proud he was of her, and to press her to hasten their marriage. But Mrs. Welland had firmly reminded him that the round of family visits was not half over, and, when he hinted at advancing the date of the wedding, had raised reproachful eyebrows and sighed out: "Twelve dozen of everything—hand-embroidered—"

Packed in the family landau they rolled from one tribal door-step to another, and Archer, when the afternoon's round was over, parted from his betrothed with the feeling that he had been shown off like a wild animal cunningly trapped. He supposed that his readings in anthropology caused him to take such a coarse view of what was after all a simple and natural demonstration of family feeling; but when he remembered that the Wellands did not expect the wedding to take place till the following autumn, and pictured what his life would be till then, a dampness fell upon his spirit.

"Tomorrow," Mrs. Welland called after him, "we'll do the Chiverses and the Dallases"; and he perceived that she was going through their two families alphabetically, and that they were only in the first quarter of the alphabet.

He had meant to tell May of the Countess Olenska's request—her command, rather—that he should call on her that afternoon; but in the brief moments when they were alone he had had more pressing things to say. Besides, it struck him as a little absurd to allude to the matter. He knew that May most particularly wanted him to be kind to her cousin; was it not that wish which had hastened the announcement of their engagement? It gave him an odd sensation to reflect that, but for the Countess's arrival, he might have been, if not still a free man, at least a man less irrevocably pledged. But May had willed it so, and he felt himself somehow relieved of further responsibility—and therefore at liberty, if he chose, to call on her cousin without telling her.

As he stood on Madame Olenska's threshold curiosity was his uppermost feeling. He was puzzled by the tone in which she had summoned him; he concluded that she was less simple than she seemed.

The door was opened by a swarthy foreign-looking maid, with a prominent bosom under a gay neckerchief, whom he vaguely fancied to be Sicilian. She welcomed him with all her white teeth, and answering his enquiries by a head-shake of incomprehension led him through the narrow hall into a low firelit drawing-room. The room was empty, and she left him, for an appreciable time, to wonder whether she had gone to find her mistress, or whether she had not understood what he was there for, and thought it might be to wind the clocks—of which he perceived that the only visible specimen had stopped. He knew that the southern races communicated with each other in the language of pantomime, and was mortified to find her shrugs and smiles so unintelligible. At length she returned with a lamp; and Archer, having meanwhile put together a phrase out of Dante and Petrarch, evoked the answer: *"La signora è fuori; ma verrà subito";* which he took to mean: "She's out—but you'll soon see."

What he saw, meanwhile, with the help of the lamp, was the faded shadowy charm of a room unlike any room he had known. He knew that the Countess Olenska had brought some of her possessions with her—bits of wreckage, she called them—and these, he supposed, were represented by some small slender tables of dark wood, a delicate little Greek bronze on the chimney-piece, and a stretch of red damask nailed on the discoloured wallpaper behind a couple of Italian-looking pictures in old frames.

Newland Archer prided himself on his knowledge of Italian art. His boyhood had been saturated with Ruskin, and he had read all the latest books: John Addington Symonds, Vernon Lee's "Euphorion," the essays of P. G. Hamerton, and a wonderful new volume called "The Renaissance" by Walter Pater. He talked easily of Botticelli, and spoke of Fra Angelico with a faint condescension. But these pictures bewildered him, for they were like nothing that he was accustomed to look at (and therefore able to see) when he travelled in Italy; and perhaps, also, his powers of observation were impaired by the oddness of finding himself in this strange empty house, where apparently no one expected him. He was sorry that he had not told May Welland of Countess Olenska's request, and a little disturbed by the thought that his betrothed might come in to see her cousin. What would she think if she found him sitting there with the air of intimacy implied by waiting alone in the dusk at a lady's fireside?

But since he had come he meant to wait; and he sank into a chair and stretched his feet to the logs.

It was odd to have summoned him in that way, and then forgotten him; but Archer felt more curious than mortified. The atmosphere of the room was so different from any he had ever breathed that self-consciousness vanished in the sense of adventure. He had been before in drawing-rooms hung with red damask, with pictures "of the Italian school"; what struck him was the way in which Medora Manson's shabby hired house, with its blighted background of pampas grass and Rogers statuettes, had, by a turn of the hand, and the skillful use of a few properties, been transformed into something intimate, "foreign," subtly suggestive of old romantic scenes and sentiments. He tried to analyse the trick, to find a clue to it in the way the chairs and tables were grouped, in the fact that only two Jacqueminot roses (of which nobody ever bought less than a dozen) had been placed in the slender vase at his elbow, and in the vague pervading perfume that was not what one put on handkerchiefs, but rather like the scent of some far-off bazaar, a smell made up of Turkish coffee and ambergris and dried roses.

His mind wandered away to the question of what May's drawing-room would look like. He knew that Mr. Welland, who was behaving "very handsomely," already had his eye on a newly built house in East Thirty-ninth Street. The neighbourhood was thought remote, and the house was built in a ghastly greenish-yellow stone that the younger architects were beginning to employ as a protest against the brownstone of which the uniform hue coated New York like a cold chocolate sauce; but the plumbing was perfect. Archer would have liked to travel, to put off the housing question; but, though the Wellands approved of an extended European honeymoon (perhaps even a winter in Egypt), they were firm as to the need of a house for the returning couple. The young man felt that his fate was sealed: for the rest of his life he would go up every evening between the cast-iron railings of that greenish-yellow doorstep, and pass through a Pompeian vestibule into a hall with a wainscoting of varnished yellow wood. But beyond that his imagination could not travel. He knew the drawing-room above had a bay window, but he could not fancy how May would deal with it. She submitted cheerfully to the purple satin and yellow tuftings of the Welland drawing-room, to its sham Buhl tables and gilt vitrines full of modern Saxe. He saw no reason to suppose that she would want anything different in her own house; and his only comfort was to reflect that she would probably let him arrange his library as he pleased—which would be, of course, with "sincere" Eastlake furniture, and the plain new bookcases without glass doors.

The round-bosomed maid came in, drew the curtains, pushed back a log, and said consolingly: "Verrà—verrà." When she had gone Archer stood up and began to wander about. Should he wait any longer? His position was becoming rather foolish. Perhaps he had misunderstood Madame Olenska—perhaps she had not invited him after all.

Down the cobblestones of the quiet street came the ring of a stepper's hoofs; they stopped before the house, and he caught the opening of a carriage door. Parting the curtains he looked out into the early dusk. A streetlamp faced him, and in its light he saw Julius Beaufort's compact English brougham, drawn by a big roan, and the banker descending from it, and helping out Madame Olenska.

Beaufort stood, hat in hand, saying something which his companion seemed to negative; then they shook hands, and he jumped into his carriage while she mounted the steps.

When she entered the room she showed no surprise at seeing Archer there; surprise seemed the emotion that she was least addicted to.

"How do you like my funny house?" she asked. "To me it's like heaven."

As she spoke she untied her little velvet bonnet and tossing it away with her long cloak stood looking at him with meditative eyes.

"You've arranged it delightfully," he rejoined, alive to the flatness of the words, but imprisoned in the conventional by his consuming desire to be simple and striking.

"Oh, it's a poor little place. My relations despise it. But at any rate it's less gloomy than the van der Luydens'."

The words gave him an electric shock, for few were the rebellious spirits who would have dared to call the stately home of the van der Luydens gloomy. Those privileged to enter it shivered there, and spoke of it as "handsome." But suddenly he was glad that she had given voice to the general shiver.

"It's delicious—what you've done here," he repeated.

"I like the little house," she admitted; "but I suppose what I like is the blessedness of its being here, in my own country and my own town; and then, of being alone in it." She spoke so low that he hardly heard the last phrase; but in his awkwardness he took it up.

"You like so much to be alone?"

"Yes; as long as my friends keep me from feeling lonely." She sat down near the fire, said: "Nastasia will bring the tea presently," and signed to him to return to his armchair, adding: "I see you've already chosen your corner."

Leaning back, she folded her arms behind her head, and looked at the fire under drooping lids.

"This is the hour I like best—don't you?"

A proper sense of his dignity caused him to answer: "I was afraid you'd forgotten the hour. Beaufort must have been very engrossing."

She looked amused. "Why—have you waited long? Mr. Beaufort took me to see a number of houses—since it seems I'm not to be allowed to stay in this one." She appeared to dismiss both Beaufort and himself from her mind, and went on: "I've never been in a city where there seems to be such a feeling against living in *des quartiers excentriques*. What does it matter where one lives? I'm told this street is respectable."

"It's not fashionable."

"Fashionable! Do you all think so much of that? Why not make one's own fashions? But I suppose I've lived too independently; at any rate, I want to do what you all do—I want to feel cared for and safe."

He was touched, as he had been the evening before when she spoke of her need of guidance.

"That's what your friends want you to feel. New York's an awfully safe place," he added with a flash of sarcasm.

"Yes, isn't it? One feels that," she cried, missing the mockery. "Being here is like—like—being taken on a holiday when one has been a good little girl and done all one's lessons."

The analogy was well meant, but did not altogether please him. He did not mind being flippant about New York, but disliked to hear any one else take the same tone. He wondered if she did not begin to see what a powerful engine it was, and how nearly it had crushed her. The Lovell Mingotts' dinner, patched up *in extremis* out of all sorts of social odds and ends, ought to have taught her the narrowness of her escape; but either she had been all along unaware of having skirted disaster, or else she had lost sight of it in the triumph of the van der Luyden evening. Archer inclined to the former theory; he fancied that her New York was still completely undifferentiated, and the conjecture nettled him.

"Last night," he said, "New York laid itself out for you. The van der Luydens do nothing by halves."

"No: how kind they are! It was such a nice party. Every one seems to have such an esteem for them."

The terms were hardly adequate; she might have spoken in that way of a tea-party at the dear old Miss Lannings'.

"The van der Luydens," said Archer, feeling himself pompous as he spoke, "are the most powerful influence in New York society. Unfortunately—owing to her health—they receive very seldom."

She unclasped her hands from behind her head, and looked at him meditatively.

"Isn't that perhaps the reason?"

"The reason—?"

"For their great influence; that they make themselves so rare."

He coloured a little, stared at her—and suddenly felt the penetration of the remark. At a stroke she had pricked the van der Luydens and they collapsed. He laughed, and sacrificed them.

Nastasia brought the tea, with handleless Japanese cups and little covered dishes, placing the tray on a low table.

"But you'll explain these things to me—you'll tell me all I ought to know," Madame Olenska continued, leaning forward to hand him his cup.

"It's you who are telling me; opening my eyes to things I'd looked at so long that I'd ceased to see them."

She detached a small gold cigarette-case from one of her bracelets, held it out to him, and took a cigarette herself. On the chimney were long spills for lighting them.

"Ah, then we can both help each other. But I want help so much more. You must tell me just what to do."

It was on the tip of his tongue to reply: "Don't be seen driving about the streets with Beaufort—" but he was being too deeply drawn into the atmosphere of the room, which was her atmosphere, and to give advice of that sort would have been like telling some one who was bargaining for attar-of-roses in Samarkand that one should always be provided with arctics for a New York winter. New York seemed much farther off than Samarkand, and if they were indeed to help each other she was rendering what might prove the first of their mutual services by making him look at his native city objectively. Viewed thus, as through the wrong end of a telescope, it looked disconcertingly small and distant; but then from Samarkand it would.

A flame darted from the logs and she bent over the fire, stretching her thin hands so close to it that a faint halo shone about the oval nails. The light touched to russet the rings of dark hair escaping from her braids, and made her pale face paler.

"There are plenty of people to tell you what to do," Archer rejoined, obscurely envious of them.

"Oh—all my aunts? And my dear old Granny?" She considered the idea impartially. "They're all a little vexed with me for setting up for myself—poor Granny especially. She wanted to keep me with her; but I had to be free—" He was impressed by this light way of speaking of the formidable Catherine, and moved by the thought of what must have given Madame Olenska this thirst for even the loneliest kind of freedom. But the idea of Beaufort gnawed him.

"I think I understand how you feel," he said. "Still, your family can advise you; explain differences; show you the way."

She lifted her thin black eyebrows. "Is New York such a labyrinth? I thought it so straight up and down—like Fifth Avenue. And with all the cross streets numbered!" She seemed to guess his faint disapproval of this, and added, with the rare smile that enchanted her whole face: "If you knew how I like it for just *that*—the straight-up-and-downness, and the big honest labels on everything!"

He saw his chance. "Everything may be labelled—but everybody is not."

"Perhaps. I may simplify too much—but you'll warn me if I do." She turned from the fire to look at him. "There are only two people here who make me feel as if they understood what I mean and could explain things to me: you and Mr. Beaufort."

Archer winced at the joining of the names, and then, with a quick readjustment, understood, sympathised and pitied. So close to the powers of evil she must have lived that she still breathed more freely in their air. But since she felt that he understood her also, his business would be to make her see Beaufort as he really was, with all he represented—and abhor it.

He answered gently: "I understand. But just at first don't let go of your old friends' hands: I mean the older women, your Granny Mingott, Mrs. Welland, Mrs. van der Luyden. They like and admire you—they want to help you."

She shook her head and sighed. "Oh, I know—I know! But on condition that they don't hear anything unpleasant. Aunt Welland put it in those very words when I tried. . . . Does no one want to know the truth here, Mr. Archer? The real loneliness is living among all these kind people who only ask one to pretend!" She lifted her hands to her face, and he saw her thin shoulders shaken by a sob.

"Madame Olenska!—Oh, don't, Ellen," he cried, starting up and bending over her. He drew down one of her hands, clasping and chafing it like a child's while he murmured reassuring words; but in a moment she freed herself, and looked up at him with wet lashes.

"Does no one cry here, either? I suppose there's no need to, in heaven," she said, straightening her loosened braids with a laugh, and bending over the teakettle. It was burnt into his consciousness that he had called her "Ellen"—called her so twice; and that she had not noticed it. Far down the inverted telescope he saw the faint white figure of May Welland—in New York.

Suddenly Nastasia put her head in to say something in her rich Italian.

Madame Olenska, again with a hand at her hair, uttered an

exclamation of assent—a flashing *"Già—già"*—and the Duke of
St. Austrey entered, piloting a tremendous blackwigged and red-
plumed lady in overflowing furs.

"My dear Countess, I've brought an old friend of mine to see
you—Mrs. Struthers. She wasn't asked to the party last night,
and she wants to know you."

The Duke beamed on the group, and Madame Olenska advanced with a murmur of welcome toward the queer couple. She
seemed to have no idea how oddly matched they were, nor what
a liberty the Duke had taken in bringing his companion—and
to do him justice, as Archer perceived, the Duke seemed as unaware of it himself.

"Of course I want to know you, my dear," cried Mrs. Struthers in a round rolling voice that matched her bold feathers and
her brazen wig. "I want to know everybody who's young and
interesting and charming. And the Duke tells me you like
music—didn't you, Duke? You're a pianist yourself, I believe?
Well, do you want to hear Sarasate play tomorrow evening at
my house? You know I've something going on every Sunday
evening—it's the day when New York doesn't know what to
do with itself, and so I say to it: 'Come and be amused.' And
the Duke thought you'd be tempted by Sarasate. You'll find a
number of your friends."

Madame Olenska's face grew brilliant with pleasure. "How
kind! How good of the Duke to think of me!" She pushed a
chair up to the tea-table and Mrs. Struthers sank into it delec-
tably. "Of course I shall be too happy to come."

"That's all right, my dear. And bring your young gentleman
with you." Mrs. Struthers extended a hail-fellow hand to Archer.
"I can't put a name to you—but I'm sure I've met you—I've
met everybody, here, or in Paris or London. Aren't you in diplomacy? All the diplomatists come to me. You like music too?
Duke, you must be sure to bring him."

The Duke said "Rather" from the depths of his beard, and
Archer withdrew with a stiffly circular bow that made him feel
as full of spine as a self-conscious school-boy among careless
and unnoticing elders.

He was not sorry for the *dénouement* of his visit: he only

wished it had come sooner, and spared him a certain waste of emotion. As he went out into the wintry night, New York again became vast and imminent, and May Welland the loveliest woman in it. He turned into his florist's to send her the daily box of lilies-of-the-valley which, to his confusion, he found he had forgotten that morning.

As he wrote a word on his card and waited for an envelope he glanced about the embowered shop, and his eye lit on a cluster of yellow roses. He had never seen any as sun-golden before, and his first impulse was to send them to May instead of the lilies. But they did not look like her—there was something too rich, too strong, in their fiery beauty. In a sudden revulsion of mood, and almost without knowing what he did, he signed to the florist to lay the roses in another long box, and slipped his card into a second envelope, on which he wrote the name of the Countess Olenska; then, just as he was turning away, he drew the card out again, and left the empty envelope on the box.

"They'll go at once?" he enquired, pointing to the roses.

The florist assured him that they would.

The next day he persuaded May to escape for a walk in the Park after luncheon. As was the custom in old-fashioned Episcopalian New York, she usually accompanied her parents to church on Sunday afternoons; but Mrs. Welland condoned her truancy, having that very morning won her over to the necessity of a long engagement, with time to prepare a hand-embroidered trousseau containing the proper number of dozens.

The day was delectable. The bare vaulting of trees along the Mall was ceiled with lapis lazuli, and arched above snow that shone like splintered crystals. It was the weather to call out May's radiance, and she burned like a young maple in the frost. Archer was proud of the glances turned on her, and the simple joy of possessorship cleared away his underlying perplexities.

"It's so delicious—waking every morning to smell lilies-of-the-valley in one's room!" she said.

"Yesterday they came late. I hadn't time in the morning—"

"But your remembering each day to send them makes me love them so much more than if you'd given a standing order, and they came every morning on the minute, like one's music-teacher—as I know Gertrude Lefferts's did, for instance, when she and Lawrence were engaged."

"Ah—they would!" laughed Archer, amused at her keenness. He looked sideways at her fruit-like cheek and felt rich and secure enough to add: "When I sent your lilies yesterday afternoon I saw some rather gorgeous yellow roses and packed them off to Madame Olenska. Was that right?"

"How dear of you! Anything of that kind delights her. It's odd she didn't mention it: she lunched with us today, and spoke of Mr. Beaufort's having sent her wonderful orchids, and cousin Henry van der Luyden a whole hamper of carnations from Skuytercliff. She seems so surprised to receive flowers. Don't people send them in Europe? She thinks it such a pretty custom."

"Oh, well, no wonder mine were overshadowed by Beaufort's," said Archer irritably. Then he remembered that he had not put a card with the roses, and was vexed at having spoken of them. He wanted to say: "I called on your cousin yesterday," but hesitated. If Madame Olenska had not spoken of his visit it might seem awkward that he should. Yet not to do so gave the affair an air of mystery that he disliked. To shake off the question he began to talk of their own plans, their future, and Mrs. Welland's insistence on a long engagement.

"If you call it long! Isabel Chivers and Reggie were engaged for two years: Grace and Thorley for nearly a year and a half. Why aren't we very well off as we are?"

It was the traditional maidenly interrogation, and he felt ashamed of himself for finding it singularly childish. No doubt she simply echoed what was said for her; but she was nearing her twenty-second birthday, and he wondered at what age "nice" women began to speak for themselves.

"Never, if we won't let them, I suppose," he mused, and recalled his mad outburst to Mr. Sillerton Jackson: "Women ought to be as free as we are—"

It would presently be his task to take the bandage from this young woman's eyes, and bid her look forth on the world. But how many generations of the women who had gone to her making had descended bandaged to the family vault? He shivered a little, remembering some of the new ideas in his scientific books, and the much-cited instance of the Kentucky cave-fish, which had ceased to develop eyes because they had no use for them. What if, when he had bidden May Welland to open hers, they could only look out blankly at blankness?

"We might be much better off. We might be altogether together—we might travel."

Her face lit up. "That would be lovely," she owned: she would love to travel. But her mother would not understand their wanting to do things so differently.

"As if the mere 'differently' didn't account for it!" the wooer insisted.

"Newland! You're so original!" she exulted.

His heart sank, for he saw that he was saying all the things that young men in the same situation were expected to say, and that she was making the answers that instinct and tradition taught her to make—even to the point of calling him original.

"Original! We're all as like each other as those dolls cut out of the same folded paper. We're like patterns stencilled on a wall. Can't you and I strike out for ourselves, May?"

He had stopped and faced her in the excitement of their discussion, and her eyes rested on him with a bright unclouded admiration.

"Mercy—shall we elope?" she laughed.

"If you would—"

"You *do* love me, Newland! I'm so happy."

"But then—why not be happier?"

"We can't behave like people in novels, though, can we?"

"Why not—why not—why not?"

She looked a little bored by his insistence. She knew very well that they couldn't, but it was troublesome to have to produce a reason. "I'm not clever enough to argue with you. But that kind of thing is rather—vulgar, isn't it?" she suggested, relieved to have hit on a word that would assuredly extinguish the whole subject.

"Are you so much afraid, then, of being vulgar?"

She was evidently staggered by this. "Of course I should hate it—so would you," she rejoined, a trifle irritably.

He stood silent, beating his stick nervously against his boot-top; and feeling that she had indeed found the right way of closing the discussion, she went on lightheartedly: "Oh, did I tell you that I showed Ellen my ring? She thinks it the most beautiful setting she ever saw. There's nothing like it in the rue de la Paix, she said. I do love you, Newland, for being so artistic!"

The next afternoon, as Archer, before dinner, sat smoking sullenly in his study, Janey wandered in on him. He had failed to stop at his club on the way up from the office where he exercised the profession of the law in the leisurely manner common to well-to-do New Yorkers of his class. He was out of spirits and slightly out of temper, and a haunting horror of doing the same thing every day at the same hour besieged his brain.

"Sameness—sameness!" he muttered, the word running through his head like a persecuting tune as he saw the familiar tall-hatted figures lounging behind the plateglass; and because he usually dropped in at the club at that hour he had gone home instead. He knew not only what they were likely to be talking about, but the part each one would take in the discussion. The Duke of course would be their principal theme; though the appearance in Fifth Avenue of a golden-haired lady in a small canary-coloured brougham with a pair of black cobs (for which Beaufort was generally thought responsible) would also doubtless be thoroughly gone into. Such "women" (as they were called) were few in New York, those driving their own carriages still fewer, and the appearance of Miss Fanny Ring in Fifth Avenue at the fashionable hour had profoundly agitated society. Only the day before, her carriage had passed Mrs. Lovell Mingott's, and the latter had instantly rung the little bell at her elbow and ordered the coachman to drive her home. "What if it had happened to Mrs. van der Luyden?" people asked each other with a shudder. Archer could hear Lawrence Lefferts, at that very hour, holding forth on the disintegration of society.

He raised his head irritably when his sister Janey entered, and then quickly bent over his book (Swinburne's "Chastelard"—just out) as if he had not seen her. She glanced at the writing-table heaped with books, opened a volume of the "Contes Drôlatiques," made a wry face over the archaic French, and sighed: "What learned things you read!"

"Well—?" he asked, as she hovered Cassandra-like before him.

"Mother's very angry."

"Angry? With whom? About what?"

"Miss Sophy Jackson has just been here. She brought word that her brother would come in after dinner: she couldn't say very much, because he forbade her to: he wishes to give all the details himself. He's with cousin Louisa van der Luyden now."

"For heaven's sake, my dear girl, try a fresh start. It would take an omniscient Deity to know what you're talking about."

"It's not a time to be profane, Newland. . . . Mother feels badly enough about your not going to church . . ."

With a groan he plunged back into his book.

"*Newland!* Do listen. Your friend Madame Olenska was at Mrs. Lemuel Struthers's party last night: she went there with the Duke and Mr. Beaufort."

At the last clause of this announcement a senseless anger swelled the young man's breast. To smother it he laughed. "Well, what of it? I knew she meant to."

Janey paled and her eyes began to project. "You knew she meant to—and you didn't try to stop her? To warn her?"

"Stop her? Warn her?" He laughed again. "I'm not engaged to be married to the Countess Olenska!" The words had a fantastic sound in his own ears.

"You're marrying into her family."

"Oh, family—family!" he jeered.

"Newland—don't you care about Family?"

"Not a brass farthing."

"Nor about what cousin Louisa van der Luyden will think?"

"Not the half of one—if she thinks such old maid's rubbish."

"Mother is not an old maid," said his virgin sister with pinched lips.

He felt like shouting back: "Yes, she is, and so are the van der Luydens, and so we all are, when it comes to being so much as brushed by the wing-tip of Reality." But he saw her long gentle face puckering into tears, and felt ashamed of the useless pain he was inflicting.

"Hang Countess Olenska! Don't be a goose, Janey—I'm not her keeper."

"No; but you *did* ask the Wellands to announce your engagement sooner so that we might all back her up; and if it hadn't been for that cousin Louisa would never have invited her to the dinner for the Duke."

"Well—what harm was there in inviting her? She was the best-looking woman in the room; she made the dinner a little less funereal than the usual van der Luyden banquet."

"You know cousin Henry asked her to please you: he persuaded cousin Louisa. And now they're so upset that they're going back to Skuytercliff tomorrow. I think, Newland, you'd better come down. You don't seem to understand how mother feels."

In the drawing-room Newland found his mother. She raised a troubled brow from her needlework to ask: "Has Janey told you?"

"Yes." He tried to keep his tone as measured as her own. "But I can't take it very seriously."

"Not the fact of having offended cousin Louisa and cousin Henry?"

"The fact that they can be offended by such a trifle as Countess Olenska's going to the house of a woman they consider common."

"*Consider—!*"

"Well, who is; but who has good music, and amuses people on Sunday evenings, when the whole of New York is dying of inanition."

"Good music? All I know is, there was a woman who got up on a table and sang the things they sing at the places you go to in Paris. There was smoking and champagne."

"Well—that kind of thing happens in other places, and the world still goes on."

"I don't suppose, dear, you're really defending the French Sunday?"

"I've heard you often enough, mother, grumble at the English Sunday when we've been in London."

"New York is neither Paris nor London."

"Oh, no, it's not!" her son groaned.

"You mean, I suppose, that society here is not as brilliant? You're right, I daresay; but we belong here, and people should respect our ways when they come among us. Ellen Olenska especially: she came back to get away from the kind of life people lead in brilliant societies."

Newland made no answer, and after a moment his mother ventured: "I was going to put on my bonnet and ask you to take me to see cousin Louisa for a moment before dinner." He frowned, and she continued: "I thought you might explain to her what you've just said: that society abroad is different . . .

that people are not as particular, and that Madame Olenska may not have realised how we feel about such things. It would be, you know, dear," she added with an innocent adroitness, "in Madame Olenska's interest if you did."

"Dearest mother, I really don't see how we're concerned in the matter. The Duke took Madame Olenska to Mrs. Struthers's—in fact he brought Mrs. Struthers to call on her. I was there when they came. If the van der Luydens want to quarrel with anybody, the real culprit is under their own roof."

"Quarrel? Newland, did you ever know of cousin Henry's quarrelling? Besides, the Duke's his guest; and a stranger too. Strangers don't discriminate: how should they? Countess Olenska is a New Yorker, and should have respected the feelings of New York."

"Well, then, if they must have a victim, you have my leave to throw Madame Olenska to them," cried her son, exasperated. "I don't see myself—or you either—offering ourselves up to expiate her crimes."

"Oh, of course you see only the Mingott side," his mother answered, in the sensitive tone that was her nearest approach to anger.

The sad butler drew back the drawing-room portières and announced: "Mr. Henry van der Luyden."

Mrs. Archer dropped her needle and pushed her chair back with an agitated hand.

"Another lamp," she cried to the retreating servant, while Janey bent over to straighten her mother's cap.

Mr. van der Luyden's figure loomed on the threshold, and Newland Archer went forward to greet his cousin.

"We were just talking about you, sir," he said.

Mr. van der Luyden seemed overwhelmed by the announcement. He drew off his glove to shake hands with the ladies, and smoothed his tall hat shyly, while Janey pushed an arm-chair forward, and Archer continued: "And the Countess Olenska."

Mrs. Archer paled.

"Ah—a charming woman. I have just been to see her," said Mr. van der Luyden, complacency restored to his brow. He sank into the chair, laid his hat and gloves on the floor beside him in the old-fashioned way, and went on: "She has a real gift for arranging flowers. I had sent her a few carnations from Skuytercliff, and I was astonished. Instead of massing them in big bunches as our head-gardener does, she had scattered them about loosely, here and there . . . I can't say how. The Duke had told me: he said: 'Go and see how cleverly she's arranged her drawing-room.' And she has. I should really like to take Louisa to see her, if the neighbourhood were not so—unpleasant."

A dead silence greeted this unusual flow of words from Mr. van der Luyden. Mrs. Archer drew her embroidery out of the basket into which she had nervously tumbled it, and Newland, leaning against the chimney-place and twisting a humming-bird-feather screen in his hand, saw Janey's gaping countenance lit up by the coming of the second lamp.

"The fact is," Mr. van der Luyden continued, stroking his long grey leg with a bloodless hand weighed down by the Patroon's great signet-ring, "the fact is, I dropped in to thank her for the very pretty note she wrote me about my flowers; and also—but this is between ourselves, of course—to give her a friendly warning about allowing the Duke to carry her off to parties with him. I don't know if you've heard—"

Mrs. Archer produced an indulgent smile. "Has the Duke been carrying her off to parties?"

"You know what these English grandees are. They're all alike. Louisa and I are very fond of our cousin—but it's hopeless to expect people who are accustomed to the European courts to trouble themselves about our little republican distinctions. The Duke goes where he's amused." Mr. van der Luyden paused, but no one spoke. "Yes—it seems he took her with him last night to Mrs. Lemuel Struthers's. Sillerton Jackson has just been to us with the foolish story, and Louisa was rather troubled. So I thought the shortest way was to go straight to Countess Olenska and explain—by the merest hint, you know—how we feel in New York about certain things. I felt I might, without indelicacy, because the evening she dined with us she rather suggested . . . 'rather let me see that she would be grateful for guidance. And she *was*."

Mr. van der Luyden looked about the room with what would
have been self-satisfaction on features less purged of the vulgar
passions. On his face it became a mild benevolence which Mrs.
Archer's countenance dutifully reflected.

"How kind you both are, dear Henry—always! Newland will
particularly appreciate what you have done because of dear May
and his new relations."

She shot an admonitory glance at her son, who said: "Immensely, sir. But I was sure you'd like Madame Olenska."

Mr. van der Luyden looked at him with extreme gentleness.
"I never ask to my house, my dear Newland," he said, "any one
whom I do not like. And so I have just told Sillerton Jackson."
With a glance at the clock he rose and added: "But Louisa will
be waiting. We are dining early, to take the Duke to the Opera."

After the portières had solemnly closed behind their visitor a
silence fell upon the Archer family.

"Gracious—how romantic!" at last broke explosively from
Janey. No one knew exactly what inspired her elliptic comments,
and her relations had long since given up trying to interpret
them.

Mrs. Archer shook her head with a sigh. "Provided it all turns
out for the best," she said, in the tone of one who knows how
surely it will not. "Newland, you must stay and see Sillerton
Jackson when he comes this evening: I really shan't know what
to say to him."

"Poor mother! But he won't come—" her son laughed,
stooping to kiss away her frown.

Some two weeks later, Newland Archer, sitting in abstracted idleness in his private compartment of the office of Letterblair, Lamson and Low, attorneys at law, was summoned by the head of the firm.

Old Mr. Letterblair, the accredited legal adviser of three generations of New York gentility, throned behind his mahogany desk in evident perplexity. As he stroked his closeclipped white whiskers and ran his hand through the rumpled grey locks above his jutting brows, his disrespectful junior partner thought how much he looked like the Family Physician annoyed with a patient whose symptoms refuse to be classified.

"My dear sir—" he always addressed Archer as "sir"—"I have sent for you to go into a little matter; a matter which, for the moment, I prefer not to mention either to Mr. Skipworth or Mr. Redwood." The gentlemen he spoke of were the other senior partners of the firm; for, as was always the case with legal associations of old standing in New York, all the partners named on the office letter-head were long since dead; and Mr. Letterblair, for example, was, professionally speaking, his own grandson.

He leaned back in his chair with a furrowed brow. "For family reasons—" he continued.

Archer looked up.

"The Mingott family," said Mr. Letterblair with an explanatory smile and bow. "Mrs. Manson Mingott sent for me yesterday. Her grand-daughter the Countess Olenska wishes to sue her husband for divorce. Certain papers have been placed in my hands." He paused and drummed on his desk. "In view of your prospective alliance with the family I should like to consult you—to consider the case with you—before taking any farther steps."

Archer felt the blood in his temples. He had seen the Countess Olenska only once since his visit to her, and then at the

Opera, in the Mingott box. During this interval she had become a less vivid and importunate image, receding from his foreground as May Welland resumed her rightful place in it. He had not heard her divorce spoken of since Janey's first random allusion to it, and had dismissed the tale as unfounded gossip. Theoretically, the idea of divorce was almost as distasteful to him as to his mother; and he was annoyed that Mr. Letterblair (no doubt prompted by old Catherine Mingott) should be so evidently planning to draw him into the affair. After all, there were plenty of Mingott men for such jobs, and as yet he was not even a Mingott by marriage.

He waited for the senior partner to continue. Mr. Letterblair unlocked a drawer and drew out a packet. "If you will run your eye over these papers—"

Archer frowned. "I beg your pardon, sir; but just because of the prospective relationship, I should prefer your consulting Mr. Skipworth or Mr. Redwood."

Mr. Letterblair looked surprised and slightly offended. It was unusual for a junior to reject such an opening.

He bowed. "I respect your scruple, sir; but in this case I believe true delicacy requires you to do as I ask. Indeed, the suggestion is not mine but Mrs. Manson Mingott's and her son's. I have seen Lovell Mingott; and also Mr. Welland. They all named you."

Archer felt his temper rising. He had been somewhat languidly drifting with events for the last fortnight, and letting May's fair looks and radiant nature obliterate the rather importunate pressure of the Mingott claims. But this behest of old Mrs. Mingott's roused him to a sense of what the clan thought they had the right to exact from a prospective son-in-law; and he chafed at the rôle.

"Her uncles ought to deal with this," he said.

"They have. The matter has been gone into by the family. They are opposed to the Countess's idea; but she is firm, and insists on a legal opinion."

The young man was silent: he had not opened the packet in his hand.

"Does she want to marry again?"

"I believe it is suggested; but she denies it."

"Then—"

"Will you oblige me, Mr. Archer, by first looking through these papers? Afterward, when we have talked the case over, I will give you my opinion."

Archer withdrew reluctantly with the unwelcome documents. Since their last meeting he had half-unconsciously collaborated with events in ridding himself of the burden of Madame Olenska. His hour alone with her by the firelight had drawn them into a momentary intimacy on which the Duke of St. Austrey's intrusion with Mrs. Lemuel Struthers, and the Countess's joyous greeting of them, had rather providentially broken. Two days later Archer had assisted at the comedy of her reinstatement in the van der Luydens' favour, and had said to himself, with a touch of tartness, that a lady who knew how to thank all-powerful elderly gentlemen to such good purpose for a bunch of flowers did not need either the private consolations or the public championship of a young man of his small compass. To look at the matter in this light simplified his own case and surprisingly furbished up all the dim domestic virtues. He could not picture May Welland, in whatever conceivable emergency, hawking about her private difficulties and lavishing her confidences on strange men; and she had never seemed to him finer or fairer than in the week that followed. He had even yielded to her wish for a long engagement, since she had found the one disarming answer to his plea for haste.

"You know, when it comes to the point, your parents have always let you have your way ever since you were a little girl," he argued; and she had answered, with her clearest look: "Yes; and that's what makes it so hard to refuse the very last thing they'll ever ask of me as a little girl."

That was the old New York note; that was the kind of answer he would like always to be sure of his wife's making. If one had habitually breathed the New York air there were times when anything less crystalline seemed stifling.

The papers he had retired to read did not tell him much in fact; but they plunged him into an atmosphere in which he choked and spluttered. They consisted mainly of an exchange of letters between Count Olenski's solicitors and a French legal firm to whom the Countess had applied for the settlement of her financial situation. There was also a short letter from the Count to his wife: after reading it, Newland Archer rose, jammed the papers back into their envelope, and reentered Mr. Letterblair's office.

"Here are the letters, sir. If you wish, I'll see Madame Olenska," he said in a constrained voice.

"Thank you—thank you, Mr. Archer. Come and dine with me tonight if you're free, and we'll go into the matter afterward: in case you wish to call on our client tomorrow."

Newland Archer walked straight home again that afternoon. It was a winter evening of transparent clearness, with an innocent young moon above the housetops; and he wanted to fill his soul's lungs with the pure radiance, and not exchange a word with any one till he and Mr. Letterblair were closeted together after dinner. It was impossible to decide otherwise than he had done: he must see Madame Olenska himself rather than let her secrets be bared to other eyes. A great wave of compassion had swept away his indifference and impatience: she stood before him as an exposed and pitiful figure, to be saved at all costs from farther wounding herself in her mad plunges against fate.

He remembered what she had told him of Mrs. Welland's request to be spared whatever was "unpleasant" in her history, and winced at the thought that it was perhaps this attitude of mind which kept the New York air so pure. "Are we only Pharisees after all?" he wondered, puzzled by the effort to reconcile his instinctive disgust at human vileness with his equally instinctive pity for human frailty.

For the first time he perceived how elementary his own principles had always been. He passed for a young man who had not been afraid of risks, and he knew that his secret love-affair with poor silly Mrs. Thorley Rushworth had not been too secret to invest him with a becoming air of adventure. But Mrs. Rushworth was "that kind of woman"; foolish, vain, clandestine by nature, and far more attracted by the secrecy and peril of the affair than by such charms and qualities as he possessed. When the fact dawned on him it nearly broke his heart, but now it seemed the redeeming feature of the case. The affair, in short, had been of the kind that most of the young men of his age had been through, and emerged from with calm consciences and an undisturbed belief in the abysmal distinction between the women one loved and respected and those one enjoyed—and pitied. In this view they were sedulously abetted by their mothers, aunts and other elderly female relatives, who all shared Mrs. Archer's belief that when "such things happened" it was undoubtedly foolish of the man, but somehow always criminal of the woman. All the elderly ladies whom Archer knew regarded any woman who loved imprudently as necessarily unscrupulous and designing, and mere simpleminded man as powerless in her clutches. The only thing to do was to persuade him, as early as possible, to marry a nice girl, and then trust to her to look after him.

In the complicated old European communities, Archer began to guess, love-problems might be less simple and less easily classified. Rich and idle and ornamental societies must produce many more such situations; and there might even be one in which a woman naturally sensitive and aloof would yet, from the force of circumstances, from sheer defencelessness and loneliness, be drawn into a tie inexcusable by conventional standards.

On reaching home he wrote a line to the Countess Olenska, asking at what hour of the next day she could receive him, and despatched it by a messenger-boy, who returned presently with a word to the effect that she was going to Skuytercliff the next morning to stay over Sunday with the van der Luydens, but that he would find her alone that evening after dinner. The note was written on a rather untidy half-sheet, without date or address, but her hand was firm and free. He was amused at the idea of her week-ending in the stately solitude of Skuytercliff, but immediately afterward felt that there, of all places, she would most feel the chill of minds rigorously averted from the "unpleasant."

He was at Mr. Letterblair's punctually at seven, glad of the pretext for excusing himself soon after dinner. He had formed his own opinion from the papers entrusted to him, and did not es-

pecially want to go into the matter with his senior partner. Mr.
Letterblair was a widower, and they dined alone, copiously and
slowly, in a dark shabby room hung with yellowing prints of
"The Death of Chatham" and "The Coronation of Napoleon."
On the sideboard, between fluted Sheraton knife-cases, stood a
decanter of Haut Brion, and another of the old Lanning port
(the gift of a client), which the wastrel Tom Lanning had sold
off a year or two before his mysterious and discreditable death
in San Francisco—an incident less publicly humiliating to the
family than the sale of the cellar.

After a velvety oyster soup came shad and cucumbers, then a
young broiled turkey with corn fritters, followed by a canvas-
back with currant jelly and a celery mayonnaise. Mr. Letterblair,
who lunched on a sandwich and tea, dined deliberately and
deeply, and insisted on his guest's doing the same. Finally, when
the closing rites had been accomplished, the cloth was removed,
cigars were lit, and Mr. Letterblair, leaning back in his chair and
pushing the port westward, said, spreading his back agreeably to
the coal fire behind him: "The whole family are against a divorce. And I think rightly."

Archer instantly felt himself on the other side of the argument. "But why, sir? If there ever was a case—"

"Well—what's the use? *She's* here—he's there; the Atlantic's
between them. She'll never get back a dollar more of her money
than what he's voluntarily returned to her: their damned heathen
marriage settlements take precious good care of that. As things
go over there, Olenski's acted generously: he might have turned
her out without a penny."

The young man knew this and was silent.

"I understand, though," Mr. Letterblair continued, "that she
attaches no importance to the money. Therefore, as the family
say, why not let well enough alone?"

Archer had gone to the house an hour earlier in full agreement
with Mr. Letterblair's view; but put into words by this selfish,
well-fed and supremely indifferent old man it suddenly became
the Pharisaic voice of a society wholly absorbed in barricading
itself against the unpleasant.

"I think that's for her to decide."

"H'm—have you considered the consequences if she decides for divorce?"

"You mean the threat in her husband's letter? What weight would that carry? It's no more than the vague charge of an angry blackguard."

"Yes; but it might make some unpleasant talk if he really defends the suit."

"Unpleasant—!" said Archer explosively.

Mr. Letterblair looked at him from under enquiring eyebrows, and the young man, aware of the uselessness of trying to explain what was in his mind, bowed acquiescently while his senior continued: "Divorce is always unpleasant."

"You agree with me?" Mr. Letterblair resumed, after a waiting silence.

"Naturally," said Archer.

"Well, then, I may count on you; the Mingotts may count on you; to use your influence against the idea?"

Archer hesitated. "I can't pledge myself till I've seen the Countess Olenska," he said at length.

"Mr. Archer, I don't understand you. Do you want to marry into a family with a scandalous divorce-suit hanging over it?"

"I don't think that has anything to do with the case."

Mr. Letterblair put down his glass of port and fixed on his young partner a cautious and apprehensive gaze.

Archer understood that he ran the risk of having his mandate withdrawn, and for some obscure reason he disliked the prospect. Now that the job had been thrust on him he did not propose to relinquish it; and, to guard against the possibility, he saw that he must reassure the unimaginative old man who was the legal conscience of the Mingotts.

"You may be sure, sir, that I shan't commit myself till I've reported to you; what I meant was that I'd rather not give an opinion till I've heard what Madame Olenska has to say."

Mr. Letterblair nodded approvingly at an excess of caution worthy of the best New York tradition, and the young man, glancing at his watch, pleaded an engagement and took leave.

Old-fashioned New York dined at seven, and the habit of after-dinner calls, though derided in Archer's set, still generally prevailed. As the young man strolled up Fifth Avenue from Waverley Place, the long thoroughfare was deserted but for a group of carriages standing before the Reggie Chiverses' (where there was a dinner for the Duke), and the occasional figure of an elderly gentleman in heavy overcoat and muffler ascending a brownstone doorstep and disappearing into a gas-lit hall. Thus, as Archer crossed Washington Square, he remarked that old Mr. du Lac was calling on his cousins the Dagonets, and turning down the corner of West Tenth Street he saw Mr. Skipworth, of his own firm, obviously bound on a visit to the Miss Lannings. A little farther up Fifth Avenue, Beaufort appeared on his doorstep, darkly projected against a blaze of light, descended to his private brougham, and rolled away to a mysterious and probably unmentionable destination. It was not an Opera night, and no one was giving a party, so that Beaufort's outing was undoubtedly of a clandestine nature. Archer connected it in his mind with a little house beyond Lexington Avenue in which beribboned window curtains and flower-boxes had recently appeared, and before whose newly painted door the canary-coloured brougham of Miss Fanny Ring was frequently seen to wait.

Beyond the small and slippery pyramid which composed Mrs. Archer's world lay the almost unmapped quarter inhabited by artists, musicians and "people who wrote." These scattered fragments of humanity had never shown any desire to be amalgamated with the social structure. In spite of odd ways they were said to be, for the most part, quite respectable; but they preferred to keep to themselves. Medora Manson, in her prosperous days, had inaugurated a "literary salon"; but it had soon died out owing to the reluctance of the literary to frequent it.

Others had made the same attempt, and there was a household

of Blenkers—an intense and voluble mother, and three blowsy daughters who imitated her—where one met Edwin Booth and Patti and William Winter, and the new Shakespearian actor George Rignold, and some of the magazine editors and musical and literary critics.

Mrs. Archer and her group felt a certain timidity concerning these persons. They were odd, they were uncertain, they had things one didn't know about in the background of their lives and minds. Literature and art were deeply respected in the Archer set, and Mrs. Archer was always at pains to tell her children how much more agreeable and cultivated society had been when it included such figures as Washington Irving, Fitz-Greene Halleck and the poet of "The Culprit Fay." The most celebrated authors of that generation had been "gentlemen"; perhaps the unknown persons who succeeded them had gentlemanly sentiments, but their origin, their appearance, their hair, their intimacy with the stage and the Opera, made any old New York criterion inapplicable to them.

"When I was a girl," Mrs. Archer used to say, "we knew everybody between the Battery and Canal Street; and only the people one knew had carriages. It was perfectly easy to place any one then; now one can't tell, and I prefer not to try."

Only old Catherine Mingott, with her absence of moral prejudices and almost *parvenu* indifference to the subtler distinctions, might have bridged the abyss; but she had never opened a book or looked at a picture, and cared for music only because it reminded her of gala nights at the *Italiens,* in the days of her triumph at the Tuileries. Possibly Beaufort, who was her match in daring, would have succeeded in bringing about a fusion; but his grand house and silk-stockinged footmen were an obstacle to informal sociability. Moreover, he was as illiterate as old Mrs. Mingott, and considered "fellows who wrote" as the mere paid purveyors of rich men's pleasures; and no one rich enough to influence his opinion had ever questioned it.

Newland Archer had been aware of these things ever since he could remember, and had accepted them as part of the structure of his universe. He knew that there were societies where painters and poets and novelists and men of science, and even great actors, were as sought after as Dukes; he had often pictured to himself what it would have been to live in the intimacy of drawing-rooms dominated by the talk of Mérimée (whose "Lettres à une Inconnue" was one of his inseparables), of Thackeray, Browning or William Morris. But such things were inconceivable in New York, and unsettling to think of. Archer knew most of the "fellows who wrote," the musicians and the painters: he met them at the Century, or at the little musical and theatrical clubs that were beginning to come into existence. He enjoyed them there, and was bored with them at the Blenkers', where they were mingled with fervid and dowdy women who passed them about like captured curiosities; and even after his most exciting talks with Ned Winsett he always came away with the feeling that if his world was small, so was theirs, and that the only way to enlarge either was to reach a stage of manners where they would naturally merge.

He was reminded of this by trying to picture the society in which the Countess Olenska had lived and suffered, and also—perhaps—tasted mysterious joys. He remembered with what amusement she had told him that her grandmother Mingott and the Wellands objected to her living in a "Bohemian" quarter given over to "people who wrote." It was not the peril but the poverty that her family disliked; but that shade escaped her, and she supposed they considered literature compromising.

She herself had no fears of it, and the books scattered about her drawing-room (a part of the house in which books were usually supposed to be "out of place"), though chiefly works of fiction, had whetted Archer's interest with such new names as those of Paul Bourget, Huysmans, and the Goncourt brothers. Ruminating on these things as he approached her door, he was once more conscious of the curious way in which she reversed his values, and of the need of thinking himself into conditions incredibly different from any that he knew if he were to be of use in her present difficulty.

Nastasia opened the door, smiling mysteriously. On the bench in the hall lay a sable-lined overcoat, a folded opera hat of dull silk with a gold J. B. on the lining, and a white silk muffler: there was no mistaking the fact that these costly articles were the property of Julius Beaufort.

Archer was angry: so angry that he came near scribbling a word on his card and going away; then he remembered that in writing to Madame Olenska he had been kept by excess of discretion from saying that he wished to see her privately. He had therefore no one but himself to blame if she had opened her doors to other visitors; and he entered the drawing-room with the dogged determination to make Beaufort feel himself in the way, and to outstay him.

The banker stood leaning against the mantelshelf, which was draped with an old embroidery held in place by brass candelabra containing church candles of yellowish wax. He had thrust his chest out, supporting his shoulders against the mantel and resting his weight on one large patent-leather foot. As Archer entered he was smiling and looking down on his hostess, who sat on a sofa placed at right angles to the chimney. A table banked with flowers formed a screen behind it, and against the orchids and azaleas which the young man recognised as tributes from the Beaufort hot-houses, Madame Olenska sat half-reclined, her head propped on a hand and her wide sleeve leaving the arm bare to the elbow.

It was usual for ladies who received in the evenings to wear what were called "simple dinner dresses": a close-fitting armour of whale-boned silk, slightly open in the neck, with lace ruffles filling in the crack, and tight sleeves with a flounce uncovering just enough wrist to show an Etruscan gold bracelet or a velvet band. But Madame Olenska, heedless of tradition, was attired in a long robe of red velvet bordered about the chin and down the front with glossy black fur. Archer remembered, on his last visit to Paris, seeing a portrait by the new painter, Carolus Duran, whose pictures were the sensation of the Salon, in which the lady wore one of these bold sheath-like robes with her chin nestling in fur. There was something perverse and provocative in the notion of fur worn in the evening in a heated drawing-room, and in the combination of a muffled throat and bare arms; but the effect was undeniably pleasing.

"Lord love us—three whole days at Skuytercliff!" Beaufort

was saying in his loud sneering voice as Archer entered. "You'd better take all your furs, and a hot-water-bottle."

"Why? Is the house so cold?" she asked, holding out her left hand to Archer in a way mysteriously suggesting that she expected him to kiss it.

"No; but the missus is," said Beaufort, nodding carelessly to the young man.

"But I thought her so kind. She came herself to invite me. Granny says I must certainly go."

"Granny would, of course. And *I* say it's a shame you're going to miss the little oyster supper I'd planned for you at Delmonico's next Sunday, with Campanini and Scalchi and a lot of jolly people."

She looked doubtfully from the banker to Archer.

"Ah—that does tempt me! Except the other evening at Mrs. Struthers's I've not met a single artist since I've been here."

"What kind of artists? I know one or two painters, very good fellows, that I could bring to see you if you'd allow me," said Archer boldly.

"Painters? Are there painters in New York?" asked Beaufort, in a tone implying that there could be none since he did not buy their pictures; and Madame Olenska said to Archer, with her grave smile: "That would be charming. But I was really thinking of dramatic artists, singers, actors, musicians. My husband's house was always full of them."

She said the words "my husband" as if no sinister associations were connected with them, and in a tone that seemed almost to sigh over the lost delights of her married life. Archer looked at her perplexedly, wondering if it were lightness or dissimulation that enabled her to touch so easily on the past at the very moment when she was risking her reputation in order to break with it.

"I do think," she went on, addressing both men, "that the *imprévu* adds to one's enjoyment. It's perhaps a mistake to see the same people every day."

"It's confoundedly dull, anyhow; New York is dying of dullness," Beaufort grumbled. "And when I try to liven it up for you, you go back on me. Come—think better of it! Sunday is your last chance, for Campanini leaves next week for Baltimore and Philadelphia; and I've a private room, and a Steinway, and they'll sing all night for me."

"How delicious! May I think it over, and write to you to-morrow morning?"

She spoke amiably, yet with the least hint of dismissal in her voice. Beaufort evidently felt it, and being unused to dismissals, stood staring at her with an obstinate line between his eyes.

"Why not now?"

"It's too serious a question to decide at this late hour."

"Do you call it late?"

She returned his glance coolly. "Yes; because I have still to talk business with Mr. Archer for a little while."

"Ah," Beaufort snapped. There was no appeal from her tone, and with a slight shrug he recovered his composure, took her hand, which he kissed with a practised air, and calling out from the threshold: "I say, Newland, if you can persuade the Countess to stop in town of course you're included in the supper," left the room with his heavy important step.

For a moment Archer fancied that Mr. Letterblair must have told her of his coming; but the irrelevance of her next remark made him change his mind.

"You know painters, then? You live in their *milieu?*" she asked, her eyes full of interest.

"Oh, not exactly. I don't know that the arts have a *milieu* here, any of them; they're more like a very thinly settled out-skirt."

"But you care for such things?"

"Immensely. When I'm in Paris or London I never miss an exhibition. I try to keep up."

She looked down at the tip of the little satin boot that peeped from her long draperies.

"I used to care immensely too: my life was full of such things. But now I want to try not to."

"You want to try not to?"

"Yes: I want to cast off all my old life, to become just like everybody else here."

Archer reddened. "You'll never be like everybody else," he said.

She raised her straight eyebrows a little. "Ah, don't say that. If you knew how I hate to be different!"

Her face had grown as sombre as a tragic mask. She leaned forward, clasping her knee in her thin hands, and looking away from him into remote dark distances.

"I want to get away from it all," she insisted.

He waited a moment and cleared his throat. "I know. Mr. Letterblair has told me."

"Ah?"

"That's the reason I've come. He asked me to—you see I'm in the firm."

She looked slightly surprised, and then her eyes brightened. "You mean you can manage it for me? I can talk to you instead of Mr. Letterblair? Oh, that will be so much easier!"

Her tone touched him, and his confidence grew with his self-satisfaction. He perceived that she had spoken of business to Beaufort simply to get rid of him; and to have routed Beaufort was something of a triumph.

"I am here to talk about it," he repeated.

She sat silent, her head still propped by the arm that rested on the back of the sofa. Her face looked pale and extinguished, as if dimmed by the rich red of her dress. She struck Archer, of a sudden, as a pathetic and even pitiful figure.

"Now we're coming to hard facts," he thought, conscious in himself of the same instinctive recoil that he had so often criticised in his mother and her contemporaries. How little practice he had had in dealing with unusual situations! Their very vocabulary was unfamiliar to him, and seemed to belong to fiction and the stage. In face of what was coming he felt as awkward and embarrassed as a boy.

After a pause Madame Olenska broke out with unexpected vehemence: "I want to be free; I want to wipe out all the past."

"I understand that."

Her face warmed. "Then you'll help me?"

"First—" he hesitated—"perhaps I ought to know a little more."

She seemed surprised. "You know about my husband—my life with him?"

He made a sign of assent.

"Well—then—what more is there? In this country are such things tolerated? I'm a Protestant—our church does not forbid divorce in such cases."

"Certainly not."

They were both silent again, and Archer felt the spectre of Count Olenski's letter grimacing hideously between them. The letter filled only half a page, and was just what he had described it to be in speaking of it to Mr. Letterblair: the vague charge of an angry blackguard. But how much truth was behind it? Only Count Olenski's wife could tell.

"I've looked through the papers you gave to Mr. Letterblair," he said at length.

"Well—can there be anything more abominable?"

"No."

She changed her position slightly, screening her eyes with her lifted hand.

"Of course you know," Archer continued, "that if your husband chooses to fight the case—as he threatens to—"

"Yes—?"

"He can say things—things that might be unpl—might be disagreeable to you: say them publicly, so that they would get about, and harm you even if—"

"If—?"

"I mean: no matter how unfounded they were."

She paused for a long interval; so long that, not wishing to keep his eyes on her shaded face, he had time to imprint on his mind the exact shape of her other hand, the one on her knee, and every detail of the three rings on her fourth and fifth fingers; among which, he noticed, a wedding ring did not appear.

"What harm could such accusations, even if he made them publicly, do me here?"

It was on his lips to exclaim: "My poor child—far more harm than anywhere else!" Instead, he answered, in a voice that sounded in his ears like Mr. Letterblair's: "New York society is a very small world compared with the one you've lived in. And it's ruled, in spite of appearances, by a few people with—well, rather old-fashioned ideas."

She said nothing, and he continued: "Our ideas about marriage and divorce are particularly old-fashioned. Our legislation favours divorce—our social customs don't."

"Never?"

"Well—not if the woman, however injured, however irreproachable, has appearances in the least degree against her, has exposed herself by an unconventional action to—to offensive insinuations—"

She drooped her head a little lower, and he waited again, intensely hoping for a flash of indignation, or at least a brief cry of denial. None came.

A little travelling clock ticked purringly at her elbow, and a log broke in two and sent up a shower of sparks. The whole hushed and brooding room seemed to be waiting silently with Archer.

"Yes," she murmured at length, "that's what my family tell me."

He winced a little. "It's not unnatural—"

"*Our* family," she corrected herself; and Archer coloured. "For you'll be my cousin soon," she continued gently.

"I hope so."

"And you take their view?"

He stood up at this, wandered across the room, stared with void eyes at one of the pictures against the old red damask, and came back irresolutely to her side. How could he say: "Yes, if what your husband hints is true, or if you've no way of disproving it?"

"Sincerely—" she interjected, as he was about to speak.

He looked down into the fire. "Sincerely, then—what should you gain that would compensate for the possibility—the certainty—of a lot of beastly talk?"

"But my freedom—is that nothing?"

It flashed across him at that instant that the charge in the letter was true, and that she hoped to marry the partner of her guilt. How was he to tell her that, if she really cherished such a plan, the laws of the State were inexorably opposed to it? The mere suspicion that the thought was in her mind made him feel harshly and impatiently toward her. "But aren't you as free as air as it is?" he returned. "Who can touch you? Mr. Letterblair tells me the financial question has been settled—"

"Oh, yes," she said indifferently.

"Well, then: is it worth while to risk what may be infinitely disagreeable and painful? Think of the newspapers—their vileness! It's all stupid and narrow and unjust—but one can't make over society."

"No," she acquiesced; and her tone was so faint and desolate that he felt a sudden remorse for his own hard thoughts.

"The individual, in such cases, is nearly always sacrificed to what is supposed to be the collective interest: people cling to any convention that keeps the family together—protects the children, if there are any," he rambled on, pouring out all the stock phrases that rose to his lips in his intense desire to cover over the ugly reality which her silence seemed to have laid bare. Since she would not or could not say the one word that would have cleared the air, his wish was not to let her feel that he was trying to probe into her secret. Better keep on the surface, in the prudent old New York way, than risk uncovering a wound he could not heal.

"It's my business, you know," he went on, "to help you to see these things as the people who are fondest of you see them. The Mingotts, the Wellands, the van der Luydens, all your friends and relations: if I didn't show you honestly how they judge such questions, it wouldn't be fair of me, would it?" He spoke insistently, almost pleading with her in his eagerness to cover up that yawning silence.

She said slowly: "No; it wouldn't be fair."

The fire had crumbled down to greyness, and one of the lamps made a gurgling appeal for attention. Madame Olenska rose, wound it up and returned to the fire, but without resuming her seat.

Her remaining on her feet seemed to signify that there was nothing more for either of them to say, and Archer stood up also.

"Very well; I will do what you wish," she said abruptly. The

blood rushed to his forehead; and, taken aback by the sudden-
ness of her surrender, he caught her two hands awkwardly
in his.

"I—I do want to help you," he said.

"You do help me. Good night, my cousin."

He bent and laid his lips on her hands, which were cold and
lifeless. She drew them away, and he turned to the door, found
his coat and hat under the faint gas-light of the hall, and plunged
out into the winter night bursting with the belated eloquence of
the inarticulate.

13

It was a crowded night at Wallack's theatre.

The play was "The Shaughraun," with Dion Boucicault in the title rôle and Harry Montague and Ada Dyas as the lovers. The popularity of the admirable English company was at its height, and the Shaughraun always packed the house. In the galleries the enthusiasm was unreserved; in the stalls and boxes, people smiled a little at the hackneyed sentiments and clap-trap situations, and enjoyed the play as much as the galleries did.

There was one episode, in particular, that held the house from floor to ceiling. It was that in which Harry Montague, after a sad, almost monosyllabic scene of parting with Miss Dyas, bade her good-bye, and turned to go. The actress, who was standing near the mantelpiece and looking down into the fire, wore a gray cashmere dress without fashionable loopings or trimmings, moulded to her tall figure and flowing in long lines about her feet. Around her neck was a narrow black velvet ribbon with the ends falling down her back.

When her wooer turned from her she rested her arms against the mantel-shelf and bowed her face in her hands. On the threshold he paused to look at her; then he stole back, lifted one of the ends of velvet ribbon, kissed it, and left the room without her hearing him or changing her attitude. And on this silent parting the curtain fell.

It was always for the sake of that particular scene that Newland Archer went to see "The Shaughraun." He thought the adieux of Montague and Ada Dyas as fine as anything he had ever seen Croisette and Bressant do in Paris, or Madge Robertson and Kendal in London; in its reticence, its dumb sorrow, it moved him more than the most famous histrionic outpourings.

On the evening in question the little scene acquired an added poignancy by reminding him—he could not have said why—of his leave-taking from Madame Olenska after their confidential talk a week or ten days earlier.

It would have been as difficult to discover any resemblance between the two situations as between the appearance of the persons concerned. Newland Archer could not pretend to anything approaching the young English actor's romantic good looks, and Miss Dyas was a tall red-haired woman of monumental build whose pale and pleasantly ugly face was utterly unlike Ellen Olenska's vivid countenance. Nor were Archer and Madame Olenska two lovers parting in heart-broken silence; they were client and lawyer separating after a talk which had given the lawyer the worst possible impression of the client's case. Wherein, then, lay the resemblance that made the young man's heart beat with a kind of retrospective excitement? It seemed to be in Madame Olenska's mysterious faculty of suggesting tragic and moving possibilities outside the daily run of experience. She had hardly ever said a word to him to produce this impression, but it was a part of her, either a projection of her mysterious and outlandish background or of something inherently dramatic, passionate and unusual in herself. Archer had always been inclined to think that chance and circumstance played a small part in shaping people's lots compared with their innate tendency to have things happen to them. This tendency he had felt from the first in Madame Olenska. The quiet, almost passive young woman struck him as exactly the kind of person to whom things were bound to happen, no matter how much she shrank from them and went out of her way to avoid them. The exciting fact was her having lived in an atmosphere so thick with drama that her own tendency to provoke it had apparently passed unperceived. It was precisely the odd absence of surprise in her that gave him the sense of her having been plucked out of a very maelstrom: the things she took for granted gave the measure of those she had rebelled against.

Archer had left her with the conviction that Count Olenski's accusation was not unfounded. The mysterious person who figured in his wife's past as "the secretary" had probably not been unrewarded for his share in her escape. The conditions from which she had fled were intolerable, past speaking of, past believing: she was young, she was frightened, she was desperate—what more natural than that she should be grateful to her rescuer? The pity was that her gratitude put her, in the law's eyes and the world's, on a par with her abominable husband. Archer had made her understand this, as he was bound to do; he had also made her understand that simplehearted kindly New York, on whose larger charity she had apparently counted, was precisely the place where she could least hope for indulgence.

To have to make this fact plain to her—and to witness her resigned acceptance of it—had been intolerably painful to him. He felt himself drawn to her by obscure feelings of jealousy and pity, as if her dumbly-confessed error had put her at his mercy, humbling yet endearing her. He was glad it was to him she had revealed her secret, rather than to the cold scrutiny of Mr. Letterblair, or the embarrassed gaze of her family. He immediately took it upon himself to assure them both that she had given up her idea of seeking a divorce, basing her decision on the fact that she had understood the uselessness of the proceeding; and with infinite relief they had all turned their eyes from the "unpleasantness" she had spared them.

"I was sure Newland would manage it," Mrs. Welland had said proudly of her future son-in-law; and old Mrs. Mingott, who had summoned him for a confidential interview, had congratulated him on his cleverness, and added impatiently: "Silly goose! I told her myself what nonsense it was. Wanting to pass herself off as Ellen Mingott and an old maid, when she has the luck to be a married woman and a Countess!"

These incidents had made the memory of his last talk with Madame Olenska so vivid to the young man that as the curtain fell on the parting of the two actors his eyes filled with tears, and he stood up to leave the theatre.

In doing so, he turned to the side of the house behind him, and saw the lady of whom he was thinking seated in a box with the Beauforts, Lawrence Lefferts and one or two other men. He had not spoken with her alone since their evening together, and had tried to avoid being with her in company; but now their eyes met, and as Mrs. Beaufort recognised him at the same time, and made her languid little gesture of invitation, it was impossible not to go into the box.

Beaufort and Lefferts made way for him, and after a few

words with Mrs. Beaufort, who always preferred to look beautiful and not have to talk, Archer seated himself behind Madame Olenska. There was no one else in the box but Mr. Sillerton Jackson, who was telling Mrs. Beaufort in a confidential undertone about Mrs. Lemuel Struthers's last Sunday reception (where some people reported that there had been dancing). Under cover of this circumstantial narrative, to which Mrs. Beaufort listened with her perfect smile, and her head at just the right angle to be seen in profile from the stalls, Madame Olenska turned and spoke in a low voice.

"Do you think," she asked, glancing toward the stage, "he will send her a bunch of yellow roses tomorrow morning?"

Archer reddened, and his heart gave a leap of surprise. He had called only twice on Madame Olenska, and each time he had sent her a box of yellow roses, and each time without a card. She had never before made any allusion to the flowers, and he supposed she had never thought of him as the sender. Now her sudden recognition of the gift, and her associating it with the tender leave-taking on the stage, filled him with an agitated pleasure.

"I was thinking of that too—I was going to leave the theatre in order to take the picture away with me," he said.

To his surprise her colour rose, reluctantly and duskily. She looked down at the mother-of-pearl opera-glass in her smoothly gloved hands, and said, after a pause: "What do you do while May is away?"

"I stick to my work," he answered, faintly annoyed by the question.

In obedience to a long-established habit, the Wellands had left the previous week for St. Augustine, where, out of regard for the supposed susceptibility of Mr. Welland's bronchial tubes, they always spent the latter part of the winter. Mr. Welland was a mild and silent man, with no opinions but with many habits. With these habits none might interfere; and one of them demanded that his wife and daughter should always go with him on his annual journey to the south. To preserve an unbroken domesticity was essential to his peace of mind; he would not have known where his hair-brushes were, or how to provide stamps for his letters, if Mrs. Welland had not been there to tell him.

As all the members of the family adored each other, and as Mr. Welland was the central object of their idolatry, it never occurred to his wife and May to let him go to St. Augustine alone; and his sons, who were both in the law, and could not leave New York during the winter, always joined him for Easter and travelled back with him.

It was impossible for Archer to discuss the necessity of May's accompanying her father. The reputation of the Mingotts' family physician was largely based on the attack of pneumonia which Mr. Welland had never had; and his insistence on St. Augustine was therefore inflexible. Originally, it had been intended that May's engagement should not be announced till her return from Florida, and the fact that it had been made known sooner could not be expected to alter Mr. Welland's plans. Archer would have liked to join the travellers and have a few weeks of sunshine and boating with his betrothed; but he too was bound by custom and conventions. Little arduous as his professional duties were, he would have been convicted of frivolity by the whole Mingott clan if he had suggested asking for a holiday in mid-winter; and he accepted May's departure with the resignation which he perceived would have to be one of the principal constituents of married life.

He was conscious that Madame Olenska was looking at him under lowered lids. "I have done what you wished—what you advised," she said abruptly.

"Ah—I'm glad," he returned, embarrassed by her broaching the subject at such a moment.

"I understand—that you were right," she went on a little breathlessly; "but sometimes life is difficult . . . perplexing . . ."

"I know."

"And I wanted to tell you that I *do* feel you were right; and that I'm grateful to you," she ended, lifting her opera-glass quickly to her eyes as the door of the box opened and Beaufort's resonant voice broke in on them.

Archer stood up, and left the box and the theatre.

Only the day before he had received a letter from May Wel-

land in which, with characteristic candour, she had asked him to
"be kind to Ellen" in their absence. "She likes you and admires
you so much—and you know, though she doesn't show it, she's
still very lonely and unhappy. I don't think Granny understands
her, or uncle Lovell Mingott either; they really think she's much
worldlier and fonder of society than she is. And I can quite see
that New York must seem dull to her, though the family won't
admit it. I think she's been used to lots of things we haven't got;
wonderful music, and picture shows, and celebrities—artists and
authors and all the clever people you admire. Granny can't understand her wanting anything but lots of dinners and clothes—
but I can see that you're almost the only person in New York
who can talk to her about what she really cares for."

His wise May—how he had loved her for that letter! But he
had not meant to act on it; he was too busy, to begin with, and
he did not care, as an engaged man, to play too conspicuously
the part of Madame Olenska's champion. He had an idea that
she knew how to take care of herself a good deal better than the
ingenuous May imagined. She had Beaufort at her feet, Mr. van
der Luyden hovering above her like a protecting deity, and any
number of candidates (Lawrence Lefferts among them) waiting
their opportunity in the middle distance. Yet he never saw her,
or exchanged a word with her, without feeling that, after all,
May's ingenuousness almost amounted to a gift of divination.
Ellen Olenska was lonely and she was unhappy.

As he came out into the lobby Archer ran across his friend Ned Winsett, the only one among what Janey called his "clever people" with whom he cared to probe into things a little deeper than the average level of club and chop-house banter.

He had caught sight, across the house, of Winsett's shabby round-shouldered back, and had once noticed his eyes turned toward the Beaufort box. The two men shook hands, and Winsett proposed a bock at a little German restaurant around the corner. Archer, who was not in the mood for the kind of talk they were likely to get there, declined on the plea that he had work to do at home; and Winsett said: "Oh, well so have I for that matter, and I'll be the Industrious Apprentice too."

They strolled along together, and presently Winsett said: "Look here, what I'm really after is the name of the dark lady in that swell box of yours—with the Beauforts, wasn't she? The one your friend Lefferts seems so smitten by."

Archer, he could not have said why, was slightly annoyed. What the devil did Ned Winsett want with Ellen Olenska's name? And above all, why did he couple it with Lefferts's? It was unlike Winsett to manifest such curiosity; but after all, Archer remembered, he was a journalist.

"It's not for an interview, I hope?" he laughed.

"Well—not for the press; just for myself," Winsett rejoined. "The fact is she's a neighbour of mine—queer quarter for such a beauty to settle in—and she's been awfully kind to my little boy, who fell down her area chasing his kitten, and gave himself a nasty cut. She rushed in bareheaded, carrying him in her arms, with his knee all beautifully bandaged, and was so sympathetic and beautiful that my wife was too dazzled to ask her name."

A pleasant glow dilated Archer's heart. There was nothing extraordinary in the tale: any woman would have done as much for a neighbour's child. But it was just like Ellen, he felt, to have rushed in bareheaded, carrying the boy in her arms, and to have dazzled poor Mrs. Winsett into forgetting to ask who she was.

"That is the Countess Olenska—a granddaughter of old Mrs. Mingott's."

"Whew—a Countess!" whistled Ned Winsett. "Well, I didn't know Countesses were so neighbourly. Mingotts ain't."

"They would be, if you'd let them."

"Ah, well—" It was their old interminable argument as to the obstinate unwillingness of the "clever people" to frequent the fashionable, and both men knew that there was no use in prolonging it.

"I wonder," Winsett broke off, "how a Countess happens to live in our slum?"

"Because she doesn't care a hang about where she lives—or about any of our little social sign-posts," said Archer, with a secret pride in his own picture of her.

"H'm—been in bigger places, I suppose," the other commented. "Well, here's my corner."

He slouched off across Broadway, and Archer stood looking after him and musing on his last words.

Ned Winsett had those flashes of penetration; they were the most interesting thing about him, and always made Archer wonder why they had allowed him to accept failure so stolidly at an age when most men are still struggling.

Archer had known that Winsett had a wife and child, but he had never seen them. The two men always met at the Century, or at some haunt of journalists and theatrical people, such as the restaurant where Winsett had proposed to go for a bock. He had given Archer to understand that his wife was an invalid; which might be true of the poor lady, or might merely mean that she was lacking in social gifts or in evening clothes, or in both. Winsett himself had a savage abhorrence of social observances: Archer, who dressed in the evening because he thought it cleaner and more comfortable to do so, and who had never stopped to consider that cleanliness and comfort are two of the costliest items in a modest budget, regarded Winsett's attitude as part of the boring "Bohemian" pose that always made fashionable people, who changed their clothes without talking about it, and were not forever harping on the number of servants one kept, seem so much simpler and less self-conscious than the others. Nevertheless, he was always stimulated by Winsett, and whenever he caught sight of the journalist's lean bearded face and melancholy eyes he would rout him out of his corner and carry him off for a long talk.

Winsett was not a journalist by choice. He was a pure man of letters, untimely born in a world that had no need of letters; but after publishing one volume of brief and exquisite literary appreciations, of which one hundred and twenty copies were sold, thirty given away, and the balance eventually destroyed by the publishers (as per contract) to make room for more marketable material, he had abandoned his real calling, and taken a subeditorial job on a women's weekly, where fashion-plates and paper patterns alternated with New England love-stories and advertisements of temperance drinks.

On the subject of "Hearth-fires" (as the paper was called) he was inexhaustibly entertaining; but beneath his fun lurked the sterile bitterness of the still young man who has tried and given up. His conversation always made Archer take the measure of his own life, and feel how little it contained; but Winsett's, after all, contained still less, and though their common fund of intellectual interests and curiosities made their talks exhilarating, their exchange of views usually remained within the limits of a pensive dilettantism.

"The fact is, life isn't much a fit for either of us," Winsett had once said. "I'm down and out; nothing to be done about it. I've got only one ware to produce, and there's no market for it here, and won't be in my time. But you're free and you're well-off. Why don't *you* get into touch? There's only one way to do it: to go into politics."

Archer threw his head back and laughed. There one saw at a flash the unbridgeable difference between men like Winsett and the others—Archer's kind. Every one in polite circles knew that, in America, "a gentleman couldn't go into politics." But, since he could hardly put it in that way to Winsett, he answered evasively: "Look at the career of the honest man in American politics! They don't want us."

"Who's 'they'? Why don't you all get together and be 'they' yourselves?"

Archer's laugh lingered on his lips in a slightly condescending smile. It was useless to prolong the discussion: everybody knew the melancholy fate of the few gentlemen who had risked their clean linen in municipal or state politics in New York. The day was past when that sort of thing was possible: the country was in possession of the bosses and the emigrant, and decent people had to fall back on sport or culture.

"Culture! Yes—if we had it! But there are just a few little local patches, dying out here and there for lack of—well, hoeing and cross-fertilising: the last remnants of the old European tradition that your forebears brought with them. But you're in a pitiful little minority: you've got no centre, no competition, no audience. You're like the pictures on the walls of a deserted house: 'The Portrait of a Gentleman.' You'll never amount to anything, any of you, till you roll up your sleeves and get right down into the muck. That, or emigrate . . . God! If I could emigrate . . ."

Archer mentally shrugged his shoulders and turned the conversation back to books, where Winsett, if uncertain, was always interesting. Emigrate! As if a gentleman could abandon his own country! One could no more do that than one could roll up one's sleeves and go down into the muck. A gentleman simply stayed at home and abstained. But you couldn't make a man like Winsett see that; and that was why the New York of literary clubs and exotic restaurants, though a first shake made it seem more of a kaleidoscope, turned out, in the end, to be a smaller box, with a more monotonous pattern, than the assembled atoms of Fifth Avenue.

The next morning Archer scoured the town in vain for more yellow roses. In consequence of this search he arrived late at the office, perceived that his doing so made no difference whatever to any one, and was filled with sudden exasperation at the elaborate futility of his life. Why should he not be, at that moment, on the sands of St. Augustine with May Welland? No one was deceived by his pretense of professional activity. In old-fashioned legal firms like that of which Mr. Letterblair was the head, and which were mainly engaged in the management of large estates and "conservative" investments, there were always two or three young men, fairly well-off, and without professional ambition, who, for a certain number of hours of each day, sat at their desks accomplishing trivial tasks, or simply reading the newspapers. Though it was supposed to be proper for them to have an occupation, the crude fact of money-making was still regarded as derogatory, and the law, being a profession, was accounted a more gentlemanly pursuit than business. But none of these young men had much hope of really advancing in his profession, or any earnest desire to do so; and over many of them the green mould of the perfunctory was already perceptibly spreading.

It made Archer shiver to think that it might be spreading over him too. He had, to be sure, other tastes and interests; he spent his vacations in European travel, cultivated the "clever people" May spoke of, and generally tried to "keep up," as he had somewhat wistfully put it to Madame Olenska. But once he was married, what would become of this narrow margin of life in which his real experiences were lived? He had seen enough of other young men who had dreamed his dream, though perhaps less ardently, and who had gradually sunk into the placid and luxurious routine of their elders.

From the office he sent a note by messenger to Madame Olenska, asking if he might call that afternoon, and begging her to let him find a reply at his club; but at the club he found nothing, nor did he receive any letter the following day. This unexpected silence mortified him beyond reason, and though the next morning he saw a glorious cluster of yellow roses behind a florist's window-pane, he left it there. It was only on the third morning that he received a line by post from the Countess Olenska. To his surprise it was dated from Skuytercliff, whither the van der Luydens had promptly retreated after putting the Duke on board his steamer.

"I ran away," the writer began abruptly (without the usual preliminaries), "the day after I saw you at the play, and these kind friends have taken me in. I wanted to be quiet, and think

things over. You were right in telling me how kind they were;
I feel myself so safe here. I wish that you were with us." She
ended with a conventional "Yours sincerely," and without any
allusion to the date of her return.

The tone of the note surprised the young man. What was
Madame Olenska running away from, and why did she feel the
need to be safe? His first thought was of some dark menace from
abroad; then he reflected that he did not know her epistolary
style, and that it might run to picturesque exaggeration. Women
always exaggerated; and moreover she was not wholly at her ease
in English, which she often spoke as if she were translating from
the French. "Je me suis évadée—" put in that way, the opening
sentence immediately suggested that she might merely have
wanted to escape from a boring round of engagements; which
was very likely true, for he judged her to be capricious, and
easily wearied of the pleasure of the moment.

It amused him to think of the van der Luydens' having carried
her off to Skuytercliff on a second visit, and this time for an
indefinite period. The doors of Skuytercliff were rarely and
grudgingly opened to visitors, and a chilly week-end was the
most ever offered to the few thus privileged. But Archer had
seen, on his last visit to Paris, the delicious play of Labiche, "Le
Voyage de M. Perrichon," and he remembered M. Perrichon's
dogged and undiscouraged attachment to the young man whom
he had pulled out of the glacier. The van der Luydens had res-
cued Madame Olenska from a doom almost as icy; and though
there were many other reasons for being attracted to her, Archer
knew that beneath them all lay the gentle and obstinate determination to go on rescuing her.

He felt a distinct disappointment on learning that she was
away; and almost immediately remembered that, only the day
before, he had refused an invitation to spend the following Sunday with the Reggie Chiverses at their house on the Hudson, a
few miles below Skuytercliff.

He had had his fill long ago of the noisy friendly parties at
Highbank, with coasting, ice-boating, sleighing, long tramps in
the snow, and a general flavour of mild flirting and milder practical jokes. He had just received a box of new books from his

London bookseller, and had preferred the prospect of a quiet Sunday at home with his spoils. But he now went into the club writing-room, wrote a hurried telegram, and told the servant to send it immediately. He knew that Mrs. Reggie didn't object to her visitors' suddenly changing their minds, and that there was always a room to spare in her elastic house.

Newland Archer arrived at the Chiverses' on Friday evening, and on Saturday went conscientiously through all the rites appertaining to a week-end at Highbank.

In the morning he had a spin in the ice-boat with his hostess and a few of the hardier guests; in the afternoon he "went over the farm" with Reggie, and listened, in the elaborately appointed stables, to long and impressive disquisitions on the horse; after tea he talked in a corner of the firelit hall with a young lady who had professed herself broken-hearted when his engagement was announced, but was now eager to tell him of her own matrimonial hopes; and finally, about midnight, he assisted in putting a gold-fish in one visitor's bed, dressed up a burglar in the bath-room of a nervous aunt, and saw in the small hours by joining in a pillow-fight that ranged from the nurseries to the basement. But on Sunday after luncheon he borrowed a cutter, and drove over to Skuytercliff.

People had always been told that the house at Skuytercliff was an Italian villa. Those who had never been to Italy believed it; so did some who had. The house had been built by Mr. van der Luyden in his youth, on his return from the "grand tour," and in anticipation of his approaching marriage with Miss Louisa Dagonet. It was a large square wooden structure, with tongued and grooved walls painted pale green and white, a Corinthian portico, and fluted pilasters between the windows. From the high ground on which it stood a series of terraces bordered by balustrades and urns descended in the steel-engraving style to a small irregular lake with an asphalt edge overhung by rare weeping conifers. To the right and left, the famous weedless lawns studded with "specimen" trees (each of a different variety) rolled away to long ranges of grass crested with elaborate cast-iron ornaments; and below, in a hollow, lay the four-roomed stone house which the first Patroon had built on the land granted him in 1612.

Against the uniform sheet of snow and the greyish winter sky the Italian villa loomed up rather grimly; even in summer it kept its distance, and the boldest coleus bed had never ventured nearer than thirty feet from its awful front. Now, as Archer rang the bell, the long tinkle seemed to echo through a mausoleum; and the surprise of the butler who at length responded to the call was as great as though he had been summoned from his final sleep.

Happily Archer was of the family, and therefore, irregular though his arrival was, entitled to be informed that the Countess Olenska was out, having driven to afternoon service with Mrs. van der Luyden exactly three quarters of an hour earlier.

"Mr. van der Luyden," the butler continued, "is in, sir; but my impression is that he is either finishing his nap or else reading yesterday's Evening Post. I heard him say, sir, on his return from church this morning, that he intended to look through the Evening Post after luncheon; if you like, sir, I might go to the library door and listen—"

But Archer, thanking him, said that he would go and meet the ladies; and the butler, obviously relieved, closed the door on him majestically.

A groom took the cutter to the stables, and Archer struck through the park to the high-road. The village of Skuytercliff was only a mile and a half away, but he knew that Mrs. van der Luyden never walked, and that he must keep to the road to meet the carriage. Presently, however, coming down a foot-path that crossed the highway, he caught sight of a slight figure in a red cloak, with a big dog running ahead. He hurried forward, and Madame Olenska stopped short with a smile of welcome.

"Ah, you've come!" she said, and drew her hand from her muff.

The red cloak made her look gay and vivid, like the Ellen Mingott of old days; and he laughed as he took her hand, and answered: "I came to see what you were running away from."

Her face clouded over, but she answered: "Ah, well—you will see, presently."

The answer puzzled him. "Why—do you mean that you've been overtaken?"

She shrugged her shoulders, with a little movement like Nastasia's, and rejoined in a lighter tone: "Shall we walk on? I'm so cold after the sermon. And what does it matter, now you're here to protect me?"

The blood rose to his temples and he caught a fold of her cloak. "Ellen—what is it? You must tell me."

"Oh, presently—let's run a race first: my feet are freezing to the ground," she cried; and gathering up the cloak she fled away across the snow, the dog leaping about her with challenging barks. For a moment Archer stood watching, his gaze delighted by the flash of the red meteor against the snow; then he started after her, and they met, panting and laughing, at a wicket that led into the park.

She looked up at him and smiled. "I knew you'd come!"

"That shows you wanted me to," he returned, with a disproportionate joy in their nonsense. The white glitter of the trees filled the air with its own mysterious brightness, and as they walked on over the snow the ground seemed to sing under their feet.

"Where did you come from?" Madame Olenska asked.

He told her, and added: "It was because I got your note."

After a pause she said, with a just perceptible chill in her voice: "May asked you to take care of me."

"I didn't need any asking."

"You mean—I'm so evidently helpless and defenceless? What a poor thing you must all think me! But women here seem not —seem never to feel the need: any more than the blessed in heaven."

He lowered his voice to ask: "What sort of a need?"

"Ah, don't ask me! I don't speak your language," she retorted petulantly.

The answer smote him like a blow, and he stood still in the path, looking down at her.

"What did I come for, if I don't speak yours?"

"Oh, my friend—!" She laid her hand lightly on his arm, and he pleaded earnestly: "Ellen—why won't you tell me what's happened?"

She shrugged again. "Does anything ever happen in heaven?"

He was silent, and they walked on a few yards without exchanging a word. Finally she said: "I will tell you—but where, where, where? One can't be alone for a minute in that great seminary of a house, with all the doors wide open, and always a servant bringing tea, or a log for the fire, or the newspaper! Is there nowhere in an American house where one may be by one's self? You're so shy, and yet you're so public. I always feel as if I were in the convent again—or on the stage, before a dreadfully polite audience that never applauds."

"Ah, you don't like us!" Archer exclaimed.

They were walking past the house of the old Patroon, with its squat walls and small square windows compactly grouped about a central chimney. The shutters stood wide, and through one of the newly-washed windows Archer caught the light of a fire.

"Why—the house is open!" he said.

She stood still. "No; only for today, at least. I wanted to see it, and Mr. van der Luyden had the fire lit and the windows opened, so that we might stop there on the way back from church this morning." She ran up the steps and tried the door. "It's still unlocked—what luck! Come in and we can have a quiet talk. Mrs. van der Luyden has driven over to see her old aunts at Rhinebeck and we shan't be missed at the house for another hour."

He followed her into the narrow passage. His spirits, which had dropped at her last words, rose with an irrational leap. The homely little house stood there, its panels and brasses shining in the firelight, as if magically created to receive them. A big bed of embers still gleamed in the kitchen chimney, under an iron pot hung from an ancient crane. Rush-bottomed arm-chairs faced each other across the tiled hearth, and rows of Delft plates stood on shelves against the walls. Archer stooped over and threw a log upon the embers.

Madame Olenska, dropping her cloak, sat down in one of the chairs. Archer leaned against the chimney and looked at her.

"You're laughing now; but when you wrote me you were unhappy," he said.

"Yes." She paused. "But I can't feel unhappy when you're here."

"I sha'n't be here long," he rejoined, his lips stiffening with the effort to say just so much and no more.

"No; I know. But I'm improvident: I live in the moment when I'm happy."

The words stole through him like a temptation, and to close his senses to it he moved away from the hearth and stood gazing out at the black tree-boles against the snow. But it was as if she too had shifted her place, and he still saw her, between himself and the trees, drooping over the fire with her indolent smile. Archer's heart was beating insubordinately. What if it were from him that she had been running away, and if she had waited to tell him so till they were here alone together in this secret room?

"Ellen, if I'm really a help to you—if you really wanted me to come—tell me what's wrong, tell me what it is you're running away from," he insisted.

He spoke without shifting his position, without even turning to look at her: if the thing was to happen, it was to happen in this way, with the whole width of the room between them, and his eyes still fixed on the outer snow.

For a long moment she was silent; and in that moment Archer imagined her, almost heard her, stealing up behind him to throw her light arms about his neck. While he waited, soul and body throbbing with the miracle to come, his eyes mechanically received the image of a heavily-coated man with his fur collar turned up who was advancing along the path to the house. The man was Julius Beaufort.

"Ah—!" Archer cried, bursting into a laugh.

Madame Olenska had sprung up and moved to his side, slipping her hand into his; but after a glance through the window her face paled and she shrank back.

"So that was it?" Archer said derisively.

"I didn't know he was here," Madame Olenska murmured. Her hand still clung to Archer's; but he drew away from her, and walking out into the passage threw open the door of the house.

"Hallo, Beaufort—this way! Madame Olenska was expecting you," he said.

During his journey back to New York the next morning, Archer relived with a fatiguing vividness his last moments at Skuytercliff.

Beaufort, though clearly annoyed at finding him with Madame Olenska, had, as usual, carried off the situation high-handedly. His way of ignoring people whose presence inconvenienced him actually gave them, if they were sensitive to it, a feeling of invisibility, of nonexistence. Archer, as the three strolled back through the park, was aware of this odd sense of disembodiment; and humbling as it was to his vanity it gave him the ghostly advantage of observing unobserved.

Beaufort had entered the little house with his usual easy assurance; but he could not smile away the vertical line between his eyes. It was fairly clear that Madame Olenska had not known that he was coming, though her words to Archer had hinted at the possibility; at any rate, she had evidently not told him where she was going when she left New York, and her unexplained departure had exasperated him. The ostensible reason of his appearance was the discovery, the very night before, of a "perfect little house," not in the market, which was really just the thing for her, but would be snapped up instantly if she didn't take it; and he was loud in mock-reproaches for the dance she had led him in running away just as he had found it.

"If only this new dodge for talking along a wire had been a little bit nearer perfection I might have told you all this from town, and been toasting my toes before the club fire at this minute, instead of tramping after you through the snow," he grumbled, disguising a real irritation under the pretence of it; and at this opening Madame Olenska twisted the talk away to the fantastic possibility that they might one day actually converse with each other from street to street, or even—incredible dream!—from one town to another. This struck from all three allusions to Edgar Poe and Jules Verne, and such platitudes as naturally rise to the lips of the most intelligent when they are talking against time, and dealing with a new invention in which it would seem ingenuous to believe too soon; and the question of the telephone carried them safely back to the big house.

Mrs. van der Luyden had not yet returned; and Archer took his leave and walked off to fetch the cutter, while Beaufort followed the Countess Olenska indoors. It was probable that, little as the van der Luydens encouraged unannounced visits, he could count on being asked to dine, and sent back to the station to catch the nine o'clock train; but more than that he would certainly not get, for it would be inconceivable to his hosts that a gentleman travelling without luggage should wish to spend the night, and distasteful to them to propose it to a person with whom they were on terms of such limited cordiality as Beaufort.

Beaufort knew all this, and must have foreseen it; and his taking the long journey for so small a reward gave the measure of his impatience. He was undeniably in pursuit of the Countess Olenska; and Beaufort had only one object in view in his pursuit of pretty women. His dull and childless home had long since palled on him; and in addition to more permanent consolations he was always in quest of amorous adventures in his own set. This was the man from whom Madame Olenska was avowedly flying: the question was whether she had fled because his importunities displeased her, or because she did not wholly trust herself to resist them; unless, indeed, all her talk of flight had been a blind, and her departure no more than a manœuvre.

Archer did not really believe this. Little as he had actually seen of Madame Olenska, he was beginning to think that he could read her face, and if not her face, her voice; and both had betrayed annoyance, and even dismay, at Beaufort's sudden appearance. But, after all, if this were the case, was it not worse than if she had left New York for the express purpose of meeting him? If she had done that, she ceased to be an object of interest, she threw in her lot with the vulgarest of dissemblers: a woman engaged in a love affair with Beaufort "classed" herself irretrievably.

No, it was worse a thousand times if, judging Beaufort, and probably despising him, she was yet drawn to him by all that gave him an advantage over the other men about her: his habit of two continents and two societies, his familiar association with artists and actors and people generally in the world's eye, and his careless contempt for local prejudices. Beaufort was vulgar, he was uneducated, he was purse-proud; but the circumstances of his life, and a certain native shrewdness, made him better worth talking to than many men, morally and socially his betters, whose horizon was bounded by the Battery and the Central Park. How should any one coming from a wider world not feel the difference and be attracted by it?

Madame Olenska, in a burst of irritation, had said to Archer that he and she did not talk the same language; and the young man knew that in some respects this was true. But Beaufort understood every turn of her dialect, and spoke it fluently: his view of life, his tone, his attitude, were merely a coarser reflection of those revealed in Count Olenski's letter. This might seem to be to his disadvantage with Count Olenski's wife; but Archer was too intelligent to think that a young woman like Ellen Olenska would necessarily recoil from everything that reminded her of her past. She might believe herself wholly in revolt against it; but what had charmed her in it would still charm her, even though it were against her will.

Thus, with a painful impartiality, did the young man make out the case for Beaufort, and for Beaufort's victim. A longing to enlighten her was strong in him; and there were moments when he imagined that all she asked was to be enlightened.

That evening he unpacked his books from London. The box was full of things he had been waiting for impatiently; a new volume of Herbert Spencer, another collection of the prolific Alphonse Daudet's brilliant tales, and a novel called "Middlemarch," as to which there had lately been interesting things said in the reviews. He had declined three dinner invitations in favour of this feast; but though he turned the pages with the sensuous joy of the book-lover, he did not know what he was reading, and one book after another dropped from his hand. Suddenly, among them, he lit on a small volume of verse which he had ordered because the name had attracted him: "The House of Life." He took it up, and found himself plunged in an atmosphere unlike any he had ever breathed in books; so warm, so rich, and yet so ineffably tender, that it gave a new and haunting beauty to the most elementary of human passions. All through the night he pursued through those enchanted pages the vision of a woman who had the face of Ellen Olenska; but when he woke the next morning, and looked out at the brownstone houses across the street, and thought of his desk in Mr. Letterblair's office, and the family pew in Grace Church, his hour in the park of Skuytercliff became as far outside the pale of probability as the visions of the night.

"Mercy, how pale you look, Newland!" Janey commented over the coffee-cups at breakfast; and his mother added: "Newland, dear, I've noticed lately that you've been coughing; I do hope you're not letting yourself be overworked?" For it was the conviction of both ladies that, under the iron despotism of his senior partners, the young man's life was spent in the most exhausting professional labours—and he had never thought it necessary to undeceive them.

The next two or three days dragged by heavily. The taste of the usual was like cinders in his mouth, and there were moments when he felt as if he were being buried alive under his future. He heard nothing of the Countess Olenska, or of the perfect little house, and though he met Beaufort at the club they merely nodded at each other across the whist-tables. It was not till the fourth evening that he found a note awaiting him on his return home. "Come late tomorrow: I must explain to you. Ellen." These were the only words it contained.

The young man, who was dining out, thrust the note into his pocket, smiling a little at the Frenchness of the "to you." After dinner he went to a play; and it was not until his return home, after midnight, that he drew Madame Olenska's missive out again and re-read it slowly a number of times. There were several ways of answering it, and he gave considerable thought to each one during the watches of an agitated night. That on which, when morning came, he finally decided was to pitch some clothes into a portmanteau and jump on board a boat that was leaving that very afternoon for St. Augustine.

When Archer walked down the sandy main street of St. Augustine to the house which had been pointed out to him as Mr. Welland's, and saw May Welland standing under a magnolia with the sun in her hair, he wondered why he had waited so long to come.

Here was the truth, here was reality, here was the life that belonged to him; and he, who fancied himself so scornful of arbitrary restraints, had been afraid to break away from his desk because of what people might think of his stealing a holiday!

Her first exclamation was: "Newland—has anything happened?" and it occurred to him that it would have been more "feminine" if she had instantly read in his eyes why he had come. But when he answered: "Yes—I found I had to see you," her happy blushes took the chill from her surprise, and he saw how easily he would be forgiven, and how soon even Mr. Letterblair's mild disapproval would be smiled away by a tolerant family.

Early as it was, the main street was no place for any but formal greetings, and Archer longed to be alone with May, and to pour out all his tenderness and his impatience. It still lacked an hour to the late Welland breakfast-time, and instead of asking him to come in she proposed that they should walk out to an old orange-garden beyond the town. She had just been for a row on the river, and the sun that netted the little waves with gold seemed to have caught her in its meshes. Across the warm brown of her cheek her blown hair glittered like silver wire; and her eyes too looked lighter, almost pale in their youthful limpidity. As she walked beside Archer with her long swinging gait her face wore the vacant serenity of a young marble athlete.

To Archer's strained nerves the vision was as soothing as the sight of the blue sky and the lazy river. They sat down on a bench under the orange-trees and he put his arm about her and kissed her. It was like drinking at a cold spring with the sun on it; but his pressure may have been more vehement than he had intended, for the blood rose to her face and she drew back as if he had startled her.

"What is it?" he asked, smiling; and she looked at him with surprise, and answered: "Nothing."

A slight embarrassment fell on them, and her hand slipped out of his. It was the only time that he had kissed her on the lips except for their fugitive embrace in the Beaufort conservatory, and he saw that she was disturbed, and shaken out of her cool boyish composure.

"Tell me what you do all day," he said, crossing his arms under his tilted-back head, and pushing his hat forward to screen the sun-dazzle. To let her talk about familiar and simple things was the easiest way of carrying on his own independent train of thought; and he sat listening to her simple chronicle of swimming, sailing and riding, varied by an occasional dance at the primitive inn when a man-of-war came in. A few pleasant people from Philadelphia and Baltimore were picknicking at the inn, and the Selfridge Merrys had come down for three weeks because Kate Merry had had bronchitis. They were planning to lay out a lawn tennis court on the sands; but no one but Kate and May had racquets, and most of the people had not even heard of the game.

All this kept her very busy, and she had not had time to do more than look at the little vellum book that Archer had sent her the week before (the "Sonnets from the Portuguese"); but she was learning by heart "How they brought the Good News from Ghent to Aix," because it was one of the first things he had ever read to her; and it amused her to be able to tell him that Kate Merry had never even heard of a poet called Robert Browning.

Presently she started up, exclaiming that they would be late for breakfast; and they hurried back to the tumble-down house with its paintless porch and unpruned hedge of plumbago and pink geraniums where the Wellands were installed for the winter. Mr. Welland's sensitive domesticity shrank from the discomforts of the slovenly southern hotel, and at immense expense, and in face of almost insuperable difficulties, Mrs. Welland was obliged, year after year, to improvise an establishment partly made up of discontented New York servants and partly drawn from the local African supply.

"The doctors want my husband to feel that he is in his own home; otherwise he would be so wretched that the climate would not do him any good," she explained, winter after winter, to the sympathising Philadelphians and Baltimoreans; and Mr. Welland, beaming across a breakfast table miraculously supplied with the most varied delicacies, was presently saying to Archer: "You see, my dear fellow, we camp—we literally camp. I tell my wife and May that I want to teach them how to rough it."

Mr. and Mrs. Welland had been as much surprised as their daughter by the young man's sudden arrival; but it had occurred to him to explain that he had felt himself on the verge of a nasty cold, and this seemed to Mr. Welland an all-sufficient reason for abandoning any duty.

"You can't be too careful, especially toward spring," he said, heaping his plate with straw-coloured griddlecakes and drowning them in golden syrup. "If I'd only been as prudent at your age May would have been dancing at the Assemblies now, instead of spending her winters in a wilderness with an old invalid."

"Oh, but I love it here, Papa; you know I do. If only Newland could stay I should like it a thousand times better than New York."

"Newland must stay till he has quite thrown off his cold," said Mrs. Welland indulgently; and the young man laughed, and said he supposed there was such a thing as one's profession.

He managed, however, after an exchange of telegrams with the firm, to make his cold last a week; and it shed an ironic light on the situation to know that Mr. Letterblair's indulgence was partly due to the satisfactory way in which his brilliant young junior partner had settled the troublesome matter of the Olenski divorce. Mr. Letterblair had let Mrs. Welland know that Mr. Archer had "rendered an invaluable service" to the whole family, and that old Mrs. Manson Mingott had been particularly pleased; and one day when May had gone for a drive with her father in the only vehicle the place produced Mrs. Welland took occasion to touch on a topic which she always avoided in her daughter's presence.

"I'm afraid Ellen's ideas are not at all like ours. She was barely eighteen when Medora Manson took her back to Europe—you remember the excitement when she appeared in black at her coming-out ball? Another of Medora's fads—really this time it was almost prophetic! That must have been at least twelve years ago; and since then Ellen has never been to America. No wonder she is completely Europeanised."

"But European society is not given to divorce: Countess Olenska thought she would be conforming to American ideas in asking for her freedom." It was the first time that the young man had pronounced her name since he had left Skuytercliff, and he felt the colour rise to his cheek.

Mrs. Welland smiled compassionately. "That is just like the extraordinary things that foreigners invent about us. They think we dine at two o'clock and countenance divorce! That is why it seems to me so foolish to entertain them when they come to New York. They accept our hospitality, and then they go home and repeat the same stupid stories."

Archer made no comment on this, and Mrs. Welland continued: "But we do most thoroughly appreciate your persuading Ellen to give up the idea. Her grandmother and her uncle Lovell could do nothing with her; both of them have written that her changing her mind was entirely due to your influence—in fact she said so to her grandmother. She has an unbounded admiration for you. Poor Ellen—she was always a wayward child. I wonder what her fate will be?"

"What we've all contrived to make it," he felt like answering. "If you'd all of you rather she should be Beaufort's mistress than some decent fellow's wife you've certainly gone the right way about it."

He wondered what Mrs. Welland would have said if he had uttered the words instead of merely thinking them. He could picture the sudden decomposure of her firm placid features, to which a lifelong mastery over trifles had given an air of factitious authority. Traces still lingered on them of a fresh beauty like her daughter's; and he asked himself if May's face was doomed to thicken into the same middle-aged image of invincible innocence.

Ah, no, he did not want May to have that kind of innocence, the innocence that seals the mind against imagination and the heart against experience!

"I verily believe," Mrs. Welland continued, "that if the horrible business had come out in the newspapers it would have been my husband's death-blow. I don't know any of the details; I only ask not to, as I told poor Ellen when she tried to talk to me about it. Having an invalid to care for, I have to keep my mind bright and happy. But Mr. Welland was terribly upset; he had a slight temperature every morning while we were waiting to hear what had been decided. It was the horror of his girl's learning that such things were possible—but of course, dear Newland, you felt that too. We all knew that you were thinking of May."

"I'm always thinking of May," the young man rejoined, rising to cut short the conversation.

He had meant to seize the opportunity of his private talk with Mrs. Welland to urge her to advance the date of his marriage. But he could think of no arguments that would move her, and with a sense of relief he saw Mr. Welland and May driving up to the door.

His only hope was to plead again with May, and on the day before his departure he walked with her to the ruinous garden of the Spanish Mission. The background lent itself to allusions to European scenes; and May, who was looking her loveliest under a wide-brimmed hat that cast a shadow of mystery over her too-clear eyes, kindled into eagerness as he spoke of Granada and the Alhambra.

"We might be seeing it all this spring—even the Easter ceremonies at Seville," he urged, exaggerating his demands in the hope of a larger concession.

"Easter in Seville? And it will be Lent next week!" she laughed.

"Why shouldn't we be married in Lent?" he rejoined; but she looked so shocked that he saw his mistake.

"Of course I didn't mean that, dearest; but soon after Easter—so that we could sail at the end of April. I know I could arrange it at the office."

She smiled dreamily upon the possibility; but he perceived that to dream of it sufficed her. It was like hearing him read aloud out of his poetry books the beautiful things that could not possibly happen in real life.

"Oh, do go on, Newland; I do love your descriptions."

"But why should they be only descriptions? Why shouldn't we make them real?"

"We shall, dearest, of course; next year." Her voice lingered over it.

"Don't you want them to be real sooner? Can't I persuade you to break away now?"

She bowed her head, vanishing from him under her conniving hat-brim.

"Why should we dream away another year? Look at me, dear! Don't you understand how I want you for my wife?"

For a moment she remained motionless; then she raised on him eyes of such despairing clearness that he half-released her waist from his hold. But suddenly her look changed and deepened inscrutably. "I'm not sure if I *do* understand," she said. "Is it—is it because you're not certain of continuing to care for me?"

Archer sprang up from his seat. "My God—perhaps—I don't know," he broke out angrily.

May Welland rose also; as they faced each other she seemed to grow in womanly stature and dignity. Both were silent for a moment, as if dismayed by the unforeseen trend of their words: then she said in a low voice: "If that is it—is there some one else?"

"Some one else—between you and me?" He echoed her words slowly, as though they were only half-intelligible and he wanted time to repeat the question to himself. She seemed to catch the uncertainty of his voice, for she went on in a deepening tone: "Let us talk frankly, Newland. Sometimes I've felt a difference in you; especially since our engagement has been announced."

"Dear—what madness!" he recovered himself to exclaim.

She met his protest with a faint smile. "If it is, it won't hurt us to talk about it." She paused, and added, lifting her head with one of her noble movements: "Or even if it's true: why shouldn't we speak of it? You might so easily have made a mistake."

He lowered his head, staring at the black leaf-pattern on the sunny path at their feet. "Mistakes are always easy to make; but if I had made one of the kind you suggest, is it likely that I should be imploring you to hasten our marriage?"

She looked downward too, disturbing the pattern with the point of her sunshade while she struggled for expression. "Yes," she said at length. "You might want—once for all—to settle the question: it's one way."

Her quiet lucidity startled him, but did not mislead him into thinking her insensible. Under her hat-brim he saw the pallor of her profile, and a slight tremor of the nostril above her resolutely steadied lips.

"Well—?" he questioned, sitting down on the bench, and looking up at her with a frown that he tried to make playful.

She dropped back into her seat and went on: "You mustn't think that a girl knows as little as her parents imagine. One hears and one notices—one has one's feelings and ideas. And of course, long before you told me that you cared for me, I'd known that there was some one else you were interested in; every one was talking about it two years ago at Newport. And once I saw you sitting together on the verandah at a dance— and when she came back into the house her face was sad, and I felt sorry for her; I remembered it afterward, when we were engaged."

Her voice had sunk almost to a whisper, and she sat clasping and unclasping her hands about the handle of her sunshade. The young man laid his upon them with a gentle pressure; his heart dilated with an inexpressible relief.

"My dear child—was *that* it? If you only knew the truth!"

She raised her head quickly. "Then there is a truth I don't know?"

He kept his hand over hers. "I meant, the truth about the old story you speak of."

"But that's what I want to know, Newland—what I ought to know. I couldn't have my happiness made out of a wrong—an unfairness—to somebody else. And I want to believe that it would be the same with you. What sort of a life could we build on such foundations?"

Her face had taken on a look of such tragic courage that he felt like bowing himself down at her feet. "I've wanted to say this for a long time," she went on. "I've wanted to tell you that, when two people really love each other, I understand that there may be situations which make it right that they should—should go against public opinion. And if you feel yourself in any way pledged . . . pledged to the person we've spoken of . . . and if there is any way . . . any way in which you can fulfill your pledge . . . even by her getting a divorce . . . Newland, don't give her up because of me!"

His surprise at discovering that her fears had fastened upon an episode so remote and so completely of the past as his love-affair with Mrs. Thorley Rushworth gave way to wonder at the generosity of her view. There was something superhuman in an attitude so recklessly unorthodox, and if other problems had not pressed on him he would have been lost in wonder at the prodigy of the Wellands' daughter urging him to marry his former mistress. But he was still dizzy with the glimpse of the precipice they had skirted, and full of a new awe at the mystery of young-girlhood.

For a moment he could not speak; then he said: "There is no pledge—no obligation whatever—of the kind you think. Such cases don't always—present themselves quite as simply as . . . But that's no matter . . . I love your generosity, because I feel as you do about those things . . . I feel that each case must be judged individually, on its own merits . . . irrespective of stupid conventionalities . . . I mean, each woman's right to her liberty—" He pulled himself up, startled by the turn his thoughts had taken, and went on, looking at her with a smile: "Since you understand so many things, dearest, can't you go a little farther, and understand the uselessness of our submitting to another form of the same foolish conventionalities? If there's no one and nothing between us, isn't that an argument for marrying quickly, rather than for more delay?"

She flushed with joy and lifted her face to his; as he bent to it he saw that her eyes were full of happy tears. But in another moment she seemed to have descended from her womanly eminence to helpless and timorous girlhood; and he understood that her courage and initiative were all for others, and that she had none for herself. It was evident that the effort of speaking had been much greater than her studied composure betrayed, and that at his first word of reassurance she had dropped back into the usual, as a too-adventurous child takes refuge in its mother's arms.

Archer had no heart to go on pleading with her; he was too much disappointed at the vanishing of the new being who had cast that one deep look at him from her transparent eyes. May seemed to be aware of his disappointment, but without knowing how to alleviate it; and they stood up and walked silently home.

17

Your cousin the Countess called on mother while you were away," Janey Archer announced to her brother on the evening of his return.

The young man, who was dining alone with his mother and sister, glanced up in surprise and saw Mrs. Archer's gaze demurely bent on her plate. Mrs. Archer did not regard her seclusion from the world as a reason for being forgotten by it; and Newland guessed that she was slightly annoyed that he should be surprised by Madame Olenska's visit.

"She had on a black velvet polonaise with jet buttons, and a tiny green monkey muff; I never saw her so stylishly dressed," Janey continued. "She came alone, early on Sunday afternoon; luckily the fire was lit in the drawing-room. She had one of those new card-cases. She said she wanted to know us because you'd been so good to her."

Newland laughed. "Madame Olenska always takes that tone about her friends. She's very happy at being among her own people again."

"Yes, so she told us," said Mrs. Archer. "I must say she seems thankful to be here."

"I hope you liked her, mother."

Mrs. Archer drew her lips together. "She certainly lays herself out to please, even when she is calling on an old lady."

"Mother doesn't think her simple," Janey interjected, her eyes screwed upon her brother's face.

"It's just my old-fashioned feeling; dear May is my ideal," said Mrs. Archer.

"Ah," said her son, "they're not alike."

Archer had left St. Augustine charged with many messages for old Mrs. Mingott; and a day or two after his return to town he called on her.

The old lady received him with unusual warmth; she was

grateful to him for persuading the Countess Olenska to give up the idea of a divorce; and when he told her that he had deserted the office without leave, and rushed down to St. Augustine simply because he wanted to see May, she gave an adipose chuckle and patted his knee with her puff-ball hand.

"Ah, ah—so you kicked over the traces, did you? And I suppose Augusta and Welland pulled long faces, and behaved as if the end of the world had come? But little May—she knew better, I'll be bound?"

"I hoped she did; but after all she wouldn't agree to what I'd gone down to ask for."

"Wouldn't she indeed? And what was that?"

"I wanted to get her to promise that we should be married in April. What's the use of our wasting another year?"

Mrs. Manson Mingott screwed up her little mouth into a grimace of mimic prudery and twinkled at him through malicious lids. "'Ask Mamma,' I suppose—the usual story. Ah, these Mingotts—all alike! Born in a rut, and you can't root 'em out of it. When I built this house you'd have thought I was moving to California! Nobody ever *had* built above Fortieth Street—no, says I, nor above the Battery either, before Christopher Columbus discovered America. No, no; not one of them wants to be different; they're as scared of it as the small-pox. Ah, my dear Mr. Archer, I thank my stars I'm nothing but a vulgar Spicer; but there's not one of my own children that takes after me but my little Ellen." She broke off, still twinkling at him, and asked, with the casual irrelevance of old age: "Now, why in the world didn't you marry my little Ellen?"

Archer laughed. "For one thing, she wasn't there to be married."

"No—to be sure; more's the pity. And now it's too late; her life is finished." She spoke with the cold-blooded complacency of the aged throwing earth into the grave of young hopes. The young man's heart grew chill, and he said hurriedly: "Can't I persuade you to use your influence with the Wellands, Mrs. Mingott? I wasn't made for long engagements."

Old Catherine beamed on him approvingly. "No; I can see that. You've got a quick eye. When you were a little boy I've no doubt you liked to be helped first." She threw back her head with a laugh that made her chins ripple like little waves. "Ah, here's my Ellen now!" she exclaimed, as the portières parted behind her.

Madame Olenska came forward with a smile. Her face looked vivid and happy, and she held out her hand gaily to Archer while she stooped to her grandmother's kiss.

"I was just saying to him, my dear: 'Now, why didn't you marry my little Ellen?' "

Madame Olenska looked at Archer, still smiling. "And what did he answer?"

"Oh, my darling, I leave you to find that out! He's been down to Florida to see his sweetheart."

"Yes, I know." She still looked at him. "I went to see your mother, to ask where you'd gone. I sent a note that you never answered, and I was afraid you were ill."

He muttered something about leaving unexpectedly, in a great hurry, and having intended to write to her from St. Augustine.

"And of course once you were there you never thought of me again!" She continued to beam on him with a gaiety that might have been a studied assumption of indifference.

"If she still needs me, she's determined not to let me see it," he thought, stung by her manner. He wanted to thank her for having been to see his mother, but under the ancestress's malicious eye he felt himself tongue-tied and constrained.

"Look at him—in such hot haste to get married that he took French leave and rushed down to implore the silly girl on his knees! That's something like a lover—that's the way handsome Bob Spicer carried off my poor mother; and then got tired of her before I was weaned—though they only had to wait eight months for me! But there—you're not a Spicer, young man; luckily for you and for May. It's only my poor Ellen that has kept any of their wicked blood; the rest of them are all model Mingotts," cried the old lady scornfully.

Archer was aware that Madame Olenska, who had seated herself at her grandmother's side, was still thoughtfully scrutinising him. The gaiety had faded from her eyes, and she said with great gentleness: "Surely, Granny, we can persuade them between us to do as he wishes."

Archer rose to go, and as his hand met Madame Olenska's he felt that she was waiting for him to make some allusion to her unanswered letter.

"When can I see you?" he asked, as she walked with him to the door of the room.

"Whenever you like; but it must be soon if you want to see the little house again. I am moving next week."

A pang shot through him at the memory of his lamplit hours in the low-studded drawing-room. Few as they had been, they were thick with memories.

"Tomorrow evening?"

She nodded. "Tomorrow; yes; but early. I'm going out."

The next day was a Sunday, and if she were "going out" on a Sunday evening it could, of course, be only to Mrs. Lemuel Struthers's. He felt a slight movement of annoyance, not so much at her going there (for he rather liked her going where she pleased in spite of the van der Luydens), but because it was the kind of house at which she was sure to meet Beaufort, where she must have known beforehand that she would meet him— and where she was probably going for that purpose.

"Very well; tomorrow evening," he repeated, inwardly resolved that he would not go early, and that by reaching her door late he would either prevent her from going to Mrs. Struthers's, or else arrive after she had started—which, all things considered, would no doubt be the simplest solution.

It was only half-past eight, after all, when he rang the bell under the wisteria; not as late as he had intended by half an hour—but a singular restlessness had driven him to her door. He reflected, however, that Mrs. Struthers's Sunday evenings were not like a ball, and that her guests, as if to minimise their delinquency, usually went early.

The one thing he had not counted on, in entering Madame Olenska's hall, was to find hats and overcoats there. Why had she bidden him to come early if she was having people to dine?

On a closer inspection of the garments besides which Nastasia was laying his own, his resentment gave way to curiosity. The overcoats were in fact the very strangest he had ever seen under a polite roof; and it took but a glance to assure himself that neither of them belonged to Julius Beaufort. One was a shaggy yellow ulster of "reach-me-down" cut, the other a very old and rusty cloak with a cape—something like what the French called a "Macfarlane." This garment, which appeared to be made for a person of prodigious size, had evidently seen long and hard wear, and its greenish-black folds gave out a moist sawdusty smell suggestive of prolonged sessions against bar-room walls. On it lay a ragged grey scarf and an odd felt hat of semiclerical shape.

Archer raised his eyebrows enquiringly at Nastasia, who raised hers in return with a fatalistic "Già!" as she threw open the drawing-room door.

The young man saw at once that his hostess was not in the room; then, with surprise, he discovered another lady standing by the fire. This lady, who was long, lean and loosely put together, was clad in raiment intricately looped and fringed, with plaids and stripes and bands of plain colour disposed in a design to which the clue seemed missing. Her hair, which had tried to turn white and only succeeded in fading, was surmounted by a Spanish comb and black lace scarf, and silk mittens, visibly darned, covered her rheumatic hands.

Beside her, in a cloud of cigar-smoke, stood the owners of the two overcoats, both in morning clothes that they had evidently not taken off since morning. In one of the two, Archer, to his surprise, recognised Ned Winsett; the other and older, who was unknown to him, and whose gigantic frame declared him to be the wearer of the "Macfarlane," had a feebly leonine head with crumpled grey hair, and moved his arms with large pawing gestures, as though he were distributing lay blessings to a kneeling multitude.

These three persons stood together on the hearth-rug, their eyes fixed on an extraordinarily large bouquet of crimson roses, with a knot of purple pansies at their base, that lay on the sofa where Madame Olenska usually sat.

"What they must have cost at this season—though of course it's the sentiment one cares about!" the lady was saying in a sighing staccato as Archer came in.

The three turned with surprise at his appearance, and the lady, advancing, held out her hand.

"Dear Mr. Archer—almost my cousin Newland!" she said. "I am the Marchioness Manson."

Archer bowed, and she continued: "My Ellen has taken me in for a few days. I came from Cuba, where I have been spending the winter with Spanish friends—such delightful distinguished people: the highest nobility of old Castile—how I wish you could know them! But I was called away by our dear great friend here, Dr. Carver. You don't know Dr. Agathon Carver, founder of the Valley of Love Community?"

Dr. Carver inclined his leonine head, and the Marchioness continued: "Ah, New York—New York—how little the life of the spirit has reached it! But I see you do know Mr. Winsett."

"Oh, yes—*I* reached him some time ago; but not by that route," Winsett said with his dry smile.

The Marchioness shook her head reprovingly. "How do you know, Mr. Winsett? The spirit bloweth where it listeth."

"List—oh, list!" interjected Dr. Carver in a stentorian murmur.

"But do sit down, Mr. Archer. We four have been having a delightful little dinner together, and my child has gone up to dress. She expects you; she will be down in a moment. We were just admiring these marvellous flowers, which will surprise her when she reappears."

Winsett remained on his feet. "I'm afraid I must be off. Please tell Madame Olenska that we shall all feel lost when she abandons our street. This house has been an oasis."

"Ah, but she won't abandon *you*. Poetry and art are the breath of life to her. It *is* poetry you write, Mr. Winsett?"

"Well, no; but I sometimes read it," said Winsett, including the group in a general nod and slipping out of the room.

"A caustic spirit—*un peu sauvage*. But so witty; Dr. Carver, you *do* think him witty?"

"I never think of wit," said Dr. Carver severely.

"Ah—ah—you never think of wit! How merciless he is to us weak mortals, Mr. Archer! But he lives only in the life of the spirit; and tonight he is mentally preparing the lecture he is to deliver presently at Mrs. Blenker's. Dr. Carver, would there be time, before you start for the Blenkers' to explain to Mr. Archer your illuminating discovery of the Direct Contact? But no; I see it is nearly nine o'clock, and we have no right to detain you while so many are waiting for your message."

Dr. Carver looked slightly disappointed at this conclusion, but, having compared his ponderous gold timepiece with Madame Olenska's little travelling-clock, he reluctantly gathered up his mighty limbs for departure.

"I shall see you later, dear friend?" he suggested to the Marchioness, who replied with a smile: "As soon as Ellen's carriage comes I will join you; I do hope the lecture won't have begun."

Dr. Carver looked thoughtfully at Archer. "Perhaps, if this young gentleman is interested in my experiences, Mrs. Blenker might allow you to bring him with you?"

"Oh, dear friend, if it were possible—I am sure she would be too happy. But I fear my Ellen counts on Mr. Archer herself."

"That," said Dr. Carver, "is unfortunate—but here is my card." He handed it to Archer, who read on it, in Gothic characters:

```
┌─────────────────────────────────┐
│                                 │
│        Agathon Carver           │
│      The Valley of Love         │
│     Kittasquattamy, N.Y.        │
│                                 │
└─────────────────────────────────┘
```

Dr. Carver bowed himself out, and Mrs. Manson, with a sigh that might have been either of regret or relief, again waved Archer to a seat.

"Ellen will be down in a moment; and before she comes, I am so glad of this quiet moment with you."

Archer murmured his pleasure at their meeting, and the Marchioness continued, in her low sighing accents: "I know everything, dear Mr. Archer—my child has told me all you have done for her. Your wise advice: your courageous firmness—thank heaven it was not too late!"

The young man listened with considerable embarrassment. Was there any one, he wondered, to whom Madame Olenska had not proclaimed his intervention in her private affairs?"

"Madame Olenska exaggerates; I simply gave her a legal opinion, as she asked me to."

"Ah, but in doing it—in doing it you were the unconscious instrument of—of—what word have we moderns for Providence, Mr. Archer?" cried the lady, tilting her head on one side and drooping her lids mysteriously. "Little did you know that at that very moment I was being appealed to: being approached, in fact—from the other side of the Atlantic!"

She glanced over her shoulder, as though fearful of being overheard, and then, drawing her chair nearer, and raising a tiny ivory fan to her lips, breathed behind it: "By the Count himself—my poor, mad, foolish Olenski; who asks only to take her back on her own terms."

"Good God!" Archer exclaimed, springing up.

"You are horrified? Yes, of course; I understand. I don't defend poor Stanislas, though he has always called me his best friend. He does not defend himself—he casts himself at her feet: in my person." She tapped her emaciated bosom. "I have his letter here."

"A letter?—Has Madame Olenska seen it?" Archer stammered, his brain whirling with the shock of the announcement.

The Marchioness Manson shook her head softly. "Time—time; I must have time. I know my Ellen—haughty, intractable; shall I say, just a shade unforgiving?"

"But, good heavens, to forgive is one thing; to go back into that hell—"

"Ah, yes," the Marchioness acquiesced. "So she describes it—my sensitive child! But on the material side, Mr. Archer, if one may stoop to consider such things; do you know what she is giving up? Those roses there on the sofa—acres like them, under glass and in the open, in his matchless terraced gardens at Nice! Jewels—historic pearls: the Sobieski emeralds—sables—

but she cares nothing for all these! Art and beauty, those she does care for, she lives for, as I always have; and those also surrounded her. Pictures, priceless furniture, music, brilliant conversation—ah, that, my dear young man, if you'll excuse me, is what you've no conception of here! And she had it all; and the homage of the greatest. She tells me she is not thought handsome in New York—good heavens! Her portrait has been painted nine times; the greatest artists in Europe have begged for the privilege. Are these things nothing? And the remorse of an adoring husband?"

As the Marchioness Manson rose to her climax her face assumed an expression of ecstatic retrospection which would have moved Archer's mirth had he not been numb with amazement.

He would have laughed if any one had foretold to him that his first sight of poor Medora Manson would have been in the guise of a messenger of Satan; but he was in no mood for laughing now, and she seemed to him to come straight out of the hell from which Ellen Olenska had just escaped.

"She knows nothing yet—of all this?" he asked abruptly.

Mrs. Manson laid a purple finger on her lips. "Nothing directly—but does she suspect? Who can tell? The truth is, Mr. Archer, I have been waiting to see you. From the moment I heard of the firm stand you had taken, and of your influence over her, I hoped it might be possible to count on your support—to convince you . . ."

"That she ought to go back? I would rather see her dead!" cried the young man violently.

"Ah," the Marchioness murmured, without visible resentment. For a while she sat in her arm-chair, opening and shutting the absurd ivory fan between her mittened fingers; but suddenly she lifted her head and listened.

"Here she comes," she said in a rapid whisper; and then, pointing to the bouquet on the sofa: "Am I to understand that you prefer *that*, Mr. Archer? After all, marriage is marriage . . . and my niece is still a wife. . . ."

What are you two plotting together, aunt Medora?" Madame Olenska cried as she came into the room. She was dressed as if for a ball. Everything about her shimmered and glimmered softly, as if her dress had been woven out of candle-beams; and she carried her head high, like a pretty woman challenging a roomful of rivals.

"We were saying, my dear, that here was something beautiful to surprise you with," Mrs. Manson rejoined, rising to her feet and pointing archly to the flowers.

Madame Olenska stopped short and looked at the bouquet. Her colour did not change, but a sort of white radiance of anger ran over her like summer lightning. "Ah," she exclaimed, in a shrill voice that the young man had never heard, "who is ridiculous enough to send me a bouquet? Why a bouquet? And why tonight of all nights? I am not going to a ball; I am not a girl engaged to be married. But some people are always ridiculous."

She turned back to the door, opened it, and called out: "Nastasia!"

The ubiquitous handmaiden promptly appeared, and Archer heard Madame Olenska say, in an Italian that she seemed to pronounce with intentional deliberateness in order that he might follow it: "Here—throw this into the dustbin!" and then, as Nastasia stared protestingly: "But no—it's not the fault of the poor flowers. Tell the boy to carry them to the house three doors away, the house of Mr. Winsett, the dark gentleman who dined here. His wife is ill—they may give her pleasure . . . The boy is out, you say? Then, my dear one, run yourself; here, put my cloak over you and fly. I want the thing out of the house immediately! And, as you live, don't say they come from me!"

She flung her velvet opera cloak over the maid's shoulders and turned back into the drawing-room, shutting the door sharply. Her bosom was rising high under its lace, and for a moment Archer thought she was about to cry; but she burst into a laugh instead, and looking from the Marchioness to Archer, asked abruptly: "And you two—have you made friends!"

"It's for Mr. Archer to say, darling; he has waited patiently while you were dressing."

"Yes—I gave you time enough: my hair wouldn't go," Madame Olenska said, raising her hand to the heaped-up curls of her *chignon*. "But that reminds me: I see Dr. Carver is gone, and you'll be late at the Blenkers'. Mr. Archer, will you put my aunt in the carriage?"

She followed the Marchioness into the hall, saw her fitted into a miscellaneous heap of overshoes, shawls and tippets, and called from the doorstep: "Mind, the carriage is to be back for me at ten!" Then she returned to the drawing-room, where Archer, on re-entering it, found her standing by the mantelpiece, examining herself in the mirror. It was not usual, in New York society, for a lady to address her parlour-maid as "my dear one," and send her out on an errand wrapped in her own opera-cloak; and Archer, through all his deeper feelings, tasted the pleasurable excitement of being in a world where action followed on emotion with such Olympian speed.

Madame Olenska did not move when he came up behind her, and for a second their eyes met in the mirror; then she turned, threw herself into her sofa-corner, and sighed out: "There's time for a cigarette."

He handed her the box and lit a spill for her; and as the flame flashed up into her face she glanced at him with laughing eyes and said: "What do you think of me in a temper?"

Archer paused a moment; then he answered with sudden resolution: "It makes me understand what your aunt has been saying about you."

"I knew she'd been talking about me. Well?"

"She said you were used to all kinds of things—splendours and amusements and excitements—that we could never hope to give you here."

Madame Olenska smiled faintly into the circle of smoke about her lips.

"Medora is incorrigibly romantic. It has made up to her for so many things!"

Archer hesitated again, and again took his risk. "Is your aunt's romanticism always consistent with accuracy?"

"You mean: does she speak the truth?" Her niece considered. "Well, I'll tell you: in almost everything she says, there's something true and something untrue. But why do you ask? What has she been telling you?"

He looked away into the fire, and then back at her shining presence. His heart tightened with the thought that this was their last evening by that fireside, and that in a moment the carriage would come to carry her away.

"She says—she pretends that Count Olenski has asked her to persuade you to go back to him."

Madame Olenska made no answer. She sat motionless, holding her cigarette in her half-lifted hand. The expression of her face had not changed; and Archer remembered that he had before noticed her apparent incapacity for surprise.

"You knew, then?" he broke out.

She was silent for so long that the ash dropped from her cigarette. She brushed it to the floor. "She has hinted about a letter: poor darling! Medora's hints—"

"Is it at your husband's request that she has arrived here suddenly?"

Madame Olenska seemed to consider this question also. "There again: one can't tell. She told me she had had a 'spiritual summons,' whatever that is, from Dr. Carver. I'm afraid she's going to marry Dr. Carver . . . poor Medora, there's always some one she wants to marry. But perhaps the people in Cuba just got tired of her! I think she was with them as a sort of paid companion. Really, I don't know why she came."

"But you do believe she has a letter from your husband?"

Again Madame Olenska brooded silently; then she said: "After all, it was to be expected."

The young man rose and went to lean against the fireplace. A sudden restlessness possessed him, and he was tongue-tied by the sense that their minutes were numbered, and that at any moment he might hear the wheels of the returning carriage.

"You know that your aunt believes you will go back?"

Madame Olenska raised her head quickly. A deep blush rose

to her face and spread over her neck and shoulders. She blushed seldom and painfully, as if it hurt her like a burn.

"Many cruel things have been believed of me," she said.

"Oh, Ellen—forgive me; I'm a fool and a brute!"

She smiled a little. "You are horribly nervous; you have your own troubles. I know you think the Wellands are unreasonable about your marriage, and of course I agree with you. In Europe people don't understand our long American engagements; I suppose they are not as calm as we are." She pronounced the "we" with a faint emphasis that gave it an ironic sound.

Archer felt the irony but did not dare to take it up. After all, she had perhaps purposely deflected the conversation from her own affairs, and after the pain his last words had evidently caused her he felt that all he could do was to follow her lead. But the sense of the waning hour made him desperate: he could not bear the thought that a barrier of words should drop between them again.

"Yes," he said abruptly; "I went south to ask May to marry me after Easter. There's no reason why we shouldn't be married then."

"And May adores you—and yet you couldn't convince her? I thought her too intelligent to be the slave of such absurd superstitions."

"She *is* too intelligent—she's not their slave."

Madame Olenska looked at him. "Well, then—I don't understand."

Archer reddened, and hurried on with a rush. "We had a frank talk—almost the first. She thinks my impatience a bad sign."

"Merciful heavens—a bad sign?"

"She thinks it means that I can't trust myself to go on caring for her. She thinks, in short, I want to marry her at once to get away from some one that I—care for more."

Madame Olenska examined this curiously. "But if she thinks that—why isn't she in a hurry too?"

"Because she's not like that: she's so much nobler. She insists all the more on the long engagement, to give me time—"

"Time to give her up for the other woman?"

"If I want to."

Madame Olenska leaned toward the fire and gazed into it with fixed eyes. Down the quiet street Archer heard the approaching trot of her horses.

"That *is* noble," she said, with a slight break in her voice.

"Yes. But it's ridiculous."

"Ridiculous? Because you don't care for any one else?"

"Because I don't mean to marry any one else."

"Ah." There was another long interval. At length she looked up at him and asked: "This other woman—does she love you?"

"Oh, there's no other woman; I mean, the person that May was thinking of is—was never—"

"Then, why, after all, are you in such haste?"

"There's your carriage," said Archer.

She half-rose and looked about her with absent eyes. Her fan and gloves lay on the sofa beside her and she picked them up mechanically.

"Yes; I suppose I must be going."

"You're going to Mrs. Struthers's?"

"Yes." She smiled and added: "I must go where I am invited, or I should be too lonely. Why not come with me?"

Archer felt that at any cost he must keep her beside him, must make her give him the rest of her evening. Ignoring her question, he continued to lean against the chimney-piece, his eyes fixed on the hand in which she held her gloves and fan, as if watching to see if he had the power to make her drop them.

"May guessed the truth," he said. "There is another woman —but not the one she thinks."

Ellen Olenska made no answer, and did not move. After a moment he sat down beside her, and, taking her hand, softly unclasped it, so that the gloves and fan fell on the sofa between them.

She started up, and freeing herself from him moved away to the other side of the hearth. "Ah, don't make love to me! Too many people have done that," she said, frowning.

Archer, changing colour, stood up also: it was the bitterest rebuke she could have given him. "I have never made love to you," he said, "and I never shall. But you are the woman I would have married if it had been possible for either of us."

"Possible for either of us?" She looked at him with unfeigned astonishment. "And you say that—when it's you who've made it impossible?"

He stared at her, groping in a blackness through which a single arrow of light tore its blinding way.

"*I've* made it impossible—?"

"You, you, *you!*" she cried, her lip trembling like a child's on the verge of tears. "Isn't it you who made me give up divorcing—give it up because you showed me how selfish and wicked it was, how one must sacrifice one's self to preserve the dignity of marriage . . . and to spare one's family the publicity, the scandal? And because my family was going to be your family—for May's sake and for yours—I did what you told me, what you proved to me that I ought to do. Ah," she broke out with a sudden laugh, "I've made no secret of having done it for you!"

She sank down on the sofa again, crouching among the festive ripples of her dress like a stricken masquerader; and the young man stood by the fireplace and continued to gaze at her without moving.

"Good God," he groaned. "When I thought—"

"You thought?"

"Ah, don't ask me what I thought!"

Still looking at her, he saw the same burning flush creep up her neck to her face. She sat upright, facing him with a rigid dignity.

"I do ask you."

"Well, then: there were things in that letter you asked me to read—"

"My husband's letter?"

"Yes."

"I had nothing to fear from that letter: absolutely nothing! All I feared was to bring notoriety, scandal, on the family—on you and May."

"Good God," he groaned again, bowing his face in his hands.

The silence that followed lay on them with the weight of things final and irrevocable. It seemed to Archer to be crushing him down like his own grave-stone; in all the wide future he saw nothing that would ever lift that load from his heart. He did not move from his place, or raise his head from his hands; his hidden eyeballs went on staring into utter darkness.

"At least I loved you—" he brought out.

On the other side of the hearth, from the sofa-corner where he supposed that she still crouched, he heard a faint stifled crying like a child's. He started up and came to her side.

"Ellen! What madness! Why are you crying? Nothing's done that can't be undone. I'm still free, and you're going to be." He had her in his arms, her face like a wet flower at his lips, and all their vain terrors shrivelling up like ghosts at sunrise. The one thing that astonished him now was that he should have stood for five minutes arguing with her across the width of the room, when just touching her made everything so simple.

She gave him back all his kiss, but after a moment he felt her stiffening in his arms, and she put him aside and stood up.

"Ah, my poor Newland—I suppose this had to be. But it doesn't in the least alter things," she said, looking down at him in her turn from the hearth.

"It alters the whole of life for me."

"No, no—it mustn't, it can't. You're engaged to May Welland; and I'm married."

He stood up too, flushed and resolute. "Nonsense! It's too late for that sort of thing. We've no right to lie to other people or to ourselves. We won't talk of your marriage; but do you see me marrying May after this?"

She stood silent, resting her thin elbows on the mantel-piece, her profile reflected in the glass behind her. One of the locks of her *chignon* had become loosened and hung on her neck; she looked haggard and almost old.

"I don't see you," she said at length, "putting that question to May. Do you?"

He gave a reckless shrug. "It's too late to do anything else."

"You say that because it's the easiest thing to say at this moment—not because it's true. In reality it's too late to do anything but what we'd both decided on."

"Ah, I don't understand you!"

She forced a pitiful smile that pinched her face instead of smoothing it. "You don't understand because you haven't yet guessed how you've changed things for me: oh, from the first— long before I knew all you'd done."

"All I'd done?"

"Yes. I was perfectly unconscious at first that people here were shy of me—that they thought I was a dreadful sort of person. It seems they had even refused to meet me at dinner. I found that out afterward; and how you'd made your mother go with you to the van der Luydens'; and how you'd insisted on announcing your engagement at the Beaufort ball, so that I might have two families to stand by me instead of one—"

At that he broke into a laugh.

"Just imagine," she said, "how stupid and unobservant I was! I knew nothing of all this till Granny blurted it out one day. New York simply meant peace and freedom to me: it was coming home. And I was so happy at being among my own people that every one I met seemed kind and good, and glad to see me. But from the very beginning," she continued, "I felt there was no one as kind as you; no one who gave me reasons that I understood for doing what at first seemed so hard and—unnecessary. The very good people didn't convince me; I felt they'd never been tempted. But you knew; you understood; you had felt the world outside tugging at one with all its golden hands —and yet you hated the things it asks of one; you hated happiness bought by disloyalty and cruelty and indifference. That was what I'd never known before—and it's better than anything I've known."

She spoke in a low even voice, without tears or visible agitation; and each word, as it dropped from her, fell into his breast like burning lead. He sat bowed over, his head between his hands, staring at the hearth-rug, and at the tip of the satin shoe that showed under her dress. Suddenly he knelt down and kissed the shoe.

She bent over him, laying her hands on his shoulders, and looking at him with eyes so deep that he remained motionless under her gaze.

"Ah, don't let us undo what you've done!" she cried. "I can't go back now to that other way of thinking. I can't love you unless I give you up."

His arms were yearning up to her; but she drew away, and they remained facing each other, divided by the distance that her words had created. Then, abruptly, his anger overflowed.

"And Beaufort? Is he to replace me?"

As the words sprang out he was prepared for an answering flare of anger; and he would have welcomed it as fuel for his own. But Madame Olenska only grew a shade paler, and stood with her arms hanging down before her, and her head slightly bent, as her way was when she pondered a question.

"He's waiting for you now at Mrs. Struthers's; why don't you go to him?" Archer sneered.

She turned to ring the bell. "I shall not go out this evening; tell the carriage to go and fetch the Signora Marchesa," she said when the maid came.

After the door had closed again Archer continued to look at her with bitter eyes. "Why this sacrifice? Since you tell me that you're lonely I've no right to keep you from your friends."

She smiled a little under her wet lashes. "I shan't be lonely now. I *was* lonely; I *was* afraid. But the emptiness and the darkness are gone; when I turn back into myself now I'm like a child going at night into a room where there's always a light."

Her tone and her look still enveloped her in a soft inaccessibility, and Archer groaned out again: "I don't understand you!"

"Yet you understand May!"

He reddened under the retort, but kept his eyes on her. "May is ready to give me up."

"What! Three days after you've entreated her on your knees to hasten your marriage?"

"She's refused; that gives me the right—"

"Ah, you've taught me what an ugly word that is," she said.

He turned away with a sense of utter weariness. He felt as

though he had been struggling for hours up the face of a steep precipice, and now, just as he had fought his way to the top, his hold had given way and he was pitching down headlong into darkness.

If he could have got her in his arms again he might have swept away her arguments; but she still held him at a distance by something inscrutably aloof in her look and attitude, and by his own awed sense of her sincerity. At length he began to plead again.

"If we do this now it will be worse afterward—worse for every one—"

"No—no—no!" she almost screamed, as if he frightened her.

At that moment the bell sent a long tinkle through the house. They had heard no carriage stopping at the door, and they stood motionless, looking at each other with startled eyes.

Outside, Nastasia's step crossed the hall, the outer door opened, and a moment later she came in carrying a telegram which she handed to the Countess Olenska.

"The lady was very happy at the flowers," Nastasia said, smoothing her apron. "She thought it was her *signor marito* who had sent them, and she cried a little and said it was a folly."

Her mistress smiled and took the yellow envelope. She tore it open and carried it to the lamp; then, when the door had closed again, she handed the telegram to Archer.

It was dated from St. Augustine, and addressed to the Countess Olenska. In it he read: "Granny's telegram successful. Papa and Mamma agree marriage after Easter. Am telegraphing Newland. Am too happy for words and love you dearly. Your grateful May."

Half an hour later, when Archer unlocked his own front-door, he found a similar envelope on the hall-table on top of his pile of notes and letters. The message inside the envelope was also from May Welland, and ran as follows: "Parents consent wedding Tuesday after Easter at twelve Grace Church eight bridesmaids please see Rector so happy love May."

Archer crumpled up the yellow sheet as if the gesture could annihilate the news it contained. Then he pulled out a small pocket-diary and turned over the pages with trembling fingers;

but he did not find what he wanted, and cramming the telegram into his pocket he mounted the stairs.

A light was shining through the door of the little hall-room which served Janey as a dressing-room and boudoir, and her brother rapped impatiently on the panel. The door opened, and his sister stood before him in her immemorial purple flannel dressing-gown, with her hair "on pins." Her face looked pale and apprehensive.

"Newland! I hope there's no bad news in that telegram? I waited on purpose, in case—" (No item of his correspondence was safe from Janey.)

He took no notice of her question. "Look here—what day is Easter this year?"

She looked shocked at such unchristian ignorance. "Easter? Newland! Why, of course, the first week in April. Why?"

"The first week?" He turned again to the pages of his diary, calculating rapidly under his breath. "The first week, did you say?" He threw back his head with a long laugh.

"For mercy's sake what's the matter?"

"Nothing's the matter, except that I'm going to be married in a month."

Janey fell upon his neck and pressed him to her purple flannel breast. "Oh Newland, how wonderful! I'm so glad! But, dearest, why do you keep on laughing? Do hush, or you'll wake Mamma."

BOOK TWO

19

The day was fresh, with a lively spring wind full of dust. All the old ladies in both families had got out their faded sables and yellowing ermines, and the smell of camphor from the front pews almost smothered the faint spring scent of the lilies banking the altar.

Newland Archer, at a signal from the sexton, had come out of the vestry and placed himself with his best man on the chancel step of Grace Church.

The signal meant that the brougham bearing the bride and her father was in sight; but there was sure to be a considerable interval of adjustment and consultation in the lobby, where the bridesmaids were already hovering like a cluster of Easter blossoms. During this unavoidable lapse of time the bridegroom, in proof of his eagerness, was expected to expose himself alone to the gaze of the assembled company; and Archer had gone through this formality as resignedly as through all the others which made of a nineteenth century New York wedding a rite that seemed to belong to the dawn of history. Everything was equally easy—or equally painful, as one chose to put it—in the path he was committed to tread, and he had obeyed the flurried injunctions of his best man as piously as other bridegrooms had obeyed his own, in the days when he had guided them through the same labyrinth.

So far he was reasonably sure of having fulfilled all his obligations. The bridesmaids' eight bouquets of white lilac and lilies-of-the-valley had been sent in due time, as well as the gold and sapphire sleeve-links of the eight ushers and the best man's cat's-eye scarf-pin; Archer had sat up half the night trying to vary the wording of his thanks for the last batch of presents from men friends and ex-lady-loves; the fees for the Bishop and the Rector were safely in the pocket of his best man; his own luggage was already at Mrs. Manson Mingott's, where the wedding-breakfast was to take place, and so were the travelling clothes into which he was to change; and a private compartment had been engaged in the train that was to carry the young couple to their unknown destination—concealment of the spot in which the bridal night was to be spent being one of the most sacred taboos of the prehistoric ritual.

"Got the ring all right?" whispered young van der Luyden Newland, who was inexperienced in the duties of a best man, and awed by the weight of his responsibility.

Archer made the gesture which he had seen so many bride-grooms make: with his ungloved right hand he felt in the pocket of his dark grey waistcoat, and assured himself that the little gold circlet (engraved inside: *Newland to May, April* ——, *187*—) was in its place; then, resuming his former attitude, his tall hat and pearl-grey gloves with black stitchings grasped in his left hand, he stood looking at the door of the church.

Overhead, Handel's March swelled pompously through the imitation stone vaulting, carrying on its waves the faded drift of the many weddings at which, with cheerful indifference, he had stood on the same chancel step watching other brides float up the nave toward other bridegrooms.

"How like a first night at the Opera!" he thought, recognising all the same faces in the same boxes (no, pews), and wondering if, when the Last Trump sounded, Mrs. Selfridge Merry would be there with the same towering ostrich feathers in her bonnet, and Mrs. Beaufort with the same diamond earrings and the same smile—and whether suitable proscenium seats were already pre-pared for them in another world.

After that there was still time to review, one by one, the fa-miliar countenances in the first rows; the women's sharp with curiosity and excitement, the men's sulky with the obligation of having to put on their frock-coats before luncheon, and fight for food at the wedding-breakfast.

"Too bad the breakfast is at old Catherine's," the bridegroom could fancy Reggie Chivers saying. "But I'm told that Lovell Mingott insisted on its being cooked by his own *chef*, so it ought to be good if one can only get at it." And he could imag-ine Sillerton Jackson adding with authority: "My dear fellow, haven't you heard? It's to be served at small tables, in the new English fashion."

Archer's eyes lingered a moment on the left-hand pew, where his mother, who had entered the church on Mr. Henry van der Luyden's arm, sat weeping softly under her Chantilly veil, her hands in her grandmother's ermine muff.

"Poor Janey!" he thought, looking at his sister, "even by screwing her head around she can see only the people in the few front pews; and they're mostly dowdy Newlands and Dagonets."

On the hither side of the white ribbon dividing off the seats reserved for the families he saw Beaufort, tall and redfaced, scrutinising the women with his arrogant stare. Beside him sat his wife, all silvery chinchilla and violets; and on the far side of the ribbon, Lawrence Lefferts's sleekly brushed head seemed to mount guard over the invisible deity of "Good Form" who presided at the ceremony.

Archer wondered how many flaws Lefferts's keen eyes would discover in the ritual of his divinity; then he suddenly recalled that he too had once thought such questions important. The things that had filled his days seemed now like a nursery parody of life, or like the wrangles of mediæval schoolmen over metaphysical terms that nobody had ever understood. A stormy discussion as to whether the wedding presents should be "shown" had darkened the last hours before the wedding; and it seemed inconceivable to Archer that grown-up people should work themselves into a state of agitation over such trifles, and that the matter should have been decided (in the negative) by Mrs. Welland's saying, with indignant tears: "I should as soon turn the reporters loose in my house." Yet there was a time when Archer had had definite and rather aggressive opinions on all such problems, and when everything concerning the manners and customs of his little tribe had seemed to him fraught with world-wide significance.

"And all the while, I suppose," he thought, "real people were living somewhere, and real things happening to them . . ."

"*There they come!*" breathed the best man excitedly; but the bridegroom knew better.

The cautious opening of the door of the church meant only that Mr. Brown the livery-stable keeper (gowned in black in his intermittent character of sexton) was taking a preliminary survey of the scene before marshalling his forces. The door was softly shut again; then after another interval it swung majestically open, and a murmur ran through the church: "The family!"

Mrs. Welland came first, on the arm of her eldest son. Her large pink face was appropriately solemn, and her plum-coloured satin with pale blue side-panels, and blue ostrich plumes in a small satin bonnet, met with general approval; but before she had settled herself with a stately rustle in the pew opposite Mrs. Archer's the spectators were craning their necks to see who was coming after her. Wild rumours had been abroad the day before to the effect that Mrs. Manson Mingott, in spite of her physical disabilities, had resolved on being present at the ceremony; and the idea was so much in keeping with her sporting character that bets ran high at the clubs as to her being able to walk up the nave and squeeze into a seat. It was known that she had insisted on sending her own carpenter to look into the possibility of taking down the end panel of the front pew, and to measure the space between the seat and the front; but the result had been discouraging, and for one anxious day her family had watched her dallying with the plan of being wheeled up the nave in her enormous Bath chair and sitting enthroned in it at the foot of the chancel.

The idea of this monstrous exposure of her person was so painful to her relations that they could have covered with gold the ingenious person who suddenly discovered that the chair was too wide to pass between the iron uprights of the awning which extended from the church door to the curbstone. The idea of doing away with this awning, and revealing the bride to the mob of dressmakers and newspaper reporters who stood outside fighting to get near the joints of the canvas, exceeded even old Catherine's courage, though for a moment she had weighed the possibility. "Why, they might take a photograph of my child *and put it in the papers!*" Mrs. Welland exclaimed when her mother's last plan was hinted to her; and from this unthinkable indecency the clan recoiled with a collective shudder. The ancestress had had to give in; but her concession was bought only by the promise that the wedding-breakfast should take place under her roof, though (as the Washington Square connection said) with the Wellands' house in easy reach it was hard to have to make a special price with Brown to drive one to the other end of nowhere.

Though all these transactions had been widely reported by the Jacksons a sporting minority still clung to the belief that old Catherine would appear in church, and there was a distinct lowering of the temperature when she was found to have been replaced by her daughter-in-law. Mrs. Lovell Mingott had the high colour and glassy stare induced in ladies of her age and habit by the effort of getting into a new dress; but once the disappointment occasioned by her mother-in-law's non-appearance had subsided, it was agreed that her black Chantilly over lilac satin, with a bonnet of Parma violets, formed the happiest contrast to Mrs. Welland's blue and plum-colour. Far different was the impression produced by the gaunt and mincing lady who followed on Mr. Mingott's arm, in a wild dishevelment of stripes and fringes and floating scarves; and as this last apparition glided into view Archer's heart contracted and stopped beating.

He had taken it for granted that the Marchioness Manson was still in Washington, where she had gone some four weeks previously with her niece, Madame Olenska. It was generally understood that their abrupt departure was due to Madame Olenska's desire to remove her aunt from the baleful eloquence of Dr. Agathon Carver, who had nearly succeeded in enlisting her as a recruit for the Valley of Love; and in the circumstances no one had expected either of the ladies to return for the wedding. For a moment Archer stood with his eyes fixed on Medora's fantastic figure, straining to see who came behind her; but the little procession was at an end, for all the lesser members of the family had taken their seats, and the eight tall ushers, gathering themselves together like birds or insects preparing for some migratory manœuvre, were already slipping through the side doors into the lobby.

"Newland—I say: *she's here!*" the best man whispered.

Archer roused himself with a start.

A long time had apparently passed since his heart had stopped
beating, for the white and rosy procession was in fact half way
up the nave, the Bishop, the Rector and two white-winged as-
sistants were hovering about the flower-banked altar, and the
first chords of the Spohr symphony were strewing their flower-
like notes before the bride.

Archer opened his eyes (but could they really have been shut,
as he imagined?), and felt his heart beginning to resume its usual
task. The music, the scent of the lilies on the altar, the vision of
the cloud of tulle and orange-blossoms floating nearer and
nearer, the sight of Mrs. Archer's face suddenly convulsed with
happy sobs, the low benedictory murmur of the Rector's voice,
the ordered evolutions of the eight pink bridesmaids and the
eight black ushers: all these sights, sounds and sensations, so
familiar in themselves, so unutterably strange and meaningl
his new relation to them, were confusedly mingled in his brain.

"My God," he thought, "*have* I got the ring?"—and once
more he went through the bridegroom's convulsive gesture.

Then, in a moment, May was beside him, such radiance
streaming from her that it sent a faint warmth through his numb-
ness, and he straightened himself and smiled into her eyes.

"Dearly beloved, we are gathered together here," the Rector
began . . .

The ring was on her hand, the Bishop's benediction had been
given, the bridesmaids were a-poise to resume their place in the
procession, and the organ was showing preliminary symptoms
of breaking out into the Mendelssohn March, without which no
newly-wedded couple had ever emerged upon New York.

"Your arm—*I say, give her your arm!*" young Newland nervously hissed; and once more Archer became aware of having
been adrift far off in the unknown. What was it that had sent
him there, he wondered? Perhaps the glimpse, among the anon-
ymous spectators in the transept, of a dark coil of hair under a
hat which, a moment later, revealed itself as belonging to an
unknown lady with a long nose, so laughably unlike the person
whose image she had evoked that he asked himself if he were
becoming subject to hallucinations.

And now he and his wife were pacing slowly down the nave,

carried forward on the light Mendelssohn ripples, the spring day beckoning to them through widely opened doors, and Mrs. Welland's chestnuts, with big white favours on their frontlets, curvetting and showing off at the far end of the canvas tunnel.

The footman, who had a still bigger white favour on his lapel, wrapped May's white cloak about her, and Archer jumped into the brougham at her side. She turned to him with a triumphant smile and their hands clasped under her veil.

"Darling!" Archer said—and suddenly the same black abyss yawned before him and he felt himself sinking into it, deeper and deeper, while his voice rambled on smoothly and cheerfully: "Yes, of course I thought I'd lost the ring; no wedding would be complete if the poor devil of a bridegroom didn't go through that. But you *did* keep me waiting, you know! I had time to think of every horror that might possibly happen."

She surprised him by turning, in full Fifth Avenue, and flinging her arms about his neck. "But none ever *can* happen now, can it, Newland, as long as we two are together?"

Every detail of the day had been so carefully thought out that the young couple, after the wedding-breakfast, had ample time to put on their travelling-clothes, descend the wide Mingott stairs between laughing bridesmaids and weeping parents, and get into the brougham under the traditional shower of rice and satin slippers; and there was still half an hour left in which to drive to the station, buy the last weeklies at the bookstall with the air of seasoned travellers, and settle themselves in the reserved compartment in which May's maid had already placed her dove-coloured travelling cloak and glaringly new dressing-bag from London.

The old du Lac aunts at Rhinebeck had put their house at the disposal of the bridal couple, with a readiness inspired by the prospect of spending a week in New York with Mrs. Archer; and Archer, glad to escape the usual "bridal suite" in a Philadelphia or Baltimore hotel, had accepted with an equal alacrity.

May was enchanted at the idea of going to the country, and childishly amused at the vain efforts of the eight bridesmaids to discover where their mysterious retreat was situated. It was thought "very English" to have a country-house lent to one, and the fact gave a last touch of distinction to what was generally conceded to be the most brilliant wedding of the year; but where the house was no one was permitted to know, except the parents of bride and groom, who, when taxed with the knowledge, pursed their lips and said mysteriously: "Ah, they didn't tell us—" which was manifestly true, since there was no need to.

Once they were settled in their compartment, and the train, shaking off the endless wooden suburbs, had pushed out into the pale landscape of spring, talk became easier than Archer had expected. May was still, in look and tone, the simple girl of yesterday, eager to compare notes with him as to the incidents of the wedding, and discussing them as impartially as a bridesmaid talking it all over with an usher. At first Archer had fancied that this detachment was the disguise of an inward tremor; but her clear eyes revealed only the most tranquil unawareness. She was alone for the first time with her husband; but her husband was only the charming comrade of yesterday. There was no one whom she liked as much, no one whom she trusted as completely, and the culminating "lark" of the whole delightful adventure of engagement and marriage was to be off with him alone on a journey, like a grownup person, like a "married woman," in fact.

It was wonderful that—as he had learned in the Mission garden at St. Augustine—such depths of feeling could coexist with such absence of imagination. But he remembered how, even then, she had surprised him by dropping back to inexpressive girlishness as soon as her conscience had been eased of its burden; and he saw that she would probably go through life dealing to the best of her ability with each experience as it came, but never anticipating any by so much as a stolen glance.

Perhaps that faculty of unawareness was what gave her eyes their transparency, and her face the look of representing a type rather than a person; as if she might have been chosen to pose for a Civic Virtue or a Greek goddess. The blood that ran so close to her fair skin might have been a preserving fluid rather than a ravaging element; yet her look of indestructible youthfulness made her seem neither hard nor dull, but only primitive and pure. In the thick of this meditation Archer suddenly felt himself looking at her with the startled gaze of a stranger, and plunged into a reminiscence of the wedding-breakfast and of Granny Mingott's immense and triumphant pervasion of it.

May settled down to frank enjoyment of the subject. "I was surprised, though—weren't you?—that aunt Medora came after all. Ellen wrote that they were neither of them well enough to take the journey; I do wish it had been she who had recovered! Did you see the exquisite old lace she sent me?"

He had known that the moment must come sooner or later, but he had somewhat imagined that by force of willing he might hold it at bay.

"Yes—I—no: yes, it was beautiful," he said, looking at her blindly, and wondering if, whenever he heard those two syllables, all his carefully built-up world would tumble about him like a house of cards.

"Aren't you tired? It will be good to have some tea when we arrive—I'm sure the aunts have got everything beautifully ready," he rattled on, taking her hand in his; and her mind rushed away instantly to the magnificent tea and coffee service of Baltimore silver which the Beauforts had sent, and which "went" so perfectly with uncle Lovell Mingott's trays and side-dishes.

In the spring twilight the train stopped at the Rhinebeck station, and they walked along the platform to the waiting carriage.

"Ah, how awfully kind of the van der Luydens—they've sent their man over from Skuytercliff to meet us," Archer exclaimed, as a sedate person out of livery approached them and relieved the maid of her bags.

"I'm extremely sorry, sir," said this emissary, "that a little accident has occurred at the Miss du Lacs': a leak in the water-tank. It happened yesterday, and Mr. van der Luyden, who heard of it this morning, sent a housemaid up by the early train to get the Patroon's house ready. It will be quite comfortable, I think you'll find, sir; and the Miss du Lacs have sent their cook over, so that it will be exactly the same as if you'd been at Rhinebeck."

Archer stared at the speaker so blankly that he repeated in

still more apologetic accents: "It'll be exactly the same, sir, I do
assure you—" and May's eager voice broke out, covering the
embarrassed silence: "The same as Rhinebeck? The Patroon's
house? But it will be a hundred thousand times better—won't
it, Newland? It's too dear and kind of Mr. van der Luyden to
have thought of it."

And as they drove off, with the maid beside the coachman,
and their shining bridal bags on the seat before them, she went
on excitedly: "Only fancy, I've never been inside it—have you?
The van der Luydens show it to so few people. But they opened
it for Ellen, it seems, and she told me what a darling little place
it was: she says it's the only house she's seen in America that
she could imagine being perfectly happy in."

"Well—that's what we're going to be, isn't it?" cried her husband gaily; and she answered with her boyish smile: "Ah, it's
just our luck beginning—the wonderful luck we're always going
to have together!"

"Of course we must dine with Mrs. Carfry, dearest," Archer said; and his wife looked at him with an anxious frown across the monumental Britannia ware of their lodging house breakfast-table.

In all the rainy desert of autumnal London there were only two people whom the Newland Archers knew; and these two they had sedulously avoided, in conformity with the old New York tradition that it was not "dignified" to force one's self on the notice of one's acquaintances in foreign countries.

Mrs. Archer and Janey, in the course of their visits to Europe, had so unflinchingly lived up to this principle, and met the friendly advances of their fellow-travellers with an air of such impenetrable reserve, that they had almost achieved the record of never having exchanged a word with a "foreigner" other than those employed in hotels and railway-stations. Their own compatriots—save those previously known or properly ac-credited—they treated with an even more pronounced disdain; so that, unless they ran across a Chivers, a Dagonet or a Mingott, their months abroad were spent in an unbroken *tête-à-tête*. But the utmost precautions are sometimes unavailing; and one night at Botzen one of the two English ladies in the room across the passage (whose names, dress and social situation were already intimately known to Janey) had knocked on the door and asked if Mrs. Archer had a bottle of liniment. The other lady—the intruder's sister, Mrs. Carfry—had been seized with a sudden attack of bronchitis; and Mrs. Archer, who never travelled without a complete family pharmacy, was fortunately able to produce the required remedy.

Mrs. Carfry was very ill, and as she and her sister Miss Harle were travelling alone they were profoundly grateful to the Ar-cher ladies, who supplied them with ingenious comforts and whose efficient maid helped to nurse the invalid back to health.

When the Archers left Botzen they had no idea of ever seeing

Mrs. Carfry and Miss Harle again. Nothing, to Mrs. Archer's mind, would have been more "undignified" than to force one's self on the notice of a "foreigner" to whom one had happened to render an accidental service. But Mrs. Carfry and her sister, to whom this point of view was unknown, and who would have found it utterly incomprehensible, felt themselves linked by an eternal gratitude to the "delightful Americans" who had been so kind at Botzen. With touching fidelity they seized every chance of meeting Mrs. Archer and Janey in the course of their continental travels, and displayed a supernatural acuteness in finding out when they were to pass through London on their way to or from the States. The intimacy became indissoluble, and Mrs. Archer and Janey, whenever they alighted at Brown's Hotel, found themselves awaited by two affectionate friends who, like themselves, cultivated ferns in Wardian cases, made macramé lace, read the memoirs of the Baroness Bunsen and had views about the occupants of the leading London pulpits. As Mrs. Archer said, it made "another thing of London" to know Mrs. Carfry and Miss Harle; and by the time that Newland became engaged the tie between the families was so firmly established that it was thought "only right" to send a wedding invitation to the two English ladies, who sent, in return, a pretty bouquet of pressed Alpine flowers under glass. And on the dock, when Newland and his wife sailed for England, Mrs. Archer's last word had been: "You must take May to see Mrs. Carfry."

Newland and his wife had had no idea of obeying this injunction; but Mrs. Carfry, with her usual acuteness, had run them down and sent them an invitation to dine; and it was over this invitation that May Archer was wrinkling her brows across the tea and muffins.

"It's all very well for you, Newland; you *know* them. But I shall feel so shy among a lot of people I've never met. And what shall I wear?"

Newland leaned back in his chair and smiled at her. She looked handsomer and more Diana-like than ever. The moist English air seemed to have deepened the bloom of her cheeks and softened the slight hardness of her virginal features; or else it was simply the inner glow of happiness, shining through like a light under ice.

"Wear, dearest? I thought a trunkful of things had come from Paris last week."

"Yes, of course. I meant to say that I shan't know *which* to wear." She pouted a little. "I've never dined out in London; and I don't want to be ridiculous."

He tried to enter into her perplexity. "But don't English-women dress just like everybody else in the evening?"

"Newland! How can you ask such funny questions? When they go to the theatre in old ball-dresses and bare heads."

"Well, perhaps they wear new ball-dresses at home; but at any rate Mrs. Carfry and Miss Harle won't. They'll wear caps like my mother's—and shawls; very soft shawls."

"Yes; but how will the other women be dressed?"

"Not as well as you, dear," he rejoined, wondering what had suddenly developed in her Janey's morbid interest in clothes.

She pushed back her chair with a sigh. "That's dear of you, Newland; but it doesn't help me much."

He had an inspiration. "Why not wear your wedding-dress? That can't be wrong, can it?"

"Oh, dearest! If I only had it here! But it's gone to Paris to be made over for next winter, and Worth hasn't sent it back."

"Oh, well—" said Archer, getting up. "Look here—the fog's lifting. If we made a dash for the National Gallery we might manage to catch a glimpse of the pictures."

The Newland Archers were on their way home, after a three months' wedding-tour which May, in writing to her girl friends, vaguely summarised as "blissful."

They had not gone to the Italian Lakes: on reflection, Archer had not been able to picture his wife in that particular setting. Her own inclination (after a month with the Paris dressmakers) was for mountaineering in July and swimming in August. This plan they punctually fulfilled, spending July at Interlaken and Grindelwald, and August at a little place called Etretat, on the Normandy coast, which some one had recommended as quaint and quiet. Once or twice, in the mountains, Archer had pointed southward and said: "There's Italy"; and May, her feet in a gentian-bed, had smiled cheerfully, and replied: "It would be lovely to go there next winter, if only you didn't have to be in New York."

But in reality travelling interested her even less than he had expected. She regarded it (once her clothes were ordered) as merely an enlarged opportunity for walking, riding, swimming, and trying her hand at the fascinating new game of lawn tennis; and when they finally got back to London (where they were to spend a fortnight while he ordered *his* clothes) she no longer concealed the eagerness with which she looked forward to sailing.

In London nothing interested her but the theatres and the shops; and she found the theatres less exciting than the Paris *cafés chantants* where, under the blossoming horse-chestnuts of the Champs Elysées, she had had the novel experience of looking down from the restaurant terrace on an audience of "cocottes," and having her husband interpret to her as much of the songs as he thought suitable for bridal ears.

Archer had reverted to all his old inherited ideas about marriage. It was less trouble to conform with the tradition and treat May exactly as all his friends treated their wives than to try to put into practice the theories with which his untrammelled bachelorhood had dallied. There was no use in trying to emancipate a wife who had not the dimmest notion that she was not free; and he had long since discovered that May's only use of the liberty she supposed herself to possess would be to lay it on the altar of her wifely adoration. Her innate dignity would always keep her from making the gift abjectly; and a day might even come (as it once had) when she would find strength to take it altogether back if she thought she were doing it for his own good. But with a conception of marriage so uncomplicated and incurious as hers such a crisis could be brought about only by something visibly outrageous in his own conduct; and the fineness of her feeling for him made that unthinkable. Whatever happened, he knew, she would always be loyal, gallant and unresentful; and that pledged him to the practice of the same virtues.

All this tended to draw him back into his old habits of mind. If her simplicity had been the simplicity of pettiness he would have chafed and rebelled; but since the lines of her character, though so few, were on the same fine mould as her face, she became the tutelary divinity of all his old traditions and reverences.

Such qualities were scarcely of the kind to enliven foreign travel, though they made her so easy and pleasant a companion; but he saw at once how they would fall into place in their proper setting. He had no fear of being oppressed by them, for his artistic and intellectual life would go on, as it always had, outside the domestic circle; and within it there would be nothing small and stifling—coming back to his wife would never be like entering a stuffy room after a tramp in the open. And when they had children the vacant corners in both their lives would be filled.

All these things went through his mind during their long slow drive from Mayfair to South Kensington, where Mrs. Carfry and her sister lived. Archer too would have preferred to escape their friends' hospitality: in conformity with the family tradition he had always travelled as a sight-seer and looker-on, affecting a haughty unconsciousness of the presence of his fellow-beings. Once only, just after Harvard, he had spent a few gay weeks at Florence with a band of queer Europeanised Americans, dancing all night with titled ladies in palaces, and gambling half the day with the rakes and dandies of the fashionable club; but it had all seemed to him, though the greatest fun in the world, as unreal as a carnival. These queer cosmopolitan women, deep in complicated love-affairs which they appeared to feel the need of retailing to every one they met, and the magnificent young officers and elderly dyed wits who were the subjects or the recipients of their confidences, were too different from the people Archer had grown up among, too much like expensive and rather malodorous hot-house exotics, to detain his imagination long. To introduce his wife into such a society was out of the question; and in the course of his travels no other had shown any marked eagerness for his company.

Not long after their arrival in London he had run across the Duke of St. Austrey, and the Duke, instantly and cordially recognising him, had said: "Look me up, won't you?"—but no proper-spirited American would have considered that a suggestion to be acted on, and the meeting was without a sequel. They had even managed to avoid May's English aunt, the banker's wife, who was still in Yorkshire; in fact, they had purposely postponed going to London till the autumn in order that their arrival during the season might not appear pushing and snobbish to these unknown relatives.

"Probably there'll be nobody at Mrs. Carfry's—London's a desert at this season, and you've made yourself much too beautiful," Archer said to May, who sat at his side in the hansom so spotlessly splendid in her sky-blue cloak edged with swansdown that it seemed wicked to expose her to the London grime.

"I don't want them to think that we dress like savages," she replied, with a scorn that Pocahontas might have resented; and he was struck again by the religious reverence of even the most unworldly American women for the social advantages of dress.

"It's their armour," he thought, "their defence against the unknown, and their defiance of it." And he understood for the first time the earnestness with which May, who was incapable of tying a ribbon in her hair to charm him, had gone through the solemn rite of selecting and ordering her extensive wardrobe.

He had been right in expecting the party at Mrs. Carfry's to be a small one. Besides their hostess and her sister, they found, in the long chilly drawing-room, only another shawled lady, a genial Vicar who was her husband, a silent lad whom Mrs. Carfry named as her nephew, and a small dark gentleman with lively eyes whom she introduced as his tutor, pronouncing a French name as she did so.

Into this dimly-lit and dim-featured group May Archer floated like a swan with the sunset on her: she seemed larger, fairer, more voluminously rustling than her husband had ever seen her; and he perceived that the rosiness and rustlingness were the tokens of an extreme and infantile shyness.

"What on earth will they expect me to talk about?" her help-less eyes implored him, at the very moment that her dazzling apparition was calling forth the same anxiety in their own bos-oms. But beauty, even when distrustful of itself, awakens con-fidence in the manly heart; and the Vicar and the French-named tutor were soon manifesting to May their desire to put her at her ease.

In spite of their best efforts, however, the dinner was a lan-guishing affair. Archer noticed that his wife's way of showing herself at her ease with foreigners was to become more uncom-promisingly local in her references, so that, though her loveliness was an encouragement to admiration, her conversation was a chill to repartee. The Vicar soon abandoned the struggle; but the tutor, who spoke the most fluent and accomplished English, gal-lantly continued to pour it out to her until the ladies, to the manifest relief of all concerned, went up to the drawing-room.

The Vicar, after a glass of port, was obliged to hurry away to a meeting, and the shy nephew, who appeared to be an invalid, was packed off to bed. But Archer and the tutor continued to sit over their wine, and suddenly Archer found himself talking as he had not done since his last symposium with Ned Winsett. The Carfry nephew, it turned out, had been threatened with consumption, and had had to leave Harrow for Switzerland, where he had spent two years in the milder air of Lake Leman. Being a bookish youth, he had been entrusted to M. Rivière, who had brought him back to England, and was to remain with him till he went up to Oxford the following spring; and M. Rivière added with simplicity that he should then have to look out for another job.

It seemed impossible, Archer thought, that he should be long without one, so varied were his interests and so many his gifts. He was a man of about thirty, with a thin ugly face (May would certainly have called him common-looking) to which the play of his ideas gave an intense expressiveness; but there was nothing frivolous or cheap in his animation.

His father, who had died young, had filled a small diplomatic post, and it had been intended that the son should follow the same career; but an insatiable taste for letters had thrown the young man into journalism, then into authorship (apparently un-successful), and at length—after other experiments and vicissi-tudes which he spared his listener—into tutoring English youths in Switzerland. Before that, however, he had lived much in Paris, frequented the Goncourt *grenier*, been advised by Maupassant not to attempt to write (even that seemed to Archer a dazzling honour!), and had often talked with Mérimée in his mother's house. He had obviously always been desperately poor and anx-ious (having a mother and an unmarried sister to provide for), and it was apparent that his literary ambitions had failed. His situation, in fact, seemed, materially speaking, no more brilliant than Ned Winsett's; but he had lived in a world in which, as he said, no one who loved ideas need hunger mentally. As it was precisely of that love that poor Winsett was starving to death, Archer looked with a sort of vicarious envy at this eager impecunious young man who had fared so richly in his poverty.

"You see, Monsieur, it's worth everything, isn't it, to keep one's intellectual liberty, not to enslave one's powers of appre-ciation, one's critical independence? It was because of that that I abandoned journalism, and took to so much duller work: tu-toring and private secretaryship. There is a good deal of drudg-ery, of course; but one preserves one's moral freedom, what we call in French one's *quant à soi*. And when one hears good talk one can join in it without compromising any opinions but one's own; or one can listen, and answer it inwardly. Ah, good conversation—there's nothing like it, is there? The air of ideas is the only air worth breathing. And so I have never regretted giving up either diplomacy or journalism—two different forms of the same self-abdication." He fixed his vivid eyes on Archer as he lit another cigarette. "*Voyez-vous*, Monsieur, to be able to look life in the face: that's worth living in a garret for, isn't it? But, after all, one must earn enough to pay for the garret; and I confess that to grow old as a private tutor—or a 'private' anything—is almost as chilling to the imagination as a second secretaryship at Bucharest. Sometimes I feel I must make a plunge: an immense plunge. Do you suppose, for instance, there would be any opening for me in America—in New York?"

Archer looked at him with startled eyes. New York, for a young man who had frequented the Goncourts and Flaubert, and who thought the life of ideas the only one worth living! He continued to stare at M. Rivière perplexedly, wondering how to tell him that his very superiorities and advantages would be the surest hindrance to success.

"New York—New York—but must it be especially New York?" he stammered, utterly unable to imagine what lucrative opening his native city could offer to a young man to whom good conversation appeared to be the only necessity.

A sudden flush rose under M. Rivière's sallow skin. "I—I thought it your metropolis: is not the intellectual life more active there?" he rejoined; then, as if fearing to give his hearer the impression of having asked a favour, he went on hastily: "One throws out random suggestions—more to one's self than to others. In reality, I see no immediate prospect—" and rising from his seat he added, without a trace of constraint: "But Mrs. Carfry will think that I ought to be taking you upstairs."

During the homeward drive Archer pondered deeply on this episode. His hour with M. Rivière had put new air into his lungs, and his first impulse had been to invite him to dine the next day; but he was beginning to understand why married men did not always immediately yield to their first impulses.

"That young tutor is an interesting fellow: we had some awfully good talk after dinner about books and things," he threw out tentatively in the hansom.

May roused herself from one of the dreamy silences into which he had read so many meanings before six months of marriage had given him the key to them.

"The little Frenchman? Wasn't he dreadfully common?" she questioned coldly; and he guessed that she nursed a secret disappointment at having been invited out in London to meet a clergyman and a French tutor. The disappointment was not occasioned by the sentiment ordinarily defined as snobbishness, but by old New York's sense of what was due to it when it risked its dignity in foreign lands. If May's parents had entertained the Carfrys in Fifth Avenue they would have offered them something more substantial than a parson and a school-master.

But Archer was on edge, and took her up.

"Common—common *where*?" he queried; and she returned with unusual readiness: "Why, I should say anywhere but in his school-room. Those people are always awkward in society. But then," she added disarmingly, "I suppose I shouldn't have known if he was clever."

Archer disliked her use of the word "clever" almost as much as her use of the word "common"; but he was beginning to fear his tendency to dwell on the things he disliked in her. After all, her point of view had always been the same. It was that of all the people he had grown up among, and he had always regarded it as necessary but negligible. Until a few months ago he had never known a "nice" woman who looked at life differently; and if a man married it must necessarily be among the nice.

"Ah—then I won't ask him to dine!" he concluded with a laugh; and May echoed, bewildered: "Goodness—ask the Carfrys' tutor?"

"Well, not on the same day with the Carfrys, if you prefer I shouldn't. But I did rather want another talk with him. He's looking for a job in New York."

Her surprise increased with her indifference: he almost fancied that she suspected him of being tainted with "foreignness."

"A job in New York? What sort of a job? People don't have French tutors: what does he want to do?"

"Chiefly to enjoy good conversation, I understand," her husband retorted perversely; and she broke into an appreciative laugh. "Oh, Newland, how funny! Isn't that *French*?"

On the whole, he was glad to have the matter settled for him by her refusing to take seriously his wish to invite M. Rivière. Another after-dinner talk would have made it difficult to avoid the question of New York; and the more Archer considered it the less he was able to fit M. Rivière into any conceivable picture of New York as he knew it.

He perceived with a flash of chilling insight that in future many problems would be thus negatively solved for him; but as he paid the hansom and followed his wife's long train into the house he took refuge in the comforting platitude that the first six months were always the most difficult in marriage. "After that I suppose we shall have pretty nearly finished rubbing off each other's angles," he reflected; but the worst of it was that May's pressure was already bearing on the very angles whose sharpness he most wanted to keep.

The small bright lawn stretched away smoothly to the big bright sea.

The turf was hemmed with an edge of scarlet geranium and coleus, and cast-iron vases painted in chocolate colour, standing at intervals along the winding path that led to the sea, looped their garlands of petunia and ivy geranium above the neatly raked gravel.

Half way between the edge of the cliff and the square wooden house (which was also chocolate-coloured, but with the tin roof of the verandah striped in yellow and brown to represent an awning) two large targets had been placed against a background of shrubbery. On the other side of the lawn, facing the targets, was pitched a real tent, with benches and garden-seats about it. A number of ladies in summer dresses and gentlemen in grey frock-coats and tall hats stood on the lawn or sat upon the benches; and every now and then a slender girl in starched muslin would step from the tent, bow in hand, and speed her shaft at one of the targets, while the spectators interrupted their talk to watch the result.

Newland Archer, standing on the verandah of the house, looked curiously down upon this scene. On each side of the shiny painted steps was a large blue china flower-pot on a bright yellow china stand. A spiky green plant filled each pot, and below the verandah ran a wide border of blue hydrangeas edged with more red geraniums. Behind him, the French windows of the drawing-rooms through which he had passed gave glimpses, between swaying lace curtains, of glassy parquet floors islanded with chintz *poufs*, dwarf armchairs, and velvet tables covered with trifles in silver.

The Newport Archery Club always held its August meeting at the Beauforts'. The sport, which had hitherto known no rival but croquet, was beginning to be discarded in favour of lawn-tennis; but the latter game was still considered too rough and inelegant for social occasions, and as an opportunity to show off pretty dresses and graceful attitudes the bow and arrow held their own.

Archer looked down with wonder at the familiar spectacle. It surprised him that life should be going on in the old way when his own reactions to it had so completely changed. It was Newport that had first brought home to him the extent of the change. In New York, during the previous winter, after he and May had settled down in the new greenish-yellow house with the bow-window and the Pompeian vestibule, he had dropped back with relief into the old routine of the office, and the renewal of this daily activity had served as a link with his former self. Then there had been the pleasurable excitement of choosing a showy grey stepper for May's brougham (the Wellands had given the carriage), and the abiding occupation and interest of arranging his new library, which, in spite of family doubts and disapprovals, had been carried out as he had dreamed, with a dark embossed paper, Eastlake book-cases and "sincere" arm-chairs and tables. At the Century he had found Winsett again, and at the Knickerbocker the fashionable young men of his own set; and what with the hours dedicated to the law and those given to dining out or entertaining friends at home, with an occasional evening at the Opera or the play, the life he was living had still seemed a fairly real and inevitable sort of business.

But Newport represented the escape from duty into an atmosphere of unmitigated holiday-making. Archer had tried to persuade May to spend the summer on a remote island off the coast of Maine (called, appropriately enough, Mount Desert), where a few hardy Bostonians and Philadelphians were camping in "native" cottages, and whence came reports of enchanting scenery and a wild, almost trapper-like existence amid woods and waters.

But the Wellands always went to Newport, where they owned one of the square boxes on the cliffs, and their son-in-law could adduce no good reason why he and May should not join them there. As Mrs. Welland rather tartly pointed out, it was hardly worth while for May to have worn herself out trying on summer clothes in Paris if she was not to be allowed to wear them; and this argument was of a kind to which Archer had as yet found no answer.

May herself could not understand his obscure reluctance to fall in with so reasonable and pleasant a way of spending the summer. She reminded him that he had always liked Newport in his bachelor days, and as this was indisputable he could only profess that he was sure he was going to like it better than ever now that they were to be there together. But as he stood on the Beaufort verandah and looked out on the brightly peopled lawn it came home to him with a shiver that he was not going to like it at all.

It was not May's fault, poor dear. If, now and then, during their travels, they had fallen slightly out of step, harmony had been restored by their return to the conditions she was used to. He had always foreseen that she would not disappoint him; and he had been right. He had married (as most young men did) because he had met a perfectly charming girl at the moment when a series of rather aimless sentimental adventures were ending in premature disgust; and she had represented peace, stability, comradeship, and the steadying sense of an unescapable duty.

He could not say that he had been mistaken in his choice, for she had fulfilled all that he had expected. It was undoubtedly gratifying to be the husband of one of the handsomest and most popular young married women in New York, especially when she was also one of the sweetest-tempered and most reasonable of wives; and Archer had never been insensible to such advantages. As for the momentary madness which had fallen upon him on the eve of his marriage, he had trained himself to regard it as the last of his discarded experiments. The idea that he could ever, in his senses, have dreamed of marrying the Countess Olenska had become almost unthinkable, and she remained in his memory simply as the most plaintive and poignant of a line of ghosts.

But all these abstractions and eliminations made of his mind a rather empty and echoing place, and he supposed that was one of the reasons why the busy animated people on the Beaufort lawn shocked him as if they had been children playing in a graveyard.

He heard a murmur of skirts beside him, and the Marchioness Manson fluttered out of the drawing-room window. As usual, she was extraordinarily festooned and bedizened, with a limp Leghorn hat anchored to her head by many windings of faded gauze, and a little black velvet parasol on a carved ivory handle absurdly balanced over her much larger hatbrim.

"My dear Newland, I had no idea that you and May had arrived! You yourself came only yesterday, you say? Ah, business—business—professional duties . . . I understand. Many husbands, I know, find it impossible to join their wives here except for the week-end." She cocked her head on one side and languished at him through screwed-up eyes. "But marriage is one long sacrifice, as I used often to remind my Ellen—"

Archer's heart stopped with the queer jerk which it had given once before, and which seemed suddenly to slam a door between himself and the outer world; but this break of continuity must have been of the briefest, for he presently heard Medora answering a question he had apparently found voice to put.

"No, I am not staying here, but with the Blenkers, in their delicious solitude at Portsmouth. Beaufort was kind enough to send his famous trotters for me this morning, so that I might have at least a glimpse of one of Regina's garden-parties; but this evening I go back to rural life. The Blenkers, dear original beings, have hired a primitive old farm-house at Portsmouth where they gather about them representative people . . ." She drooped slightly beneath her protecting brim, and added with a faint blush: "This week Dr. Agathon Carver is holding a series of Inner Thought meetings there. A contrast indeed to this gay scene of worldly pleasure—but then I have always lived on contrasts! To me the only death is monotony. I always say to Ellen: Beware of monotony; it's the mother of all the deadly sins. But my poor child is going through a phase of exaltation, of abhorrence of the world. You know, I suppose, that she has declined all invitations to stay at Newport, even with her grandmother Mingott? I could hardly persuade her to come with me to the Blenkers', if you will believe it! The life she leads is morbid, unnatural. Ah, if she had only listened to me when it was still possible . . . When the door was still open . . . But shall we go down and watch this absorbing match? I hear your May is one of the competitors."

Strolling toward them from the tent Beaufort advanced over the lawn, tall, heavy, too tightly buttoned into a London frock-coat, with one of his own orchids in its buttonhole. Archer, who had not seen him for two or three months, was struck by the change in his appearance. In the hot summer light his florid-ness seemed heavy and bloated, and but for his erect square-shouldered walk he would have looked like an over-fed and over-dressed old man.

There were all sorts of rumours afloat about Beaufort. In the spring he had gone off on a long cruise to the West Indies in his new steam-yacht, and it was reported that, at various points where he had touched, a lady resembling Miss Fanny Ring had been seen in his company. The steam-yacht, built in the Clyde, and fitted with tiled bath-rooms and other unheard-of luxuries, was said to have cost him half a million; and the pearl necklace which he had presented to his wife on his return was as magnificent as such expiatory offerings are apt to be. Beaufort's fortune was substantial enough to stand the strain; and yet the disquieting rumours persisted, not only in Fifth Avenue but in Wall Street. Some people said he had speculated unfortunately in railways, others that he was being bled by one of the most insatiable members of her profession; and to every report of threatened insolvency Beaufort replied by a fresh extravagance: the building of a new row of orchid-houses, the purchase of a new string of race-horses, or the addition of a new Meissonnier or Cabanel to his picture-gallery.

He advanced toward the Marchioness and Newland with his usual half-sneering smile. "Hullo, Medora! Did the trotters do their business? Forty minutes, eh? . . . Well, that's not so bad, considering your nerves had to be spared." He shook hands with Archer, and then, turning back with them, placed himself on Mrs. Manson's other side, and said, in a low voice, a few words which their companion did not catch.

The Marchioness replied by one of her queer foreign jerks, and a *"Que voulez-vous?"* which deepened Beaufort's frown; but he produced a good semblance of a congratulatory smile as he glanced at Archer to say: "You know May's going to carry off the first prize."

"Ah, then it remains in the family," Medora rippled; and at that moment they reached the tent and Mrs. Beaufort met them in a girlish cloud of mauve muslin and floating veils.

May Welland was just coming out of the tent. In her white dress, with a pale green ribbon about the waist and a wreath of ivy on her hat, she had the same Diana-like aloofness as when she had entered the Beaufort ball-room on the night of her engagement. In the interval not a thought seemed to have passed behind her eyes or a feeling through her heart; and though her husband knew that she had the capacity for both he marvelled afresh at the way in which experience dropped away from her.

She had her bow and arrow in her hand, and placing herself on the chalk-mark traced on the turf she lifted the bow to her shoulder and took aim. The attitude was so full of a classic grace that a murmur of appreciation followed her appearance, and Archer felt the glow of proprietorship that so often cheated him into momentary well-being. Her rivals—Mrs. Reggie Chivers, the Merry girls, and divers rosy Thorleys, Dagonets and Mingotts, stood behind her in a lovely anxious group, brown heads and golden bent above the scores, and pale muslins and flower-wreathed hats mingled in a tender rainbow. All were young and pretty, and bathed in summer bloom; but not one had the nymphlike ease of his wife, when, with tense muscles and happy frown, she bent her soul upon some feat of strength.

"Gad," Archer heard Lawrence Lefferts say, "not one of the lot holds the bow as she does"; and Beaufort retorted: "Yes; but that's the only kind of target she'll ever hit."

Archer felt irrationally angry. His host's contemptuous tribute to May's "niceness" was just what a husband should have wished to hear said of his wife. The fact that a coarseminded man found her lacking in attraction was simply another proof of her quality; yet the words sent a faint shiver through his heart. What if "niceness" carried to that supreme degree were only a negation, the curtain dropped before an emptiness? As he looked at May, returning flushed and calm from her final bull's-eye, he had the feeling that he had never yet lifted that curtain.

She took the congratulations of her rivals and of the rest of
the company with the simplicity that was her crowning grace.
No one could ever be jealous of her triumphs because she managed to give the feeling that she would have been just as serene
if she had missed them. But when her eyes met her husband's
her face glowed with the pleasure she saw in his.

Mrs. Welland's basket-work poney-carriage was waiting for
them, and they drove off among the dispersing carriages, May
handling the reins and Archer sitting at her side.

The afternoon sunlight still lingered upon the bright lawns
and shrubberies, and up and down Bellevue Avenue rolled a
double line of victorias, dog-carts, landaus and "vis-à-vis," carrying well-dressed ladies and gentlemen away from the Beaufort
garden-party, or homeward from their daily afternoon turn
along the Ocean Drive.

"Shall we go to see Granny?" May suddenly proposed. "I
should like to tell her myself that I've won the prize. There's
lots of time before dinner."

Archer acquiesced, and she turned the ponies down Narragansett Avenue, crossed Spring Street and drove out toward the
rocky moorland beyond. In this unfashionable region Catherine
the Great, always indifferent to precedent and thrifty of purse,
had built herself in her youth a many-peaked and cross-beamed
cottage-orné on a bit of cheap land overlooking the bay. Here,
in a thicket of stunted oaks, her verandahs spread themselves
above the island-dotted waters. A winding drive led up between
iron stags and blue glass balls embedded in mounds of geraniums to a front door of highly-varnished walnut under a striped
verandah-roof; and behind it ran a narrow hall with a black and
yellow star-patterned parquet floor, upon which opened four
small square rooms with heavy flock-papers under ceilings on
which an Italian house-painter had lavished all the divinities of
Olympus. One of these rooms had been turned into a bedroom
by Mrs. Mingott when the burden of flesh descended on her,
and in the adjoining one she spent her days, enthroned in a large
armchair between the open door and window, and perpetually
waving a palm-leaf fan which the prodigious projection of her
bosom kept so far from the rest of her person that the air it set

in motion stirred only the fringe of the anti-macassars on the chair-arms.

Since she had been the means of hastening his marriage old Catherine had shown to Archer the cordiality which a service rendered excites toward the person served. She was persuaded that irrepressible passion was the cause of his impatience; and being an ardent admirer of impulsiveness (when it did not lead to the spending of money) she always received him with a genial twinkle of complicity and a play of allusion to which May seemed fortunately impervious.

She examined and appraised with much interest the diamond-tipped arrow which had been pinned on May's bosom at the conclusion of the match, remarking that in her day a filigree brooch would have been thought enough, but that there was no denying that Beaufort did things handsomely.

"Quite an heirloom, in fact, my dear," the old lady chuckled. "You must leave it in fee to your eldest girl." She pinched May's white arm and watched the colour flood her face. "Well, well, what have I said to make you shake out the red flag? Ain't there going to be any daughters—only boys, eh? Good gracious, look at her blushing again all over her blushes! What—can't I say that either? Mercy me—when my children beg me to have all those gods and goddesses painted out overhead I always say I'm too thankful to have somebody about me that *nothing* can shock!"

Archer burst into a laugh, and May echoed it, crimson to the eyes.

"Well, now tell me all about the party, please, my dears, for I shall never get a straight word about it out of that silly Medora," the ancestress continued; and, as May exclaimed: "Cousin Medora? But I thought she was going back to Portsmouth?" she answered placidly: "So she is—but she's got to come here first to pick up Ellen. Ah—you didn't know Ellen had come to spend the day with me? Such fol-de-rol, her not coming for the summer; but I gave up arguing with young people about fifty years ago. Ellen—*Ellen!*" she cried in her shrill old voice, trying to bend forward far enough to catch a glimpse of the lawn beyond the verandah.

There was no answer, and Mrs. Mingott rapped impatiently with her stick on the shiny floor. A mulatto maid-servant in a bright turban, replying to the summons, informed her mistress that she had seen "Miss Ellen" going down the path to the shore; and Mrs. Mingott turned to Archer.

"Run down and fetch her, like a good grandson; this pretty lady will describe the party to me," she said; and Archer stood up as if in a dream.

He had heard the Countess Olenska's name pronounced often enough during the year and a half since they had last met, and was even familiar with the main incidents of her life in the interval. He knew that she had spent the previous summer at Newport, where she appeared to have gone a great deal into society, but that in the autumn she had suddenly sub-let the "perfect house" which Beaufort had been at such pains to find for her, and decided to establish herself in Washington. There, during the winter, he had heard of her (as one always heard of pretty women in Washington) as shining in the "brilliant diplomatic society" that was supposed to make up for the social short-comings of the Administration. He had listened to these accounts, and to various contradictory reports on her appearance, her conversation, her point of view and her choice of friends, with the detachment with which one listens to reminiscences of some one long since dead; not till Medora suddenly spoke her name at the archery match had Ellen Olenska become a living presence to him again. The Marchioness's foolish lisp had called up a vision of the little fire-lit drawing-room and the sound of the carriage-wheels returning down the deserted street. He thought of a story he had read, of some peasant children in Tuscany lighting a bunch of straw in a wayside cavern, and revealing old silent images in their painted tomb . . .

The way to the shore descended from the bank on which the house was perched to a walk above the water planted with weeping willows. Through their veil Archer caught the glint of the Lime Rock, with its white-washed turret and the tiny house in which the heroic light-house keeper, Ida Lewis, was living her last venerable years. Beyond it lay the flat reaches and ugly

government chimneys of Goat Island, the bay spreading northward in a shimmer of gold to Prudence Island with its low growth
of oaks, and the shores of Conanicut faint in the sunset haze.

From the willow walk projected a slight wooden pier ending
in a sort of pagoda-like summer-house; and in the pagoda a lady
stood, leaning against the rail, her back to the shore. Archer
stopped at the sight as if he had waked from sleep. That vision
of the past was a dream, and the reality was what awaited him
in the house on the bank overhead: was Mrs. Welland's pony-
carriage circling around and around the oval at the door, was
May sitting under the shameless Olympians and glowing with
secret hopes, was the Welland villa at the far end of Bellevue
Avenue, and Mr. Welland, already dressed for dinner, and pacing
the drawing-room floor, watch in hand, with dyspeptic impatience—for it was one of the houses in which one always
knew exactly what is happening at a given hour.

"What am I? A son-in-law—" Archer thought.

The figure at the end of the pier had not moved. For a long
moment the young man stood half way down the bank, gazing
at the bay furrowed with the coming and going of sailboats,
yacht-launches, fishing-craft and the trailing black coal-barges
hauled by noisy tugs. The lady in the summer-house seemed to
be held by the same sight. Beyond the grey bastions of Fort
Adams a long-drawn sunset was splintering up into a thousand
fires, and the radiance caught the sail of a catboat as it beat out
through the channel between the Lime Rock and the shore. Archer, as he watched, remembered the scene in the Shaughraun,
and Montague lifting Ada Dyas's ribbon to his lips without her
knowing that he was in the room.

"She doesn't know—she hasn't guessed. Shouldn't I know if
she came up behind me, I wonder?" he mused; and suddenly he
said to himself: "If she doesn't turn before that sail crosses the
Lime Rock light I'll go back."

The boat was gliding out on the receding tide. It slid before
the Lime Rock, blotted out Ida Lewis's little house, and passed
across the turret in which the light was hung. Archer waited till
a wide space of water sparkled between the last reef of the island

and the stern of the boat; but still the figure in the summer-house did not move.

He turned and walked up the hill.

"I'm sorry you didn't find Ellen—I should have liked to see her again," May said as they drove home through the dusk. "But perhaps she wouldn't have cared—she seems so changed."

"Changed?" echoed her husband in a colourless voice, his eyes fixed on the ponies' twitching ears.

"So indifferent to her friends, I mean; giving up New York and her house, and spending her time with such queer people. Fancy how hideously uncomfortable she must be at the Blenk-ers'! She says she does it to keep cousin Medora out of mischief: to prevent her marrying dreadful people. But I sometimes think we've always bored her."

Archer made no answer, and she continued, with a tinge of hardness that he had never before noticed in her frank fresh voice: "After all, I wonder if she wouldn't be happier with her husband."

He burst into a laugh. *"Sancta simplicitas!"* he exclaimed; and as she turned a puzzled frown on him he added: "I don't think I ever heard you say a cruel thing before."

"Cruel?"

"Well—watching the contortions of the damned is supposed to be a favourite sport of the angels; but I believe even they don't think people happier in hell."

"It's a pity she ever married abroad then," said May, in the placid tone with which her mother met Mr. Welland's vagaries; and Archer felt himself gently relegated to the category of un-reasonable husbands.

They drove down Bellevue Avenue and turned in between the chamfered wooden gate-posts surmounted by cast-iron lamps which marked the approach to the Welland villa. Lights were already shining through its windows, and Archer, as the carriage stopped, caught a glimpse of his father-in-law, exactly as he had pictured him, pacing the drawing-room, watch in hand and wearing the pained expression that he had long since found to be much more efficacious than anger.

The young man, as he followed his wife into the hall, was conscious of a curious reversal of mood. There was something about the luxury of the Welland house and the density of the Welland atmosphere, so charged with minute observances and exactions, that always stole into his system like a narcotic. The heavy carpets, the watchful servants, the perpetually reminding tick of disciplined clocks, the perpetually renewed stack of cards and invitations on the hall table, the whole chain of tyrannical trifles binding one hour to the next, and each member of the household to all the others, made any less systematised and affluent existence seem unreal and precarious. But now it was the Welland house, and the life he was expected to lead in it, that had become unreal and irrelevant, and the brief scene on the shore, when he had stood irresolute, halfway down the bank, was as close to him as the blood in his veins.

All night he lay awake in the big chintz bedroom at May's side, watching the moonlight slant along the carpet, and thinking of Ellen Olenska driving home across the gleaming beaches behind Beaufort's trotters.

"A party for the Blenkers—the Blenkers?"

Mr. Welland laid down his knife and fork and looked anxiously and incredulously across the luncheon-table at his wife, who, adjusting her gold eye-glasses, read aloud, in the tone of high comedy: "Professor and Mrs. Emerson Sillerton request the pleasure of Mr. and Mrs. Welland's company at the meeting of the Wednesday Afternoon Club on August 25th at 3 o'clock punctually. To meet Mrs. and the Misses Blenker.

"Red Gables, Catherine Street.   R. S. V. P."

"Good gracious—" Mr. Welland gasped, as if a second reading had been necessary to bring the monstrous absurdity of the thing home to him.

"Poor Amy Sillerton—you never can tell what her husband will do next," Mrs. Welland sighed. "I suppose he's just discovered the Blenkers."

Professor Emerson Sillerton was a thorn in the side of Newport society; and a thorn that could not be plucked out, for it grew on a venerable and venerated family tree. He was, as people said, a man who had had "every advantage." His father was Sillerton Jackson's uncle, his mother a Pennilow of Boston; on each side there was wealth and position, and mutual suitability. Nothing—as Mrs. Welland had often remarked—nothing on earth obliged Emerson Sillerton to be an archæologist, or indeed a Professor of any sort, or to live in Newport in winter, or do any of the other revolutionary things that he did. But at least, if he was going to break with tradition and flout society in the face, he need not have married poor Amy Dagonet, who had a right to expect "something different," and money enough to keep her own carriage.

No one in the Mingott set could understand why Amy Sillerton had submitted so tamely to the eccentricities of a husband who filled the house with long-haired men and short-haired women, and, when he travelled, took her to explore tombs in

Yucatan instead of going to Paris or Italy. But there they were, set in their ways, and apparently unaware that they were different from other people; and when they gave one of their dreary annual garden-parties every family on the Cliffs, because of the Sillerton-Pennilow-Dagonet connection, had to draw lots and send an unwilling representative.

"It's a wonder," Mrs. Welland remarked, "that they didn't choose the Cup Race day! Do you remember, two years ago, their giving a party for a black man on the day of Julia Mingott's *thé dansant*? Luckily this time there's nothing else going on that I know of—for of course some of us will have to go."

Mr. Welland sighed nervously. " 'Some of us,' my dear— more than one? Three o'clock is such a very awkward hour. I have to be here at half-past three to take my drops: it's really no use trying to follow Bencomb's new treatment if I don't do it systematically; and if I join you later, of course I shall miss my drive." At the thought he laid down his knife and fork again, and a flush of anxiety rose to his finely-wrinkled cheek.

"There's no reason why you should go at all, my dear," his wife answered with a cheerfulness that had become automatic. "I have some cards to leave at the other end of Bellevue Avenue, and I'll drop in at about half-past three and stay long enough to make poor Amy feel that she hasn't been slighted." She glanced hesitatingly at her daughter. "And if Newland's afternoon is provided for perhaps May can drive you out with the ponies, and try their new russet harness."

It was a principle in the Welland family that people's days and hours should be what Mrs. Welland called "provided for." The melancholy possibility of having to "kill time" (especially for those who did not care for whist or solitaire) was a vision that haunted her as the spectre of the unemployed haunts the philanthropist. Another of her principles was that parents should never (at least visibly) interfere with the plans of their married children; and the difficulty of adjusting this respect for May's independence with the exigency of Mr. Welland's claims could be overcome only by the exercise of an ingenuity which left not a second of Mrs. Welland's own time unprovided for.

"Of course I'll drive with Papa—I'm sure Newland will find something to do," May said, in a tone that gently reminded her husband of his lack of response. It was a cause of constant distress to Mrs. Welland that her son-in-law showed so little foresight in planning his days. Often already, during the fortnight that he had passed under her roof, when she enquired how he meant to spend his afternoon, he had answered paradoxically: "Oh, I think for a change I'll just save it instead of spending it—" and once, when she and May had had to go on a long-postponed round of afternoon calls, he had confessed to having lain all the afternoon under a rock on the beach below the house.

"Newland never seems to look ahead," Mrs. Welland once ventured to complain to her daughter; and May answered serenely: "No; but you see it doesn't matter, because when there's nothing particular to do he reads a book."

"Ah, yes—like his father!" Mrs. Welland agreed, as if allowing for an inherited oddity; and after that the question of Newland's unemployment was tacitly dropped.

Nevertheless, as the day for the Sillerton reception approached, May began to show a natural solicitude for his welfare, and to suggest a tennis match at the Chiverses', or a sail on Julius Beaufort's cutter, as a means of atoning for her temporary desertion. "I shall be back by six, you know, dear: Papa never drives later than that—" and she was not reassured till Archer said that he thought of hiring a run-about and driving up the island to a stud-farm to look at a second horse for her brougham. They had been looking for this horse for some time, and the suggestion was so acceptable that May glanced at her mother as if to say: "You see he knows how to plan out his time as well as any of us."

The idea of the stud-farm and the brougham horse had germinated in Archer's mind on the very day when the Emerson Sillerton invitation had first been mentioned; but he had kept it to himself as if there were something clandestine in the plan, and discovery might prevent its execution. He had, however, taken the precaution to engage in advance a runabout with a pair of old livery-stable trotters that could still do their eighteen miles on level roads; and at two o'clock, hastily deserting the luncheon-table, he sprang into the light carriage and drove off.

The day was perfect. A breeze from the north drove little puffs of white cloud across an ultramarine sky, with a bright sea running under it. Bellevue Avenue was empty at that hour, and after dropping the stable-lad at the corner of Mill Street Archer turned down the Old Beach Road and drove across Eastman's Beach.

He had the feeling of unexplained excitement with which, on half-holidays at school, he used to start off into the unknown. Taking his pair at an easy gait, he counted on reaching the stud-farm, which was not far beyond Paradise Rocks, before three o'clock; so that, after looking over the horse (and trying him if he seemed promising) he would still have four golden hours to dispose of.

As soon as he heard of the Sillerton's party he had said to himself that the Marchioness Manson would certainly come to Newport with the Blenkers, and that Madame Olenska might again take the opportunity of spending the day with her grand-mother. At any rate, the Blenker habitation would probably be deserted, and he would be able, without indiscretion, to satisfy a vague curiosity concerning it. He was not sure that he wanted to see the Countess Olenska again; but ever since he had looked at her from the path above the bay he had wanted, irrationally and indescribably, to see the place she was living in, and to follow the movements of her imagined figure as he had watched the real one in the summer-house. The longing was with him day and night, an incessant undefinable craving, like the sudden whim of a sick man for food or drink once tasted and long since forgotten. He could not see beyond the craving, or picture what it might lead to, for he was not conscious of any wish to speak to Madame Olenska or to hear her voice. He simply felt that if he could carry away the vision of the spot of earth she walked on, and the way the sky and sea enclosed it, the rest of the world might seem less empty.

When he reached the stud-farm a glance showed him that the horse was not what he wanted; nevertheless he took a turn behind it in order to prove to himself that he was not in a hurry. But at three o'clock he shook out the reins over the trotters and turned into the by-roads leading to Portsmouth. The wind had dropped and a faint haze on the horizon showed that a fog was waiting to steal up the Saconnet on the turn of the tide; but all about him fields and woods were steeped in golden light.

He drove past grey-shingled farm-houses in orchards, past hay-fields and groves of oak, past villages with white steeples rising sharply into the fading sky; and at last, after stopping to ask the way of some men at work in a field, he turned down a lane between high banks of goldenrod and brambles. At the end of the lane was the blue glimmer of the river; to the left, standing in front of a clump of oaks and maples, he saw a long tumble-down house with white paint peeling from its clap-boards.

On the road-side facing the gateway stood one of the open sheds in which the New Englander shelters his farming imple-ments and visitors "hitch" their "teams." Archer, jumping down, led his pair into the shed, and after tying them to a post turned toward the house. The patch of lawn before it had relapsed into a hay-field; but to the left an overgrown box-garden full of dahlias and rusty rose-bushes encircled a ghostly summer-house of trellis-work that had once been white, sur-mounted by a wooden Cupid who had lost his bow and arrow but continued to take ineffectual aim.

Archer leaned for a while against the gate. No one was in sight, and not a sound came from the open windows of the house: a grizzled Newfoundland dozing before the door seemed as ineffectual a guardian as the arrowless Cupid. It was strange to think that this place of silence and decay was the home of the turbulent Blenkers; yet Archer was sure that he was not mistaken.

For a long time he stood there, content to take in the scene, and gradually falling under its drowsy spell; but at length he roused himself to the sense of the passing time. Should he look his fill and then drive away? He stood irresolute, wishing sud-denly to see the inside of the house, so that he might picture the room that Madame Olenska sat in. There was nothing to prevent his walking up to the door and ringing the bell; if, as he sup-posed, she was away with the rest of the party, he could easily give his name, and ask permission to go into the sitting-room to write a message.

But instead, he crossed the lawn and turned toward the box-garden. As he entered it he caught sight of something bright-coloured in the summer-house, and presently made it out to be a pink parasol. The parasol drew him like a magnet: he was sure it was hers. He went into the summer-house, and sitting down on the rickety seat picked up the silken thing and looked at its carved handle, which was made of some rare wood that gave out an aromatic scent. Archer lifted the handle to his lips.

He heard a rustle of skirts against the box, and sat motionless, leaning on the parasol handle with clasped hands, and letting the rustle come nearer without lifting his eyes. He had always known that this must happen . . .

"Oh, Mr. Archer!" exclaimed a loud young voice; and looking up he saw before him the youngest and largest of the Blenker girls, blonde and blowsy, in bedraggled muslin. A red blotch on one of her cheeks seemed to show that it had recently been pressed against a pillow, and her half-awakened eyes stared at him hospitably but confusedly.

"Gracious—where did you drop from? I must have been sound asleep in the hammock. Everybody else has gone to Newport. Did you ring?" she incoherently enquired.

Archer's confusion was greater than hers. "I—no—that is, I was just going to. I had to come up the island to see about a horse, and I drove over on a chance of finding Mrs. Blenker and your visitors. But the house seemed empty—so I sat down to wait."

Miss Blenker, shaking off the fumes of sleep, looked at him with increasing interest. "The house *is* empty. Mother's not here, or the Marchioness—or anybody but me." Her glance became faintly reproachful. "Didn't you know that Professor and Mrs. Sillerton are giving a garden-party for mother and all of us this afternoon? It was too unlucky that I couldn't go; but I've had a sore throat, and mother was afraid of the drive home this evening. Did you ever know anything so disappointing? Of course," she added gaily, "I shouldn't have minded half as much if I'd known you were coming."

Symptoms of a lumbering coquetry became visible in her, and Archer found the strength to break in: "But Madame Olenska —has she gone to Newport too?"

Miss Blenker looked at him with surprise. "Madame Olenska—didn't you know she'd been called away?"

"Called away?—"

"Oh, my best parasol! I lent it to that goose of a Katie, because it matched her ribbons, and the careless thing must have dropped it here. We Blenkers are all like that . . . real Bohemians!" Recovering the sunshade with a powerful hand she unfurled it and suspended its rosy dome above her head. "Yes, Ellen was called away yesterday: she lets us call her Ellen, you know. A telegram came from Boston: she said she might be gone for two days. I do *love* the way she does her hair, don't you?" Miss Blenker rambled on.

Archer continued to stare through her as though she had been transparent. All he saw was the trumpery parasol that arched its pinkness above her giggling head.

After a moment he ventured: "You don't happen to know why Madame Olenska went to Boston? I hope it was not on account of bad news?"

Miss Blenker took this with a cheerful incredulity. "Oh, I don't believe so. She didn't tell us what was in the telegram. I think she didn't want the Marchioness to know. She's so romantic-looking, isn't she? Doesn't she remind you of Mrs. Scott-Siddons when she reads 'Lady Geraldine's Courtship'? Did you never hear her?"

Archer was dealing hurriedly with crowding thoughts. His whole future seemed suddenly to be unrolled before him; and passing down its endless emptiness he saw the dwindling figure of a man to whom nothing was ever to happen. He glanced about him at the unpruned garden, the tumble-down house, and the oak-grove under which the dusk was gathering. It had seemed so exactly the place in which he ought to have found Madame Olenska; and she was far away, and even the pink sunshade was not hers . . .

He frowned and hesitated. "You don't know, I suppose—I shall be in Boston tomorrow. If I could manage to see her—"

He felt that Miss Blenker was losing interest in him, though her smile persisted. "Oh, of course; how lovely of you! She's staying at the Parker House; it must be horrible there in this weather."

After that Archer was but intermittently aware of the remarks they exchanged. He could only remember stoutly resisting her entreaty that he should await the returning family and have high tea with them before he drove home. At length, with his hostess still at his side, he passed out of range of the wooden Cupid, unfastened his horses and drove off. At the turn of the lane he saw Miss Blenker standing at the gate and waving the pink parasol.

The next morning, when Archer got out of the Fall River train, he emerged upon a steaming midsummer Boston. The streets near the station were full of the smell of beer and coffee and decaying fruit and a shirt-sleeved populace moved through them with the intimate abandon of boarders going down the passage to the bathroom.

Archer found a cab and drove to the Somerset Club for breakfast. Even the fashionable quarters had the air of untidy domesticity to which no excess of heat ever degrades the European cities. Care-takers in calico lounged on the door-steps of the wealthy, and the Common looked like a pleasure-ground on the morrow of a Masonic picnic. If Archer had tried to imagine Ellen Olenska in improbable scenes he could not have called up any into which it was more difficult to fit her than this heat-prostrated and deserted Boston.

He breakfasted with appetite and method, beginning with a slice of melon, and studying a morning paper while he waited for his toast and scrambled eggs. A new sense of energy and activity had possessed him ever since he had announced to May the night before that he had business in Boston, and should take the Fall River boat that night and go on to New York the following evening. It had always been understood that he would return to town early in the week, and when he got back from his expedition to Portsmouth a letter from the office, which fate had conspicuously placed on a corner of the hall table, sufficed to justify his sudden change of plan. He was even ashamed of the ease with which the whole thing had been done: it reminded him, for an uncomfortable moment, of Lawrence Lefferts's masterly contrivances for securing his freedom. But this did not long trouble him, for he was not in an analytic mood.

After breakfast he smoked a cigarette and glanced over the Commercial Advertiser. While he was thus engaged two or three men he knew came in, and the usual greetings were exchanged:

it was the same world after all, though he had such a queer sense of having slipped through the meshes of time and space.

He looked at his watch, and finding that it was half-past nine got up and went into the writing-room. There he wrote a few lines, and ordered a messenger to take a cab to the Parker House and wait for the answer. He then sat down behind another newspaper and tried to calculate how long it would take a cab to get to the Parker House.

"The lady was out, sir," he suddenly heard a waiter's voice at his elbow; and he stammered: "Out?—" as if it were a word in a strange language.

He got up and went into the hall. It must be a mistake: she could not be out at that hour. He flushed with anger at his own stupidity: why had he not sent the note as soon as he arrived?

He found his hat and stick and went forth into the street. The city had suddenly become as strange and vast and empty as if he were a traveller from distant lands. For a moment he stood on the door-step hesitating; then he decided to go to the Parker House. What if the messenger had been misinformed, and she were still there?

He started to walk across the Common; and on the first bench, under a tree, he saw her sitting. She had a grey silk sunshade over her head—how could he ever have imagined her with a pink one? As he approached he was struck by her listless attitude: she sat there as if she had nothing else to do. He saw her drooping profile, and the knot of hair fastened low in the neck under her dark hat, and the long wrinkled glove on the hand that held the sunshade. He came a step or two nearer, and she turned and looked at him.

"Oh"—she said; and for the first time he noticed a startled look on her face; but in another moment it gave way to a slow smile of wonder and contentment.

"Oh"—she murmured again, on a different note, as he stood looking down at her; and without rising she made a place for him on the bench.

"I'm here on business—just got here," Archer explained; and, without knowing why, he suddenly began to feign astonishment at seeing her. "But what on earth are *you* doing in this wilderness?" He had really no idea what he was saying: he felt as if he were shouting at her across endless distances, and she might vanish again before he could overtake her.

"I? Oh, I'm here on business too," she answered, turning her head toward him so that they were face to face. The words hardly reached him: he was aware only of her voice, and of the startling fact that not an echo of it had remained in his memory. He had not even remembered that it was low-pitched, with a faint roughness on the consonants.

"You do your hair differently," he said, his heart beating as if he had uttered something irrevocable.

"Differently? No—it's only that I do it as best I can when I'm without Nastasia."

"Nastasia; but isn't she with you?"

"No; I'm alone. For two days it was not worth while to bring her."

"You're alone—at the Parker House?"

She looked at him with a flash of her old malice. "Does it strike you as dangerous?"

"No; not dangerous—"

"But unconventional? I see; I suppose it is." She considered a moment. "I hadn't thought of it, because I've just done something so much more unconventional." The faint tinge of irony lingered in her eyes. "I've just refused to take back a sum of money—that belonged to me."

Archer sprang up and moved a step or two away. She had furled her parasol and sat absently drawing patterns on the gravel. Presently he came back and stood before her.

"Some one—has come here to meet you?"

"Yes."

"With this offer?"

She nodded.

"And you refused—because of the conditions?"

"I refused," she said after a moment.

He sat down by her again. "What were the conditions?"

"Oh, they were not onerous: just to sit at the head of his table now and then."

There was another interval of silence. Archer's heart had slammed itself shut in the queer way it had, and he sat vainly groping for a word.

"He wants you back—at any price?"

"Well—a considerable price. At least the sum is considerable for me."

He paused again, beating about the question he felt he must put.

"It was to meet him here that you came?"

She stared, and then burst into a laugh. "Meet him—my husband? *Here?* At this season he's always at Cowes or Baden."

"He sent some one?"

"Yes."

"With a letter?"

She shook her head. "No; just a message. He never writes. I don't think I've had more than one letter from him." The allusion brought the colour to her cheek, and it reflected itself in Archer's vivid blush.

"Why does he never write?"

"Why should he? What does one have secretaries for?"

The young man's blush deepened. She had pronounced the word as if it had no more significance than any other in her vocabulary. For a moment it was on the tip of his tongue to ask: "Did he send his secretary, then?" But the remembrance of Count Olenski's only letter to his wife was too present to him. He paused again, and then took another plunge.

"And the person?"—

"The emissary? The emissary," Madame Olenska rejoined, still smiling, "might, for all I care, have left already; but he has insisted on waiting till this evening . . . in case . . . on the chance . . ."

"And you came out here to think the chance over?"

"I came out to get a breath of air. The hotel's too stifling. I'm taking the afternoon train back to Portsmouth."

They sat silent, not looking at each other, but straight ahead at the people passing along the path. Finally she turned her eyes again to his face and said: "You're not changed."

He felt like answering: "I was, till I saw you again;" but instead he stood up abruptly and glanced about him at the untidy sweltering park.

"This is horrible. Why shouldn't we go out a little on the bay? There's a breeze, and it will be cooler. We might take the steamboat down to Point Arley." She glanced up at him hesitatingly and he went on: "On a Monday morning there won't be anybody on the boat. My train doesn't leave till evening: I'm going back to New York. Why shouldn't we?" he insisted, looking down at her; and suddenly he broke out: "Haven't we done all we could?"

"Oh"—she murmured again. She stood up and reopened her sunshade, glancing about her as if to take counsel of the scene, and assure herself of the impossibility of remaining in it. Then her eyes returned to his face. "You mustn't say things like that to me," she said.

"I'll say anything you like; or nothing. I won't open my mouth unless you tell me to. What harm can it do to anybody? All I want is to listen to you," he stammered.

She drew out a little gold-faced watch on an enamelled chain. "Oh, don't calculate," he broke out; "give me the day! I want to get you away from that man. At what time was he coming?"

Her colour rose again. "At eleven."

"Then you must come at once."

"You needn't be afraid—if I don't come."

"Nor you either—if you do. I swear I only want to hear about you, to know what you've been doing. It's a hundred years since we've met—it may be another hundred before we meet again."

She still wavered, her anxious eyes on his face. "Why didn't you come down to the beach to fetch me, the day I was at Granny's?" she asked.

"Because you didn't look round—because you didn't know I was there. I swore I wouldn't unless you looked round." He laughed as the childishness of the confession struck him.

"But I didn't look round on purpose."

"On purpose?"

"I knew you were there; when you drove in I recognised the ponies. So I went down to the beach."

"To get away from me as far as you could?"

She repeated in a low voice: "To get away from you as far as I could."

He laughed out again, this time in boyish satisfaction. "Well, you see it's no use. I may as well tell you," he added, "that the business I came here for was just to find you. But, look here, we must start or we shall miss our boat."

"Our boat?" She frowned perplexedly, and then smiled. "Oh, but I must go back to the hotel first: I must leave a note—"

"As many notes as you please. You can write here." He drew out a note-case and one of the new stylographic pens. "I've even got an envelope—you see how everything's predestined! There —steady the thing on your knee, and I'll get the pen going in a second. They have to be humoured; wait—" He banged the hand that held the pen against the back of the bench. "It's like jerking down the mercury in a thermometer: just a trick. Now try—"

She laughed, and bending over the sheet of paper which he had laid on his note-case, began to write. Archer walked away a few steps, staring with radiant unseeing eyes at the passersby, who, in their turn, paused to stare at the unwonted sight of a fashionably-dressed lady writing a note on her knee on a bench in the Common.

Madame Olenska slipped the sheet into the envelope, wrote a name on it, and put it into her pocket. Then she too stood up.

They walked back toward Beacon Street, and near the club Archer caught sight of the plush-lined "herdic" which had carried his note to the Parker House, and whose driver was reposing from this effort by bathing his brow at the corner hydrant.

"I told you everything was predestined! Here's a cab for us. You see!" They laughed, astonished at the miracle of picking up a public conveyance at that hour, and in that unlikely spot, in a city where cab-stands were still a "foreign" novelty.

Archer, looking at his watch, saw that there was time to drive to the Parker House before going to the steamboat landing. They rattled through the hot streets and drew up at the door of the hotel.

Archer held out his hand for the letter. "Shall I take it in?" he asked; but Madame Olenska, shaking her head, sprang out and disappeared through the glazed doors. It was barely half-past ten; but what if the emissary, impatient for her reply, and not knowing how else to employ his time, were already seated among the travellers with cooling drinks at their elbows of whom Archer had caught a glimpse as she went in?

He waited, pacing up and down before the herdic. A Sicilian youth with eyes like Nastasia's offered to shine his boots, and an Irish matron to sell him peaches; and every few moments the doors opened to let out hot men with straw hats tilted far back, who glanced at him as they went by. He marvelled that the door should open so often, and that all the people it let out should look so like each other, and so like all the other hot men who, at that hour, through the length and breadth of the land, were passing continuously in and out of the swinging doors of hotels.

And then, suddenly, came a face that he could not relate to the other faces. He caught but a flash of it, for his pacings had carried him to the farthest point of his beat, and it was in turning back to the hotel that he saw, in a group of typical countenances—the lank and weary, the round and surprised, the lantern-jawed and mild—this other face that was so many more things at once, and things so different. It was that of a young man, pale too, and half-extinguished by the heat, or worry, or both, but somehow, quicker, vivider, more conscious; or perhaps seeming so because he was so different. Archer hung a moment on a thin thread of memory, but it snapped and floated off with the disappearing face—apparently that of some foreign business man, looking doubly foreign in such a setting. He vanished in the stream of passers-by, and Archer resumed his patrol.

He did not care to be seen watch in hand within view of the hotel, and his unaided reckoning of the lapse of time led him to conclude that, if Madame Olenska was so long in reappearing, it could only be because she had met the emissary and been waylaid by him. At the thought Archer's apprehension rose to anguish.

"If she doesn't come soon I'll go in and find her," he said.

The doors swung open again and she was at his side. They got into the herdic, and as it drove off he took out his watch and saw that she had been absent just three minutes. In the clatter of loose windows that made talk impossible they bumped over the disjointed cobblestones to the wharf.

Seated side by side on a bench of the half-empty boat they found that they had hardly anything to say to each other, or rather that what they had to say communicated itself best in the blessed silence of their release and their isolation.

As the paddle-wheels began to turn, and wharves and shipping to recede through the veil of heat, it seemed to Archer that everything in the old familiar world of habit was receding also. He longed to ask Madame Olenska if she did not have the same feeling: the feeling that they were starting on some long voyage from which they might never return. But he was afraid to say it, or anything else that might disturb the delicate balance of her trust in him. In reality he had no wish to betray that trust. There had been days and nights when the memory of their kiss had burned and burned on his lips; the day before even, on the drive to Portsmouth, the thought of her had run through him like fire; but now that she was beside him, and they were drifting forth into this unknown world, they seemed to have reached the kind of deeper nearness that a touch may sunder.

As the boat left the harbour and turned seaward a breeze stirred about them and the bay broke up into long oily undulations, then into ripples tipped with spray. The fog of sultriness still hung over the city, but ahead lay a fresh world of ruffled waters, and distant promontories with light-houses in the sun. Madame Olenska, leaning back against the boat-rail, drank in the coolness between parted lips. She had wound a long veil about her hat, but it left her face uncovered, and Archer was struck by the tranquil gaiety of her expression. She seemed to take their adventure as a matter of course, and to be neither in fear of unexpected encounters, nor (what was worse) unduly elated by their possibility.

In the bare dining-room of the inn, which he had hoped

they would have to themselves, they found a strident party of
innocent-looking young men and women—school-teachers on a
holiday, the landlord told them—and Archer's heart sank at the
idea of having to talk through their noise.

"This is hopeless—I'll ask for a private room," he said; and
Madame Olenska, without offering any objection, waited while
he went in search of it. The room opened on a long wooden
verandah, with the sea coming in at the windows. It was bare
and cool, with a table covered with a coarse checkered cloth and
adorned by a bottle of pickles and a blueberry pie under a cage.
No more guileless-looking *cabinet particulier* ever offered its
shelter to a clandestine couple: Archer fancied he saw the sense
of its reassurance in the faintly amused smile with which Madame Olenska sat down opposite to him. A woman who had
run away from her husband—and reputedly with another man
—was likely to have mastered the art of taking things for
granted; but something in the quality of her composure took the
edge from his irony. By being so quiet, so unsurprised and so
simple she had managed to brush away the conventions and
make him feel that to seek to be alone was the natural thing for
two old friends who had so much to say to each other. . . .

They lunched slowly and meditatively, with mute intervals between rushes of talk; for, the spell once broken, they had much
to say, and yet moments when saying became the mere accom-
paniment to long duologues of silence. Archer kept the talk from
his own affairs, not with conscious intention but because he did
not want to miss a word of her history; and leaning on the table,
her chin resting on her clasped hands, she talked to him of the
year and a half since they had met.

She had grown tired of what people called "society"; New
York was kind, it was almost oppressively hospitable; she should
never forget the way in which it had welcomed her back; but
after the first flush of novelty she had found herself, as she
phrased it, too "different" to care for the things it cared about
—and so she had decided to try Washington, where one was
supposed to meet more varieties of people and of opinion. And
on the whole she should probably settle down in Washington,
and make a home there for poor Medora, who had worn out
the patience of all her other relations just at the time when she
most needed looking after and protecting from matrimonial
perils.

"But Dr. Carver—aren't you afraid of Dr. Carver? I hear he's
been staying with you at the Blenkers'."

She smiled. "Oh, the Carver danger is over. Dr. Carver is a
very clever man. He wants a rich wife to finance his plans, and
Medora is simply a good advertisement as a convert."

"A convert to what?"

"To all sorts of new and crazy social schemes. But, do you
know, they interest me more than the blind conformity to
tradition—somebody else's tradition—that I see among our own
friends. It seems stupid to have discovered America only to make
it into a copy of another country." She smiled across the table.
"Do you suppose Christopher Columbus would have taken all
that trouble just to go to the Opera with the Selfridge Merrys?"

Archer changed colour. "And Beaufort—do you say these things to Beaufort?" he asked abruptly.

"I haven't seen him for a long time. But I used to; and he understands."

"Ah, it's what I've always told you; you don't like us. And you like Beaufort because he's so unlike us." He looked about the bare room and out at the bare beach and the row of stark white village houses strung along the shore. "We're damnably dull. We've no character, no colour, no variety.—I wonder," he broke out, "why you don't go back?"

Her eyes darkened, and he expected an indignant rejoinder. But she sat silent, as if thinking over what he had said, and he grew frightened lest she should answer that she wondered too.

At length she said: "I believe it's because of you."

It was impossible to make the confession more dispassionately, or in a tone less encouraging to the vanity of the person addressed. Archer reddened to the temples, but dared not move or speak: it was as if her words had been some rare butterfly that the least motion might drive off on startled wings, but that might gather a flock about it if it were left undisturbed.

"At least," she continued, "it was you who made me understand that under the dullness there are things so fine and sensitive and delicate that even those I most cared for in my other life look cheap in comparison. I don't know how to explain myself"—she drew together her troubled brows—"but it seems as if I'd never before understood with how much that is hard and shabby and base the most exquisite pleasures may be paid."

"Exquisite pleasures—it's something to have had them!" he felt like retorting; but the appeal in her eyes kept him silent.

"I want," she went on, "to be perfectly honest with you—and with myself. For a long time I've hoped this chance would come: that I might tell you how you've helped me, what you've made of me—"

Archer sat staring beneath frowning brows. He interrupted her with a laugh. "And what do you make out that you've made of me?"

She paled a little. "Of you?"

"Yes: for I'm of your making much more than you ever were of mine. I'm the man who married one woman because another one told him to."

Her paleness turned to a fugitive flush. "I thought—you promised—you were not to say such things today."

"Ah—how like a woman! None of you will ever see a bad business through!"

She lowered her voice. "*Is* it a bad business—for May?"

He stood in the window, drumming against the raised sash, and feeling in every fibre the wistful tenderness with which she had spoken her cousin's name.

"For that's the thing we've always got to think of—haven't we—by your own showing?" she insisted.

"My own showing?" he echoed, his blank eyes still on the sea.

"Or if not," she continued, pursuing her own thought with a painful application, "if it's not worth while to have given up, to have missed things, so that others may be saved from disillusionment and misery—then everything I came home for, everything that made my other life seem by contrast so bare and so poor because no one there took account of them—all these things are a sham or a dream—"

He turned around without moving from his place. "And in that case there's no reason on earth why you shouldn't go back?" he concluded for her.

Her eyes were clinging to him desperately. "Oh, *is* there no reason?"

"Not if you staked your all on the success of my marriage. My marriage," he said savagely, "isn't going to be a sight to keep you here." She made no answer, and he went on: "What's the use? You gave me my first glimpse of a real life, and at the same moment you asked me to go on with a sham one. It's beyond human enduring—that's all."

"Oh, don't say that; when I'm enduring it!" she burst out, her eyes filling.

Her arms had dropped along the table, and she sat with her face abandoned to his gaze as if in the recklessness of a desperate peril. The face exposed her as much as if it had been her whole person, with the soul behind it: Archer stood dumb, overwhelmed by what it suddenly told him.

"You too—oh, all this time, you too?"

For answer, she let the tears on her lids overflow and run slowly downward.

Half the width of the room was still between them, and neither made any show of moving. Archer was conscious of a curious indifference to her bodily presence: he would hardly have been aware of it if one of the hands she had flung out on the table had not drawn his gaze as on the occasion when, in the little Twenty-third Street house, he had kept his eye on it in order not to look at her face. Now his imagination spun about the hand as about the edge of a vortex; but still he made no effort to draw nearer. He had known the love that is fed on caresses and feeds them; but this passion that was closer than his bones was not to be superficially satisfied. His one terror was to do anything which might efface the sound and impression of her words; his one thought, that he should never again feel quite alone.

But after a moment the sense of waste and ruin overcame him. There they were, close together and safe and shut in; yet so chained to their separate destinies that they might as well have been half the world apart.

"What's the use—when you will go back?" he broke out, a great hopeless *How on earth can I keep you?* crying out to her beneath his words.

She sat motionless, with lowered lids. "Oh—I shan't go yet!"

"Not yet? Some time, then? Some time that you already foresee?"

At that she raised her clearest eyes. "I promise you: not as long as you hold out. Not as long as we can look straight at each other like this."

He dropped into his chair. What her answer really said was: "If you lift a finger you'll drive me back: back to all the abominations you know of, and all the temptations you half guess." He understood it as clearly as if she had uttered the words, and the thought kept him anchored to his side of the table in a kind of moved and sacred submission.

"What a life for you!—" he groaned.

"Oh—as long as it's a part of yours."

"And mine a part of yours?"

She nodded.

"And that's to be all—for either of us?"

"Well; it *is* all, isn't it?"

At that he sprang up, forgetting everything but the sweetness of her face. She rose too, not as if to meet him or to flee from him, but quietly, as though the worst of the task were done and she had only to wait; so quietly that, as he came close, her outstretched hands acted not as a check but as a guide to him. They fell into his, while her arms, extended but not rigid, kept him far enough off to let her surrendered face say the rest.

They may have stood in that way for a long time, or only for a few moments; but it was long enough for her silence to communicate all she had to say, and for him to feel that only one thing mattered. He must do nothing to make this meeting their last; he must leave their future in her care, asking only that she should keep fast hold of it.

"Don't—don't be unhappy," she said, with a break in her voice, as she drew her hands away; and he answered: "You won't go back—you won't go back?" as if it were the one possibility he could not bear.

"I won't go back," she said; and turning away she opened the door and led the way into the public dining-room.

The strident school-teachers were gathering up their possessions preparatory to a straggling flight to the wharf; across the beach lay the white steam-boat at the pier; and over the sunlit waters Boston loomed in a line of haze.

Once more on the boat, and in the presence of others, Archer felt a tranquillity of spirit that surprised as much as it sustained him.

The day, according to any current valuation, had been a rather ridiculous failure; he had not so much as touched Madame Olenska's hand with his lips, or extracted one word from her that gave promise of farther opportunities. Nevertheless, for a man sick with unsatisfied love, and parting for an indefinite period from the object of his passion, he felt himself almost humiliatingly calm and comforted. It was the perfect balance she had held between their loyalty to others and their honesty to themselves that had so stirred and yet tranquillized him; a balance not artfully calculated, as her tears and her falterings showed, but resulting naturally from her unabashed sincerity. It filled him with a tender awe, now the danger was over, and made him thank the fates that no personal vanity, no sense of playing a part before sophisticated witnesses, had tempted him to tempt her. Even after they had clasped hands for good-bye at the Fall River station, and he had turned away alone, the conviction remained with him of having saved out of their meeting much more than he had sacrificed.

He wandered back to the club, and went and sat alone in the deserted library, turning and turning over in his thoughts every separate second of their hours together. It was clear to him, and it grew more clear under closer scrutiny, that if she should finally decide on returning to Europe—returning to her husband—it would not be because her old life tempted her, even on the new terms offered. No: she would go only if she felt herself becoming a temptation to Archer, a temptation to fall away from the standard they had both set up. Her choice would be to stay near him as long as he did not ask her to come nearer; and it depended on himself to keep her just there, safe but secluded.

In the train these thoughts were still with him. They enclosed him in a kind of golden haze, through which the faces about him looked remote and indistinct: he had a feeling that if he spoke to his fellow-travellers they would not understand what he was saying. In this state of abstraction he found himself, the following morning, waking to the reality of a stifling September day in New York. The heat-withered faces in the long train streamed past him, and he continued to stare at them through the same golden blur; but suddenly, as he left the station, one of the faces detached itself, came closer and forced itself upon his consciousness. It was, as he instantly recalled, the face of the young man he had seen, the day before, passing out of the Parker House, and had noted as not conforming to type, as not having an American hotel face.

The same thing struck him now; and again he became aware of a dim stir of former associations. The young man stood looking about him with the dazed air of the foreigner flung upon the harsh mercies of American travel; then he advanced toward Archer, lifted his hat, and said in English: "Surely, Monsieur, we met in London?"

"Ah, to be sure: in London!" Archer grasped his hand with curiosity and sympathy. "So you *did* get here, after all?" he exclaimed, casting a wondering eye on the astute and haggard little countenance of young Carfry's French tutor.

"Oh, I got here—yes," M. Rivière smiled with drawn lips. "But not for long; I return the day after tomorrow." He stood grasping his light valise in one neatly gloved hand, and gazing anxiously, perplexedly, almost appealingly, into Archer's face.

"I wonder, Monsieur, since I've had the good luck to run across you, if I might—"

"I was just going to suggest it: come to luncheon, won't you? Down town, I mean: if you'll look me up in my office I'll take you to a very decent restaurant in that quarter."

M. Rivière was visibly touched and surprised. "You're too kind. But I was only going to ask if you would tell me how to reach some sort of conveyance. There are no porters, and no one here seems to listen—"

"I know: our American stations must surprise you. When you ask for a porter they give you chewing-gum. But if you'll come along I'll extricate you; and you must really lunch with me, you know."

The young man, after a just perceptible hesitation, replied, with profuse thanks, and in a tone that did not carry complete conviction, that he was already engaged; but when they had reached the comparative reassurance of the street he asked if he might call that afternoon.

Archer, at ease in the midsummer leisure of the office, fixed an hour and scribbled his address, which the Frenchman pocketed with reiterated thanks and a wide flourish of his hat. A horse-car received him, and Archer walked away.

Punctually at the hour M. Rivière appeared, shaved, smoothed-out, but still unmistakably drawn and serious. Archer was alone in his office, and the young man, before accepting the seat he proffered, began abruptly: "I believe I saw you, sir, yesterday in Boston."

The statement was insignificant enough, and Archer was about to frame an assent when his words were checked by something mysterious yet illuminating in his visitor's insistent gaze.

"It is extraordinary, very extraordinary," M. Rivière continued, "that we should have met in the circumstances in which I find myself."

"What circumstances?" Archer asked, wondering a little crudely if he needed money.

M. Rivière continued to study him with tentative eyes. "I have come, not to look for employment, as I spoke of doing when we last met, but on a special mission—"

"Ah—!" Archer exclaimed. In a flash the two meetings had connected themselves in his mind. He paused to take in the situation thus suddenly lighted up for him, and M. Rivière also remained silent, as if aware that what he had said was enough.

"A special mission," Archer at length repeated.

The young Frenchman, opening his palms, raised them slightly, and the two men continued to look at each other across the office-desk till Archer roused himself to say: "Do sit down"; whereupon M. Rivière bowed, took a distant chair, and again waited.

"It was about this mission that you wanted to consult me?" Archer finally asked.

M. Rivière bent his head. "Not in my own behalf: on that score I—I have fully dealt with myself. I should like—if I may—to speak to you about the Countess Olenska."

Archer had known for the last few minutes that the words were coming; but when they came they sent the blood rushing to his temples as if he had been caught by a bent-back branch in a thicket.

"And on whose behalf," he said, "do you wish to do this?"

M. Rivière met the question sturdily. "Well—I might say *hers*, if it did not sound like a liberty. Shall I say instead: on behalf of abstract justice?"

Archer considered him ironically. "In other words: you are Count Olenski's messenger?"

He saw his blush more darkly reflected in M. Rivière's sallow countenance. "Not to *you*, Monsieur. If I come to you, it is on quite other grounds."

"What right have you, in the circumstances, to *be* on any other ground?" Archer retorted. "If you're an emissary you're an emissary."

The young man considered. "My mission is over: as far as the Countess Olenska goes, it has failed."

"I can't help that," Archer rejoined on the same note of irony.

"No: but you can help—" M. Rivière paused, turned his hat about in his still carefully gloved hands, looked into its lining and then back at Archer's face. "You can help, Monsieur, I am convinced, to make it equally a failure with her family."

Archer pushed back his chair and stood up. "Well—and by God I will!" he exclaimed. He stood with his hands in his pockets, staring down wrathfully at the little Frenchman, whose face, though he too had risen, was still an inch or two below the line of Archer's eyes.

M. Rivière paled to his normal hue: paler than that his complexion could hardly turn.

"Why the devil," Archer explosively continued, "should you have thought—since I suppose you're appealing to me on the ground of my relationship to Madame Olenska—that I should take a view contrary to the rest of her family?"

The change of expression in M. Rivière's face was for a time his only answer. His look passed from timidity to absolute distress: for a young man of his usually resourceful mien it would have been difficult to appear more disarmed and defenceless. "Oh, Monsieur—"

"I can't imagine," Archer continued, "why you should have come to me when there are others so much nearer to the Countess; still less why you thought I should be more accessible to the arguments I suppose you were sent over with."

M. Rivière took this onslaught with a disconcerting humility. "The arguments I want to present to you, Monsieur, are my own and not those I was sent over with."

"Then I see still less reason for listening to them."

M. Rivière again looked into his hat, as if considering whether these last words were not a sufficiently broad hint to put it on and be gone. Then he spoke with sudden decision. "Monsieur—will you tell me one thing? Is it my right to be here that you question? Or do you perhaps believe the whole matter to be already closed?"

His quiet insistence made Archer feel the clumsiness of his own bluster. M. Rivière had succeeded in imposing himself: Archer, reddening slightly, dropped into his chair again, and signed to the young man to be seated.

"I beg your pardon: but why isn't the matter closed?"

M. Rivière gazed back at him with anguish. "You do, then, agree with the rest of the family that, in face of the new proposals I have brought, it is hardly possible for Madame Olenska not to return to her husband?"

"Good God!" Archer exclaimed; and his visitor gave out a low murmur of confirmation.

"Before seeing her, I saw—at Count Olenski's request—Mr. Lovell Mingott, with whom I had several talks before going to Boston. I understand that he represents his mother's view; and that Mrs. Manson Mingott's influence is great throughout her family."

Archer sat silent, with the sense of clinging to the edge of a sliding precipice. The discovery that he had been excluded from a share in these negotiations, and even from the knowledge that they were on foot, caused him a surprise hardly dulled by the acuter wonder of what he was learning. He saw in a flash that if the family had ceased to consult him it was because some deep tribal instinct warned them that he was no longer on their side; and he recalled, with a start of comprehension, a remark of May's during their drive home from Mrs. Manson Mingott's on the day of the Archery Meeting: "Perhaps, after all, Ellen would be happier with her husband."

Even in the tumult of new discoveries Archer remembered his indignant exclamation, and the fact that since then his wife had never named Madame Olenska to him. Her careless allusion had no doubt been the straw held up to see which way the wind blew; the result had been reported to the family, and thereafter Archer had been tacitly omitted from their counsels. He admired the tribal discipline which made May bow to this decision. She would not have done so, he knew, had her conscience protested; but she probably shared the family view that Madame Olenska would be better off as an unhappy wife than as a separated one, and that there was no use in discussing the case with Newland, who had an awkward way of suddenly not seeming to take the most fundamental things for granted.

Archer looked up and met his visitor's anxious gaze. "Don't you know, Monsieur—is it possible you don't know—that the family begin to doubt if they have the right to advise the Countess to refuse her husband's last proposals?"

"The proposals you brought?"

"The proposals I brought."

It was on Archer's lips to exclaim that whatever he knew or did not know was no concern of M. Rivière's; but something in the humble and yet courageous tenacity of M. Rivière's gaze made him reject this conclusion, and he met the young man's question with another. "What is your object in speaking to me of this?"

He had not to wait a moment for the answer. "To beg you, Monsieur—to beg you with all the force I'm capable of—not to let her go back.—Oh, don't let her!" M. Rivière exclaimed.

Archer looked at him with increasing astonishment. There was no mistaking the sincerity of his distress or the strength of his determination: he had evidently resolved to let everything go by the board but the supreme need of thus putting himself on record. Archer considered.

"May I ask," he said at length, "if this is the line you took with the Countess Olenska?"

M. Rivière reddened, but his eyes did not falter. "No, Monsieur: I accepted my mission in good faith. I really believed—for reasons I need not trouble you with—that it would be better for Madame Olenska to recover her situation, her fortune, the social consideration that her husband's standing gives her."

"So I supposed: you could hardly have accepted such a mission otherwise."

"I should not have accepted it."

"Well, then—?" Archer paused again, and their eyes met in another protracted scrutiny.

"Ah, Monsieur, after I had seen her, after I had listened to her, I knew she was better off here."

"You knew—?"

"Monsieur, I discharged my mission faithfully: I put the Count's arguments, I stated his offers, without adding any comment of my own. The Countess was good enough to listen patiently; she carried her goodness so far as to see me twice; she considered impartially all I had come to say. And it was in the course of these two talks that I changed my mind, that I came to see things differently."

"May I ask what led to this change?"

"Simply seeing the change in *her*," M. Rivière replied.

"The change in her? Then you knew her before?"

The young man's colour again rose. "I used to see her in her husband's house. I have known Count Olenski for many years. You can imagine that he would not have sent a stranger on such a mission."

Archer's gaze, wandering away to the blank walls of the office, rested on a hanging calendar surmounted by the rugged features of the President of the United States. That such a conversation should be going on anywhere within the millions of square miles subject to his rule seemed as strange as anything that the imagination could invent.

"The change—what sort of a change?"

"Ah, Monsieur, if I could tell you!" M. Rivière paused. "*Tenez*—the discovery, I suppose, of what I'd never thought of before: that she's an American. And that if you're an American of *her* kind—of your kind—things that are accepted in certain other societies, or at least put up with as part of a general convenient give-and-take—become unthinkable, simply unthinkable. If Madame Olenska's relations understood what these things were, their opposition to her returning would no doubt be as unconditional as her own; but they seem to regard her husband's wish to have her back as proof of an irresistible longing for domestic life." M. Rivière paused, and then added: "Whereas it's far from being as simple as that."

Archer looked back to the President of the United States, and then down at his desk and at the papers scattered on it. For a second or two he could not trust himself to speak. During this interval he heard M. Rivière's chair pushed back, and was aware that the young man had risen. When he glanced up again he saw that his visitor was as moved as himself.

"Thank you," Archer said simply.

"There's nothing to thank me for, Monsieur: it is I, rather—" M. Rivière broke off, as if speech for him too were difficult. "I should like, though," he continued in a firmer voice, "to add one thing. You asked me if I was in Count Olenski's employ. I am at this moment: I returned to him, a few months ago, for reasons of private necessity such as may happen to any one who has persons, ill and older persons, dependent on him. But from the moment that I have taken the step of coming here to say these things to you I consider myself discharged, and I shall tell him so on my return, and give him the reasons. That's all, Monsieur."

M. Rivière bowed and drew back a step.

"Thank you," Archer said again, as their hands met.

Every year on the fifteenth of October Fifth Avenue opened its shutters, unrolled its carpets and hung up its triple layer of window-curtains.

By the first of November this household ritual was over, and society had begun to look about and take stock of itself. By the fifteenth the season was in full blast, Opera and theatres were putting forth their new attractions, dinner-engagements were accumulating, and dates for dances being fixed. And punctually at about this time Mrs. Archer always said that New York was very much changed.

Observing it from the lofty stand-point of a nonparticipant, she was able, with the help of Mr. Sillerton Jackson and Miss Sophy, to trace each new crack in its surface, and all the strange weeds pushing up between the ordered rows of social vegetables. It had been one of the amusements of Archer's youth to wait for this annual pronouncement of his mother's, and to hear her enumerate the minute signs of disintegration that his careless gaze had overlooked. For New York, to Mrs. Archer's mind, never changed without changing for the worse; and in this view Miss Sophy Jackson heartily concurred.

Mr. Sillerton Jackson, as became a man of the world, suspended his judgment and listened with an amused impartiality to the lamentations of the ladies. But even he never denied that New York had changed; and Newland Archer, in the winter of the second year of his marriage, was himself obliged to admit that if it had not actually changed it was certainly changing.

These points had been raised, as usual, at Mrs. Archer's Thanksgiving dinner. At the date when she was officially enjoined to give thanks for the blessings of the year it was her habit to take a mournful though not embittered stock of her world, and wonder what there was to be thankful for. At any rate, not the state of society; society, if it could be said to exist, was rather a spectacle on which to call down Biblical

imprecations—and in fact, every one knew what the Reverend
Dr. Ashmore meant when he chose a text from Jeremiah (chap.
ii., verse 25) for his Thanksgiving sermon. Dr. Ashmore, the new
Rector of St. Matthew's, had been chosen because he was very
"advanced": his sermons were considered bold in thought and
novel in language. When he fulminated against fashionable society he always spoke of its "trend"; and to Mrs. Archer it was
terrifying and yet fascinating to feel herself part of a community
that was trending.

"There's no doubt that Dr. Ashmore is right: there *is* a
marked trend," she said, as if it were something visible and meas-
urable, like a crack in a house.

"It was odd, though, to preach about it on Thanksgiving,"
Miss Jackson opined; and her hostess drily rejoined: "Oh, he
means us to give thanks for what's left."

Archer had been wont to smile at these annual vaticinations
of his mother's; but this year even he was obliged to acknowledge, as he listened to an enumeration of the changes, that the
"trend" was visible.

"The extravagance in dress—" Miss Jackson began. "Sillerton
took me to the first night of the Opera, and I can only tell you
that Jane Merry's dress was the only one I recognised from last
year; and even that had had the front panel changed. Yet I know
she got it out from Worth only two years ago, because my seam-
stress always goes in to make over her Paris dresses before she
wears them."

"Ah, Jane Merry is one of *us*," said Mrs. Archer sighing, as
if it were not such an enviable thing to be in an age when ladies
were beginning to flaunt abroad their Paris dresses as soon as
they were out of the Custom House, instead of letting them
mellow under lock and key, in the manner of Mrs. Archer's
contemporaries.

"Yes; she's one of the few. In my youth," Miss Jackson rejoined, "it was considered vulgar to dress in the newest fashions;
and Amy Sillerton has always told me that in Boston the rule
was to put away one's Paris dresses for two years. Old Mrs.
Baxter Pennilow, who did everything handsomely, used to im-
port twelve a year, two velvet, two satin, two silk, and the other

six of poplin and the finest cashmere. It was a standing order, and as she was ill for two years before she died they found forty-eight Worth dresses that had never been taken out of tissue paper; and when the girls left off their mourning they were able to wear the first lot at the Symphony concerts without looking in advance of the fashion."

"Ah, well, Boston is more conservative than New York; but I always think it's a safe rule for a lady to lay aside her French dresses for one season," Mrs. Archer conceded.

"It was Beaufort who started the new fashion by making his wife clap her new clothes on her back as soon as they arrived: I must say at times it takes all Regina's distinction not to look like . . . like . . ." Miss Jackson glanced around the table, caught Janey's bulging gaze, and took refuge in an unintelligible murmur.

"Like her rivals," said Mr. Sillerton Jackson, with the air of producing an epigram.

"Oh,—" the ladies murmured; and Mrs. Archer added, partly to distract her daughter's attention from forbidden topics: "Poor Regina! Her Thanksgiving hasn't been a very cheerful one, I'm afraid. Have you heard the rumours about Beaufort's speculations, Sillerton?"

Mr. Jackson nodded carelessly. Every one had heard the rumours in question, and he scorned to confirm a tale that was already common property.

A gloomy silence fell upon the party. No one really liked Beaufort, and it was not wholly unpleasant to think the worst of his private life; but the idea of his having brought financial dishonour on his wife's family was too shocking to be enjoyed even by his enemies. Archer's New York tolerated hypocrisy in private relations; but in business matters it exacted a limpid and impeccable honesty. It was a long time since any well-known banker had failed discreditably; but every one remembered the social extinction visited on the heads of the firm when the last event of the kind had happened. It would be the same with the Beauforts, in spite of his power and her popularity; not all the leagued strength of the Dallas connection would save poor Regina if there were any truth in the reports of her husband's un-lawful speculations.

The talk took refuge in less ominous topics; but everything they touched on seemed to confirm Mrs. Archer's sense of an accelerated trend.

"Of course, Newland, I know you let dear May go to Mrs. Struthers's Sunday evenings—" she began; and May interposed gaily: "Oh, you know, everybody goes to Mrs. Struthers's now; and she was invited to Granny's last reception."

It was thus, Archer reflected, that New York managed its transitions: conspiring to ignore them till they were well over, and then, in all good faith, imagining that they had taken place in a preceding age. There was always a traitor in the citadel; and after he (or generally she) had surrendered the keys, what was the use of pretending that it was impregnable? Once people had tasted of Mrs. Struthers's easy Sunday hospitality they were not likely to sit at home remembering that her champagne was trans-muted Shoe-Polish.

"I know, dear, I know," Mrs. Archer sighed. "Such things have to be, I suppose, as long as *amusement* is what people go out for; but I've never quite forgiven your cousin Madame Olen-ska for being the first person to countenance Mrs. Struthers."

A sudden blush rose to young Mrs. Archer's face; it surprised her husband as much as the other guests about the table. "Oh, *Ellen*—" she murmured, much in the same accusing and yet deprecating tone in which her parents might have said: "Oh, *the Blenkers*—."

It was the note which the family had taken to sounding on the mention of the Countess Olenska's name, since she had sur-prised and inconvenienced them by remaining obdurate to her husband's advances; but on May's lips it gave food for thought, and Archer looked at her with the sense of strangeness that sometimes came over him when she was most in the tone of her environment.

His mother, with less than her usual sensitiveness to atmos-phere, still insisted: "I've always thought that people like the Countess Olenska, who have lived in aristocratic societies, ought to help us to keep up our social distinctions, instead of ignoring them."

May's blush remained permanently vivid: it seemed to have a significance beyond that implied by the recognition of Madame Olenska's social bad faith.

"I've no doubt we all seem alike to foreigners," said Miss Jackson tartly.

"I don't think Ellen cares for society; but nobody knows exactly what she does care for," May continued, as if she had been groping for something noncommittal.

"Ah, well—" Mrs. Archer sighed again.

Everybody knew that the Countess Olenska was no longer in the good graces of her family. Even her devoted champion, old Mrs. Manson Mingott, had been unable to defend her refusal to return to her husband. The Mingotts had not proclaimed their disapproval aloud: their sense of solidarity was too strong. They had simply, as Mrs. Welland said, "let poor Ellen find her own level"—and that, mortifyingly and incomprehensibly, was in the dim depths where the Blenkers prevailed, and "people who wrote" celebrated their untidy rites. It was incredible, but it was a fact, that Ellen, in spite of all her opportunities and her privileges, had become simply "Bohemian." The fact enforced the contention that she had made a fatal mistake in not returning to Count Olenski. After all, a young woman's place was under her husband's roof, especially when she had left it in circumstances that . . . well . . . if one had cared to look into them . . .

"Madame Olenska is a great favourite with the gentlemen," said Miss Sophy, with her air of wishing to put forth something conciliatory when she knew that she was planting a dart.

"Ah, that's the danger that a young woman like Madame Olenska is always exposed to," Mrs. Archer mournfully agreed; and the ladies, on this conclusion, gathered up their trains to seek the carcel globes of the drawing-room, while Archer and Mr. Sillerton Jackson withdrew to the Gothic library.

Once established before the grate, and consoling himself for the inadequacy of the dinner by the perfection of his cigar, Mr. Jackson became portentous and communicable.

"If the Beaufort smash comes," he announced, "there are go-ing to be disclosures."

Archer raised his head quickly: he could never hear the name without the sharp vision of Beaufort's heavy figure, opulently furred and shod, advancing through the snow at Skuytercliff.

"There's bound to be," Mr. Jackson continued, "the nastiest kind of a cleaning up. He hasn't spent all his money on Regina."

"Oh, well—that's discounted, isn't it? My belief is he'll pull out yet," said the young man, wanting to change the subject.

"Perhaps—perhaps. I know he was to see some of the influ-ential people today. Of course," Mr. Jackson reluctantly con-ceded, "it's to be hoped they can tide him over—this time anyhow. I shouldn't like to think of poor Regina's spending the rest of her life in some shabby foreign watering-place for bankrupts."

Archer said nothing. It seemed to him so natural—however tragic—that money ill-gotten should be cruelly expiated, that his mind, hardly lingering over Mrs. Beaufort's doom, wandered back to closer questions. What was the meaning of May's blush when the Countess Olenska had been mentioned?

Four months had passed since the midsummer day that he and Madame Olenska had spent together; and since then he had not seen her. He knew that she had returned to Washington, to the little house which she and Medora Manson had taken there: he had written to her once—a few words, asking when they were to meet again—and she had even more briefly replied: "Not yet."

Since then there had been no farther communication between them, and he had built up within himself a kind of sanctuary in which she throned among his secret thoughts and longings. Little by little it became the scene of his real life, of his only rational activities; thither he brought the books he read, the ideas and feelings which nourished him, his judgments and his visions. Outside it, in the scene of his actual life, he moved with a grow-ing sense of unreality and insufficiency, blundering against familiar prejudices and traditional points of view as an absent-minded man goes on bumping into the furniture of his own room. Absent—that was what he was: so absent from everything most densely real and near to those about him that it sometimes startled him to find they still imagined he was there.

He became aware that Mr. Jackson was clearing his throat preparatory to farther revelations.

"I don't know, of course, how far your wife's family are aware of what people say about—well, about Madame Olenska's refusal to accept her husband's latest offer."

Archer was silent, and Mr. Jackson obliquely continued: "It's a pity—it's certainly a pity—that she refused it."

"A pity? In God's name, why?"

Mr. Jackson looked down his leg to the unwrinkled sock that joined it to a glossy pump.

"Well—to put it on the lowest ground—what's she going to live on now?"

"Now—?"

"If Beaufort—"

Archer sprang up, his fist banging down on the black walnut-edge of the writing-table. The wells of the brass double-inkstand danced in their sockets.

"What the devil do you mean, sir?"

Mr. Jackson, shifting himself slightly in his chair, turned a tranquil gaze on the young man's burning face.

"Well—I have it on pretty good authority—in fact, on old Catherine's herself—that the family reduced Countess Olenska's allowance considerably when she definitely refused to go back to her husband; and as, by this refusal, she also forfeits the money settled on her when she married—which Olenski was ready to make over to her if she returned—why, what the devil do *you* mean, my dear boy, by asking me what *I* mean?" Mr. Jackson good-humouredly retorted.

Archer moved toward the mantelpiece and bent over to knock his ashes into the grate.

"I don't know anything of Madame Olenska's private affairs; but I don't need to, to be certain that what you insinuate—"

"Oh, *I* don't: it's Lefferts, for one," Mr. Jackson interposed.

"Lefferts—who made love to her and got snubbed for it!" Archer broke out contemptuously.

"Ah—*did* he?" snapped the other, as if this were exactly the fact he had been laying a trap for. He still sat sideways from the fire, so that his hard old gaze held Archer's face as if in a spring of steel.

"Well, well: it's a pity she didn't go back before Beaufort's cropper," he repeated. "If she goes *now*, and if he fails, it will only confirm the general impression: which isn't by any means peculiar to Lefferts, by the way."

"Oh, she won't go back now: less than ever!" Archer had no sooner said it than he had once more the feeling that it was exactly what Mr. Jackson had been waiting for.

The old gentleman considered him attentively. "That's your opinion, eh? Well, no doubt you know. But everybody will tell you that the few pennies Medora Manson has left are all in Beaufort's hands; and how the two women are to keep their heads above water unless he does, I can't imagine. Of course, Madame Olenska may still soften old Catherine, who's been the most inexorably opposed to her staying; and old Catherine could make her any allowance she chooses. But we all know that she hates parting with good money; and the rest of the family have no particular interest in keeping Madame Olenska here."

Archer was burning with unavailing wrath: he was exactly in the state when a man is sure to do something stupid, knowing all the while that he is doing it.

He saw that Mr. Jackson had been instantly struck by the fact that Madame Olenska's differences with her grandmother and her other relations were not known to him, and that the old gentleman had drawn his own conclusions as to the reasons for Archer's exclusion from the family councils. This fact warned Archer to go warily; but the insinuations about Beaufort made him reckless. He was mindful, however, if not of his own danger, at least of the fact that Mr. Jackson was under his mother's roof, and consequently his guest. Old New York scrupulously observed the etiquette of hospitality, and no discussion with a guest was ever allowed to degenerate into a disagreement.

"Shall we go up and join my mother?" he suggested curtly, as Mr. Jackson's last cone of ashes dropped into the brass ashtray at his elbow.

On the drive homeward May remained oddly silent; through the darkness, he still felt her enveloped in her menacing blush. What its menace meant he could not guess: but he was sufficiently warned by the fact that Madame Olenska's name had evoked it.

They went upstairs, and he turned into the library. She usually followed him; but he heard her passing down the passage to her bedroom.

"May!" he called out impatiently; and she came back, with a slight glance of surprise at his tone.

"This lamp is smoking again; I should think the servants might see that it's kept properly trimmed," he grumbled nervously.

"I'm so sorry: it shan't happen again," she answered, in the firm bright tone she had learned from her mother; and it exasperated Archer to feel that she was already beginning to humour him like a younger Mr. Welland. She bent over to lower the wick, and as the light struck up on her white shoulders and the clear curves of her face he thought: "How young she is! For what endless years this life will have to go on!"

He felt, with a kind of horror, his own strong youth and the bounding blood in his veins. "Look here," he said suddenly, "I may have to go to Washington for a few days—soon; next week perhaps."

Her hand remained on the key of the lamp as she turned to him slowly. The heat from its flame had brought back a glow to her face, but it paled as she looked up.

"On business?" she asked, in a tone which implied that there could be no other conceivable reason, and that she had put the question automatically, as if merely to finish his own sentence.

"On business, naturally. There's a patent case coming up before the Supreme Court—" He gave the name of the inventor, and went on furnishing details with all Lawrence Lefferts's practised glibness, while she listened attentively, saying at intervals: "Yes, I see."

"The change will do you good," she said simply, when he had finished; "and you must be sure to go and see Ellen," she added, looking him straight in the eyes with her cloudless smile, and speaking in the tone she might have employed in urging him not to neglect some irksome family duty.

It was the only word that passed between them on the subject; but in the code in which they had both been trained it meant: "Of course you understand that I know all that people have been saying about Ellen, and heartily sympathise with my family in their effort to get her to return to her husband. I also know that, for some reason you have not chosen to tell me, you have advised her against this course, which all the older men of the family, as well as our grandmother, agree in approving; and that it is owing to your encouragement that Ellen defies us all, and exposes herself to the kind of criticism of which Mr. Sillerton Jackson probably gave you, this evening, the hint that has made you so irritable. . . . Hints have indeed not been wanting; but since you appear unwilling to take them from others, I offer you this one myself, in the only form in which well-bred people of our kind can communicate unpleasant things to each other: by letting you understand that I know you mean to see Ellen when you are in Washington, and are perhaps going there expressly for that purpose; and that, since you are sure to see her, I wish you to do so with my full and explicit approval—and to take the opportunity of letting her know what the course of conduct you have encouraged her in is likely to lead to."

Her hand was still on the key of the lamp when the last word of this mute message reached him. She turned the wick down, lifted off the globe, and breathed on the sulky flame.

"They smell less if one blows them out," she explained, with her bright housekeeping air. On the threshold she turned and paused for his kiss.

Wall Street, the next day, had more reassuring reports of Beaufort's situation. They were not definite, but they were hopeful. It was generally understood that he could call on powerful influences in case of emergency, and that he had done so with success; and that evening, when Mrs. Beaufort appeared at the Opera wearing her old smile and a new emerald necklace, society drew a breath of relief.

New York was inexorable in its condemnation of business irregularities. So far there had been no exception to its tacit rule that those who broke the law of probity must pay; and every one was aware that even Beaufort and Beaufort's wife would be offered up unflinchingly to this principle. But to be obliged to offer them up would be not only painful but inconvenient. The disappearance of the Beauforts would leave a considerable void in their compact little circle; and those who were too ignorant or too careless to shudder at the moral catastrophe bewailed in advance the loss of the best ball-room in New York.

Archer had definitely made up his mind to go to Washington. He was waiting only for the opening of the law-suit of which he had spoken to May, so that its date might coincide with that of his visit; but on the following Tuesday he learned from Mr. Letterblair that the case might be postponed for several weeks. Nevertheless, he went home that afternoon determined in any event to leave the next evening. The chances were that May, who knew nothing of his professional life, and had never shown any interest in it, would not learn of the postponement, should it take place, nor remember the names of the litigants if they were mentioned before her; and at any rate he could no longer put off seeing Madame Olenska. There were too many things that he must say to her.

On the Wednesday morning, when he reached his office, Mr. Letterblair met him with a troubled face. Beaufort, after all, had not managed to "tide over"; but by setting afloat the rumour that he had done so he had reassured his depositors, and heavy payments had poured into the bank till the previous evening, when disturbing reports again began to predominate. In consequence, a run on the bank had begun, and its doors were likely to close before the day was over. The ugliest things were being said of Beaufort's dastardly manœuvre, and his failure promised to be one of the most discreditable in the history of Wall Street.

The extent of the calamity left Mr. Letterblair white and incapacitated. "I've seen bad things in my time; but nothing as bad as this. Everybody we know will be hit, one way or another. And what will be done about Mrs. Beaufort? What *can* be done about her? I pity Mrs. Manson Mingott as much as anybody: coming at her age, there's no knowing what effect this affair may have on her. She always believed in Beaufort—she made a friend of him! And there's the whole Dallas connection: poor Mrs. Beaufort is related to every one of you. Her only chance would be to leave her husband—yet how can any one tell her so? Her duty is at his side; and luckily she seems always to have been blind to his private weaknesses."

There was a knock, and Mr. Letterblair turned his head sharply. "What is it? I can't be disturbed."

A clerk brought in a letter for Archer and withdrew. Recognising his wife's hand, the young man opened the envelope and read: "Won't you please come up town as early as you can? Granny had a slight stroke last night. In some mysterious way she found out before any one else this awful news about the bank. Uncle Lovell is away shooting, and the idea of the disgrace has made poor Papa so nervous that he has a temperature and can't leave his room. Mamma needs you dreadfully, and I do hope you can get away at once and go straight to Granny's."

Archer handed the note to his senior partner, and a few minutes later was crawling northward in a crowded horse-car, which he exchanged at Fourteenth Street for one of the high staggering omnibuses of the Fifth Avenue line. It was after twelve o'clock when this laborious vehicle dropped him at old Catherine's. The sitting-room window on the ground floor, where she usually throned, was tenanted by the inadequate figure of her daughter, Mrs. Welland, who signed a haggard welcome as she caught sight of Archer; and at the door he was met by May. The hall wore the unnatural appearance peculiar to well-kept houses suddenly invaded by illness: wraps and furs lay in heaps on the chairs, a doctor's bag and overcoat were on the table, and beside them letters and cards had already piled up unheeded.

May looked pale but smiling: Dr. Bencomb, who had just come for the second time, took a more hopeful view, and Mrs. Mingott's dauntless determination to live and get well was already having an effect on her family. May led Archer into the old lady's sitting-room, where the sliding doors opening into the bedroom had been drawn shut, and the heavy yellow damask portières dropped over them; and here Mrs. Welland communicated to him in horrified undertones the details of the catastrophe. It appeared that the evening before something dreadful and mysterious had happened. At about eight o'clock, just after Mrs. Mingott had finished the game of solitaire that she always played after dinner, the door-bell had rung, and a lady so thickly veiled that the servants did not immediately recognise her had asked to be received.

The butler, hearing a familiar voice, had thrown open the sitting-room door, announcing: "Mrs. Julius Beaufort"—and had then closed it again on the two ladies. They must have been together, he thought, about an hour. When Mrs. Mingott's bell rang Mrs. Beaufort had already slipped away unseen, and the old lady, white and vast and terrible, sat alone in her great chair, and signed to the butler to help her into her room. She seemed, at that time, though obviously distressed, in complete control of her body and brain. The mulatto maid put her to bed, brought her a cup of tea as usual, laid everything straight in the room, and went away; but at three in the morning the bell rang again, and the two servants, hastening in at this unwonted summons (for old Catherine usually slept like a baby), had found their mistress sitting up against her pillows with a crooked smile on her face and one little hand hanging limp from its huge arm.

The stroke had clearly been a slight one, for she was able to articulate and to make her wishes known; and soon after the doctor's first visit she had begun to regain control of her facial muscles. But the alarm had been great; and proportionately great was the indignation when it was gathered from Mrs. Mingott's fragmentary phrases that Regina Beaufort had come to ask her —incredible effrontery!—to back up her husband, see them through—not to "desert" them, as she called it—in fact to induce the whole family to cover and condone their monstrous dishonour.

"I said to her: 'Honour's always been honour, and honesty honesty, in Manson Mingott's house, and will be till I'm carried out of it feet first,' " the old woman had stammered into her daughter's ear, in the thick voice of the partly paralysed. "And when she said: 'But my name, Auntie—my name's Regina Dallas,' I said: 'It was Beaufort when he covered you with jewels, and it's got to stay Beaufort now that he's covered you with shame.' "

So much, with tears and gasps of horror, Mrs. Welland imparted, blanched and demolished by the unwonted obligation of having at last to fix her eyes on the unpleasant and the discreditable. "If only I could keep it from your father-in-law: he always says: 'Augusta, for pity's sake, don't destroy my last illusions'—and how am I to prevent his knowing these horrors?" the poor lady wailed.

"After all, Mamma, he won't have *seen* them," her daughter suggested; and Mrs. Welland sighed: "Ah, no; thank heaven he's safe in bed. And Dr. Bencomb has promised to keep him there till poor Mamma is better, and Regina has been got away somewhere."

Archer had seated himself near the window and was gazing out blankly at the deserted thoroughfare. It was evident that he had been summoned rather for the moral support of the stricken ladies than because of any specific aid that he could render. Mr. Lovell Mingott had been telegraphed for, and messages were being despatched by hand to the members of the family living in New York; and meanwhile there was nothing to do but to discuss in hushed tones the consequences of Beaufort's dishonour and of his wife's unjustifiable action.

Mrs. Lovell Mingott, who had been in another room writing notes, presently reappeared, and added her voice to the discussion. In *their* day, the elder ladies agreed, the wife of a man who had done anything disgraceful in business had only one idea: to efface herself, to disappear with him. "There was the case of poor Grandmamma Spicer; your great-grandmother, May. Of course," Mrs. Welland hastened to add, "your great-grandfather's money difficulties were private—losses at cards, or signing a note for somebody—I never quite knew, because Mamma would never speak of it. But she was brought up in the country because her mother had to leave New York after the disgrace, whatever it was: they lived up the Hudson alone, winter and summer, till Mamma was sixteen. It would never have occurred to Grandmamma Spicer to ask the family to 'countenance' her, as I understand Regina calls it; though a private disgrace is nothing compared to the scandal of ruining hundreds of innocent people."

"Yes, it would be more becoming in Regina to hide her own countenance than to talk about other people's," Mrs. Lovell Mingott agreed. "I understand that the emerald necklace she wore at the Opera last Friday had been sent on approval from Ball and Black's in the afternoon. I wonder if they'll ever get it back?"

Archer listened unmoved to the relentless chorus. The idea of absolute financial probity as the first law of a gentleman's code was too deeply ingrained in him for sentimental considerations to weaken it. An adventurer like Lemuel Struthers might build up the millions of his Shoe Polish on any number of shady dealings; but unblemished honesty was the *noblesse oblige* of old financial New York. Nor did Mrs. Beaufort's fate greatly move Archer. He felt, no doubt, more sorry for her than her indignant relatives; but it seemed to him that the tie between husband and wife, even if breakable in prosperity, should be indissoluble in misfortune. As Mr. Letterblair had said, a wife's place was at her husband's side when he was in trouble; but society's place was not at his side, and Mrs. Beaufort's cool assumption that it was seemed almost to make her his accomplice. The mere idea of a woman's appealing to her family to screen her husband's business dishonour was inadmissible, since it was the one thing that the Family, as an institution, could not do.

The mulatto maid called Mrs. Lovell Mingott into the hall, and the latter came back in a moment with a frowning brow.

"She wants me to telegraph for Ellen Olenska. I had written to Ellen, of course, and to Medora; but now it seems that's not enough. I'm to telegraph to her immediately, and to tell her that she's to come alone."

The announcement was received in silence. Mrs. Welland sighed resignedly, and May rose from her seat and went to gather up some newspapers that had been scattered on the floor.

"I suppose it must be done," Mrs. Lovell Mingott continued, as if hoping to be contradicted; and May turned back toward the middle of the room.

"Of course it must be done," she said. "Granny knows what she wants, and we must carry out all her wishes. Shall I write the telegram for you, Auntie? If it goes at once Ellen can probably catch tomorrow morning's train." She pronounced the syllables of the name with a peculiar clearness, as if she had tapped on two silver bells.

"Well, it can't go at once. Jasper and the pantry-boy are both out with notes and telegrams."

May turned to her husband with a smile. "But here's Newland, ready to do anything. Will you take the telegram, Newland? There'll be just time before luncheon."

Archer rose with a murmur of readiness, and she seated herself at old Catherine's rosewood "Bonheur du Jour," and wrote out the message in her large immature hand. When it was written she blotted it neatly and handed it to Archer.

"What a pity," she said, "that you and Ellen will cross each other on the way!—Newland," she added, turning to her mother and aunt, "is obliged to go to Washington about a patent lawsuit that is coming up before the Supreme Court. I suppose Uncle Lovell will be back by tomorrow night, and with Granny improving so much it doesn't seem right to ask Newland to give up an important engagement for the firm—does it?"

She paused, as if for an answer, and Mrs. Welland hastily declared: "Oh, of course not, darling. Your Granny would be the last person to wish it." As Archer left the room with the telegram, he heard his mother-in-law add, presumably to Mrs.

Lovell Mingott: "But why on earth she should make you tele-graph for Ellen Olenska—" and May's clear voice rejoin: "Per-haps it's to urge on her again that after all her duty is with her husband."

The outer door closed on Archer and he walked hastily away toward the telegraph office.

Ol—ol—howjer spell it, anyhow?" asked the tart young lady to whom Archer had pushed his wife's telegram across the brass ledge of the Western Union office.

"Olenska—O-len-ska," he repeated, drawing back the message in order to print out the foreign syllables above May's rambling script.

"It's an unlikely name for a New York telegraph office; at least in this quarter," an unexpected voice observed; and turning around Archer saw Lawrence Lefferts at his elbow, pulling an imperturbable moustache and affecting not to glance at the message.

"Hallo, Newland: thought I'd catch you here. I've just heard of old Mrs. Mingott's stroke; and as I was on my way to the house I saw you turning down this street and nipped after you. I suppose you've come from there?"

Archer nodded, and pushed his telegram under the lattice.

"Very bad, eh?" Lefferts continued. "Wiring to the family, I suppose. I gather it *is* bad, if you're including Countess Olenska."

Archer's lips stiffened; he felt a savage impulse to dash his fist into the long vain handsome face at his side.

"Why?" he questioned.

Lefferts, who was known to shrink from discussion, raised his eye-brows with an ironic grimace that warned the other of the watching damsel behind the lattice. Nothing could be worse "form" the look reminded Archer, than any display of temper in a public place.

Archer had never been more indifferent to the requirements of form; but his impulse to do Lawrence Lefferts a physical injury was only momentary. The idea of bandying Ellen Olenska's name with him at such a time, and on whatsoever provocation, was unthinkable. He paid for his telegram, and the two young men went out together into the street. There Archer, having regained his self-control, went on: "Mrs. Mingott is much better: the doctor feels no anxiety whatever"; and Lefferts, with profuse expressions of relief, asked him if he had heard that there were beastly bad rumours again about Beaufort. . . .

That afternoon the announcement of the Beaufort failure was in all the papers. It overshadowed the report of Mrs. Manson Mingott's stroke, and only the few who had heard of the mysterious connection between the two events thought of ascribing old Catherine's illness to anything but the accumulation of flesh and years.

The whole of New York was darkened by the tale of Beaufort's dishonour. There had never, as Mr. Letterblair said, been a worse case in his memory, nor, for that matter, in the memory of the far-off Letterblair who had given his name to the firm. The bank had continued to take in money for a whole day after its failure was inevitable; and as many of its clients belonged to one or another of the ruling clans, Beaufort's duplicity seemed doubly cynical. If Mrs. Beaufort had not taken the tone that such misfortunes (the word was her own) were "the test of friendship," compassion for her might have tempered the general indignation against her husband. As it was—and especially after the object of her nocturnal visit to Mrs. Manson Mingott had become known—her cynicism was held to exceed his; and she had not the excuse—nor her detractors the satisfaction—of pleading that she was "a foreigner." It was some comfort (to those whose securities were not in jeopardy) to be able to remind themselves that Beaufort *was*; but, after all, if a Dallas of South Carolina took his view of the case, and glibly talked of his soon being "on his feet again," the argument lost its edge, and there was nothing to do but to accept this awful evidence of the indissolubility of marriage. Society must manage to get on without the Beauforts, and there was an end of it—except indeed for such hapless victims of the disaster as Medora Manson, the poor old Miss Lannings, and certain other misguided ladies of good family who, if only they had listened to Mr. Henry van der Luyden . . .

"The best thing the Beauforts can do," said Mrs. Archer, summing it up as if she were pronouncing a diagnosis and prescribing a course of treatment, "is to go and live at Regina's little place in North Carolina. Beaufort has always kept a racing stable, and he had better breed trotting horses. I should say he had all the qualities of a successful horsedealer." Every one agreed with her, but no one condescended to enquire what the Beauforts really meant to do.

The next day Mrs. Manson Mingott was much better: she recovered her voice sufficiently to give orders that no one should mention the Beauforts to her again, and asked—when Dr. Bencomb appeared—what in the world her family meant by making such a fuss about her health.

"If people of my age *will* eat chicken-salad in the evening what are they to expect?" she enquired; and, the doctor having opportunely modified her dietary, the stroke was transformed into an attack of indigestion. But in spite of her firm tone old Catherine did not wholly recover her former attitude toward life. The growing remoteness of old age, though it had not diminished her curiosity about her neighbours, had blunted her never very lively compassion for their troubles; and she seemed to have no difficulty in putting the Beaufort disaster out of her mind. But for the first time she became absorbed in her own symptoms, and began to take a sentimental interest in certain members of her family to whom she had hitherto been contemptuously indifferent.

Mr. Welland, in particular, had the privilege of attracting her notice. Of her sons-in-law he was the one she had most consistently ignored; and all his wife's efforts to represent him as a man of forceful character and marked intellectual ability (if he had only "chosen") had been met with a derisive chuckle. But his eminence as a valetudinarian now made him an object of engrossing interest, and Mrs. Mingott issued an imperial summons to him to come and compare diets as soon as his temperature permitted; for old Catherine was now the first to recognise that one could not be too careful about temperatures.

—

Twenty-four hours after Madame Olenska's summons a telegram announced that she would arrive from Washington on the
evening of the following day. At the Wellands', where the Newland Archers chanced to be lunching, the question as to who
should meet her at Jersey City was immediately raised; and the
material difficulties amid which the Welland household struggled
as if it had been a frontier outpost, lent animation to the debate.
It was agreed that Mrs. Welland could not possibly go to Jersey
City because she was to accompany her husband to old Catherine's that afternoon, and the brougham could not be spared,
since, if Mr. Welland were "upset" by seeing his mother-in-law
for the first time after her attack, he might have to be taken home
at a moment's notice. The Welland sons would of course be
"down town," Mr. Lovell Mingott would be just hurrying back
from his shooting, and the Mingott carriage engaged in meeting
him; and one could not ask May, at the close of a winter afternoon, to go alone across the ferry to Jersey City, even in her
own carriage. Nevertheless, it might appear inhospitable—and
contrary to old Catherine's express wishes—if Madame Olenska
were allowed to arrive without any of the family being at the
station to receive her. It was just like Ellen, Mrs. Welland's tired
voice implied, to place the family in such a dilemma. "It's always
one thing after another," the poor lady grieved, in one of her
rare revolts against fate; "the only thing that makes me think
Mamma must be less well than Dr. Bencomb will admit is this
morbid desire to have Ellen come at once, however inconvenient
it is to meet her."

The words had been thoughtless, as the utterances of impatience often are; and Mr. Welland was upon them with a pounce.

"Augusta," he said, turning pale and laying down his fork,
"have you any other reason for thinking that Bencomb is less
to be relied on than he was? Have you noticed that he has been
less conscientious than usual in following up my case or your
mother's?"

It was Mrs. Welland's turn to grow pale as the endless consequences of her blunder unrolled themselves before her; but
she managed to laugh, and take a second helping of scalloped

oysters, before she said, struggling back into her old armour of cheerfulness: "My dear, how could you imagine such a thing? I only meant that, after the decided stand Mamma took about its being Ellen's duty to go back to her husband, it seems strange that she should be seized with this sudden whim to see her, when there are half a dozen other grandchildren that she might have asked for. But we must never forget that Mamma, in spite of her wonderful vitality, is a very old woman."

Mr. Welland's brow remained clouded, and it was evident that his perturbed imagination had fastened at once on this last remark. "Yes: your mother's a very old woman; and for all we know Bencomb may not be as successful with very old people. As you say, my dear, it's always one thing after another; and in another ten or fifteen years I suppose I shall have the pleasing duty of looking about for a new doctor. It's always better to make such a change before it's absolutely necessary." And having arrived at this Spartan decision Mr. Welland firmly took up his fork.

"But all the while," Mrs. Welland began again, as she rose from the luncheon-table, and led the way into the wilderness of purple satin and malachite known as the back drawing-room, "I don't see how Ellen's to be got here tomorrow evening; and I do like to have things settled for at least twenty-four hours ahead."

Archer turned from the fascinated contemplation of a small painting representing two Cardinals carousing, in an octagonal ebony frame set with medallions of onyx.

"Shall I fetch her?" he proposed. "I can easily get away from the office in time to meet the brougham at the ferry, if May will send it there." His heart was beating excitedly as he spoke.

Mrs. Welland heaved a sigh of gratitude, and May, who had moved away to the window, turned to shed on him a beam of approval. "So you see, Mamma, everything *will* be settled twenty-four hours in advance," she said, stooping over to kiss her mother's troubled forehead.

———

May's brougham awaited her at the door, and she was to drive Archer to Union Square, where he could pick up a Broadway car to carry him to the office. As she settled herself in her corner she said: "I didn't want to worry Mamma by raising fresh obstacles; but how can you meet Ellen tomorrow, and bring her back to New York, when you're going to Washington?"

"Oh, I'm not going," Archer answered.

"Not going? Why, what's happened?" Her voice was as clear as a bell, and full of wifely solicitude.

"The case is off—postponed."

"Postponed? How odd! I saw a note this morning from Mr. Letterblair to Mamma saying that he was going to Washington tomorrow for the big patent case that he was to argue before the Supreme Court. You said it was a patent case, didn't you?"

"Well—that's it: the whole office can't go. Letterblair decided to go this morning."

"Then it's *not* postponed?" she continued, with an insistence so unlike her that he felt the blood rising to his face, as if he were blushing for her unwonted lapse from all the traditional delicacies.

"No: but my going is," he answered, cursing the unnecessary explanations that he had given when he had announced his intention of going to Washington, and wondering where he had read that clever liars give details, but that the cleverest do not. It did not hurt him half as much to tell May an untruth as to see her trying to pretend that she had not detected him.

"I'm not going till later on: luckily for the convenience of your family," he continued, taking base refuge in sarcasm. As he spoke he felt that she was looking at him, and he turned his eyes to hers in order not to appear to be avoiding them. Their glances met for a second, and perhaps let them into each other's meanings more deeply than either cared to go.

"Yes; it *is* awfully convenient," May brightly agreed, "that you should be able to meet Ellen after all; you saw how much Mamma appreciated your offering to do it."

"Oh, I'm delighted to do it." The carriage stopped, and as he jumped out she leaned to him and laid her hand on his. "Good-bye, dearest," she said, her eyes so blue that he wondered after-ward if they had shone on him through tears.

He turned away and hurried across Union Square, repeating to himself, in a sort of inward chant: "It's all of two hours from Jersey City to old Catherine's. It's all of two hours—and it may be more."

29

His wife's dark blue brougham (with the wedding varnish still on it) met Archer at the ferry, and conveyed him luxuriously to the Pennsylvania terminus in Jersey City.

It was a sombre snowy afternoon, and the gas-lamps were lit in the big reverberating station. As he paced the platform, waiting for the Washington express, he remembered that there were people who thought there would one day be a tunnel under the Hudson through which the trains of the Pennsylvania railway would run straight into New York. They were of the brotherhood of visionaries who likewise predicted the building of ships that would cross the Atlantic in five days, the invention of a flying machine, lighting by electricity, telephonic communication without wires, and other Arabian Night marvels.

"I don't care which of their visions comes true," Archer mused, "as long as the tunnel isn't built yet." In his senseless school-boy happiness he pictured Madame Olenska's descent from the train, his discovery of her a long way off, among the throngs of meaningless faces, her clinging to his arm as he guided her to the carriage, their slow approach to the wharf among slipping horses, laden carts, vociferating teamsters, and then the startling quiet of the ferry-boat, where they would sit side by side under the snow, in the motionless carriage, while the earth seemed to glide away under them, rolling to the other side of the sun. It was incredible, the number of things he had to say to her, and in what eloquent order they were forming themselves on his lips . . .

The clanging and groaning of the train came nearer, and it staggered slowly into the station like a prey-laden monster into its lair. Archer pushed forward, elbowing through the crowd, and staring blindly into window after window of the high-hung carriages. And then, suddenly, he saw Madame Olenska's pale and surprised face close at hand, and had again the mortified sensation of having forgotten what she looked like.

They reached each other, their hands met, and he drew her arm through his. "This way—I have the carriage," he said.

After that it all happened as he had dreamed. He helped her into the brougham with her bags, and had afterward the vague recollection of having properly reassured her about her grandmother and given her a summary of the Beaufort situation (he was struck by the softness of her: "Poor Regina!"). Meanwhile the carriage had worked its way out of the coil about the station, and they were crawling down the slippery incline to the wharf, menaced by swaying coal-carts, bewildered horses, dishevelled express-wagons, and an empty hearse—ah, that hearse! She shut her eyes as it passed, and clutched at Archer's hand.

"If only it doesn't mean—poor Granny!"

"Oh, no, no—she's much better—she's all right, really. There—we've passed it!" he exclaimed, as if that made all the difference. Her hand remained in his, and as the carriage lurched across the gang-plank onto the ferry he bent over, unbuttoned her tight brown glove, and kissed her palm as if he had kissed a relic. She disengaged herself with a faint smile, and he said: "You didn't expect me today?"

"Oh, no."

"I meant to go to Washington to see you. I'd made all my arrangements—I very nearly crossed you in the train."

"Oh—" she exclaimed, as if terrified by the narrowness of their escape.

"Do you know—I hardly remembered you?"

"Hardly remembered me?"

"I mean: how shall I explain? I—it's always so. *Each time you happen to me all over again.*"

"Oh, yes: I know! I know!"

"Does it—do I too: to you?" he insisted.

She nodded, looking out of the window.

"Ellen—Ellen—Ellen!"

She made no answer, and he sat in silence, watching her profile grow indistinct against the snow-streaked dusk beyond the window. What had she been doing in all those four long months, he wondered? How little they knew of each other, after all! The precious moments were slipping away, but he had forgotten

everything that he had meant to say to her and could only help-
lessly brood on the mystery of their remoteness and their prox-
imity, which seemed to be symbolised by the fact of their sitting
so close to each other, and yet being unable to see each other's
faces.

"What a pretty carriage! Is it May's?" she asked, suddenly
turning her face from the window.

"Yes."

"It was May who sent you to fetch me, then? How kind of
her!"

He made no answer for a moment; then he said explosively:
"Your husband's secretary came to see me the day after we met
in Boston."

In his brief letter to her he had made no allusion to M. Rivière's visit, and his intention had been to bury the incident in
his bosom. But her reminder that they were in his wife's carriage
provoked him to an impulse of retaliation. He would see if she
liked his reference to Rivière any better than he liked hers to
May! As on certain other occasions when he had expected to
shake her out of her usual composure, she betrayed no sign of
surprise: and at once he concluded: "He writes to her, then."

"M. Rivière went to see you?"

"Yes: didn't you know?"

"No," she answered simply.

"And you're not surprised?"

She hesitated. "Why should I be? He told me in Boston that
he knew you; that he'd met you in England I think."

"Ellen—I must ask you one thing."

"Yes."

"I wanted to ask it after I saw him, but I couldn't put it in a
letter. It was Rivière who helped you to get away—when you
left your husband?"

His heart was beating suffocatingly. Would she meet this
question with the same composure?

"Yes: I owe him a great debt," she answered, without the least
tremor in her quiet voice.

Her tone was so natural, so almost indifferent, that Archer's
turmoil subsided. Once more she had managed, by her sheer

simplicity, to make him feel stupidly conventional just when he thought he was flinging convention to the winds.

"I think you're the most honest woman I ever met!" he exclaimed.

"Oh, no—but probably one of the least fussy," she answered, a smile in her voice.

"Call it what you like: you look at things as they are."

"Ah—I've had to. I've had to look at the Gorgon."

"Well—it hasn't blinded you! You've seen that she's just an old bogey like all the others."

"She doesn't blind one; but she dries up one's tears."

The answer checked the pleading on Archer's lips: it seemed to come from depths of experience beyond his reach. The slow advance of the ferry-boat had ceased, and her bows bumped against the piles of the slip with a violence that made the brougham stagger, and flung Archer and Madame Olenska against each other. The young man, trembling, felt the pressure of her shoulder, and passed his arm about her.

"If you're not blind, then, you must see that this can't last."

"What can't?"

"Our being together—and not together."

"No. You ought not to have come today," she said in an altered voice; and suddenly she turned, flung her arms about him and pressed her lips to his. At the same moment the carriage began to move, and a gas-lamp at the head of the slip flashed its light into the window. She drew away, and they sat silent and motionless while the brougham struggled through the congestion of carriages about the ferry-landing. As they gained the street Archer began to speak hurriedly.

"Don't be afraid of me: you needn't squeeze yourself back into your corner like that. A stolen kiss isn't what I want. Look: I'm not even trying to touch the sleeve of your jacket. Don't suppose that I don't understand your reasons for not wanting to let this feeling between us dwindle into an ordinary hole-and-corner love-affair. I couldn't have spoken like this yesterday, because when we've been apart, and I'm looking forward to seeing you, every thought is burnt up in a great flame. But then you come; and you're so much more than I remembered, and what I want of you is so much more than an hour or two every now and then, with wastes of thirsty waiting between, that I can sit perfectly still beside you, like this, with that other vision in my mind, just quietly trusting to it to come true."

For a moment she made no reply; then she asked, hardly above a whisper: "What do you mean by trusting to it to come true?"

"Why—you know it will, don't you?"

"Your vision of you and me together?" She burst into a sudden hard laugh. "You choose your place well to put it to me!"

"Do you mean because we're in my wife's brougham? Shall we get out and walk, then? I don't suppose you mind a little snow?"

She laughed again, more gently. "No; I shan't get out and walk, because my business is to get to Granny's as quickly as I can. And you'll sit beside me, and we'll look, not at visions, but at realities."

"I don't know what you mean by realities. The only reality to me is this."

She met the words with a long silence, during which the carriage rolled down an obscure side-street and then turned into the searching illumination of Fifth Avenue.

"Is it your idea, then, that I should live with you as your mistress—since I can't be your wife?" she asked.

The crudeness of the question startled him: the word was one that women of his class fought shy of, even when their talk flitted closest about the topic. He noticed that Madame Olenska pronounced it as if it had a recognised place in her vocabulary, and he wondered if it had been used familiarly in her presence in the horrible life she had fled from. Her question pulled him up with a jerk, and he floundered.

"I want—I want somehow to get away with you into a world where words like that—categories like that—won't exist. Where we shall be simply two human beings who love each other, who are the whole of life to each other; and nothing else on earth will matter."

She drew a deep sigh that ended in another laugh. "Oh, my dear—where is that country? Have you ever been there?" she asked; and as he remained sullenly dumb she went on: "I know so many who've tried to find it; and, believe me, they all got out by mistake at wayside stations: at places like Boulogne, or Pisa, or Monte Carlo—and it wasn't at all different from the old world they'd left, but only rather smaller and dingier and more promiscuous."

He had never heard her speak in such a tone, and he remembered the phrase she had used a little while before.

"Yes, the Gorgon *has* dried your tears," he said.

"Well, she opened my eyes too; it's a delusion to say that she blinds people. What she does is just the contrary—she fastens their eyelids open, so that they're never again in the blessed darkness. Isn't there a Chinese torture like that? There ought to be. Ah, believe me, it's a miserable little country!"

The carriage had crossed Forty-second Street: May's sturdy brougham-horse was carrying them northward as if he had been a Kentucky trotter. Archer choked with the sense of wasted minutes and vain words.

"Then what, exactly, is your plan for us?" he asked.

"For *us*? But there's no *us* in that sense! We're near each other only if we stay far from each other. Then we can be ourselves. Otherwise we're only Newland Archer, the husband of Ellen Olenska's cousin, and Ellen Olenska, the cousin of Newland Archer's wife, trying to be happy behind the backs of the people who trust them."

"Ah, I'm beyond that," he groaned.

"No, you're not! You've never been beyond. And *I* have," she said, in a strange voice, "and I know what it looks like there."

He sat silent, dazed with inarticulate pain. Then he groped in the darkness of the carriage for the little bell that signalled orders to the coachman. He remembered that May rang twice when she wished to stop. He pressed the bell, and the carriage drew up beside the curbstone.

"Why are we stopping? This is not Granny's," Madame Olenska exclaimed.

"No: I shall get out here," he stammered, opening the door and jumping to the pavement. By the light of a street-lamp he saw her startled face, and the instinctive motion she made to detain him. He closed the door, and leaned for a moment in the window.

"You're right: I ought not to have come today," he said, lowering his voice so that the coachman should not hear. She bent forward, and seemed about to speak; but he had already called out the order to drive on, and the carriage rolled away while he stood on the corner. The snow was over, and a tingling wind had sprung up, that lashed his face as he stood gazing. Suddenly he felt something stiff and cold on his lashes, and perceived that he had been crying, and that the wind had frozen his tears.

He thrust his hands in his pockets, and walked at a sharp pace down Fifth Avenue to his own house.

30

That evening when Archer came down before dinner he found the drawing-room empty.

He and May were dining alone, all the family engagements having been postponed since Mrs. Manson Mingott's illness; and as May was the more punctual of the two he was surprised that she had not preceded him. He knew that she was at home, for while he dressed he had heard her moving about in her room; and he wondered what had delayed her.

He had fallen into the way of dwelling on such conjectures as a means of tying his thoughts fast to reality. Sometimes he felt as if he had found the clue to his father-in-law's absorption in trifles; perhaps even Mr. Welland, long ago, had had escapes and visions, and had conjured up all the hosts of domesticity to defend himself against them.

When May appeared he thought she looked tired. She had put on the low-necked and tightly-laced dinner-dress which the Mingott ceremonial exacted on the most informal occasions, and had built her fair hair into its usual accumulated coils; and her face, in contrast, was wan and almost faded. But she shone on him with her usual tenderness, and her eyes had kept the blue dazzle of the day before.

"What became of you, dear?" she asked. "I was waiting at Granny's, and Ellen came alone, and said she had dropped you on the way because you had to rush off on business. There's nothing wrong?"

"Only some letters I'd forgotten, and wanted to get off before dinner."

"Ah—" she said; and a moment afterward: "I'm sorry you didn't come to Granny's—unless the letters were urgent."

"They were," he rejoined, surprised at her insistence. "Besides, I don't see why I should have gone to your grandmother's. I didn't know you were there."

She turned and moved to the looking-glass above the mantelpiece. As she stood there, lifting her long arm to fasten a puff that had slipped from its place in her intricate hair, Archer was struck by something languid and inelastic in her attitude, and wondered if the deadly monotony of their lives had laid its weight on her also. Then he remembered that, as he had left the house that morning, she had called over the stairs that she would meet him at her grandmother's so that they might drive home together. He had called back a cheery "Yes!" and then, absorbed in other visions, had forgotten his promise. Now he was smitten with compunction, yet irritated that so trifling an omission should be stored up against him after nearly two years of marriage. He was weary of living in a perpetual tepid honeymoon, without the temperature of passion yet with all its exactions. If May had spoken out her grievances (he suspected her of many) he might have laughed them away; but she was trained to conceal imaginary wounds under a Spartan smile.

To disguise his own annoyance he asked how her grandmother was, and she answered that Mrs. Mingott was still improving, but had been rather disturbed by the last news about the Beauforts.

"What news?"

"It seems they're going to stay in New York. I believe he's going into an insurance business, or something. They're looking about for a small house."

The preposterousness of the case was beyond discussion, and they went in to dinner. During dinner their talk moved in its usual limited circle; but Archer noticed that his wife made no allusion to Madame Olenska, nor to old Catherine's reception of her. He was thankful for the fact, yet felt it to be vaguely ominous.

They went up to the library for coffee, and Archer lit a cigar and took down a volume of Michelet. He had taken to history in the evenings since May had shown a tendency to ask him to read aloud whenever she saw him with a volume of poetry: not that he disliked the sound of his own voice, but because he could always foresee her comments on what he read. In the days of their engagement she had simply (as he now perceived) echoed what he told her; but since he had ceased to provide her with opinions she had begun to hazard her own, with results destructive to his enjoyment of the works commented on.

Seeing that he had chosen history she fetched her workbasket, drew up an arm-chair to the green-shaded student lamp, and uncovered a cushion she was embroidering for his sofa. She was not a clever needle-woman; her large capable hands were made for riding, rowing and open-air activities; but since other wives embroidered cushions for their husbands she did not wish to omit this last link in her devotion.

She was so placed that Archer, by merely raising his eyes, could see her bent above her work-frame, her ruffled elbow-sleeves slipping back from her firm round arms, the betrothal sapphire shining on her left hand above her broad gold wedding-ring, and the right hand slowly and laboriously stabbing the canvas. As she sat thus, the lamplight full on her clear brow, he said to himself with a secret dismay that he would always know the thoughts behind it, that never, in all the years to come, would she surprise him by an unexpected mood, by a new idea, a weakness, a cruelty or an emotion. She had spent her poetry and romance on their short courting: the function was exhausted because the need was past. Now she was simply ripening into a copy of her mother, and mysteriously, by the very process, trying to turn him into a Mr. Welland. He laid down his book and stood up impatiently; and at once she raised her head.

"What's the matter?"

"The room is stifling: I want a little air."

He had insisted that the library curtains should draw backward and forward on a rod, so that they might be closed in the evening, instead of remaining nailed to a gilt cornice, and immovably looped up over layers of lace, as in the drawing-room; and he pulled them back and pushed up the sash, leaning out into the icy night. The mere fact of not looking at May, seated beside his table, under his lamp, the fact of seeing other houses, roofs, chimneys, of getting the sense of other lives outside his own, other cities beyond New York, and a whole world beyond his world, cleared his brain and made it easier to breathe.

After he had leaned out into the darkness for a few minutes he heard her say: "Newland! Do shut the window. You'll catch your death."

He pulled the sash down and turned back. "Catch my death!" he echoed; and he felt like adding: "But I've caught it already. I *am* dead—I've been dead for months and months."

And suddenly the play of the word flashed up a wild suggestion. What if it were *she* who was dead! If she were going to die—to die soon—and leave him free! The sensation of standing there, in that warm familiar room, and looking at her, and wishing her dead, was so strange, so fascinating and overmastering, that its enormity did not immediately strike him. He simply felt that chance had given him a new possibility to which his sick soul might cling. Yes, May might die—people did: young people, healthy people like herself: she might die, and set him suddenly free.

She glanced up, and he saw by her widening eyes that there must be something strange in his own.

"Newland! Are you ill?"

He shook his head and turned toward his arm-chair. She bent over her work-frame, and as he passed he laid his hand on her hair. "Poor May!" he said.

"Poor? Why poor?" she echoed with a strained laugh.

"Because I shall never be able to open a window without worrying you," he rejoined, laughing also.

For a moment she was silent; then she said very low, her head bowed over her work: "I shall never worry if you're happy."

"Ah, my dear; and I shall never be happy unless I can open the windows!"

"In *this* weather?" she remonstrated; and with a sigh he buried his head in his book.

Six or seven days passed. Archer heard nothing from Madame Olenska, and became aware that her name would not be mentioned in his presence by any member of the family. He did not try to see her; to do so while she was at old Catherine's guarded bedside would have been almost impossible. In the uncertainty of the situation he let himself drift, conscious, somewhere below the surface of his thoughts, of a resolve which had come to him when he had leaned out from his library window into the icy night. The strength of that resolve made it easy to wait and make no sign.

Then one day May told him that Mrs. Manson Mingott had asked to see him. There was nothing surprising in the request, for the old lady was steadily recovering, and she had always openly declared that she preferred Archer to any of her other grandsons-in-law. May gave the message with evident pleasure: she was proud of old Catherine's appreciation of her husband.

There was a moment's pause, and then Archer felt it incumbent on him to say: "All right. Shall we go together this afternoon?"

His wife's face brightened, but she instantly answered: "Oh, you'd much better go alone. It bores Granny to see the same people too often."

Archer's heart was beating violently when he rang old Mrs. Mingott's bell. He had wanted above all things to go alone, for he felt sure the visit would give him the chance of saying a word in private to the Countess Olenska. He had determined to wait till the chance presented itself naturally; and here it was, and here he was on the doorstep. Behind the door, behind the curtains of the yellow damask room next to the hall, she was surely awaiting him; in another moment he should see her, and be able to speak to her before she led him to the sick-room.

He wanted only to put one question: after that his course would be clear. What he wished to ask was simply the date of her return to Washington; and that question she could hardly refuse to answer.

But in the yellow sitting-room it was the mulatto maid who waited. Her white teeth shining like a keyboard, she pushed back the sliding doors and ushered him into old Catherine's presence.

The old woman sat in a vast throne-like arm-chair near her bed. Beside her was a mahogany stand bearing a cast bronze lamp with an engraved globe, over which a green paper shade had been balanced. There was not a book or a newspaper in reach, nor any evidence of feminine employment: conversation had always been Mrs. Mingott's sole pursuit, and she would have scorned to feign an interest in fancywork.

Archer saw no trace of the slight distortion left by her stroke. She merely looked paler, with darker shadows in the folds and recesses of her obesity; and, in the fluted mob-cap tied by a starched bow between her first two chins, and the muslin kerchief crossed over her billowing purple dressing-gown, she seemed like some shrewd and kindly ancestress of her own who might have yielded too freely to the pleasures of the table.

She held out one of the little hands that nestled in a hollow of her huge lap like pet animals, and called to the maid: "Don't let in any one else. If my daughters call, say I'm asleep."

The maid disappeared, and the old lady turned to her grandson.

"My dear, am I perfectly hideous?" she asked gaily, launching out one hand in search of the folds of muslin on her inaccessible bosom. "My daughters tell me it doesn't matter at my age—as if hideousness didn't matter all the more the harder it gets to conceal!"

"My dear, you're handsomer than ever!" Archer rejoined in the same tone; and she threw back her head and laughed.

"Ah, but not as handsome as Ellen!" she jerked out, twinkling at him maliciously; and before he could answer she added: "Was she so awfully handsome the day you drove her up from the ferry?"

He laughed, and she continued: "Was it because you told her so that she had to put you out on the way? In my youth young men didn't desert pretty women unless they were made to!" She gave another chuckle, and interrupted it to say almost querulously: "It's a pity she didn't marry you; I always told her so. It would have spared me all this worry. But who ever thought of sparing their grandmother worry?"

Archer wondered if her illness had blurred her faculties; but suddenly she broke out: "Well, it's settled, anyhow: she's going to stay with me, whatever the rest of the family say! She hadn't been here five minutes before I'd have gone down on my knees to keep her—if only, for the last twenty years, I'd been able to see where the floor was!"

Archer listened in silence, and she went on: "They'd talked me over, as no doubt you know: persuaded me, Lovell, and Letterblair, and Augusta Welland, and all the rest of them, that I must hold out and cut off her allowance, till she was made to see that it was her duty to go back to Olenski. They thought they'd convinced me when the secretary, or whatever he was, came out with the last proposals: handsome proposals I confess they were. After all, marriage is marriage, and money's money —both useful things in their way . . . and I didn't know what to answer—" She broke off and drew a long breath, as if speaking had become an effort. "But the minute I laid eyes on her, I said: 'You sweet bird, you! Shut you up in that cage again? Never!' And now it's settled that she's to stay here and nurse her Granny as long as there's a Granny to nurse. It's not a gay prospect, but she doesn't mind; and of course I've told Letterblair that she's to be given her proper allowance."

The young man heard her with veins aglow; but in his confusion of mind he hardly knew whether her news brought joy or pain. He had so definitely decided on the course he meant to pursue that for the moment he could not readjust his thoughts. But gradually there stole over him the delicious sense of difficulties deferred and opportunities miraculously provided. If Ellen had consented to come and live with her grandmother it must surely be because she had recognised the impossibility of giving him up. This was her answer to his final appeal of the other day: if she would not take the extreme step he had urged, she had at last yielded to half-measures. He sank back into the thought with the involuntary relief of a man who has been ready to risk everything, and suddenly tastes the dangerous sweetness of security.

"She couldn't have gone back—it was impossible!" he exclaimed.

"Ah, my dear, I always knew you were on her side; and that's why I sent for you today, and why I said to your pretty wife, when she proposed to come with you: 'No, my dear, I'm pining

to see Newland, and I don't want anybody to share our trans-
ports.' For you see, my dear—" she drew her head back as far
as its tethering chins permitted, and looked him full in the
eyes—"you see, we shall have a fight yet. The family don't want
her here, and they'll say it's because I've been ill, because I'm a
weak old woman, that she's persuaded me. I'm not well enough
yet to fight them one by one, and you've got to do it for me."

"I?" he stammered.

"You. Why not?" she jerked back at him, her round eyes
suddenly as sharp as pen-knives. Her hand fluttered from its
chair-arm and lit on his with a clutch of little pale nails like bird-
claws. "Why not?" she searchingly repeated.

Archer, under the exposure of her gaze, had recovered his
self-possession.

"Oh, I don't count—I'm too insignificant."

"Well, you're Letterblair's partner, ain't you? You've got to
get at them through Letterblair. Unless you've got a reason,"
she insisted.

"Oh, my dear, I back you to hold your own against them all
without my help; but you shall have it if you need it," he reassured her.

"Then we're safe!" she sighed; and smiling on him with all
her ancient cunning she added, as she settled her head among
the cushions: "I always knew you'd back us up, because they
never quote you when they talk about its being her duty to go
home."

He winced a little at her terrifying perspicacity, and longed
to ask: "And May—do they quote her?" But he judged it safer
to turn the question.

"And Madame Olenska? When am I to see her?" he said.

The old lady chuckled, crumpled her lids, and went through
the pantomime of archness. "Not today. One at a time, please.
Madame Olenska's gone out."

He flushed with disappointment, and she went on: "She's
gone out, my child: gone in my carriage to see Regina Beaufort."

She paused for this announcement to produce its effect.
"That's what she's reduced me to already. The day after she got
here she put on her best bonnet, and told me, as cool as a cu-

cumber, that she was going to call on Regina Beaufort. 'I don't know her; who is she?' says I. 'She's your grand-niece, and a most unhappy woman,' she says. 'She's the wife of a scoundrel,' I answered. 'Well,' she says, 'and so am I, and yet all my family want me to go back to him.' Well, that floored me, and I let her go; and finally one day she said it was raining too hard to go out on foot, and she wanted me to lend her my carriage. 'What for?' I asked her; and she said: 'To go and see cousin Regina'—*cousin*! Now, my dear, I looked out of the window, and saw it wasn't raining a drop; but I understood her, and I let her have the carriage. . . . After all, Regina's a brave woman, and so is she; and I've always liked courage above everything."

Archer bent down and pressed his lips on the little hand that still lay on his.

"Eh—eh—eh! Whose hand did you think you were kissing, young man—your wife's, I hope?" the old lady snapped out with her mocking cackle; and as he rose to go she called out after him: "Give her her Granny's love; but you'd better not say anything about our talk."

31

Archer had been stunned by old Catherine's news. It was only natural that Madame Olenska should have hastened from Washington in response to her grandmother's summons; but that she should have decided to remain under her roof—especially now that Mrs. Mingott had almost regained her health—was less easy to explain.

Archer was sure that Madame Olenska's decision had not been influenced by the change in her financial situation. He knew the exact figure of the small income which her husband had allowed her at their separation. Without the addition of her grandmother's allowance it was hardly enough to live on, in any sense known to the Mingott vocabulary; and now that Medora Manson, who shared her life, had been ruined, such a pittance would barely keep the two women clothed and fed. Yet Archer was convinced that Madame Olenska had not accepted her grandmother's offer from interested motives.

She had the heedless generosity and the spasmodic extravagance of persons used to large fortunes, and indifferent to money; but she could go without many things which her relations considered indispensable, and Mrs. Lovell Mingott and Mrs. Welland had often been heard to deplore that any one who had enjoyed the cosmopolitan luxuries of Count Olenski's establishments should care so little about "how things were done." Moreover, as Archer knew, several months had passed since her allowance had been cut off; yet in the interval she had made no effort to regain her grandmother's favour. Therefore if she had changed her course it must be for a different reason.

He did not have far to seek for that reason. On the way from the ferry she had told him that he and she must remain apart; but she had said it with her head on his breast. He knew that there was no calculated coquetry in her words; she was fighting her fate as he had fought his, and clinging desperately to her resolve that they should not break faith with the people who trusted them. But during the ten days which had elapsed since her return to New York she had perhaps guessed from his silence, and from the fact of his making no attempt to see her, that he was meditating a decisive step, a step from which there was no turning back. At the thought, a sudden fear of her own weakness might have seized her, and she might have felt that, after all, it was better to accept the compromise usual in such cases, and follow the line of least resistance.

An hour earlier, when he had rung Mrs. Mingott's bell, Archer had fancied that his path was clear before him. He had meant to have a word alone with Madame Olenska, and failing that, to learn from her grandmother on what day, and by which train, she was returning to Washington. In that train he intended to join her, and travel with her to Washington, or as much farther as she was willing to go. His own fancy inclined to Japan. At any rate she would understand at once that, wherever she went, he was going. He meant to leave a note for May that should cut off any other alternative.

He had fancied himself not only nerved for this plunge but eager to take it; yet his first feeling on hearing that the course of events was changed had been one of relief. Now, however, as he walked home from Mrs. Mingott's, he was conscious of a growing distaste for what lay before him. There was nothing unknown or unfamiliar in the path he was presumably to tread; but when he had trodden it before it was as a free man, who was accountable to no one for his actions, and could lend himself with an amused detachment to the game of precautions and prevarications, concealments and compliances, that the part required. This procedure was called "protecting a woman's honour"; and the best fiction, combined with the after-dinner talk of his elders, had long since initiated him into every detail of its code.

Now he saw the matter in a new light, and his part in it seemed singularly diminished. It was, in fact, that which, with a secret fatuity, he had watched Mrs. Thorley Rushworth play toward a fond and unperceiving husband: a smiling, bantering, humouring, watchful and incessant lie. A lie by day, a lie by night, a lie in every touch and every look; a lie in every caress and every quarrel; a lie in every word and in every silence.

It was easier, and less dastardly on the whole, for a wife to play such a part toward her husband. A woman's standard of truthfulness was tacitly held to be lower: she was the subject creature, and versed in the arts of the enslaved. Then she could always plead moods and nerves, and the right not to be held too strictly to account; and even in the most strait-laced societies the laugh was always against the husband.

But in Archer's little world no one laughed at a wife deceived, and a certain measure of contempt was attached to men who continued their philandering after marriage. In the rotation of crops there was a recognised season for wild oats; but they were not to be sown more than once.

Archer had always shared this view: in his heart he thought Lefferts despicable. But to love Ellen Olenska was not to become a man like Lefferts: for the first time Archer found himself face to face with the dread argument of the individual case. Ellen Olenska was like no other woman, he was like no other man: their situation, therefore, resembled no one else's, and they were answerable to no tribunal but that of their own judgment.

Yes, but in ten minutes more he would be mounting his own doorstep; and there were May, and habit, and honour, and all the old decencies that he and his people had always believed in . . .

At his corner he hesitated, and then walked on down Fifth Avenue.

Ahead of him, in the winter night, loomed a big unlit house. As he drew near he thought how often he had seen it blazing with lights, its steps awninged and carpeted, and carriages waiting in double line to draw up at the curbstone. It was in the conservatory that stretched its dead-black bulk down the side street that he had taken his first kiss from May; it was under the myriad candles of the ball-room that he had seen her appear, tall and silver-shining as a young Diana.

Now the house was as dark as the grave, except for a faint flare of gas in the basement, and a light in one upstairs room where the blind had not been lowered. As Archer reached the corner he saw that the carriage standing at the door was Mrs. Manson Mingott's. What an opportunity for Sillerton Jackson, if he should chance to pass! Archer had been greatly moved by old Catherine's account of Madame Olenska's attitude toward Mrs. Beaufort; it made the righteous reprobation of New York seem like a passing by on the other side. But he knew well enough what construction the clubs and drawing-rooms would put on Ellen Olenska's visits to her cousin.

He paused and looked up at the lighted window. No doubt the two women were sitting together in that room: Beaufort had probably sought consolation elsewhere. There were even rumours that he had left New York with Fanny Ring; but Mrs. Beaufort's attitude made the report seem improbable.

Archer had the nocturnal perspective of Fifth Avenue almost to himself. At that hour most people were indoors, dressing for dinner; and he was secretly glad that Ellen's exit was likely to be unobserved. As the thought passed through his mind the door opened, and she came out. Behind her was a faint light, such as might have been carried down the stairs to show her the way. She turned to say a word to some one; then the door closed, and she came down the steps.

"Ellen," he said in a low voice, as she reached the pavement.

She stopped with a slight start, and just then he saw two young men of fashionable cut approaching. There was a familiar air about their overcoats and the way their smart silk mufflers were folded over their white ties; and he wondered how youths of their quality happened to be dining out so early. Then he remembered that the Reggie Chiverses, whose house was a few doors above, were taking a large party that evening to see Adelaide Neilson in Romeo and Juliet, and guessed that the two were of the number. They passed under a lamp, and he recognised Lawrence Lefferts and a young Chivers.

A mean desire not to have Madame Olenska seen at the Beauforts' door vanished as he felt the penetrating warmth of her hand.

"I shall see you now—we shall be together," he broke out, hardly knowing what he said.

"Ah," she answered, "Granny has told you?"

While he watched her he was aware that Lefferts and Chivers, on reaching the farther side of the street corner, had discreetly struck away across Fifth Avenue. It was the kind of masculine solidarity that he himself often practised; now he sickened at their connivance. Did she really imagine that he and she could live like this? And if not, what else did she imagine?

"Tomorrow I must see you—somewhere where we can be alone," he said, in a voice that sounded almost angry to his own ears.

She wavered, and moved toward the carriage.

"But I shall be at Granny's—for the present that is," she added, as if conscious that her change of plans required some explanation.

"Somewhere where we can be alone," he insisted.

She gave a faint laugh that grated on him.

"In New York? But there are no churches . . . no monuments."

"There's the Art Museum—in the Park," he explained, as she looked puzzled. "At half-past two. I shall be at the door . . ."

She turned away without answering and got quickly into the carriage. As it drove off she leaned forward and he thought she waved her hand in the obscurity. He stared after her in a turmoil of contradictory feelings. It seemed to him that he had been speaking not to the woman he loved but to another, a woman he was indebted to for pleasures already wearied of: it was hateful to find himself the prisoner of this hackneyed vocabulary.

"She'll come!" he said to himself, almost contemptuously.

Avoiding the popular "Wolfe collection," whose anecdotic canvases filled one of the main galleries of the queer wilderness of cast-iron and encaustic tiles known as the Metropolitan Museum, they had wandered down a passage to the room where the "Cesnola antiquities" mouldered in unvisited loneliness.

They had this melancholy retreat to themselves, and seated on the divan enclosing the central steam-radiator, they were staring silently at the glass cabinets mounted in ebonised wood which contained the recovered fragments of Ilium.

"It's odd," Madame Olenska said, "I never came here before."

"Ah, well—. Some day, I suppose, it will be a great Museum."

"Yes," she assented absently.

She stood up and wandered across the room. Archer, remaining seated, watched the light movements of her figure, so girlish even under its heavy furs, the cleverly planted heron wing in her fur cap, and the way a dark curl lay like a flattened vine spiral on each cheek above the ear. His mind, as always when they first met, was wholly absorbed in the delicious details that made her herself and no other. Presently he rose and approached the case before which she stood. Its glass shelves were crowded with small broken objects—hardly recognisable domestic utensils, ornaments and personal trifles—made of glass, of clay, of discoloured bronze and other time-blurred substances.

"It seems cruel," she said, "that after a while nothing matters . . . any more than these little things, that used to be necessary and important to forgotten people, and now have to be guessed at under a magnifying glass and labelled: 'Use unknown.'"

"Yes; but meanwhile—"

"Ah, meanwhile—"

As she stood there, in her long sealskin coat, her hands thrust in a small round muff, her veil drawn down like a transparent mask to the tip of her nose, and the bunch of violets he had brought her stirring with her quickly-taken breath, it seemed incredible that this pure harmony of line and colour should ever suffer the stupid law of change.

"Meanwhile everything matters—that concerns you," he said.

She looked at him thoughtfully, and turned back to the divan. He sat down beside her and waited; but suddenly he heard a step echoing far off down the empty rooms, and felt the pressure of the minutes.

"What is it you wanted to tell me?" she asked, as if she had received the same warning.

"What I wanted to tell you?" he rejoined. "Why, that I be-lieve you came to New York because you were afraid."

"Afraid?"

"Of my coming to Washington."

She looked down at her muff, and he saw her hands stir in it uneasily.

"Well—?"

"Well—yes," she said.

"You *were* afraid? You knew—?"

"Yes: I knew . . ."

"Well, then?" he insisted.

"Well, then: this is better, isn't it?" she returned with a long questioning sigh.

"Better—?"

"We shall hurt others less. Isn't it, after all, what you always wanted?"

"To have you here, you mean—in reach and yet out of reach? To meet you in this way, on the sly? It's the very reverse of what I want. I told you the other day what I wanted."

She hesitated. "And you still think this—worse?"

"A thousand times!" He paused. "It would be easy to lie to you; but the truth is I think it detestable."

"Oh, so do I!" she cried with a deep breath of relief.

He sprang up impatiently. "Well, then—it's my turn to ask: what is it, in God's name, that you think better?"

She hung her head and continued to clasp and unclasp her hands in her muff. The step drew nearer, and a guardian in a braided cap walked listlessly through the room like a ghost stalk-ing through a necropolis. They fixed their eyes simultaneously on the case opposite them, and when the official figure had van-ished down a vista of mummies and sarcophagi Archer spoke again.

"What do you think better?"

Instead of answering she murmured: "I promised Granny to stay with her because it seemed to me that here I should be safer."

"From me?"

She bent her head slightly, without looking at him.

"Safer from loving me?"

Her profile did not stir, but he saw a tear overflow on her lashes and hang in a mesh of her veil.

"Safer from doing irreparable harm. Don't let us be like all the others!" she protested.

"What others? I don't profess to be different from my kind. I'm consumed by the same wants and the same longings."

She glanced at him with a kind of terror, and he saw a faint colour steal into her cheeks.

"Shall I—once come to you; and then go home?" she suddenly hazarded in a low clear voice.

The blood rushed to the young man's forehead. "Dearest!" he said, without moving. It seemed as if he held his heart in his hands, like a full cup that the least motion might overbrim.

Then her last phrase struck his ear and his face clouded. "Go home? What do you mean by going home?"

"Home to my husband."

"And you expect me to say yes to that?"

She raised her troubled eyes to his. "What else is there? I can't stay here and lie to the people who've been good to me."

"But that's the very reason why I ask you to come away!"

"And destroy their lives, when they've helped me to remake mine?"

Archer sprang to his feet and stood looking down on her in inarticulate despair. It would have been easy to say: "Yes, come; come once." He knew the power she would put in his hands if she consented; there would be no difficulty then in persuading her not to go back to her husband.

But something silenced the word on his lips. A sort of passionate honesty in her made it inconceivable that he should try to draw her into that familiar trap. "If I were to let her come," he said to himself, "I should have to let her go again." And that was not to be imagined.

But he saw the shadow of the lashes on her wet cheek, and wavered.

"After all," he began again, "we have lives of our own. . . . There's no use attempting the impossible. You're so unprejudiced about some things, so used, as you say, to looking at the

Gorgon, that I don't know why you're afraid to face our case, and see it as it really is—unless you think the sacrifice is not worth making."

She stood up also, her lips tightening under a rapid frown.

"Call it that, then—I must go," she said, drawing her little watch from her bosom.

She turned away, and he followed and caught her by the wrist. "Well, then: come to me once," he said, his head turning suddenly at the thought of losing her; and for a second or two they looked at each other almost like enemies.

"When?" he insisted. "Tomorrow?"

She hesitated. "The day after."

"Dearest—!" he said again.

She had disengaged her wrist; but for a moment they continued to hold each other's eyes, and he saw that her face, which had grown very pale, was flooded with a deep inner radiance. His heart beat with awe: he felt that he had never before beheld love visible.

"Oh, I shall be late—good-bye. No, don't come any farther than this," she cried, walking hurriedly away down the long room, as if the reflected radiance in his eyes had frightened her. When she reached the door she turned for a moment to wave a quick farewell.

Archer walked home alone. Darkness was falling when he let himself into his house, and he looked about at the familiar objects in the hall as if he viewed them from the other side of the grave.

The parlour-maid, hearing his step, ran up the stairs to light the gas on the upper landing.

"Is Mrs. Archer in?"

"No, sir; Mrs. Archer went out in the carriage after luncheon, and hasn't come back."

With a sense of relief he entered the library and flung himself down in his armchair. The parlour-maid followed, bringing the student lamp and shaking some coals onto the dying fire. When she left he continued to sit motionless, his elbows on his knees, his chin on his clasped hands, his eyes fixed on the red grate.

He sat there without conscious thoughts, without sense of the lapse of time, in a deep and grave amazement that seemed to suspend life rather than quicken it. "This was what had to be, then . . . this was what had to be," he kept repeating to himself, as if he hung in the clutch of doom. What he had dreamed of had been so different that there was a mortal chill in his rapture.

The door opened and May came in.

"I'm dreadfully late—you weren't worried, were you?" she asked, laying her hand on his shoulder with one of her rare caresses.

He looked up astonished. "Is it late?"

"After seven. I believe you've been asleep!" She laughed, and drawing out her hat pins tossed her velvet hat on the sofa. She looked paler than usual, but sparkling with an unwonted animation.

"I went to see Granny, and just as I was going away Ellen came in from a walk; so I stayed and had a long talk with her. It was ages since we'd had a real talk. . . ." She had dropped into her usual armchair, facing his, and was running her fingers through her rumpled hair. He fancied she expected him to speak.

"A really good talk," she went on, smiling with what seemed to Archer an unnatural vividness. "She was so dear—just like the old Ellen. I'm afraid I haven't been fair to her lately. I've sometimes thought—"

Archer stood up and leaned against the mantelpiece, out of the radius of the lamp.

"Yes, you've thought—?" he echoed as she paused.

"Well, perhaps I haven't judged her fairly. She's so different —at least on the surface. She takes up such odd people—she seems to like to make herself conspicuous. I suppose it's the life she's led in that fast European society; no doubt we seem dreadfully dull to her. But I don't want to judge her unfairly."

She paused again, a little breathless with the unwonted length of her speech, and sat with her lips slightly parted and a deep blush on her cheeks.

Archer, as he looked at her, was reminded of the glow which had suffused her face in the Mission Garden at St. Augustine. He became aware of the same obscure effort in her, the same reaching out toward something beyond the usual range of her vision.

"She hates Ellen," he thought, "and she's trying to overcome the feeling, and to get me to help her to overcome it."

The thought moved him, and for a moment he was on the point of breaking the silence between them, and throwing himself on her mercy.

"You understand, don't you," she went on, "why the family have sometimes been annoyed? We all did what we could for her at first; but she never seemed to understand. And now this idea of going to see Mrs. Beaufort, of going there in Granny's carriage! I'm afraid she's quite alienated the van der Luydens . . ."

"Ah," said Archer with an impatient laugh. The open door had closed between them again.

"It's time to dress; we're dining out, aren't we?" he asked, moving from the fire.

She rose also, but lingered near the hearth. As he walked past her she moved forward impulsively, as though to detain him: their eyes met, and he saw that hers were of the same swimming blue as when he had left her to drive to Jersey City.

She flung her arms about his neck and pressed her cheek to his.

"You haven't kissed me today," she said in a whisper; and he felt her tremble in his arms.

32

"At the court of the Tuileries," said Mr. Sillerton Jackson with his reminiscent smile, "such things were pretty openly tolerated."

The scene was the van der Luydens' black walnut dining-room in Madison Avenue, and the time the evening after Newland Archer's visit to the Museum of Art. Mr. and Mrs. van der Luyden had come to town for a few days from Skuytercliff, whither they had precipitately fled at the announcement of Beaufort's failure. It had been represented to them that the disarray into which society had been thrown by this deplorable affair made their presence in town more necessary than ever. It was one of the occasions when, as Mrs. Archer put it, they "owed it to society" to show themselves at the Opera, and even to open their own doors.

"It will never do, my dear Louisa, to let people like Mrs. Lemuel Struthers think they can step into Regina's shoes. It is just at such times that new people push in and get a footing. It was owing to the epidemic of chicken-pox in New York the winter Mrs. Struthers first appeared that the married men slipped away to her house while their wives were in the nursery. You and dear Henry, Louisa, must stand in the breach as you always have."

Mr. and Mrs. van der Luyden could not remain deaf to such a call, and reluctantly but heroically they had come to town, unmuffled the house, and sent out invitations for two dinners and an evening reception.

On this particular evening they had invited Sillerton Jackson, Mrs. Archer and Newland and his wife to go with them to the Opera, where Faust was being sung for the first time that winter. Nothing was done without ceremony under the van der Luyden roof, and though there were but four guests the repast had begun at seven punctually, so that the proper sequence of courses might be served without haste before the gentlemen settled down to their cigars.

Archer had not seen his wife since the evening before. He had left early for the office, where he had plunged into an accumulation of unimportant business. In the afternoon one of the senior partners had made an unexpected call on his time; and he had reached home so late that May had preceded him to the van der Luydens', and sent back the carriage.

Now, across the Skuytercliff carnations and the massive plate, she struck him as pale and languid; but her eyes shone, and she talked with exaggerated animation.

The subject which had called forth Mr. Sillerton Jackson's favourite allusion had been brought up (Archer fancied not without intention) by their hostess. The Beaufort failure, or rather the Beaufort attitude since the failure, was still a fruitful theme for the drawing-room moralist; and after it had been thoroughly examined and condemned Mrs. van der Luyden had turned her scrupulous eyes on May Archer.

"Is it possible, dear, that what I hear is true? I was told your grandmother Mingott's carriage was seen standing at Mrs. Beaufort's door." It was noticeable that she no longer called the offending lady by her Christian name.

May's colour rose, and Mrs. Archer put in hastily: "If it was, I'm convinced it was there without Mrs. Mingott's knowledge."

"Ah, you think—?" Mrs. van der Luyden paused, sighed, and glanced at her husband.

"I'm afraid," Mr. van der Luyden said, "that Madame Olenska's kind heart may have led her into the imprudence of calling on Mrs. Beaufort."

"Or her taste for peculiar people," put in Mrs. Archer in a dry tone, while her eyes dwelt innocently on her son's.

"I'm sorry to think it of Madame Olenska," said Mrs. van der Luyden; and Mrs. Archer murmured: "Ah, my dear—and after you'd had her twice at Skuytercliff!"

It was at this point that Mr. Jackson seized the chance to place his favourite allusion.

"At the Tuileries," he repeated, seeing the eyes of the company expectantly turned on him, "the standard was excessively

lax in some respects; and if you'd asked where Morny's money
came from—! Or who paid the debts of some of the Court
beauties . . ."

"I hope, dear Sillerton," said Mrs. Archer, "you are not suggesting that we should adopt such standards?"

"I never suggest," returned Mr. Jackson imperturbably. "But
Madame Olenska's foreign bringing-up may make her less
particular—"

"Ah," the two elder ladies sighed.

"Still, to have kept her grandmother's carriage at a defaulter's
door!" Mr. van der Luyden protested; and Archer guessed that
he was remembering, and resenting, the hampers of carnations
he had sent to the little house in Twenty-third Street.

"Of course I've always said that she looks at things quite
differently," Mrs. Archer summed up.

A flush rose to May's forehead. She looked across the table
at her husband, and said precipitately: "I'm sure Ellen meant it
kindly."

"Imprudent people are often kind," said Mrs. Archer, as if
the fact were scarcely an extenuation; and Mrs. van der Luyden
murmured: "If only she had consulted some one—"

"Ah, that she never did!" Mrs. Archer rejoined.

At this point Mr. van der Luyden glanced at his wife, who
bent her head slightly in the direction of Mrs. Archer; and the
glimmering trains of the three ladies swept out of the door while
the gentlemen settled down to their cigars. Mr. van der Luyden
supplied short ones on Opera nights; but they were so good that
they made his guests deplore his inexorable punctuality.

Archer, after the first act, had detached himself from the party
and made his way to the back of the club box. From there he
watched, over various Chivers, Mingott and Rushworth shoulders, the same scene that he had looked at, two years previously,
on the night of his first meeting with Ellen Olenska. He had
half-expected her to appear again in old Mrs. Mingott's box, but
it remained empty; and he sat motionless, his eyes fastened on
it, till suddenly Madame Nilsson's pure soprano broke out into
"*M'ama, non m'ama . . .*"

Archer turned to the stage, where, in the familiar setting of giant roses and pen-wiper pansies, the same large blonde victim was succumbing to the same small brown seducer.

From the stage his eyes wandered to the point of the horse-shoe where May sat between two older ladies, just as, on that former evening, she had sat between Mrs. Lovell Mingott and her newly-arrived "foreign" cousin. As on that evening, she was all in white; and Archer, who had not noticed what she wore, recognised the blue-white satin and old lace of her wedding dress.

It was the custom, in old New York, for brides to appear in this costly garment during the first year or two of marriage: his mother, he knew, kept hers in tissue paper in the hope that Janey might some day wear it, though poor Janey was reaching the age when pearl grey poplin and no bridesmaids would be thought more "appropriate."

It struck Archer that May, since their return from Europe, had seldom worn her bridal satin, and the surprise of seeing her in it made him compare her appearance with that of the young girl he had watched with such blissful anticipations two years earlier.

Though May's outline was slightly heavier, as her goddesslike build had foretold, her athletic erectness of carriage, and the girl-ish transparency of her expression, remained unchanged: but for the slight languor that Archer had lately noticed in her she would have been the exact image of the girl playing with the bouquet of lilies-of-the-valley on her betrothal evening. The fact seemed an additional appeal to his pity: such innocence was as moving as the trustful clasp of a child. Then he remembered the passionate generosity latent under that incurious calm. He re-called her glance of understanding when he had urged that their engagement should be announced at the Beaufort ball; he heard the voice in which she had said, in the Mission garden: "I couldn't have my happiness made out of a wrong—a wrong to some one else;" and an uncontrollable longing seized him to tell her the truth, to throw himself on her generosity, and ask for the freedom he had once refused.

Newland Archer was a quiet and self-controlled young man.

Conformity to the discipline of a small society had become almost his second nature. It was deeply distasteful to him to do anything melodramatic and conspicuous, anything Mr. van der Luyden would have deprecated and the club box condemned as bad form. But he had become suddenly unconscious of the club box, of Mr. van der Luyden, of all that had so long enclosed him in the warm shelter of habit. He walked along the semi-circular passage at the back of the house, and opened the door of Mrs. van der Luyden's box as if it had been a gate into the unknown.

"*M'ama!*" thrilled out the triumphant Marguerite; and the occupants of the box looked up in surprise at Archer's entrance. He had already broken one of the rules of his world, which forbade the entering of a box during a solo.

Slipping between Mr. van der Luyden and Sillerton Jackson, he leaned over his wife.

"I've got a beastly headache; don't tell any one, but come home, won't you?" he whispered.

May gave him a glance of comprehension, and he saw her whisper to his mother, who nodded sympathetically; then she murmured an excuse to Mrs. van der Luyden, and rose from her seat just as Marguerite fell into Faust's arms. Archer, while he helped her on with her Opera cloak, noticed the exchange of a significant smile between the older ladies.

As they drove away May laid her hand shyly on his. "I'm so sorry you don't feel well. I'm afraid they've been overworking you again at the office."

"No—it's not that: do you mind if I open the window?" he returned confusedly, letting down the pane on his side. He sat staring out into the street, feeling his wife beside him as a silent watchful interrogation, and keeping his eyes steadily fixed on the passing houses. At their door she caught her skirt in the step of the carriage, and fell against him.

"Did you hurt yourself?" he asked, steadying her with his arm.

"No; but my poor dress—see how I've torn it!" she exclaimed. She bent to gather up a mud-stained breadth, and followed him up the steps into the hall. The servants had not expected them so early, and there was only a glimmer of gas on the upper landing.

Archer mounted the stairs, turned up the light, and put a match to the brackets on each side of the library mantelpiece. The curtains were drawn, and the warm friendly aspect of the room smote him like that of a familiar face met during an unavowable errand.

He noticed that his wife was very pale, and asked if he should get her some brandy.

"Oh, no," she exclaimed with a momentary flush, as she took off her cloak. "But hadn't you better go to bed at once?" she added, as he opened a silver box on the table and took out a cigarette.

Archer threw down the cigarette and walked to his usual place by the fire.

"No; my head is not as bad as that." He paused. "And there's something I want to say; something important—that I must tell you at once."

She had dropped into an armchair, and raised her head as he spoke. "Yes, dear?" she rejoined, so gently that he wondered at the lack of wonder with which she received this preamble.

"May—" he began, standing a few feet from her chair, and looking over at her as if the slight distance between them were an unbridgeable abyss. The sound of his voice echoed uncannily through the homelike hush, and he repeated: "There is something I've got to tell you . . . about myself . . ."

She sat silent, without a movement or a tremor of her lashes. She was still extremely pale, but her face had a curious tranquillity of expression that seemed drawn from some secret inner source.

Archer checked the conventional phrases of self-accusal that were crowding to his lips. He was determined to put the case baldly, without vain recrimination or excuse.

"Madame Olenska—" he said; but at the name his wife raised her hand as if to silence him. As she did so the gaslight struck on the gold of her wedding-ring.

"Oh, why should we talk about Ellen tonight?" she asked, with a slight pout of impatience.

"Because I ought to have spoken before."

Her face remained calm. "Is it really worth while, dear? I know I've been unfair to her at times—perhaps we all have. You've understood her, no doubt, better than we did: you've always been kind to her. But what does it matter, now it's all over?"

Archer looked at her blankly. Could it be possible that the sense of unreality in which he felt himself imprisoned had communicated itself to his wife?

"All over—what do you mean?" he asked in an indistinct stammer.

May still looked at him with transparent eyes. "Why—since she's going back to Europe so soon; since Granny approves and understands, and has arranged to make her independent of her husband—"

She broke off, and Archer, grasping the corner of the mantelpiece in one convulsed hand, and steadying himself against it, made a vain effort to extend the same control to his reeling thoughts.

"I supposed," he heard his wife's even voice go on, "that you had been kept at the office this evening about the business arrangements. It was settled this morning, I believe." She lowered her eyes under his unseeing stare, and another fugitive flush passed over her face.

He understood that his own eyes must be unbearable, and turning away, rested his elbows on the mantel-shelf and covered his face. Something drummed and clanged furiously in his ears; he could not tell if it were the blood in his veins, or the tick of the clock on the mantel.

May sat without moving or speaking while the clock slowly measured out five minutes. A lump of coal fell forward in the grate, and hearing her rise to push it back, Archer at length turned and faced her.

"It's impossible," he exclaimed.

"Impossible—?"

"How do you know—what you've just told me?"

"I saw Ellen yesterday—I told you I'd seen her at Granny's."

"It wasn't then that she told you?"

"No; I had a note from her this afternoon.—Do you want to see it?"

He could not find his voice, and she went out of the room, and came back almost immediately.

"I thought you knew," she said simply.

She laid a sheet of paper on the table, and Archer put out his hand and took it up. The letter contained only a few lines.

"May dear, I have at last made Granny understand that my visit to her could be no more than a visit; and she has been as kind and generous as ever. She sees now that if I return to Europe I must live by myself, or rather with poor Aunt Medora, who is coming with me. I am hurrying back to Washington to pack up, and we sail next week. You must be very good to Granny when I'm gone—as good as you've always been to me. Ellen.

"If any of my friends wish to urge me to change my mind, please tell them it would be utterly useless."

Archer read the letter over two or three times; then he flung it down and burst out laughing.

The sound of his laugh startled him. It recalled Janey's midnight fright when she had caught him rocking with incomprehensible mirth over May's telegram announcing that the date of their marriage had been advanced.

"Why did she write this?" he asked, checking his laugh with a supreme effort.

May met the question with her unshaken candour. "I suppose because we talked things over yesterday—"

"What things?"

"I told her I was afraid I hadn't been fair to her—hadn't always understood how hard it must have been for her here, alone among so many people who were relations and yet strangers; who felt the right to criticise, and yet didn't always know the circumstances." She paused. "I knew you'd been the one friend she could always count on; and I wanted her to know that you and I were the same—in all our feelings."

She hesitated, as if waiting for him to speak, and then added slowly: "She understood my wishing to tell her this. I think she understands everything."

She went up to Archer, and taking one of his cold hands pressed it quickly against her cheek.

"My head aches too; good-night, dear," she said, and turned to the door, her torn and muddy wedding-dress dragging after her across the room.

33

It was, as Mrs. Archer smilingly said to Mrs. Welland, a great event for a young couple to give their first big dinner.

The Newland Archers, since they had set up their household, had received a good deal of company in an informal way. Archer was fond of having three or four friends to dine, and May welcomed them with the beaming readiness of which her mother had set her the example in conjugal affairs. Her husband questioned whether, if left to herself, she would ever have asked any one to the house; but he had long given up trying to disengage her real self from the shape into which tradition and training had moulded her. It was expected that well-off young couples in New York should do a good deal of informal entertaining, and a Welland married to an Archer was doubly pledged to the tradition.

But a big dinner, with a hired *chef* and two borrowed footmen, with Roman punch, roses from Henderson's, and *menus* on gilt-edged cards, was a different affair, and not to be lightly undertaken. As Mrs. Archer remarked, the Roman punch made all the difference; not in itself but by its manifold implications —since it signified either canvas-backs or terrapin, two soups, a hot and a cold sweet, full *dècolletage* with short sleeves, and guests of a proportionate importance.

It was always an interesting occasion when a young pair launched their first invitations in the third person, and their summons was seldom refused even by the seasoned and sought-after. Still, it was admittedly a triumph that the van der Luydens, at May's request, should have stayed over in order to be present at her farewell dinner for the Countess Olenska.

The two mothers-in-law sat in May's drawing-room on the afternoon of the great day, Mrs. Archer writing out the *menus* on Tiffany's thickest gilt-edged bristol, while Mrs. Welland superintended the placing of the palms and standard lamps.

Archer, arriving late from his office, found them still there. Mrs. Archer had turned her attention to the name-cards for the table, and Mrs. Welland was considering the effect of bringing forward the large gilt sofa, so that another "corner" might be created between the piano and the window.

May, they told him, was in the dining-room inspecting the mound of Jacqueminot roses and maidenhair in the centre of the long table, and the placing of the Maillard bonbons in openwork silver baskets between the candelabra. On the piano stood a large basket of orchids which Mr. van der Luyden had had sent from Skuytercliff. Everything was, in short, as it should be on the approach of so considerable an event.

Mrs. Archer ran thoughtfully over the list, checking off each name with her sharp gold pen.

"Henry van der Luyden—Louisa—the Lovell Mingotts—the Reggie Chiverses—Lawrence Lefferts and Gertrude—(yes, I suppose May was right to have them)—the Selfridge Merrys, Sillerton Jackson, Van Newland and his wife. (How time passes! It seems only yesterday that he was your best man, Newland) —and Countess Olenska—yes, I think that's all. . . ."

Mrs. Welland surveyed her son-in-law affectionately. "No one can say, Newland, that you and May are not giving Ellen a handsome send-off."

"Ah, well," said Mrs. Archer, "I understand May's wanting her cousin to tell people abroad that we're not quite barbarians."

"I'm sure Ellen will appreciate it. She was to arrive this morning, I believe. It will make a most charming last impression. The evening before sailing is usually so dreary," Mrs. Welland cheerfully continued.

Archer turned toward the door, and his mother-in-law called to him: "Do go in and have a peep at the table. And don't let May tire herself too much." But he affected not to hear, and sprang up the stairs to his library. The room looked at him like an alien countenance composed into a polite grimace; and he perceived that it had been ruthlessly "tidied," and prepared, by a judicious distribution of ash-trays and cedar-wood boxes, for the gentlemen to smoke in.

"Ah, well," he thought, "it's not for long—" and he went on to his dressing-room.

Ten days had passed since Madame Olenska's departure from New York. During those ten days Archer had had no sign from her but that conveyed by the return of a key wrapped in tissue paper, and sent to his office in a sealed envelope addressed in her hand. This retort to his last appeal might have been interpreted as a classic move in a familiar game; but the young man chose to give it a different meaning. She was still fighting against her fate; but she was going to Europe, and she was not returning to her husband. Nothing, therefore, was to prevent his following her; and once he had taken the irrevocable step, and had proved to her that it was irrevocable, he believed she would not send him away.

This confidence in the future had steadied him to play his part in the present. It had kept him from writing to her, or betraying, by any sign or act, his misery and mortification. It seemed to him that in the deadly silent game between them the trumps were still in his hands; and he waited.

There had been, nevertheless, moments sufficiently difficult to pass; as when Mr. Letterblair, the day after Madame Olenska's departure, had sent for him to go over the details of the trust which Mrs. Manson Mingott wished to create for her granddaughter. For a couple of hours Archer had examined the terms of the deed with his senior, all the while obscurely feeling that if he had been consulted it was for some reason other than the obvious one of his cousinship; and that the close of the conference would reveal it.

"Well, the lady can't deny that it's a handsome arrangement," Mr. Letterblair had summed up, after mumbling over a summary of the settlement. "In fact I'm bound to say she's been treated pretty handsomely all round."

"All round?" Archer echoed with a touch of derision. "Do you refer to her husband's proposal to give her back her own money?"

Mr. Letterblair's bushy eyebrows went up a fraction of an

inch. "My dear sir, the law's the law; and your wife's cousin was married under the French law. It's to be presumed she knew what that meant."

"Even if she did, what happened subsequently—." But Archer paused. Mr. Letterblair had laid his pen-handle against his big corrugated nose, and was looking down it with the expression assumed by virtuous elderly gentlemen when they wish their youngers to understand that virtue is not synonymous with ignorance.

"My dear sir, I've no wish to extenuate the Count's transgressions; but—but on the other side . . . I wouldn't put my hand in the fire . . . well, that there hadn't been tit for tat . . . with the young champion. . . ." Mr. Letterblair unlocked a drawer and pushed a folded paper toward Archer. "This report, the result of discreet enquiries . . ." And then, as Archer made no effort to glance at the paper or to repudiate the suggestion, the lawyer somewhat flatly continued: "I don't say it's conclusive, you observe; far from it. But straws show . . . and on the whole it's eminently satisfactory for all parties that this dignified solution has been reached."

"Oh, eminently," Archer assented, pushing back the paper.

A day or two later, on responding to a summons from Mrs. Manson Mingott, his soul had been more deeply tried.

He had found the old lady depressed and querulous.

"You know she's deserted me?" she began at once; and without waiting for his reply: "Oh, don't ask me why! She gave so many reasons that I've forgotten them all. My private belief is that she couldn't face the boredom. At any rate that's what Augusta and my daughters-in-law think. And I don't know that I altogether blame her. Olenski's a finished scoundrel; but life with him must have been a good deal gayer than it is in Fifth Avenue. Not that the family would admit that: they think Fifth Avenue is Heaven with the rue de la Paix thrown in. And poor Ellen, of course, has no idea of going back to her husband. She held out as firmly as ever against that. So she's to settle down in Paris with that fool Medora. . . . Well, Paris is Paris; and you can keep a carriage there on next to nothing. But she was as gay as a bird, and I shall miss her." Two tears, the parched tears of the old, rolled down her puffy cheeks and vanished in the abysses of her bosom.

"All I ask is," she concluded, "that they shouldn't bother me any more. I must really be allowed to digest my gruel. . . ." And she twinkled a little wistfully at Archer.

It was that evening, on his return home, that May announced her intention of giving a farewell dinner to her cousin. Madame Olenska's name had not been pronounced between them since the night of her flight to Washington; and Archer looked at his wife with surprise.

"A dinner—why?" he interrogated.

Her colour rose. "But you like Ellen—I thought you'd be pleased."

"It's awfully nice—your putting it in that way. But I really don't see—"

"I mean to do it, Newland," she said, quietly rising and going to her desk. "Here are the invitations all written. Mother helped me—she agrees that we ought to." She paused, embarrassed and yet smiling, and Archer suddenly saw before him the embodied image of the Family.

"Oh, all right," he said, staring with unseeing eyes at the list of guests that she had put in his hand.

When he entered the drawing-room before dinner May was stooping over the fire and trying to coax the logs to burn in their unaccustomed setting of immaculate tiles.

The tall lamps were all lit, and Mr. van der Luyden's orchids had been conspicuously disposed in various receptacles of modern porcelain and knobby silver. Mrs. Newland Archer's drawing-room was generally thought a great success. A gilt bamboo *jardinière*, in which the primulas and cinerarias were punctually renewed, blocked the access to the bay window (where the old-fashioned would have preferred a bronze reduction of the Venus of Milo); the sofas and arm-chairs of pale brocade were cleverly grouped about little plush tables densely covered with silver toys, porcelain animals and efflorescent photograph frames; and tall rosy-shaded lamps shot up like tropical flowers among the palms.

"I don't think Ellen has ever seen this room lighted up," said May, rising flushed from her struggle, and sending about her a glance of pardonable pride. The brass tongs which she had propped against the side of the chimney fell with a crash that drowned her husband's answer; and before he could restore them Mr. and Mrs. van der Luyden were announced.

The other guests quickly followed, for it was known that the van der Luydens liked to dine punctually. The room was nearly full, and Archer was engaged in showing to Mrs. Selfridge Merry a small highly-varnished Verbeckhoven "Study of Sheep," which Mr. Welland had given May for Christmas, when he found Madame Olenska at his side.

She was excessively pale, and her pallor made her dark hair seem denser and heavier than ever. Perhaps that, or the fact that she had wound several rows of amber beads about her neck, reminded him suddenly of the little Ellen Mingott he had danced with at children's parties, when Medora Manson had first brought her to New York.

The amber beads were trying to her complexion, or her dress was perhaps unbecoming: her face looked lustreless and almost ugly, and he had never loved it as he did at that minute. Their hands met, and he thought he heard her say: "Yes, we're sailing tomorrow in the Russia—"; then there was an unmeaning noise of opening doors, and after an interval May's voice: "Newland! Dinner's been announced. Won't you please take Ellen in?"

Madame Olenska put her hand on his arm, and he noticed that the hand was ungloved, and remembered how he had kept his eyes fixed on it the evening that he had sat with her in the little Twenty-third Street drawing-room. All the beauty that had forsaken her face seemed to have taken refuge in the long pale fingers and faintly dimpled knuckles on his sleeve, and he said to himself: "If it were only to see her hand again I should have to follow her—."

It was only at an entertainment ostensibly offered to a "foreign visitor" that Mrs. van der Luyden could suffer the dimi-

nution of being placed on her host's left. The fact of Madame
Olenska's "foreignness" could hardly have been more adroitly
emphasised than by this farewell tribute; and Mrs. van der Luyden accepted her displacement with an affability which left no
doubt as to her approval. There were certain things that had to
be done, and if done at all, done handsomely and thoroughly;
and one of these, in the old New York code, was the tribal rally
around a kinswoman about to be eliminated from the tribe.
There was nothing on earth that the Wellands and Mingotts
would not have done to proclaim their unalterable affection for
the Countess Olenska now that her passage for Europe was engaged; and Archer, at the head of his table, sat marvelling at the
silent untiring activity with which her popularity had been re-
trieved, grievances against her silenced, her past countenanced,
and her present irradiated by the family approval. Mrs. van der
Luyden shone on her with the dim benevolence which was her
nearest approach to cordiality, and Mr. van der Luyden, from
his seat at May's right, cast down the table glances plainly intended to justify all the carnations he had sent from Skuytercliff.

Archer, who seemed to be assisting at the scene in a state of
odd imponderability, as if he floated somewhere between chandelier and ceiling, wondered at nothing so much as his own share
in the proceedings. As his glance travelled from one placid well-
fed face to another he saw all the harmless-looking people engaged upon May's canvas-backs as a band of dumb conspirators,
and himself and the pale woman on his right as the centre of
their conspiracy. And then it came over him, in a vast flash made
up of many broken gleams, that to all of them he and Madame
Olenska were lovers, lovers in the extreme sense peculiar to "foreign" vocabularies. He guessed himself to have been, for months,
the centre of countless silently observing eyes and patiently listening ears, he understood that, by means as yet unknown to
him, the separation between himself and the partner of his guilt
had been achieved, and that now the whole tribe had rallied
about his wife on the tacit assumption that nobody knew anything, or had ever imagined anything, and that the occasion of
the entertainment was simply May Archer's natural desire to
take an affectionate leave of her friend and cousin.

It was the old New York way of taking life "without effusion of blood": the way of people who dreaded scandal more than disease, who placed decency above courage, and who considered that nothing was more ill-bred than "scenes," except the behaviour of those who gave rise to them.

As these thoughts succeeded each other in his mind Archer felt like a prisoner in the centre of an armed camp. He looked about the table, and guessed at the inexorableness of his captors from the tone in which, over the asparagus from Florida, they were dealing with Beaufort and his wife. "It's to show me," he thought, "what would happen to *me*—" and a deathly sense of the superiority of implication and analogy over direct action, and of silence over rash words, closed in on him like the doors of the family vault.

He laughed, and met Mrs. van der Luyden's startled eyes.

"You think it laughable?" she said with a pinched smile. "Of course poor Regina's idea of remaining in New York has its ridiculous side, I suppose;" and Archer muttered: "Of course."

At this point, he became conscious that Madame Olenska's other neighbour had been engaged for some time with the lady on his right. At the same moment he saw that May, serenely enthroned between Mr. van der Luyden and Mr. Selfridge Merry, had cast a quick glance down the table. It was evident that the host and the lady on his right could not sit through the whole meal in silence. He turned to Madame Olenska, and her pale smile met him. "Oh, do let's see it through," it seemed to say.

"Did you find the journey tiring?" he asked in a voice that surprised him by its naturalness; and she answered that, on the contrary, she had seldom travelled with fewer discomforts.

"Except, you know, the dreadful heat in the train," she added; and he remarked that she would not suffer from that particular hardship in the country she was going to.

"I never," he declared with intensity, "was more nearly frozen than once, in April, in the train between Calais and Paris."

She said she did not wonder, but remarked that, after all, one could always carry an extra rug, and that every form of travel had its hardships; to which he abruptly returned that he thought them all of no account compared with the blessedness of getting away. She changed colour, and he added, his voice suddenly rising in pitch: "I mean to do a lot of travelling myself before long." A tremor crossed her face, and leaning over to Reggie Chivers, he cried out: "I say, Reggie, what do you say to a trip round the world: now, next month, I mean? I'm game if you are—" at which Mrs. Reggie piped up that she could not think of letting Reggie go till after the Martha Washington Ball she was getting up for the Blind Asylum in Easter week; and her husband placidly observed that by that time he would have to be practising for the International Polo match.

But Mr. Selfridge Merry had caught the phrase "round the world," and having once circled the globe in his steam-yacht, he seized the opportunity to send down the table several striking items concerning the shallowness of the Mediterranean ports. Though, after all, he added, it didn't matter; for when you'd seen Athens and Smyrna and Constantinople, what else was there? And Mrs. Merry said she could never be too grateful to Dr. Bencomb for having made them promise not to go to Naples on account of the fever.

"But you must have three weeks to do India properly," her husband conceded, anxious to have it understood that he was no frivolous globe-trotter.

And at this point the ladies went up to the drawing-room.

In the library, in spite of weightier presences, Lawrence Lefferts predominated.

The talk, as usual, had veered around to the Beauforts, and even Mr. van der Luyden and Mr. Selfridge Merry, installed in the honorary arm-chairs tacitly reserved for them, paused to listen to the younger man's philippic.

Never had Lefferts so abounded in the sentiments that adorn Christian manhood and exalt the sanctity of the home. Indignation lent him a scathing eloquence, and it was clear that if others had followed his example, and acted as he talked, society would never have been weak enough to receive a foreign upstart like Beaufort—no, sir, not even if he'd married a van der Luyden or a Lanning instead of a Dallas. And what chance would there have been, Lefferts wrathfully questioned, of his marrying into such a family as the Dallases, if he had not already wormed his way into certain houses, as people like Mrs. Lemuel Struthers had managed to worm theirs in his wake? If society chose to open its doors to vulgar women the harm was not great, though the gain was doubtful; but once it got in the way of tolerating men of obscure origin and tainted wealth the end was total disintegration—and at no distant date.

"If things go on at this pace," Lefferts thundered, looking like a young prophet dressed by Poole, and who had not yet been stoned, "we shall see our children fighting for invitations to swindlers' houses, and marrying Beaufort's bastards."

"Oh, I say—draw it mild!" Reggie Chivers and young Newland protested, while Mr. Selfridge Merry looked genuinely alarmed, and an expression of pain and disgust settled on Mr. van der Luyden's sensitive face.

"Has he got any?" cried Mr. Sillerton Jackson, pricking up his ears; and while Lefferts tried to turn the question with a laugh, the old gentleman twittered into Archer's ear: "Queer, those fellows who are always wanting to set things right. The people who have the worst cooks are always telling you they're poisoned when they dine out. But I hear there are pressing reasons for our friend Lawrence's diatribe:—typewriter this time, I understand. . . ."

The talk swept past Archer like some senseless river running and running because it did not know enough to stop. He saw, on the faces about him, expressions of interest, amusement and even mirth. He listened to the younger men's laughter, and to the praise of the Archer Madeira, which Mr. van der Luyden and Mr. Merry were thoughtfully celebrating. Through it all he was dimly aware of a general attitude of friendliness toward himself, as if the guard of the prisoner he felt himself to be were trying to soften his captivity; and the perception increased his passionate determination to be free.

In the drawing-room, where they presently joined the ladies, he met May's triumphant eyes, and read in them the conviction that everything had "gone off" beautifully. She rose from Madame Olenska's side, and immediately Mrs. van der Luyden beckoned the latter to a seat on the gilt sofa where she throned. Mrs. Selfridge Merry bore across the room to join them, and it became clear to Archer that here also a conspiracy of rehabilitation and obliteration was going on. The silent organisation which held his little world together was determined to put itself on record as never for a moment having questioned the propriety of Madame Olenska's conduct, or the completeness of Archer's domestic felicity. All these amiable and inexorable persons were resolutely engaged in pretending to each other that they had never heard of, suspected, or even conceived possible, the least hint to the contrary; and from this tissue of elaborate mutual dissimulation Archer once more disengaged the fact that New York believed him to be Madame Olenska's lover. He caught the glitter of victory in his wife's eyes, and for the first time understood that she shared the belief. The discovery roused a laughter of inner devils that reverberated through all his efforts to discuss the Martha Washington ball with Mrs. Reggie Chivers and little Mrs. Newland; and so the evening swept on, running and running like a senseless river that did not know how to stop.

At length he saw that Madame Olenska had risen and was saying good-bye. He understood that in a moment she would be gone, and tried to remember what he had said to her at dinner; but he could not recall a single word they had exchanged.

She went up to May, the rest of the company making a circle about her as she advanced. The two young women clasped hands; then May bent forward and kissed her cousin.

"Certainly our hostess is much the handsomer of the two," Archer heard Reggie Chivers say in an undertone to young Mrs. Newland; and he remembered Beaufort's coarse sneer at May's ineffectual beauty.

A moment later he was in the hall, putting Madame Olenska's cloak about her shoulders.

Through all his confusion of mind he had held fast to the resolve to say nothing that might startle or disturb her. Convinced that no power could now turn him from his purpose he had found strength to let events shape themselves as they would. But as he followed Madame Olenska into the hall he thought with a sudden hunger of being for a moment alone with her at the door of her carriage.

"Is your carriage here?" he asked; and at that moment Mrs. van der Luyden, who was being majestically inserted into her sables, said gently: "We are driving dear Ellen home."

Archer's heart gave a jerk, and Madame Olenska, clasping her cloak and fan with one hand, held out the other to him. "Good-bye," she said.

"Good-bye—but I shall see you soon in Paris," he answered aloud—it seemed to him that he had shouted it.

"Oh," she murmured, "if you and May could come—!"

Mr. van der Luyden advanced to give her his arm, and Archer turned to Mrs. van der Luyden. For a moment, in the billowy darkness inside the big landau, he caught the dim oval of a face, eyes shining steadily—and she was gone.

As he went up the steps he crossed Lawrence Lefferts coming down with his wife. Lefferts caught his host by the sleeve, drawing back to let Gertrude pass.

"I say, old chap: do you mind just letting it be understood that I'm dining with you at the club tomorrow night? Thanks so much, you old brick! Good-night."

"It *did* go off beautifully, didn't it?" May questioned from the threshold of the library.

Archer roused himself with a start. As soon as the last carriage had driven away, he had come up to the library and shut himself in, with the hope that his wife, who still lingered below, would go straight to her room. But there she stood, pale and drawn, yet radiating the factitious energy of one who has passed beyond fatigue.

"May I come and talk it over?" she asked.

"Of course, if you like. But you must be awfully sleepy—"

"No, I'm not sleepy. I should like to sit with you a little."

"Very well," he said, pushing her chair near the fire.

She sat down and he resumed his seat; but neither spoke for a long time. At length Archer began abruptly: "Since you're not tired, and want to talk, there's something I must tell you. I tried to the other night—."

She looked at him quickly. "Yes, dear. Something about yourself?"

"About myself. You say you're not tired: well, I am. Horribly tired . . ."

In an instant she was all tender anxiety. "Oh, I've seen it coming on, Newland! You've been so wickedly overworked—"

"Perhaps it's that. Anyhow, I want to make a break—"

"A break? To give up the law?"

"To go away, at any rate—at once. On a long trip, ever so far off—away from everything—"

He paused, conscious that he had failed in his attempt to speak with the indifference of a man who longs for a change, and is yet too weary to welcome it. Do what he would, the chord of eagerness vibrated. "Away from everything—" he repeated.

"Ever so far? Where, for instance?" she asked.

"Oh, I don't know. India—or Japan."

She stood up, and as he sat with bent head, his chin propped on his hands, he felt her warmly and fragrantly hovering over him.

"As far as that? But I'm afraid you can't, dear . . ." she said in an unsteady voice. "Not unless you'll take me with you." And then, as he was silent, she went on, in tones so clear and evenly-pitched that each separate syllable tapped like a little hammer on his brain: "That is, if the doctors will let me go . . . but I'm afraid they won't. For you see, Newland, I've been sure since this morning of something I've been so longing and hoping for—"

He looked up at her with a sick stare, and she sank down, all dew and roses, and hid her face against his knee.

"Oh, my dear," he said, holding her to him while his cold hand stroked her hair.

There was a long pause, which the inner devils filled with strident laughter; then May freed herself from his arms and stood up.

"You didn't guess—?"

"Yes—I; no. That is, of course I hoped—"

They looked at each other for an instant and again fell silent; then, turning his eyes from hers, he asked abruptly: "Have you told any one else?"

"Only Mamma and your mother." She paused, and then added hurriedly, the blood flushing up to her forehead: "That is—and Ellen. You know I told you we'd had a long talk one afternoon—and how dear she was to me."

"Ah—" said Archer, his heart stopping.

He felt that his wife was watching him intently. "Did you *mind* my telling her first, Newland?"

"Mind? Why should I?" He made a last effort to collect himself. "But that was a fortnight ago, wasn't it? I thought you said you weren't sure till today."

Her colour burned deeper, but she held his gaze. "No; I wasn't sure then—but I told her I was. And you see I was right!" she exclaimed, her blue eyes wet with victory.

Newland Archer sat at the writing-table in his library in East Thirty-ninth Street.

He had just got back from a big official reception for the inauguration of the new galleries at the Metropolitan Museum, and the spectacle of those great spaces crowded with the spoils of the ages, where the throng of fashion circulated through a series of scientifically catalogued treasures, had suddenly pressed on a rusted spring of memory.

"Why, this used to be one of the old Cesnola rooms," he heard some one say; and instantly everything about him vanished, and he was sitting alone on a hard leather divan against a radiator, while a slight figure in a long sealskin cloak moved away down the meagrely-fitted vista of the old Museum.

The vision had roused a host of other associations, and he sat looking with new eyes at the library which, for over thirty years, had been the scene of his solitary musings and of all the family confabulations.

It was the room in which most of the real things of his life had happened. There his wife, nearly twenty-six years ago, had broken to him, with a blushing circumlocution that would have caused the young women of the new generation to smile, the news that she was to have a child; and there their eldest boy, Dallas, too delicate to be taken to church in midwinter, had been christened by their old friend the Bishop of New York, the ample magnificent irreplaceable Bishop, so long the pride and ornament of his diocese. There Dallas had first staggered across the floor shouting "Dad," while May and the nurse laughed behind the door; there their second child, Mary (who was so like her mother), had announced her engagement to the dullest and most reliable of Reggie Chivers's many sons; and there Archer had kissed her through her wedding veil before they went down to the motor which was to carry them to Grace Church—for in a world where all else had reeled on its foundations the "Grace Church wedding" remained an unchanged institution.

It was in the library that he and May had always discussed the future of the children: the studies of Dallas and his young brother Bill, Mary's incurable indifference to "accomplishments," and passion for sport and philanthropy, and the vague leanings toward "art" which had finally landed the restless and curious Dallas in the office of a rising New York architect.

The young men nowadays were emancipating themselves from the law and business and taking up all sorts of new things. If they were not absorbed in state politics or municipal reform, the chances were that they were going in for Central American archæology, for architecture or landscape-engineering; taking a keen and learned interest in the prerevolutionary buildings of their own country, studying and adapting Georgian types, and protesting at the meaningless use of the word "Colonial." Nobody nowadays had "Colonial" houses except the millionaire grocers of the suburbs.

But above all—sometimes Archer put it above all—it was in that library that the Governor of New York, coming down from Albany one evening to dine and spend the night, had turned to his host, and said, banging his clenched fist on the table and gnashing his eye-glasses: "Hang the professional politician! You're the kind of man the country wants, Archer. If the stable's ever to be cleaned out, men like you have got to lend a hand in the cleaning."

"Men like you—" how Archer had glowed at the phrase! How eagerly he had risen up at the call! It was an echo of Ned Winsett's old appeal to roll his sleeves up and get down into the muck; but spoken by a man who set the example of the gesture, and whose summons to follow him was irresistible.

Archer, as he looked back, was not sure that men like himself *were* what his country needed, at least in the active service to which Theodore Roosevelt had pointed; in fact, there was reason to think it did not, for after a year in the State Assembly he had not been re-elected, and had dropped back thankfully into obscure if useful municipal work, and from that again to the writ-

ing of occasional articles in one of the reforming weeklies that
were trying to shake the country out of its apathy. It was little
enough to look back on; but when he remembered to what the
young men of his generation and his set had looked forward—
the narrow groove of money-making, sport and society to which
their vision had been limited—even his small contribution to the
new state of things seemed to count, as each brick counts in a
well-built wall. He had done little in public life; he would always
be by nature a contemplative and a dilettante; but he had had
high things to contemplate, great things to delight in; and one
great man's friendship to be his strength and pride.

He had been, in short, what people were beginning to call "a
good citizen." In New York, for many years past, every new
movement, philanthropic, municipal or artistic, had taken account of his opinion and wanted his name. People said: "Ask
Archer" when there was a question of starting the first school
for crippled children, reorganising the Museum of Art, founding
the Grolier Club, inaugurating the new Library, or getting up a
new society of chamber music. His days were full, and they were
filled decently. He supposed it was all a man ought to ask.

Something he knew he had missed: the flower of life. But he
thought of it now as a thing so unattainable and improbable that
to have repined would have been like despairing because one
had not drawn the first prize in a lottery. There were a hundred
million tickets in *his* lottery, and there was only one prize; the
chances had been too decidedly against him. When he thought
of Ellen Olenska it was abstractly, serenely, as one might think
of some imaginary beloved in a book or a picture: she had become the composite vision of all that he had missed. That vision,
faint and tenuous as it was, had kept him from thinking of other
women. He had been what was called a faithful husband; and
when May had suddenly died—carried off by the infectious
pneumonia through which she had nursed their youngest child
—he had honestly mourned her. Their long years together had
shown him that it did not so much matter if marriage was a dull
duty, as long as it kept the dignity of a duty: lapsing from that,
it became a mere battle of ugly appetites. Looking about him,

he honoured his own past, and mourned for it. After all, there was good in the old ways.

His eyes, making the round of the room—done over by Dallas with English mezzotints, Chippendale cabinets, bits of chosen blue-and-white and pleasantly shaded electric lamps—came back to the old Eastlake writing-table that he had never been willing to banish, and to his first photograph of May, which still kept its place beside his inkstand.

There she was, tall, round-bosomed and willowy, in her starched muslin and flapping Leghorn, as he had seen her under the orange-trees in the Mission garden. And as he had seen her that day, so she had remained; never quite at the same height, yet never far below it: generous, faithful, unwearied; but so lacking in imagination, so incapable of growth, that the world of her youth had fallen into pieces and rebuilt itself without her ever being conscious of the change. This hard bright blindness had kept her immediate horizon apparently unaltered. Her incapacity to recognise change made her children conceal their views from her as Archer concealed his; there had been, from the first, a joint pretence of sameness, a kind of innocent family hypocrisy, in which father and children had unconsciously collaborated. And she had died thinking the world a good place, full of loving and harmonious households like her own, and resigned to leave it because she was convinced that, whatever happened, Newland would continue to inculcate in Dallas the same principles and prejudices which had shaped his parents' lives, and that Dallas in turn (when Newland followed her) would transmit the sacred trust to little Bill. And of Mary she was sure as of her own self. So, having snatched little Bill from the grave, and given her life in the effort, she went contentedly to her place in the Archer vault in St. Mark's, where Mrs. Archer already lay safe from the terrifying "trend" which her daughter-in-law had never even become aware of.

Opposite May's portrait stood one of her daughter. Mary Chivers was as tall and fair as her mother, but large-waisted, flat-chested and slightly slouching, as the altered fashion required. Mary Chivers's mighty feats of athleticism could not have been performed with the twenty-inch waist that May Archer's azure sash so easily spanned. And the difference seemed symbolic; the mother's life had been as closely girt as her figure. Mary, who was no less conventional, and no more intelligent, yet led a larger life and held more tolerant views. There was good in the new order too.

The telephone clicked, and Archer, turning from the photographs, unhooked the transmitter at his elbow. How far they were from the days when the legs of the brass-buttoned messenger boy had been New York's only means of quick communication!

"Chicago wants you."

Ah—it must be a long-distance from Dallas, who had been sent to Chicago by his firm to talk over the plan of the Lakeside palace they were to build for a young millionaire with ideas. The firm always sent Dallas on such errands.

"Hallo, Dad—Yes: Dallas. I say—how do you feel about sailing on Wednesday? Mauretania: Yes, next Wednesday as ever is. Our client wants me to look at some Italian gardens before we settle anything, and has asked me to nip over on the next boat. I've got to be back on the first of June—" the voice broke into a joyful conscious laugh—"so we must look alive. I say, Dad, I want your help: do come."

Dallas seemed to be speaking in the room: the voice was as near by and natural as if he had been lounging in his favourite arm-chair by the fire. The fact would not ordinarily have surprised Archer, for long-distance telephoning had become as much a matter of course as electric lighting and five-day Atlantic voyages. But the laugh did startle him; it still seemed wonderful that across all those miles and miles of country—forest, river, mountain, prairie, roaring cities and busy indifferent millions— Dallas's laugh should be able to say: "Of course, whatever happens, I must get back on the first, because Fanny Beaufort and I are to be married on the fifth."

The voice began again: "Think it over? No, sir: not a minute. You've got to say yes now. Why not, I'd like to know? If you can allege a single reason—No; I knew it. Then it's a go, eh? Because I count on you to ring up the Cunard office first thing tomorrow; and you'd better book a return on a boat from Marseilles. I say, Dad; it'll be our last time together, in this kind of way—. Oh, good! I knew you would."

Chicago rang off, and Archer rose and began to pace up and down the room.

It would be their last time together in this kind of way: the boy was right. They would have lots of other "times" after Dallas's marriage, his father was sure; for the two were born comrades, and Fanny Beaufort, whatever one might think of her, did not seem likely to interfere with their intimacy. On the contrary, from what he had seen of her, he thought she would be naturally included in it. Still, change was change, and differences were differences, and much as he felt himself drawn toward his future daughter-in-law, it was tempting to seize this last chance of being alone with his boy.

There was no reason why he should not seize it, except the profound one that he had lost the habit of travel. May had disliked to move except for valid reasons, such as taking the children to the sea or in the mountains: she could imagine no other motive for leaving the house in Thirty-ninth Street or their comfortable quarters at the Wellands' in Newport. After Dallas had taken his degree she had thought it her duty to travel for six months; and the whole family had made the old-fashioned tour through England, Switzerland and Italy. Their time being limited (no one knew why) they had omitted France. Archer remembered Dallas's wrath at being asked to contemplate Mont Blanc instead of Rheims and Chartres. But Mary and Bill wanted mountain-climbing, and had already yawned their way in Dallas's wake through the English cathedrals; and May, always fair to her children, had insisted on holding the balance evenly between their athletic and artistic proclivities. She had indeed proposed that her husband should go to Paris for a fortnight, and join them on the Italian lakes after they had "done" Switzerland; but Archer had declined. "We'll stick together," he said; and May's face had brightened at his setting such a good example to Dallas.

Since her death, nearly two years before, there had been no reason for his continuing in the same routine. His children had urged him to travel: Mary Chivers had felt sure it would do him good to go abroad and "see the galleries." The very mysteriousness of such a cure made her the more confident of its efficacy. But Archer had found himself held fast by habit, by memories, by a sudden startled shrinking from new things.

Now, as he reviewed his past, he saw into what a deep rut he had sunk. The worst of doing one's duty was that it apparently unfitted one for doing anything else. At least that was the view that the men of his generation had taken. The trenchant divisions between right and wrong, honest and dishonest, respectable and the reverse, had left so little scope for the unforeseen. There are moments when a man's imagination, so easily subdued to what it lives in, suddenly rises above its daily level, and surveys the long windings of destiny. Archer hung there and wondered. . . .

What was left of the little world he had grown up in, and whose standards had bent and bound him? He remembered a sneering prophecy of poor Lawrence Lefferts's, uttered years ago in that very room: "If things go on at this rate, our children will be marrying Beaufort's bastards."

It was just what Archer's eldest son, the pride of his life, was doing; and nobody wondered or reproved. Even the boy's Aunt Janey, who still looked so exactly as she used to in her elderly youth, had taken her mother's emeralds and seed-pearls out of their pink cotton-wool, and carried them with her own twitching hands to the future bride; and Fanny Beaufort, instead of looking disappointed at not receiving a "set" from a Paris jeweller, had exclaimed at their old-fashioned beauty, and declared that when she wore them she should feel like an Isabey miniature.

Fanny Beaufort, who had appeared in New York at eighteen, after the death of her parents, had won its heart much as Madame Olenska had won it thirty years earlier; only instead of being distrustful and afraid of her, society took her joyfully for granted. She was pretty, amusing and accomplished: what more did any one want? Nobody was narrow-minded enough to rake up against her the half-forgotten facts of her father's past and her own origin. Only the older people remembered so obscure an incident in the business life of New York as Beaufort's failure, or the fact that after his wife's death he had been quietly married to the notorious Fanny Ring, and had left the country with his new wife, and a little girl who inherited her beauty. He was subsequently heard of in Constantinople, then in Russia; and a dozen years later American travellers were handsomely entertained by him in Buenos Ayres, where he represented a large insurance agency. He and his wife died there in the odour of prosperity; and one day their orphaned daughter had appeared in New York in charge of May Archer's sister-in-law, Mrs. Jack Welland, whose husband had been appointed the girl's guardian. The fact threw her into almost cousinly relationship with Newland Archer's children, and nobody was surprised when Dallas's engagement was announced.

Nothing could more clearly give the measure of the distance that the world had travelled. People nowadays were too busy—busy with reforms and "movements," with fads and fetishes and frivolities—to bother much about their neighbours. And of what account was anybody's past, in the huge kaleidoscope where all the social atoms spun around on the same plane?

Newland Archer, looking out of his hotel window at the stately gaiety of the Paris streets, felt his heart beating with the confusion and eagerness of youth.

It was long since it had thus plunged and reared under his widening waistcoat, leaving him, the next minute, with an empty breast and hot temples. He wondered if it was thus that his son's conducted itself in the presence of Miss Fanny Beaufort—and decided that it was not. "It functions as actively, no doubt, but the rhythm is different," he reflected, recalling the cool composure with which the young man had announced his engagement, and taken for granted that his family would approve.

"The difference is that these young people take it for granted that they're going to get whatever they want, and that we almost always took it for granted that we shouldn't. Only, I wonder—the thing one's so certain of in advance: can it ever make one's heart beat as wildly?"

It was the day after their arrival in Paris, and the spring sunshine held Archer in his open window, above the wide silvery prospect of the Place Vendôme. One of the things he had stipulated—almost the only one—when he had agreed to come abroad with Dallas, was that, in Paris, he shouldn't be made to go to one of the new-fangled "palaces."

"Oh, all right—of course," Dallas good-naturedly agreed. "I'll take you to some jolly old-fashioned place—the Bristol say—" leaving his father speechless at hearing that the century-long home of kings and emperors was now spoken of as an old-fashioned inn, where one went for its quaint inconveniences and lingering local colour.

Archer had pictured often enough, in the first impatient years, the scene of his return to Paris; then the personal vision had faded, and he had simply tried to see the city as the setting of Madame Olenska's life. Sitting alone at night in his library, after the household had gone to bed, he had evoked the radiant outbreak of spring down the avenues of horse-chestnuts, the flowers and statues in the public gardens, the whiff of lilacs from the flower-carts, the majestic roll of the river under the great bridges, and the life of art and study and pleasure that filled each mighty artery to bursting. Now the spectacle was before him in its glory, and as he looked out on it he felt shy, old-fashioned, inadequate: a mere grey speck of a man compared with the ruthless magnificent fellow he had dreamed of being. . . .

Dallas's hand came down cheerily on his shoulder. "Hullo, father: this is something like, isn't it?" They stood for a while looking out in silence, and then the young man continued: "By the way, I've got a message for you: the Countess Olenska expects us both at half-past five."

He said it lightly, carelessly, as he might have imparted any casual item of information, such as the hour at which their train was to leave for Florence the next evening. Archer looked at him, and thought he saw in his gay young eyes a gleam of his great-grandmother Mingott's malice.

"Oh, didn't I tell you?" Dallas pursued. "Fanny made me swear to do three things while I was in Paris: get her the score of the last Debussy songs, go to the Grand-Guignol and see Madame Olenska. You know she was awfully good to Fanny when Mr. Beaufort sent her over from Buenos Ayres to the Assomption. Fanny hadn't any friends in Paris, and Madame Olen-

THE AGE OF INNOCENCE 293

ska used to be kind to her and trot her about on holidays. I believe she was a great friend of the first Mrs. Beaufort's. And she's our cousin, of course. So I rang her up this morning, before I went out, and told her you and I were here for two days and wanted to see her."

Archer continued to stare at him. "You told her I was here?"

"Of course—why not?" Dallas's eye brows went up whimsically. Then, getting no answer, he slipped his arm through his father's with a confidential pressure.

"I say, father: what was she like?"

Archer felt his colour rise under his son's unabashed gaze. "Come, own up: you and she were great pals, weren't you? Wasn't she most awfully lovely?"

"Lovely? I don't know. She was different."

"Ah—there you have it! That's what it always comes to, doesn't it? When she comes, *she's different*—and one doesn't know why. It's exactly what I feel about Fanny."

His father drew back a step, releasing his arm. "About Fanny? But, my dear fellow—I should hope so! Only I don't see—"

"Dash it, Dad, don't be prehistoric! Wasn't she—once—your Fanny?"

Dallas belonged body and soul to the new generation. He was the first-born of Newland and May Archer, yet it had never been possible to inculcate in him even the rudiments of reserve. "What's the use of making mysteries? It only makes people want to nose 'em out," he always objected when enjoined to discretion. But Archer, meeting his eyes, saw the filial light under their banter.

"My Fanny—?"

"Well, the woman you'd have chucked everything for: only you didn't," continued his surprising son.

"I didn't," echoed Archer with a kind of solemnity.

"No: you date, you see, dear old boy. But mother said—"

"Your mother?"

"Yes: the day before she died. It was when she sent for me alone—you remember? She said she knew we were safe with you, and always would be, because once, when she asked you to, you'd given up the thing you most wanted."

Archer received this strange communication in silence. His eyes remained unseeingly fixed on the thronged sunlit square below the window. At length he said in a low voice: "She never asked me."

"No. I forgot. You never did ask each other anything, did you? And you never told each other anything. You just sat and watched each other, and guessed at what was going on underneath. A deaf-and-dumb asylum, in fact! Well, I back your generation for knowing more about each other's private thoughts than we ever have time to find out about our own.—I say, Dad," Dallas broke off, "you're not angry with me? If you are, let's make it up and go and lunch at Henri's. I've got to rush out to Versailles afterward."

Archer did not accompany his son to Versailles. He preferred to spend the afternoon in solitary roamings through Paris. He had to deal all at once with the packed regrets and stifled memories of an inarticulate lifetime.

After a little while he did not regret Dallas's indiscretion. It seemed to take an iron band from his heart to know that, after all, some one had guessed and pitied. . . . And that it should have been his wife moved him indescribably. Dallas, for all his affectionate insight, would not have understood that. To the boy, no doubt, the episode was only a pathetic instance of vain frustration, of wasted forces. But was it really no more? For a long time Archer sat on a bench in the Champs Elysées and wondered, while the stream of life rolled by. . . .

A few streets away, a few hours away, Ellen Olenska waited. She had never gone back to her husband, and when he had died, some years before, she had made no change in her way of living. There was nothing now to keep her and Archer apart—and that afternoon he was to see her.

He got up and walked across the Place de la Concorde and the Tuileries gardens to the Louvre. She had once told him that she often went there, and he had a fancy to spend the intervening time in a place where he could think of her as perhaps having lately been. For an hour or more he wandered from gallery to gallery through the dazzle of afternoon light, and one by one

the pictures burst on him in their half-forgotten splendour, filling his soul with the long echoes of beauty. After all, his life had
been too starved. . . .

Suddenly, before an effulgent Titian, he found himself saying:
"But I'm only fifty-seven—" and then he turned away. For such
summer dreams it was too late; but surely not for a quiet har-
vest of friendship, of comradeship, in the blessed hush of her
nearness.

He went back to the hotel, where he and Dallas were to meet;
and together they walked again across the Place de la Concorde
and over the bridge that leads to the Chamber of Deputies.

Dallas, unconscious of what was going on in his father's mind,
was talking excitedly and abundantly of Versailles. He had had
but one previous glimpse of it, during a holiday trip in which
he had tried to pack all the sights he had been deprived of when
he had had to go with the family to Switzerland; and tumultuous
enthusiasm and cock-sure criticism tripped each other up on his
lips.

As Archer listened, his sense of inadequacy and inexpres-
siveness increased. The boy was not insensitive, he knew; but he
had the facility and self-confidence that came of looking at fate
not as a master but as an equal. "That's it: they feel equal to
things—they know their way about," he mused, thinking of his
son as the spokesman of the new generation which had swept
away all the old landmarks, and with them the sign-posts and
the danger-signal.

Suddenly Dallas stopped short, grasping his father's arm.
"Oh, by Jove," he exclaimed.

They had come out into the great tree-planted space before
the Invalides. The dome of Mansart floated ethereally above the
budding trees and the long grey front of the building: drawing
up into itself all the rays of afternoon light, it hung there like
the visible symbol of the race's glory.

Archer knew that Madame Olenska lived in a square near one
of the avenues radiating from the Invalides; and he had pictured
the quarter as quiet and almost obscure, forgetting the central
splendour that lit it up. Now, by some queer process of association, that golden light became for him the pervading illumi-

nation in which she lived. For nearly thirty years, her life—of which he knew so strangely little—had been spent in this rich atmosphere that he already felt to be too dense and yet too stimulating for his lungs. He thought of the theatres she must have been to, the pictures she must have looked at, the sober and splendid old houses she must have frequented, the people she must have talked with, the incessant stir of ideas, curiosities, images and associations thrown out by an intensely social race in a setting of immemorial manners; and suddenly he remembered the young Frenchman who had once said to him: "Ah, good conversation—there is nothing like it, is there?"

Archer had not seen M. Rivière, or heard of him, for nearly thirty years; and that fact gave the measure of his ignorance of Madame Olenska's existence. More than half a lifetime divided them, and she had spent the long interval among people he did not know, in a society he but faintly guessed at, in conditions he would never wholly understand. During that time he had been living with his youthful memory of her; but she had doubtless had other and more tangible companionship. Perhaps she too had kept her memory of him as something apart; but if she had, it must have been like a relic in a small dim chapel, where there was not time to pray every day. . . .

They had crossed the Place des Invalides, and were walking down one of the thoroughfares flanking the building. It was a quiet quarter, after all, in spite of its splendour and its history; and the fact gave one an idea of the riches Paris had to draw on, since such scenes as this were left to the few and the indifferent.

The day was fading into a soft sun-shot haze, pricked here and there by a yellow electric light, and passers were rare in the little square into which they had turned. Dallas stopped again, and looked up.

"It must be here," he said, slipping his arm through his father's with a movement from which Archer's shyness did not shrink; and they stood together looking up at the house.

It was a modern building, without distinctive character, but many-windowed, and pleasantly balconied up its wide cream-coloured front. On one of the upper balconies, which hung well above the rounded tops of the horse-chestnuts in the square, the awnings were still lowered, as though the sun had just left it.

"I wonder which floor—?" Dallas conjectured; and moving toward the *porte-cochère* he put his head into the porter's lodge, and came back to say: "The fifth. It must be the one with the awnings."

Archer remained motionless, gazing at the upper windows as if the end of their pilgrimage had been attained.

"I say, you know, it's nearly six," his son at length reminded him.

The father glanced away at an empty bench under the trees.

"I believe I'll sit there a moment," he said.

"Why—aren't you well?" his son exclaimed.

"Oh, perfectly. But I should like you, please, to go up without me."

Dallas paused before him, visibly bewildered. "But, I say, Dad: do you mean you won't come up at all?"

"I don't know," said Archer slowly.

"If you don't she won't understand."

"Go, my boy; perhaps I shall follow you."

Dallas gave him a long look through the twilight.

"But what on earth shall I say?"

"My dear fellow, don't you always know what to say?" his father rejoined with a smile.

"Very well. I shall say you're old-fashioned, and prefer walking up the five flights because you don't like lifts."

His father smiled again. "Say I'm old-fashioned: that's enough."

Dallas looked at him again, and then, with an incredulous gesture, passed out of sight under the vaulted doorway.

Archer sat down on the bench and continued to gaze at the awninged balcony. He calculated the time it would take his son to be carried up in the lift to the fifth floor, to ring the bell, and be admitted to the hall, and then ushered into the drawing-room. He pictured Dallas entering that room with his quick assured step and his delightful smile, and wondered if the people were right who said that his boy "took after him."

Then he tried to see the persons already in the room—for probably at that sociable hour there would be more than one—

and among them a dark lady, pale and dark, who would look up quickly, half rise, and hold out a long thin hand with three rings on it. . . . . He thought she would be sitting in a sofa-corner near the fire, with azaleas banked behind her on a table.

"It's more real to me here than if I went up," he suddenly heard himself say; and the fear lest that last shadow of reality should lose its edge kept him rooted to his seat as the minutes succeeded each other.

He sat for a long time on the bench in the thickening dusk, his eyes never turning from the balcony. At length a light shone through the windows, and a moment later a man-servant came out on the balcony, drew up the awnings, and closed the shutters.

At that, as if it had been the signal he waited for, Newland Archer got up slowly and walked back alone to his hotel.

EXPLANATORY NOTES

A true appreciation of *The Age of Innocence* depends on an understanding of Wharton's subtle methods of intermingling the characterization of individuals, the delineation of each individual's position in society, and the dramatization of conflicts, such as that between tradition and experimentation. In this novel, Wharton presents three main levels of Old New York society. The van der Luydens represent the most ancient level, composed of well-established families of Dutch ancestry. Although they occupy the most powerful rung on the social ladder, their era seems to be nearly over. The next rung belongs to families of Dutch-Yankee heritage, such as the Mingotts, the Wellands, and the Archers. The newest arrivals, quickly moving up the ladder, are represented by characters such as Beaufort and Mrs. Struthers. The specifics of a family's home—its location, the nature of its decoration, and the literature and art that its members prefer—help identify a character's position in a world that is beginning to change.

Although some of the following notes merely explain terms unfamiliar to the modern reader, many call attention to the way in which a particular term contributes to a theme that runs throughout the novel. Wharton refers to actual performances, theaters, and actors not only to create a detailed setting but also to amplify the implications of her own narrative. In addition to references to the private home and public theater are those that define the individual's relationship to society. Wharton makes an analogy between the fashionable world of Old New York and ancient tribes in order to emphasize the benefits and limitations common to both types of communal body: in each, the individual must sacrifice a certain amount of freedom in order to enjoy the group's protection and security. As Wharton describes a character's involvement in military service and political or civic activities, she asks us to consider the responsibilities of citizens to contribute to the growth and rectitude of their community. Such references reveal Wharton's concern in this novel with the nature of change over time, with evolution, and with an examination of the processes that contribute to survival or lead to extinction.

BOOK ONE

CHAPTER 1

page

3 [Christine Nilsson] A Swedish soprano (1843–1921) who debuted as Marguerite in Charles Gounod's *Faust* at the Academy of Music on November 1, 1871.

3 [Faust] Charles Gounod's opera in five acts (1859), based on the familiar legend. Like Faust, Newland Archer will be tempted to sacrifice something of inestimable value based on reality for a fleeting passion that is a product of his imagination.

3 [Academy of Music in New York] Theater located on Fourteenth Street, in Union Square. It opened in 1854 and held regular opera seasons until 1886. It had a seating capacity of 4,600, but the boxes were monopolized by families belonging to the old-line aristocracy, the descendants of the Dutch and early English settlers.

3 [a new Opera House] The Metropolitan, which opened on October 22, 1883, on a site bounded by Broadway, Thirty-ninth Street, Seventh Avenue, and Fortieth Street.

3 ["new people"] Those such as Jay Gould, J. P. Morgan, Cornelius Vanderbilt, and William Rockefeller, who made their fortunes in finance or industry. They were considered "new" to the descendants of the first settlers, who lived near Washington Square, the area first inhabited by wealthy New Yorkers. The "new people" welcomed the Metropolitan Opera House, which provided them with a theater in which they did not have to compete with the old-line aristocracy for boxes.

3 [broughams] Closed, four-wheeled carriages pulled by a single horse.

3 [landau] An elegant four-wheeled carriage pulled by a pair of horses. It had two large folding hoods that could be raised to form a covered compartment.

3 ["Brown *coupé*"] The coupe is another variation on the four-wheeled horse-drawn carriage. Isaac Brown, the sexton of Grace Church, which all of fashionable New York attended, provided a fleet of coaches that would carry his clients home from evening entertainments, such as the opera or private parties.

4 [finial-topped chairs] A finial is a decorative knob, often in the form of an acorn or urn, that is applied to furniture.

4 [*M'ama . . . non m'ama*] Italian: "He loves me . . . he loves me

not." Marguerite sings this song and plucks the petals from a daisy as Faust tries to seduce her. Nineteenth-century books on the language of flowers associate the daisy with beauty and innocence.

4 [Faust-Capoul] Victor Capoul played Faust to Christine Nilsson's Marguerite in the 1871 production.

5 [tulle tucker] Tulle is a fine netlike fabric; the tucker is a piece of fabric that fashionable women in New York wore to make the low-cut necklines of their European dresses more modest.

5 [lilies-of-the-valley] Small bell-shaped white flowers. According to nineteenth-century books on the language of flowers, lilies-of-the-valley are associated with delicate simplicity, a return of happiness, or a heart that is withering in secret. While Newland would probably associate May's flowers only with the delicate simplicity he sees in her, Wharton would have been familiar with all these associations. Newland is not only blind to all but one side of May and the flowers that he associates with her, but also to the "withering" of her heart as a result of his desire for Ellen. Throughout the novel, May is associated with flowers that suggest purity; in contrast, Ellen is associated with more exotic flowers.

5 [Luther Burbank's far-off prodigies] Luther Burbank (1849–1926), an American horticulturist who created many new varieties of flowers by cross-breeding. Wharton, a serious gardener who would have been familiar with Burbank's hybrids, refers to such experiments in breeding as her first example of the process of change over time; in so doing, she suggests the theme of evolution.

5 [muslin chemisette] Muslin is a plain-woven fabric that was often used in the nineteenth century for undergarments; a chemisette is an underbodice that was often worn with a jumper-style dress to cover the arms and neck.

6 [Lohengrin] A three-act opera by Richard Wagner (1813–1883) that includes the traditional wedding march.

7 ["Josephine look"] A reference to a style of dress associated with Josephine, empress of France from 1804 until 1809, when Emperor Napoleon divorced her. The "unusual dress" that Ellen Olenska is wearing could have been in the style of one of the negligéelike dresses worn by women in France after the French Revolution (1789–1795) and popular throughout the early 1800s, or one more particularly associated with Josephine, a gown with a long heavy train but a filmy underdress. The negligée-style dress, characterized by its low neckline, broke with the tradition of constraining clothing. Such a dress would have caught people's attention in 1870s

New York, during a time when most women were wearing uncomfortable bustles and corsets.

CHAPTER 2

11 [brown sandstone] The regular building material used in New York City in the middle of the nineteenth century. The stone, which is pink when first cut and turns brown as it weathers, was mined from quarries close to New York, in Portland, Connecticut, and Little Falls, New Jersey. The availability of the material and the development of technology, such as the steam cutting processes, explain brownstone's popularity at the time. Only the very wealthy, however, could afford houses built completely of brownstone; others settled for "brownstone fronts," brick houses with a thin veneer of the fashionable material.

11 [frock-coat] A double-breasted coat with long skirts of equal length in front and back; during the nineteenth century, it was considered standard afternoon attire for males.

11 [Central Park] Park that runs two and a half miles north and south, from Fifty-ninth Street to One Hundred Tenth Street, and one-half mile east and west, from Fifth Avenue to Central Park West. It was opened to the public soon after the Civil War. Development of New York City moved north from Washington Square, near Eighth Street; therefore, Fifty-ninth Street, in the early and middle 1800s, was, not surprisingly, considered a "wilderness."

11 [pre-Revolutionary furniture] Dates from the period, before the French Revolution, during which Louis XVI reigned.

11 [Tuileries of Louis Napoleon] Gardens in Paris along the right bank of the Seine from the Louvre to the Place de la Concorde. Louis-Napoléon (Napoléon III), the son of Napoléon Bonaparte's brother, ruled France during the period known as the Second Empire (1852–1871).

11 [Thirty-fourth Street] During the 1840s and 1850s, the Second Avenue area of the street was very fashionable; by the 1860s, the fashionable section had shifted west to Fifth Avenue. After the Civil War, Thirty-fourth Street became the home of many of the wealthiest New Yorkers, including A. T. Stewart, who built his mansion at the corner of this street and Fifth Avenue.

11 [Imperial namesake] Catherine the Great, Empress of Russia from 1762 to 1796.

11 [Mme. Taglioni] Marie Taglioni (1804–1884), one of the most famous ballerinas of the 1830s and 1840s.

12 [*chef*] As Wharton indicates in Chapter V, whether a family invests in a chef depends on the values of its members. In general, families such as the Mansons and Mingotts are said to care for "eating and clothes and money"; therefore, Mrs. Mingott's son feels he must compensate for his mother's unusual decision not to have a chef.

13 [Mephistopheles-and-Martha scenes] During the third act of *Faust*. Martha is Marguerite's guardian; Mephistopheles attempts to seduce her in order to give Faust the chance to speak to Marguerite.

13 ["*double entendre*"] French: a phrase that has two different senses, with one of them being somewhat indelicate.

14 [fan of eagle feathers] Feathers were so often used during the nineteenth century for fashionable items such as fans and hats that by 1883 approximately five million birds were killed each year to meet the demand; that the eagle is the national bird of the United States and was being hunted to near extinction suggests that Wharton is making a comment on the price paid for fashion.

15 [knickerbockers and pantalettes] Knickerbockers are knee breeches worn by boys and pantalettes are leg coverings of lace and ruffles that extend below the hems of girls' dresses.

CHAPTER 3

16 ["crash"] Coarse linen cloth.

16 ["*droit de cité*"] A French phrase that refers to the pleasure associated with membership in a society, particularly the privilege of holding the rights one is entitled to as a member.

17 [gloxinias] Bell-shaped flowers that range in color from purple to white.

17 [Kew] Kew Gardens (Royal Botanical Gardens), located near London; one of the major botanical gardens in the world.

18 [Veuve Clicquot] Champagne produced by the firm of Veuve-Clicquot-Ponsardin in Reims, France.

18 [the Jewel Song] Air sung by Marguerite in the middle of Act III of *Faust*.

18 [*coiffées*] French: refers to hairdressing, from the verb *coiffer* (to do somebody's hair); the women who arrive at Beaufort's balls are not given the opportunity to rearrange their hair once they arrive.

18 [*bouton d'or*] French: buttercup, or king-cup, a flower associated with riches; reference to the yellow-gold color scheme.

18 [camellias] Roselike flowers that are usually white, pink, or red; nineteenth-century books on the language of flowers state that they are associated with unpretending excellence.

18 [Buhl and malachite] Buhl refers to a style of inlaying contrasting wood or brass into a background of veneer, wood, or tortoiseshell. The style was employed by André-Charles Boulle (1642–1732), a French cabinetmaker, and has come to be known in English as Buhl. Malachite is a bright copper-green stone with black veins.

19 ["Love Victorious," the much-discussed nude of Bouguereau] Adolphe-William Bouguereau (1825–1905), a French painter who won the Prix de Rome in 1850, was well known for his nudes.

19 [aigrettes] Feathers or plumes from the egret, a kind of heron.

19 [glacé gloves] Gloves with a glossy surface.

CHAPTER 4

22 [University Place and lower Fifth Avenue] University Place runs parallel to Fifth Avenue, north from Washington Square. "Lower Fifth Avenue" refers to the southern tip of the street, its oldest section; residential New York City, beginning in 1850, grew northward from this area.

22 [Second Empire] The period from 1852 to 1871 when France was under the rule of Napoléon III; during this time the country was a leader in the arts.

22 [immense accretion of flesh . . . like a flood of lava on a doomed city] The first of Wharton's references to Pompeii, an ancient city in Italy that was destroyed by the eruption of Mount Vesuvius in 79 A.D. Here Wharton associates Mrs. Mingott with this city frozen in time; later she associates Newland with the city.

23 [damask portière] Damask is a heavy, patterned fabric often used for draperies or upholstery; a portiere is a curtain made to hang over a door.

23 ["Monsieur de Camors"] Novel (1867) by the popular French author and playwright Octave Feuillet (1821–1890). Newland sees Mrs. Mingott's bedroom as the kind that would provide the perfect setting for the secret rendezvous of Louis de Camors and the wife of General de Campvallon, Camors's benefactor; Archer is fully aware, however, that no such affairs have taken place in Mrs. Mingott's house despite its unconventional design.

25 [Madison Square] Area in New York City just north of the intersection of Fifth Avenue and Broadway; it runs from Twenty-third

Street north to Twenty-sixth Street. Whereas Washington Square was the home for the old-line aristocracy, Madison Square was the home for the nouveaux riches.

26 [Fifth Avenue] One of the most fashionable streets in New York; it became known as a "street of palaces" during the 1850s and as Millionaires' Row in the 1890s.

CHAPTER 5

27 [canvas-back] A kind of wild North American duck.

27 [terrapin] An edible North American turtle.

27 ["The Marble Faun"] A romance written by Nathaniel Hawthorne (1804–1864) and published in 1860.

27 [Madeira] A white wine produced on the island of Madeira, about 400 miles northwest of the coast of Africa. Having "gone round the Cape" is a reference to the good quality of the wine.

28 [Wardian cases] Domed glass cases used for growing plants indoors; they were popular during the middle of the nineteenth century.

28 [Ouida's novels . . . Dickens . . . Thackeray . . . and Bulwer] Since Thackeray and Bulwer wrote about the upper classes at the same time Dickens was writing about the lower and middle classes, Wharton is making a comment on the reading tastes of the Archer women: not surprisingly, they prefer to read fiction in which the characters are members of their own class. Even when they did read about peasants, they chose novels such as Ouida's, in which they were presented with a romanticized version of lower-class life.

28 [Ruskin] John Ruskin (1819–1900), a critic and writer on art and its relationship to society.

28 [Reynolds] Sir Joshua Reynolds (1723–1792), an English painter and writer on art. Knighted in 1769, he was considered the greatest portrait painter of his day.

28 [*embonpoint*] French: literally, in good condition; slang, overweight.

29 [shad . . . roe] Shad is a fish of the herring family, once abundant in the United States, and very popular during the nineteenth century. Shad roe, the eggs of the fish, is considered a delicacy; the fact that Mrs. Archer's cook always burns the best part of the dinner is evidence of the family's indifference to good food.

31 [Siren Isle] A reference to one of the episodes in *The Odyssey*, the epic by the ancient Greek poet Homer, in which Odysseus and his

crew must battle to keep their ship from crashing into the rocks that the Sirens, with their enchanting songs, lure them toward.

31 [*esprit de corps*] French: the common spirit, loyalty, and solidarity manifested by individuals in a group, in this case a family.

CHAPTER 6

35 [chintz-curtained] Chintz is a cotton cloth with a glazed finish, generally with a floral or other decorative pattern.

37 [books on Primitive Man . . . Idyls of the King . . . Ulysses and the Lotus Eaters] Wharton contrasts the books that Newland reads with those he tries to introduce to May. In addition to the classics, Newland reads books that question long-accepted beliefs; he is familiar with books on primitive man, texts on anthropology and evolution, such as *On the Origin of Species* (1859) and *The Descent of Man and Selection in Relation to Sex* (1871) by Charles Darwin (1809–1882). Instead of introducing May to such books, he talks with her about safer subjects such as the poems of Alfred Tennyson (1809–1892; British poet laureate 1850–1892). Tennyson's *Idyls of the King* is based on the King Arthur legend; his "The Lotus Eaters" is based on the Greek epic *The Odyssey.*

37 [Thackeray's heroes] Reference to the upper-class heroes in novels by Thackeray.

38 [Babes in the Wood] Title of a ballad (1593) whose plot often appears in books of fairy tales. The story involves a wicked uncle who plans to murder his nephew and niece in order to obtain their property. He hires murderers to abandon the children in a forest, where they die.

40 [General Burgoyne's sword after the battle of Saratoga] During the American Revolution, the British General John Burgoyne (1722–1792) surrendered to General Horatio Gates on October 17, 1777, at Saratoga, New York. The victory for the Americans, which Wharton's own great-grandfather contributed to, is seen as a turning point in the war.

40 [Washington Square] Area of New York City first developed as a residential area for the wealthiest members of society. During the nineteenth century, numbers 1 through 13 Washington Square were known as "the Row." Construction of row houses moved northward from Washington Square as the nouveaux riches settled in New York.

40 [Pitts] English family of William Pitt the Elder (1708–1778) and

his son William Pitt the Younger (1759–1806). Each had his turn as British prime minister.

40 [Foxes] English family of Charles James Fox (1749–1806), a leader of the British Whig Party. He had opposed King George III during the American Revolution.

40 [Count de Grasse] François Joseph Paul (1722–1788), a French naval officer who led the French Atlantic fleet in the American Revolution. His defeat of Charles Cornwallis in the Battle of Chesapeake Bay (September 5–9, 1781) helped lead the Americans to victory.

40 [first Dutch governor of Manhattan] Peter Minuit, who bought Manhattan Island from the Indians in 1626.

40 [Chippendale] Furniture in the manner of Thomas Chippendale (1718–1779), an English furniture maker who published the highly influential *Gentleman and Cabinet-Maker's Director* in 1754, 1759, and 1762. That the Lannings live among such antique American furniture and heirlooms is an indication of their aristocratic position and the fact that they have inherited old money.

41 [Channel Island] The four Channel Islands lie in the English Channel between England and France.

41 [Cornwallis] Charles Cornwallis (1783–1805), a British general in the American Revolution. His surrender at Yorktown, Virginia, on October 19, 1781, virtually ended the war.

41 [Gloucestershire] County in west-central England, immediately east of Wales.

41 ["Patroon"] Title given to a landlord in the Dutch colony of New Netherland from 1629 until 1664, when the colony came under British control. The van der Luydens descend from the first Dutch landlord and therefore are entitled to the highest social position.

CHAPTER 7

42 [ormolu mantel ornaments] Ornaments with an overlay of gold or of an alloy of copper, zinc, and tin that has a gold color.

42 [Gainsborough's "Lady Angelica du Lac"] Portrait by the English painter Thomas Gainsborough (1727–1788).

42 [Huntington] Daniel Huntington (1816–1906), an American painter born in New York City, well known for his portraits of prominent people.

42 [Venetian point] Type of needlepoint lace that has been made in Venice since the fifteenth century.

42 [Cabanel] Alexandre Cabanel (1823–1889), a French painter who won the Prix de Rome in 1845.

42 [rep curtain] Rep is a ribbed or striped fabric.

44 ["the [New York] Times] The newspaper begun by Henry Jarvis Raymond and George Jones on September 18, 1851. It became authoritative in 1871–1873 when it exposed William Marcy Tweed, the leader of a corrupt New York political machine. In the course of the novel, Wharton refers to corruption in all levels of government; she suggests that men like Archer, who were initially opposed to political involvement since it was considered to lie outside of the boundaries of conventional gentlemanly behavior, eventually entered politics in order to repair the damage done by men such as Tweed.

44 [minute-gun] Gun fired at intervals of a minute as a sign of mourning or distress.

44 [Patience] A game of solitaire; rather than playing a game in which they would compete against each other, Mr. and Mrs. van der Luyden play solitaire simultaneously.

46 [International Cup Race] A yacht race, possibly what is known today as the America's Cup, the top prize in international yacht racing. The New York Yacht Club, founded in 1844, held the cup from 1851 to 1983.

46 [seventeen-hand chestnuts] A hand is a unit of measurement, usually used for the height of horses, equal to four inches.

47 [Esther interceding with Ahasuerus] A reference to the Old Testament Book of Esther, in which Queen Esther wines and dines King Ahasuerus and successfully convinces him to stop a plot to destroy the Jews.

47 [C-spring barouche] Four-wheeled or two-wheeled carriage.

47 [Patti] Adelina Patti (1843–1913), an Italian soprano who toured the United States before debuting at Covent Garden in 1861.

47 [the Sonnambula] *The Sleepwalker*, an opera in two acts by Vincenzo Bellini (1801–1835), Sicily's most famous composer. *La Sonnambula*, first performed in 1831, was very popular during the nineteenth century. It's ironic that one of the favorite operas of a society of which many members unthinkingly follow conventions is entitled *The Sleepwalker*.

CHAPTER 8

48 [American mourning] A reference to nineteenth-century rules that
   dictated dress according to one's relation to the deceased; while
   close relatives were supposed to wear black for a period of years,
   more distant relatives wore clothes trimmed in black.

49 [Neapolitan love-songs] Reference to Naples, Italy. Throughout
   this paragraph, Wharton emphasizes Ellen's unconventional up-
   bringing, her exposure to lands and customs that would have
   seemed odd to her peers.

49 [Papal title . . . Marchioness] *Marchioness* is a title given to a wife
   or widow of a marquis, or in the Italian form, a marchese.

49 [Manzoni] Writer considered one of Italy's greatest novelists, Ales-
   sandro Manzoni (1785–1873).

49 ["drawing from the model"] Refers to drawing the figure of a live
   human model, generally a nude. That Ellen has had such experience
   is particularly shocking since women, especially in the United
   States, were not permitted to draw or paint from live models.

49 [Cowes] Port and yachting center on the northern shore of the Isle
   of Wight, England.

49 [Transylvania] Region in Eastern Europe known as the home of
   Count Dracula, the vampire in the 1897 novel of that name by the
   British author Bram Stoker (1847–1912).

50 [Debrett] Reference to *Debrett's Peerage of England, Scotland and
   Ireland* (1st ed. 1803).

50 [Sèvres] High-quality porcelain manufactured in Sèvres, France.

50 [George II plate] Antique plated silver.

50 ["Lowestoft" (East India Company)] Fine porcelain, often referred
   to as Chinese Export Porcelain since it was made in China for
   export to the United States during the eighteenth and nineteenth
   centuries; possession generally suggests that the family had made
   money as merchants in the "China trade."

50 [Crown Derby] Porcelain manufactured in Derby, England, from
   1784 to 1848.

51 [Isabey] Jean-Baptiste Isabey (1767–1855), was a French painter
   best known for his miniatures.

53 [Diana] Roman goddess known in Greek as Artemis, associated
   with the moon, light, hunting, and virginity; since she was often
   associated with human fertility, as well, she was worshipped by
   women for success in marriage and childbirth. Wharton's descriptions of May as Diana-like can be accounted for to some extent by

the fact that she was reading Sir James George Frazer's *The Golden Bough* (1914), a fourteen-volume work on anthropology, while she was writing *The Age of Innocence*. Frazer's work is a collection of myths, customs, and magical practices presented in a manner that supports his belief in human progress over time.

CHAPTER 9

55 [stucco house with a giant wisteria] Stucco is a compound similar to plaster, often used as an inexpensive way to repair exterior brick or brownstone walls by covering the surface entirely. Such an exterior indicates that Ellen is living in a less than fashionable neighborhood. Wisteria is an ornamental vine.

55 [cast-iron balcony] Casting, an inexpensive process of pouring molten metal into a mold, could be used to create carved effects, as was popular throughout the nineteenth century.

55 [West Twenty-third Street] Street near Madison Square that was fashionable during the late 1840s and early 1850s.

57 [Dante and Petrarch] Dante Alighieri (1265–1321) and Francesco Petrarch (1304–1374), Italian poets of idealized love that is never consummated.

57 [John Addington Symonds] English poet (1840–1893) and art historian.

57 [Vernon Lee] The pseudonym of Violet Paget (1856–1935), a French novelist and writer of aesthetic theory whom Wharton met in 1894.

57 [P. G. Hamerton] Philip Gilbert Hamerton (1834–1894), English art critic and essayist.

57 ["The Renaissance" by Walter Pater] Pater (1839–1894) was an English essayist and critic who published *Studies in the History of the Renaissance* (1873), with essays on such artists as Botticelli and Leonardo da Vinci.

57 [Botticelli] Sandro Botticelli (c. 1445–1510), an Italian painter whose reputation was revived in the second half of the nineteenth century by critics such as Pater and Ruskin.

57 [Fra Angelico] Italian painter and Dominican monk (c. 1400–1455) whose paintings were exclusively religious; his reputation as an artist declined during the same period in which Botticelli's increased.

58 [pampas grass] Popular name for a grass native to South America that was introduced to Europe as an ornament during the nine-

teenth century; it is a silvery color and grows to twelve or fourteen feet.

58 [Rogers statuettes] John Rogers (1829–1904) was an American sculptor who had a studio on Twelfth Street, west of Fifth Avenue. He found success selling plaster statues of sentimental genre groupings, such as *Checkers up at the Farm* (1875) or *Weighing the Baby* (1876), in general stores and by mail. Between 1860 and 1893 he created seventy-seven groups that were widely reproduced.

58 [Jacqueminot roses] A red rose named for a French soldier, J. F. Jacqueminot (1787–1865).

58 [ambergris] A waxy substance used in perfumes; it is secreted by the intestines of sperm whales.

58 [East Thirty-ninth Street] Street in a newer section of New York, removed from longer-established areas such as Washington or Madison Square.

58 [Pompeian vestibule] A style of room modeled after houses discovered in excavations of the ruins of Pompeii. The home that Newland imagines living in after marrying May contains a lobby modeled after homes in which life was frozen in time. Wharton's reference suggests that Newland fears marriage will bury him as the volcanic ash buried the inhabitants of Pompeii.

58 [wainscoting] Paneling that covers a wall up to a height of about thirty-six inches.

58 [vitrines] A vitrine is a cabinet with glass doors and sometimes glass sides and top used to display such things as china.

58 [modern Saxe] An imitation of Vieux (or "Old") Saxe, a high-quality porcelain produced at a factory near Dresden, Germany. Vieux Saxe, also known as Meissen, was considered the finest porcelain in Europe during the early 1700s.

59 ["sincere" Eastlake furniture] Charles Lock Eastlake (1836–1906) was an English architect who wrote a popular book entitled *Hints on Household Taste* (first published in 1872 in America). During the late nineteenth century, Eastlake became a household word associated with Victorian taste. Archer's library will contain new machine-made furniture rather than the antique handcrafted furniture found in the homes of old-money families such as the Lannings.

59 [*verrà—verrà*] Italian: "She will come—she will come."

59 [stepper] A horse that moves with a showy action.

60 [*des quartiers excentriques*] French phrase used to describe an area

that is distant or remote from the main body of a city, often occupied by artists or students.

61 [spills] Slips of wood or paper used to light candles or fires.

62 [attar-of-roses] Fragrant oil made from rose petals.

62 [Samarkand] One of the oldest cities of Central Asia, known for
perfumes.

62 [arctics] Protective rubber coverings for shoes.

64 [*Già*] Italian: of course, absolutely.

64 [Sarasate] Pablo de Sarasate (1844–1908), a Spanish violinist and
composer who made frequent concert tours in Europe and North
and South America during the second half of the nineteenth
century.

64 [hail-fellow hand] "Hail fellow" was a familiar greeting between
people who knew each other very well.

65 [yellow roses] According to nineteenth-century books on the language of flowers, associated with infidelity.

CHAPTER 10

66 [Episcopalian New York] The old aristocracy of New York, those
members of society who were descendants of the founding fathers,
belonged to the Episcopal Church, an Anglican denomination that
broke from the Church of England in 1789.

67 [Kentucky cave-fish] Fish without eyes that live in Kentucky's
Mammoth cave and were used to illustrate Darwin's theory of natural selection.

68 [rue de la Paix] A fashionable street in Paris, near one of the squares
on the Right Bank of the Seine, the Place Vendôme.

69 [canary-coloured brougham] Wharton's way of suggesting that
Fanny Ring, the "golden-haired lady" in the carriage, is Beaufort's
mistress.

69 [Swinburne's "Chastelard"] Charles Algernon Swinburne (1837–
1909) was an English poet and critic; *Chastelard* (1865) is the first
of his three plays based on the life of Mary Queen of Scots.

69 ["Contes Drôlatiques"] *Droll Stories*, originally published in
France in 1832; written by the novelist Honoré de Balzac (1799–
1850).

69 [Cassandra-like] In Greek legend, Cassandra received the gift of
prophecy from the god Apollo; she was the daughter of Priam,
King of Troy, and with her gift, foresaw the fall of her homeland.

70 [brass farthing] A farthing represents very little value, one-fourth of a penny.

71 [French Sunday] The French, or Continental, Sunday devoted to promenade and family outings, in contrast to the traditional English Sunday, devoted to church and rest.

73 [humming-bird-feather screen] An oval or square screen attached to a pole of five to six feet. The screen, which was meant to shield one's face from the fire, could be raised or lowered on the pole. Although these screens often featured needlework, this particular one is made of feathers.

CHAPTER 11

75 [mahogany] A common wood for Chippendale furniture.

78 [Pharisees] Self-righteous people, hypocrites; originally, the name of an ancient Jewish sect whose members were characterized by a strict observance of traditions and written laws as well as a sense of superiority.

80 ["The Death of Chatham" (1779–1781)] A painting by John Singleton Copley (1738–1815), an American artist.

80 ["The Coronation of Napoleon"] A painting (1805–1807) by Jacques-Louis David (1748–1825), a French artist whose works commemorate many of Napoléon's achievements.

80 [Sheraton knife-cases] These cases, made by or in the style of Thomas Sheraton (1751–1806), were often attached to or set on top of a chest of drawers in the dining room. They became popular during the eighteenth century.

80 [Haut Brion] Fine red wine from Bordeaux, France.

CHAPTER 12

82 [Waverley Place] A street (now spelled "Waverly") in the Greenwich Village section of New York City. It runs east and west, just north of Washington Square.

82 [Lexington Avenue] During the 1850s this street, which runs north and south, was the eastern border of the fashionable residential area, near Madison Square; the western border was Sixth Avenue.

83 [Edwin Booth] American actor (1833–1893) who specialized in Shakespearean tragedy. His younger brother, John Wilkes Booth, assassinated President Lincoln.

83 [William Winter] The major drama critic for the *New York Tribune* from 1865 to 1909.

83 [George Rignold] London actor who made his New York debut in Shakespeare's *Henry V.*

83 [Washington Irving, Fitz-Greene Halleck and the poet of "The Culprit Fay"] Irving (1783–1859) was one of America's first professional authors, as well as one of the first to achieve international fame. His most famous work, *The Sketch Book* (1819–1820), includes the familiar tales "The Legend of Sleepy Hollow" and "Rip Van Winkle." Halleck (1790–1867) was an American poet who collaborated with Joseph Rodman Drake (1795–1820), the author of "The Culprit Fay," on the "Croaker Papers" (1819); Halleck was a member of the Knickerbocker Group of New York City writers who named themselves after Washington Irving's *Knickerbocker's History of New York* (1809). Wharton mentions Irving and Halleck in her autobiography as members of a small group of writers that her parents respected; they considered the work of these men "safe." It is surprising that Wharton puts Drake in the same company as these two, for she singles him out in the autobiography as an example of a writer who was neither a member of high society nor a very good poet. It is significant, however, that she does not identify him by name.

83 [Battery and Canal Street] The area south of Washington Square, in which New York City originated. In the early nineteenth century, what became Canal Street was still a canal. The Battery was one of the most fashionable residential areas in the late eighteenth and early nineteenth centuries, but during the course of the nineteenth century, New York's fashionable society moved to the north and this area came to be populated by warehouses, saloons, and boardinghouses for sailors and men who worked on the nearby docks. By the 1850s, the area was inhabited primarily by immigrants.

83 [*parvenu*] French: from the verb meaning "to arrive"; refers to a person of unknown origin who has accumulated wealth and attained a position above his or her original class.

83 [*Italiens*] A European nightclub.

84 [Mérimée . . . Browning . . . William Morris] Prosper Mérimée (1803–1870), a French author who is most famous for his short stories and his novelettes. *Lettres à une Inconnue* ("Letters to an Unknown Girl"), one of Newland's "inseparables," is a volume of Mérimée's correspondence with one of his many lovers, published

in 1874. Robert Browning (1812–1889), an English poet well known for his dramatic monologues. William Morris (1834–1896), an English poet and designer who founded the Socialist League in 1884 and edited its journal *Commonweal*. As this list shows, Newland's tastes are very eclectic; in contrast to his mother and Janey, who prefer novels about their own class, he enjoys reading literature about worlds unfamiliar to him.

84 [the Century] A New York men's club consisting of writers and artists, located on Fifteenth Street and founded in 1847; its name is a reference to the one hundred original members. It is very adventuresome of Newland to belong to this club.

84 ["Bohemian" quarter] A place populated by creative individuals, such as artists, authors, and actors, who live without much regard for society's conventions.

84 [Paul Bourget] French writer (1852–1935) who published poetry, criticism, and novels. Wharton first met her friend Bourget in 1893.

84 [Huysmans] Charles Marie Georges Huysmans (1848–1907), a French novelist.

84 [Goncourt brothers] Edmond Louis Antoine Huot de Goncourt (1822–1896) and Jules Alfred Huot (1830–1870), French novelists whose names are synonymous with realism. Most of their novels were written collaboratively.

85 [armour of whale-boned silk] While strips of whalebone were used to make a dress fit perfectly and stay in place, Wharton suggests that their rigidity provides some degree of protection to the body they enclosed.

85 [Etruscan gold bracelet] A spiral bracelet modeled after those worn by women in Rome during the period of the Etruscan Monarchy (753–509 BC).

85 [Carolus Duran] Emile-Auguste (1838–1917), French portrait painter who became very successful in the 1870s.

85 [the Salon] Annual art exhibition of the French Royal Academy of Painting and Sculpture held in the Louvre, Paris; in 1881, the exhibitions, which had become increasingly conservative during the nineteenth century, were taken over by the Societé des Artistes Francais. Other salons were established during the last two decades of the nineteenth century to exhibit work of artists such as the Impressionists.

86 [Delmonico's] A fashionable New York gourmet restaurant.

86 [Campanini] Italo Campanini (1845–1896), Italian tenor who made

his New York opera debut in 1873; in 1883 he appeared in the New York Metropolitan's opening performance of *Faust*.

86 [Scalchi] Sofia Scalchi (1850–1922), Italian contralto.

86 [*imprévu*] French: unexpected.

89 [Protestant] While Ellen is identifying herself as a Protestant, in contrast to a Roman Catholic, whose church *did* forbid divorce, even Protestants of the day were opposed to divorce.

CHAPTER 13

93 [Wallack's theatre] The second of three theaters in New York that were operated by James W. Wallack and, afterward, his son Lester.

93 ["The Shaughraun"] A three-act play by Dion Boucicault set in Ireland; the title is Anglo-Irish for "vagabond." It opened at Wallack's on November 14, 1874, and enjoyed the longest run of any play at the theater during the 1870s.

93 [Dion Boucicault] Irish-born playwright (1820–1890), actor, and manager, whose dramas were very popular in the United States during the late nineteenth century. Boucicault played the title character, Conn, in the Wallack production.

93 [Harry Montague] Henry James Montague (1843–1878), an English-born actor who played Captain Molyneux in the 1874 Wallack production of *The Shaughraun*.

93 [Ada Dyas] One of the leading women in Wallack's theater company; she played Claire Ffolliott, Captain Molyneux's love interest, in the 1874 production.

93 [one episode] Although the play is a comedy, Wharton, in order to amplify the theme of renunciation in her narrative, concentrates on an episode in which the lovers, Molyneux and Claire, part.

93 [Croisette and Bressant] Sophie Croizette, a French actress, and Jean-Baptiste Bressant, a French actor, who performed in the Comédie Française during the 1870s.

93 [Madge Robertson and Kendal] Mrs. Kendal (née Margaret Robertson, 1848–1935) and Mr. Kendal (né William Hunter Grimston, 1843–1917), a famous English acting team of the late nineteenth century.

96 [St. Augustine] The oldest city in the United States, founded by Spain in 1565. Situated in northeast Florida, the city was a popular resort on account of its mild climate and historical attractions.

CHAPTER 14

100 [Broadway] Street that runs north from Battery Park, crosses Fifth
Avenue, and continues northwest. Lower Broadway (that area
closest to Battery Park) was New York's best-known section of
town at the beginning of the nineteenth century. The street was
paved in 1809 and sidewalks were installed beyond Washington
Square. The A. T. Stewart Store, one of the world's first depart-
ment stores, located at Broadway and Chambers Street, opened in
1846; by the 1850s Broadway was the New York street most famous for fashionable shops and hotels.

102 [the bosses] A reference to corrupt New York City officials and
politicians, probably "Boss" Tweed in particular, who took advantage of opportunities for fraud that accompanied the rise of
industry and an increase in the city population during the 1860s
and 1870s. William Marcy Tweed was a politician who made
money by collecting kickbacks from contractors; he was arrested
in 1871 after having stolen somewhere between seventy-five million
and two hundred million dollars.

104 [Labiche] Eugène Marin Labiche (1815–1888), a prolific French
dramatist.

104 ["Le Voyage de M. Perrichon"] Labiche play (1860) set in
Switzerland.

CHAPTER 15

107 [Evening Post] The *Saturday Evening Post*, a weekly periodical that
was established in 1821 by Charles Alexander and Samuel Coate
Atkinson. It began by printing news and editorials along with literature, but by the 1870s its space was devoted primarily to fiction.

109 [Delft plates] Ceramics made in Delft, Holland.

111 [Jules Verne] French writer (1828–1905) who is considered one of
the founders of science fiction for his books about fantastic jour-
neys and technology that seemed unbelievable at the time.

113 [Herbert Spencer] English philosopher (1820–1903) and social sci-
entist who anticipated the concepts of Darwin. His philosophy
combined aspects of utilitarianism and evolution; he was actually
the first to use the phrase "survival of the fittest." Wharton shows
Newland's interest in the latest developments in social science at
the same time that she amplifies the novel's concern with evolution.

113 [Alphonse Daudet] French writer (1840–1897) of poems, short stories, and plays.

113 ["Middlemarch"] A novel containing many references to science and philosophy by George Eliot (Mary Anne Evans, 1819–1880). It was published serially during 1871 and 1872.

113 ["The House of Life"] Sequence of sonnets written by Dante Gabriel Rossetti (1828–1882), a London-born poet and painter whose father was a political exile from Italy.

114 [Grace Church] Gothic-revival church of white marble designed by James Renwick, Jr., built from 1843 to 1846. This Episcopal church, which all of fashionable New York attended during the nineteenth century, is located at the intersection of Broadway and East Tenth Street.

CHAPTER 16

116 ["Sonnets from the Portuguese"] Sequence of love poems by English poet Elizabeth Barrett Browning (1806–1861).

116 ["How they brought the Good News from Ghent to Aix"] A poem by Robert Browning.

116 [plumbago] A plant that grows in the southern United States; it is sometimes called leadwort because of the color of its flowers.

117 [Assemblies] Fashionable social gatherings.

CHAPTER 17

124 [polonaise] A type of gown worn in the 1870s, characterized by its bustle and overskirt, which was draped up.

124 [jet buttons] Black buttons made of a form of coal found on the Yorkshire coast of England; the material was considered very fashionable during the 1870s and 1880s and was used not only for buttons but also for lockets, broaches, and bracelets.

124 [green monkey muff] Muffs were worn as an accessory by many women in the second half of the nineteenth century. Ellen's appears to be made of the long, silky hair of a monkey, a fashionable trimming at the turn of the century.

125 [Fortieth Street] The uppermost limits of New York City in the first half of the nineteenth century.

126 [French leave] Originally a custom in eighteenth-century France of leaving a gathering without saying good-bye to the host or hostess;

the phrase has come to be used to describe anything done without asking permission or giving notice.

128 [ulster] A double-breasted coat with a cape; such coats were originally made of a coarse woolen cloth produced in Ulster, Ireland.

128 ["Macfarlane"] A cloth topcoat with slits at the side.

128 [morning clothes] The usual outfit worn early in the day by fashionable men in the second half of the nineteenth century; the outfit consisted of a shirt with a wing collar, a scarf or cravat, a gray vest, a frock coat, gray striped trousers, gray gloves and spats, and a top hat.

129 [cousin] In some later editions, *cousin* was changed to *nephew.*

129 [old Castile] The center of a region in Spain that led the Christian fight against the Moors.

129 [Valley of Love Community] The name of Dr. Carver's community suggests a similarity to the Oneida community, established in 1848, between Syracuse and Utica, New York. Until 1879, this community, led by John Humphrey Noyes, practiced economic communism and rejected monogamy.

129 [*un peu sauvage*] French: literally, a bit wild, but here used to describe Winsett's sarcasm.

130 [Direct Contact] A specific form of spiritualism. In the United States a spiritualism movement began after 1848, when Margaret and Kate Fox reported the rapping of spirits inside their home in Hydesville, New York. During the second half of the nineteenth century, this somewhat eccentric movement gained a small following, but never lost its association with charlatanry.

CHAPTER 18

134 [tippets] Flat collars of fur, silk, or velvet, with long ends that hang down in the front; a very popular fashion accessory in the first half of the nineteenth century.

142 [*signor marito*] Italian: husband.

BOOK TWO

CHAPTER 19

147 [camphor] A moth-proofing substance with a strong smell; it was said to be an antaphrodisiac, quite ironic considering that the smell is present at a wedding.

147 [cat's-eye] Cat's-eye is a precious quartz stone that, when held up to light at the right angle, resembles the eye of a cat.

148 [Handel's March] A piece of music written by the English composer George Friderick Handel (1685–1759).

148 [proscenium seats] Seats close to the dramatic action, in between the curtain and the orchestra.

149 [Chantilly veil] A veil made of the delicate lace produced in Chantilly, France; here, probably an heirloom.

149 [silvery chinchilla] Expensive fur of a rodent that lives in the Andes Mountains of South America.

150 [Bath chair] A large chair on wheels, which originated in fashionable Bath, England, home to many health resorts.

151 [Parma violets] Light or deep purple flowers associated with the city of Parma, in northern Italy.

152 [Spohr] German composer and violinist Louis Spohr (1784–1859), one of the most famous musical figures of the first half of the nineteenth century.

152 [Mendelssohn March] A traditional wedding anthem written by German composer Felix Mendelssohn (1809–1847).

153 [favours] Ribbons or rosettes.

154 [Civic Virtue or a Greek goddess] The suggestion is that May would make a good model for a modern statue or a mural that personified good citizenship or some abstract virtue. The reference implies both May's strength and her purity.

CHAPTER 20

157 [Britannia ware] Flatware and domestic articles, such as teapots, made of a white metal that has a blue tint.

157 [tête-à-tête] French: literally "head-to-head," an intimate conversation between two people.

157 [Botzen] German name for Bolzano, in northern Italy.

158 [macramé lace] Lace made by knotting thread in a decorative pattern.

158 [Baroness Bunsen] Frances Waddington Bunsen (1791–1876) published a two-volume memoir of her husband, the baron (1791–1860), in 1868.

159 [Worth] Paris was the capital of the fashion industry for women during the nineteenth century, and Worth was the head of the industry in Paris. In America, fashionable wealthy women purchased their gowns from Worth each year.

159 [National Gallery] Art museum in London, established in 1824.

159 [Italian Lakes] Lakes, such as Como and Maggiore, in the southern Alps; popular tourist resorts in the late nineteenth century.

159 [Interlaken] Swiss city that became popular with tourists in the nineteenth century as interest in the Alps grew.

159 [Grindelwald] Mountain resort in Switzerland.

160 [gentian-bed] Gentians are common plants with tubular flowers.

160 [lawn tennis] an outdoor version of court tennis.

160 [*cafés chantants*] French: literally, singing cafés—cafés in which customers are entertained with music.

160 [Champs Élysées] Famous broad boulevard on the right bank of the Seine in Paris that runs from the Tuileries Gardens to the Arc de Triomphe, at which twelve avenues intersect.

160 ["cocottes"] French: lovers.

161 [Mayfair] A fashionable district in London bounded on the east by Regent Street, on the west by Hyde Park, on the south by Piccadilly Circus, and on the north by Oxford Street.

161 [South Kensington] A section of London that is home to many colleges and museums, including the Victoria and Albert Museum, established in 1857 and called the South Kensington Museum until 1899.

162 [hansom] A two-wheeled vehicle with room for two people inside the cab; the driver sits on an elevated seat behind the passengers, from which he holds the reins, which go over the roof of the cab.

162 [swansdown] The underplumage of a swan; this soft material was often used for trimming dresses and other garments.

163 [Harrow] A private secondary school for boys from wealthy and titled families; it was established in 1571 and is located about twelve miles northwest of London.

163 [Lake Leman] Also called Lake Geneva; on the border between southwest Switzerland and eastern France.

164 [Goncourt *grenier*] A literary salon held in the home of the Goncourt brothers in Auteuil, a district in western Paris. The first official meeting of the *grenier* took place in the attic rooms on February 1, 1885, and since this section of *The Age of Innocence* is set in the 1870s, Wharton's reference appears to be an anachronism.

164 [Maupassant] Guy de Maupassant (1850–1893), French novelist and short-story writer.

164 [*quant à soi*] French: dignity.

164 [*voyez-vous*] French: You see.

165 [Flaubert] Gustave Flaubert (1821–1880), French novelist well known for *Madame Bovary* (1856).

CHAPTER 21

168 [*poufs*] French: low padded seats, cushions, or sofas.

168 [Newport] A seaside town on Aquidneck Island, Rhode Island; sometimes referred to as "America's First Resort."

169 [Knickerbocker] A very exclusive gentlemen's club; membership was available only to those coming from the most distinguished families in New York.

169 [Mount Desert] A beautiful island off the coast of Maine that began to attract tourists in 1855; steamboat service from Boston to the island was established in 1868.

171 [Leghorn hat] A large straw hat.

171 [Portsmouth] City on the northern end of Aquidneck Island.

171 [trotters] Carriage horses bred and trained for speed and endurance; during the second half of the nineteenth century, wealthy New Yorkers invested quite a bit of money in the best horses and enjoyed showing them off in Central Park.

172 [Clyde] River in Scotland noted for shipbuilding.

172 [Meissonnier] Jean-Louis-Ernest Meissonier (1815–1891), very successful French painter, lithographer, and sculptor.

172 [*Que voulez-vous?*] French: What do you want?

174 [Bellevue Avenue] Street in Newport along which a number of mansions were built during the second half of the nineteenth century; these include Kingscote (1839), Château-sur-Mer (1852, enlarged 1872), and Beechwood (1851–1852). The street runs north to south, parallel to the Atlantic coast.

174 [victorias] Open carriages popular during the second half of the nineteenth century, with low floors that made them easy to enter.

174 [dog-carts] Two-wheeled carriages pulled by a single horse; they have two seats arranged back to back with a space in between for carrying dogs.

174 ["vis-à-vis"] In French, literally, "face to face"; a carriage with room for two people who sit facing one another.

174 [Ocean Drive] Another street in Newport along which many mansions are situated.

174 [Narragansett Avenue] Newport street named after the Narragansett tribe of the Wampanoag Indians.

174 [Spring Street] Street that runs near Newport Harbor. According

to May and Archer's route, Catherine Mingott's cottage must be near the west coast of Aquidneck Island, away from the fashionable center of Newport.

174 [*cottage-orné*] Large, picturesque country residence.

174 [flock-papers] Textured wallpaper that is covered with flock, a powdered wool or cloth.

175 [anti-macassars] Coverings for pieces of furniture that are simply decorative or, more typically, meant as a protection against dirt or grease, particularly Macassar, a type of hair oil used during the nineteenth century.

175 [filigree brooch] A pin that displays delicate, intricate jewel work.

176 [the Administration] Either that of Ulysses S. Grant, who served as president from 1869 to 1877, or Rutherford B. Hayes, who served from 1877 to 1881. Both were known for their corruption.

176 [Lime Rock] Location of a lighthouse between Goat Island and the coast of Newport; legend has it that Ida Lewis, who succeeded her father as lighthouse keeper, was responsible for many rescues.

177 [Goat Island] Small island off the west coast of Aquidneck Island, at the mouth of Newport Harbor.

177 [Prudence Island] Large island in Narragansett Bay, opposite Portsmouth on Aquidneck Island.

177 [Conanicut] Large island to the west of the Aquidneck and Goat Islands.

177 [Fort Adams] Granite fort dating from the American Revolution, located on the west coast of Aquidneck Island, at the opening of Newport Harbor.

177 [catboat] A broad-beamed boat with a single sail, designed for shallow waters.

178 [*Sancta simplicitas!*] Latin: literally, holy simplicity. The phrase indicates astonishment at another's display of naïveté.

CHAPTER 22

181 [Yucatan] State in Mexico; the tombs referred to are those of the Mayans, the native inhabitants of the area before it was colonized by the Spanish during the early 1500s.

181 [the Cliffs] Area of Newport on the east side of Aquidneck Island, along the Atlantic coast, removed from the center of the city; a path along the coast is called the Cliff Walk.

181 [*thé dansant*] French: tea dance; a form of afternoon entertainment at which tea is served and the guests dance.

182 [run-about] Small, light vehicle pulled by a horse.

183 [Eastman's Beach] Also called Easton's Beach, First Beach, or Newport Beach. It runs for three-quarters of a mile along the Atlantic coast.

184 [Saconnet] River between Aquidneck Island and part of the Rhode Island mainland.

184 [goldenrod] Plant with small clusters of yellow flowers; it blooms in the late summer and the fall. While some books on the language of flowers associate it with encouragement, others associate it with precaution.

184 [dahlias] American herbs that produce rayed flowers of many different colors; according to nineteenth-century books on the language of flowers, they are consistently associated with elegance and dignity.

184 [Newfoundland] Large breed of dog named after a Canadian province; its long, thick coat is usually black.

186 [Mrs. Scott-Siddons] Mary Frances Scott-Siddons (1844–1896), an English actress.

186 ["Lady Geraldine's Courtship?"] Poem by Elizabeth Barrett Browning, in which she complimented the poetry of her future husband.

187 [Parker House] Boston hotel located at the corner of Tremont and School streets, opposite King's Chapel. Established in 1856 by Harvey Parker, it is one of the oldest hotels in the United States.

CHAPTER 23

188 [Fall River] Manufacturing city in Massachusetts, close to Narragansett Bay and the border with Rhode Island.

188 [Somerset Club] Boston's oldest and most exclusive gentlemen's club, founded in 1851.

188 [Common] The Boston Common, a forty-five-acre public park located below the Massachusetts State House.

188 [Masonic picnic] A reference to the Society of Freemasons, a political organization for men that held its meetings in secret, not in such public areas as the Boston Common.

188 [Commercial Advertiser] Daily New York newspaper that focused on shipping, manufacturing, and retail news.

191 [Baden] Resort town in Austria, about fifteen miles southwest of Vienna.

193 [stylographic pens] Fountain pens introduced in the second half of

the nineteenth century; the point of such a pen is supplied with
ink from a reservoir in the stem.

193 [Beacon Street] One of the main streets in Boston, along which are
a number of mansions, including the Sears Mansion, home of the
Somerset Club; it borders one side of the city's common.

193 ["herdic"] A two- or four-wheeled carriage with an entrance at the
rear and seats on the sides; it is named after the inventor, Peter
Herdic, of Pennsylvania.

196 [*cabinet particulier*] French: private room or office.

CHAPTER 25

204 [horse-car] A horse-drawn public vehicle on rails that had the capacity to hold thirty to forty passengers. By the middle of the
nineteenth century, these cars had replaced the ordinary omnibus
in major cities, for they provided a relatively smooth ride, since
they ran on rails, and moved about twice as fast as the omnibus.

CHAPTER 26

210 [the season] A reference to the indoor entertainments attended by
members of New York's upper class during the winter months.

211 [Jeremiah (chapter ii., verse 25)] "Keep your feet from going un-
shod and your throat from thirst. But you said, 'It is hopeless, for
I have loved strangers, and after them I will go.'"

211 [front panel] A panel is a triangular piece of cloth in a skirt; by
simply replacing the front panel, one could change the look of an
older dress.

212 [Symphony concerts] The Boston Music Hall, at the intersection
of Winter Street and Bumstead Place, was constructed in 1852. Mrs.
Pennilow would not have heard the famous Boston Symphony Orchestra there, however, for it was not founded until 1881. The Boston Music Hall was the home of the orchestra until October 15,
1900, when Symphony Hall, at the corner of Huntington and Massachusetts Avenue, was opened.

CHAPTER 27

221 [omnibuses] Public vehicles pulled by horses; they held twelve passengers and ran along fixed routes. The first omnibus in the United
States started operation in New York City in 1829.

224 [*noblesse oblige*] French: literally, nobility obligates. The phrase
    refers to the behavior, such as generosity and honor, expected of
    individuals in the upper ranks of society.
225 [rosewood "Bonheur du Jour"] Rosewood, a dark brown wood
    with stripes of darker brown or black, was often imported from
    India or the East Indies and used for furniture throughout the
    nineteenth century. The bonheur du jour is a small writing table
    or desk.

CHAPTER 28

227 [Western Union] Telegraph company organized in 1856 by Hiram
    Sibley and Ezra Cornell. By 1861 the company, which had a virtual
    monopoly on the business until the 1870s, had established the
    country's first transcontinental telegraph line.
231 [Spartan] A reference to the courage and self-denying discipline
    associated with the inhabitants of Sparta, a city in ancient Greece.
    Wharton's irony is at work here in her reference to the hypochon-
    driacal Mr. Welland.
232 [Union Square] Before the Civil War, an elegant area that served
    as New York's center for theater; it is located between Park Ave-
    nue South and Broadway, north of Fourteenth Street.

CHAPTER 29

234 [Pennsylvania terminus] In 1871, the United Companies of New
    Jersey supplied the Pennsylvania Railroad, the major transportation
    system on the Atlantic seaboard and in the Great Lakes region,
    with a terminus on the New York Harbor.
234 [Arabian Night] A reference to the collection of fantasy-filled an-
    cient tales, originally written in Arabic, entitled *The Arabian
    Nights' Entertainment* or *A Thousand and One Nights*.
234 [teamsters] Drivers or owners of teams of horses.
237 [Gorgon] Monster of classical myth that would turn one to stone
    upon sight of it.
239 [Forty-second Street] Ellen and Archer are headed toward Granny
    Mingott's home, located near Central Park, which begins at Fifty-
    ninth Street.

CHAPTER 30

242 [Michelet] Jules Michelet (1798–1874), French historian whose great work is the *Histoire de France* (1833–1867).

CHAPTER 31

253 [Adelaide Neilson] English actress (1848–1880) who made her New York debut in 1872 as Juliet.

254 [the Art Museum—in the Park] The Metropolitan Museum of Art was organized in January 1870, with John Taylor Johnston as president and William Cullen Bryant and General John A. Dix as vice presidents. Its first exhibits were housed in a rented brownstone on Fifth Avenue, near Fifty-third Street. In 1874, ground was broken for the Central Park site, between Seventy-ninth and Eighty-fourth Streets. Since the building "in the Park" did not open until March 30, 1880, Wharton's reference is an anachronism.

254 [encaustic tiles] Tiles decorated with patterns formed by different colored clays.

254 ["Cesnola antiquities"] A reference to Johnston's first big purchase for the museum. He paid $60,000 for about 10,000 objects, ranging from spearheads to statues, from Phoenician, Greek, Assyrian, and Egyptian tombs on the island of Cyprus, pillaged by General Louis Palma di Cesnola.

255 [ebonised wood] Wood that has been stained or polished to give it a deep black color.

255 [Ilium] Latin name for Troy, an ancient city in Asia Minor, site of the Trojan War.

CHAPTER 32

263 [Morny's money] Reference to the duke de Morny (1811–1865), French politician and half-brother of Napoléon III.

265 [Marguerite fell into Faust's arms] End of Act III of *Faust*.

CHAPTER 33

270 [Tiffany's thickest gilt-edged bristol] Bristol is a kind of decorative board with a smooth surface. Tiffany's, located on the west side of Union Square, at Fifteenth Street, was the store at which fashion-

able New York purchased its jewelry, engraved cards, and decorative items.

274 [*jardinière*] An ornamental stand for plants or flowers.

274 [primulas] Also known as primroses, showy flowers associated with inconstancy, modest worth, or a request that one have confidence in the owner or giver.

274 [cinerarias] Daisylike flowers.

274 [Venus of Milo] A replica of the marble statue of Aphrodite, the goddess of love. The original, which is missing the arms of the goddess, dates from the fourth or fifth century B.C. Discovered on the island of Milos in 1820, it has since been permanently installed at the Louvre.

275 [Verbeckhoven "Study of Sheep"] Eugene Joseph Verbeckhoven (1798–1881), Belgian painter, famous for his paintings of animals.

278 [Blind Asylum] In her autobiography, *A Backward Glance*, Wharton mentions that her father, George Frederic Jones, was a director on the board of the Blind Asylum, one of New York's main charitable organizations.

278 [Smyrna] Also known as Izmir; Turkey's second-largest port, located on the Aegean Sea. It has been settled since the third millennium B.C.

278 [Constantinople] An ancient city founded as Byzantium in the seventh century B.C.

279 [Poole] While Paris was the center of the women's fashion industry, London was the center of the industry for men. Poole was one of the best-known London tailors.

CHAPTER 34

285 [Georgian] A specific type of Colonial architecture, employed by builders in the United States from 1730–1830.

285 ["Colonial"] a loose term referring to a number of styles of architecture of the American Colonies.

285 [Governor of New York] Theodore Roosevelt (1859–1919), twenty-sixth president of the United States (1901–1909), was governor of New York from 1899 to 1900. Wharton had great respect for this powerful friend of hers.

286 [reforming weeklies] Weekly magazines that focused on movements for political and/or social change. While Thomas J. Creamer's New York *Citizen* focused on political reform, periodicals such as the New York *Voice* (1884–1906) endorsed the temperance

movement. Some of the major turn-of-the-century reformers called for utopian socialism, the exposure of corruption and vice in business and politics (the "muckraking" movement), women's rights, and labor unions; each movement used the press in its attempts to persuade others to join its cause.

286 [Grolier Club] New York gentlemen's book club founded in 1884; Wharton's reference suggests that she associates the organization of such a club with some progress, or evolution, taking place in New York society.

286 [new Library] The New York Public Library, established in 1895, designed by Carrere and Hastings, and built between 1902 and 1909. It is located on Fifth Avenue, between Fortieth and Forty-second Streets.

287 [English mezzotints] Prints produced from copper plates by a process invented by Ludwig von Siegen in 1642. The height of the English mezzotint industry was established during the eighteenth century.

287 [St. Mark's] Second-oldest church (1795–1799) in New York City, located at the corner of Stuyvesant Street and Second Avenue.

288 [Lakeside] Along the shore of Lake Michigan; Chicago is one of the Midwestern cities that was rapidly developing at the turn of the century.

288 [Mauretania] A popular ship of the Cunard lines from 1906 to 1934; from 1907 to 1929 it held the Blue Ribbon, a metaphorical rank for the fastest Atlantic crossing.

288 [five-day Atlantic voyages] A contrast to the voyages of the 1850s, which took twice as long, and a reference to the "visionaries" Archer thinks of at the beginning of Chapter XXIX as he waits for Ellen at the Pennsylvania terminus. Throughout this chapter, Wharton emphasizes how some things that were deemed unimaginable thirty years earlier have come to pass.

288 [Cunard office] Reference to the Cunard Line of steamships. It was founded by Sir Samuel Cunard (1787–1865), a British shipowner, in 1840. After 1848, the company ran ten ships on a weekly schedule. In the 1850s, Cunard competed with the Collins line, which set a record by traveling from Liverpool to New York in ten days and four hours. During the twentieth century, the Cunard Line ran the fastest luxury liners.

291 [reforms and "movements"] Programs associated with what has been called the Progressive Era, at the turn of the century. By this time gentlemen of the upper class, unlike their ancestors, had be-

come engaged in politics; they worked to repair the damage effected by postbellum corruption.

291 [Place Vendôme] Oblong square in Paris, on the Right Bank of the Seine, designed by Jules Hardouin-Mansart (1646–1708).

292 [Debussy] Claude Debussy (1862–1918), an iconoclastic French composer whose works include the *Prélude à l'après-midi d'un faune* (1894) and *La mer* (1904).

292 [Grand-Guignol] A theater in Paris, founded in 1897 by Oscar Metenier and taken over by Max Maurey in 1899. It had a reputation for staging violent, terrifying plays.

295 [Titian] Tiziano Vecellio (c. 1485–1576), great Italian painter.

295 [Chamber of Deputies] Lower house of the French parliament; Archer and his son are crossing from the Right to the Left bank of the Seine.

295 [Invalides] Hôtel des Invalides, on the Left Bank of the Seine, was founded in 1671 by Louis XIV as a home for disabled soldiers.

295 [dome of Mansart] Gold-plated dome of the Church of Saint-Louis-des-Invalides, the work of the French architect Jules Hardouin-Mansart. The tomb of Napoléon is located under the dome.

297 [*porte-cochère*] Driveway that leads to an inner court.

FOR THE BEST IN PAPERBACKS, LOOK FOR THE

In every corner of the world, on every subject under the sun, Penguin represents quality and variety—the very best in publishing today.

For complete information about books available from Penguin—including Puffins, Penguin Classics, and Arkana—and how to order them, write to us at the appropriate address below. Please note that for copyright reasons the selection of books varies from country to country.